A RURAL NOIR BY TIM SEELEY + MIKE NORTON

REVIVAL

VOLUME 6: THY LOYAL SONS & DAUGHTERS

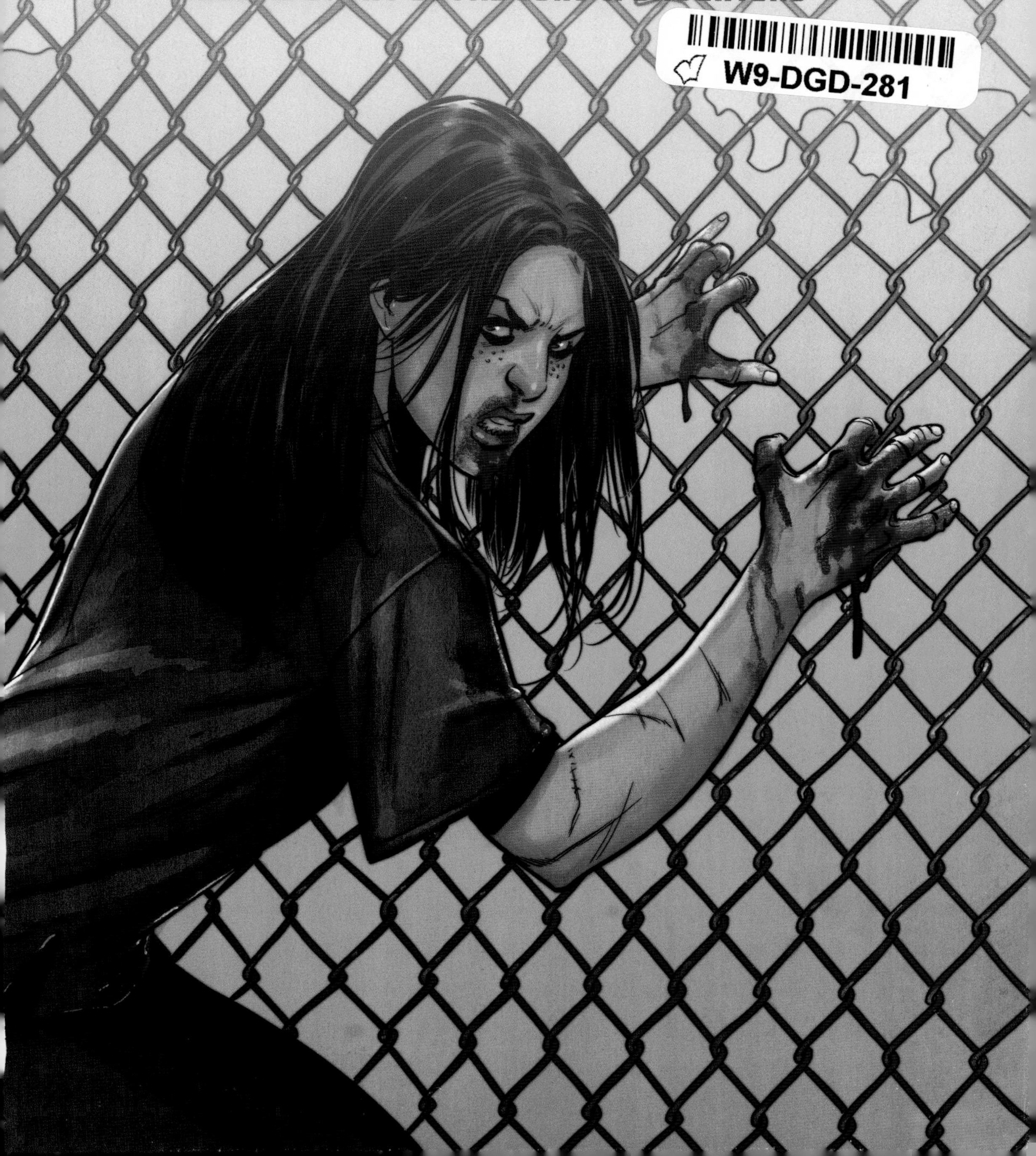

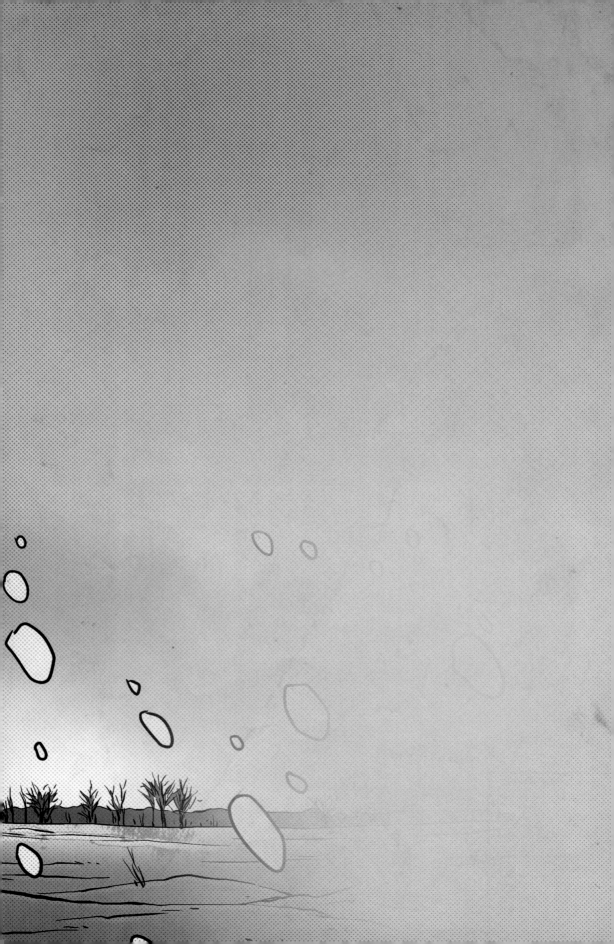

STORY BY:
TIM SEELEY

ART BY:
MIKE NORTON

COLORS BY
MARK ENGLERT

LETTERS BY
CRANK!

CHAPTER ART BY
JENNY FRISON

EDITED BY
4 STAR STUDIOS

DESIGN BY
SEAN DOVE

ADDITIONAL ART BY EMILIO LAISO

FOR MORE INFO CHECK OUT
WWW.REVIVALCOMIC.COM

ALSO CHECK OUT THE SOUNDTRACK BY
SONO MORTI AT **SONOMORTI.BANDCAMP.COM**

IMAGE COMICS, INC.
Robert Kirkman – Chief Operating Officer
Erik Larsen – Chief Financial Officer
Todd McFarlane – President
Marc Silvestri – Chief Executive Officer
Jim Valentino – Vice-President

Eric Stephenson – Publisher
Corey Murphy – Director of Sales
Jeff Boison – Director of Publishing Planning & Book Trade Sales
Jeremy Sullivan – Director of Digital Sales
Kat Salazar – Director of PR & Marketing
Emily Miller – Director of Operations
Branwyn Bigglestone – Senior Accounts Manager
Sarah Mello – Accounts Manager
Drew Gill – Art Director
Jonathan Chan – Production Manager
Meredith Wallace – Print Manager
Brian Skelly – Publicity Assistant
Randy Okamura – Marketing Production Designer
David Brothers – Branding Manager
Ally Power – Content Manager
Addison Duke – Production Artist
Vincent Kukua – Production Artist
Sasha Head – Production Artist
Tricia Ramos – Production Artist
Jeff Stang – Direct Market Sales Representative
Emilio Bautista – Digital Sales Associate
Chloe Ramos-Peterson – Administrative Assistant
IMAGECOMICS.COM

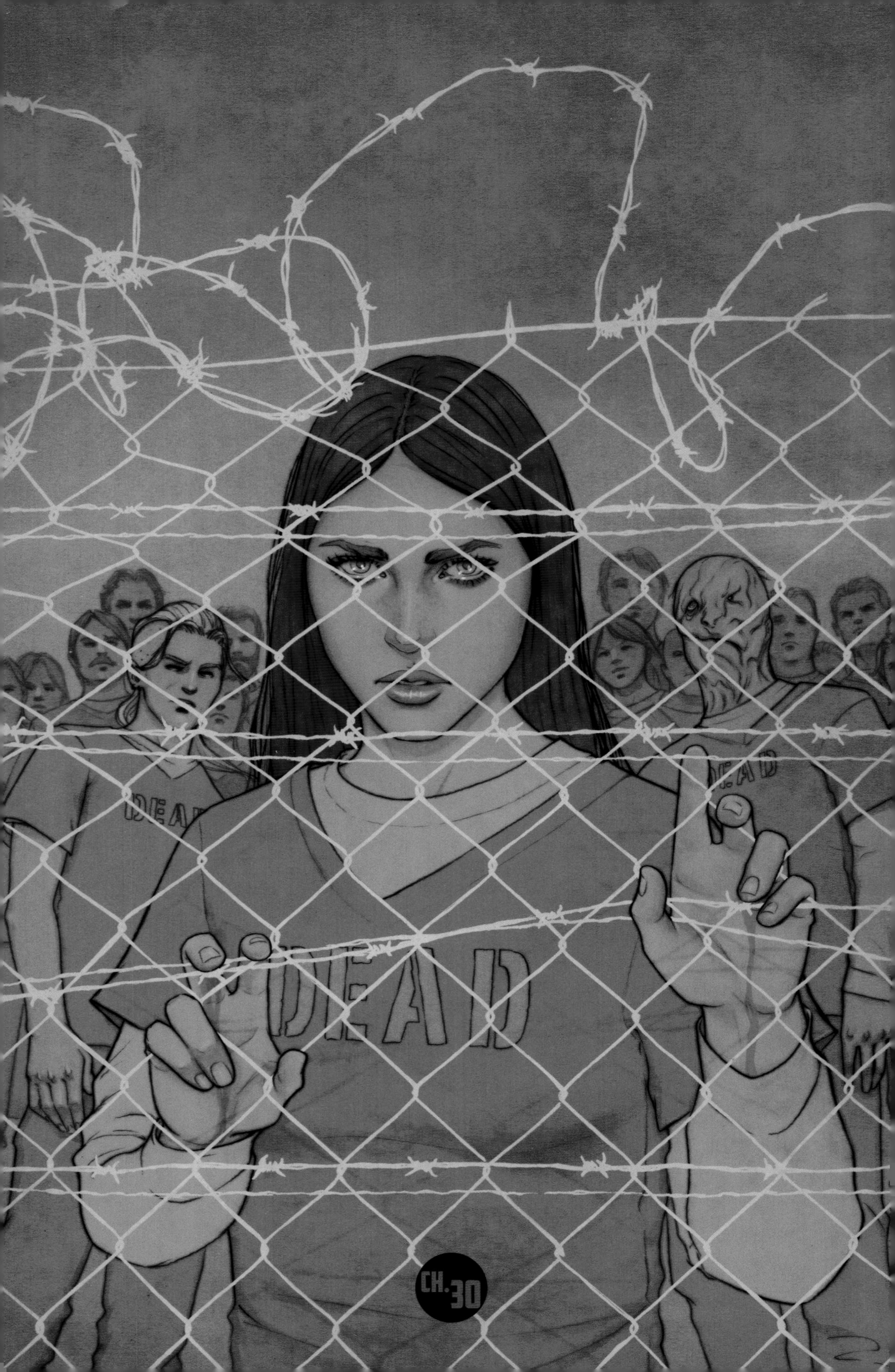
DEAD
DEAD
DEAD
CH.30

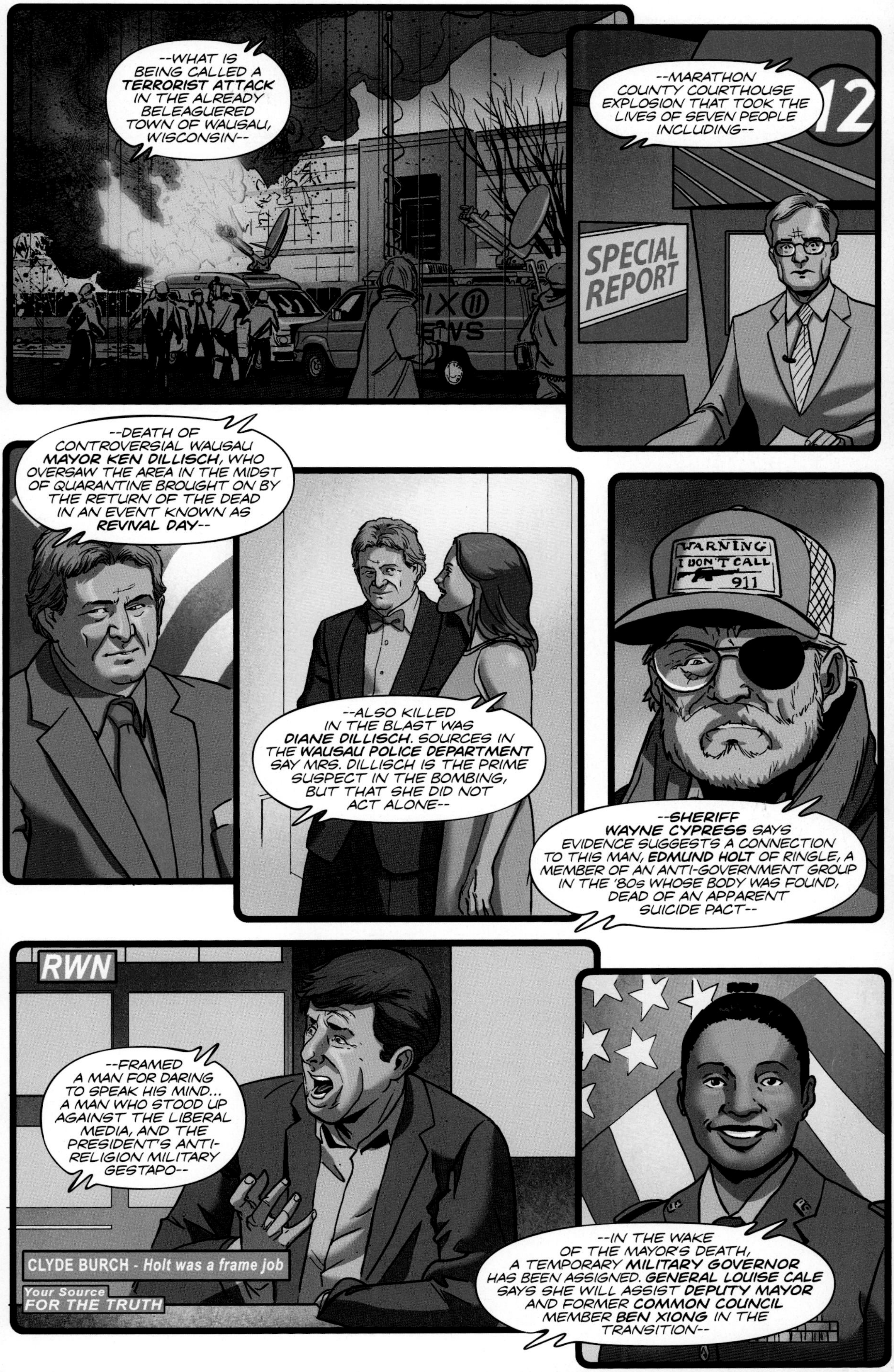
--WHAT IS BEING CALLED A TERRORIST ATTACK IN THE ALREADY BELEAGUERED TOWN OF WAUSAU, WISCONSIN--
--MARATHON COUNTY COURTHOUSE EXPLOSION THAT TOOK THE LIVES OF SEVEN PEOPLE INCLUDING--
12
SPECIAL REPORT
--DEATH OF CONTROVERSIAL WAUSAU MAYOR KEN DILLISCH, WHO OVERSAW THE AREA IN THE MIDST OF QUARANTINE BROUGHT ON BY THE RETURN OF THE DEAD IN AN EVENT KNOWN AS REVIVAL DAY--
--ALSO KILLED IN THE BLAST WAS DIANE DILLISCH. SOURCES IN THE WAUSAU POLICE DEPARTMENT SAY MRS. DILLISCH IS THE PRIME SUSPECT IN THE BOMBING, BUT THAT SHE DID NOT ACT ALONE--
WARNING I DON'T CALL 911
--SHERIFF WAYNE CYPRESS SAYS EVIDENCE SUGGESTS A CONNECTION TO THIS MAN, EDMUND HOLT OF RINGLE, A MEMBER OF AN ANTI-GOVERNMENT GROUP IN THE '80s WHOSE BODY WAS FOUND, DEAD OF AN APPARENT SUICIDE PACT--
RWN
--FRAMED A MAN FOR DARING TO SPEAK HIS MIND... A MAN WHO STOOD UP AGAINST THE LIBERAL MEDIA, AND THE PRESIDENT'S ANTI-RELIGION MILITARY GESTAPO--
CLYDE BURCH - Holt was a frame job
Your Source FOR THE TRUTH
--IN THE WAKE OF THE MAYOR'S DEATH, A TEMPORARY MILITARY GOVERNOR HAS BEEN ASSIGNED. GENERAL LOUISE CALE SAYS SHE WILL ASSIST DEPUTY MAYOR AND FORMER COMMON COUNCIL MEMBER BEN XIONG IN THE TRANSITION--

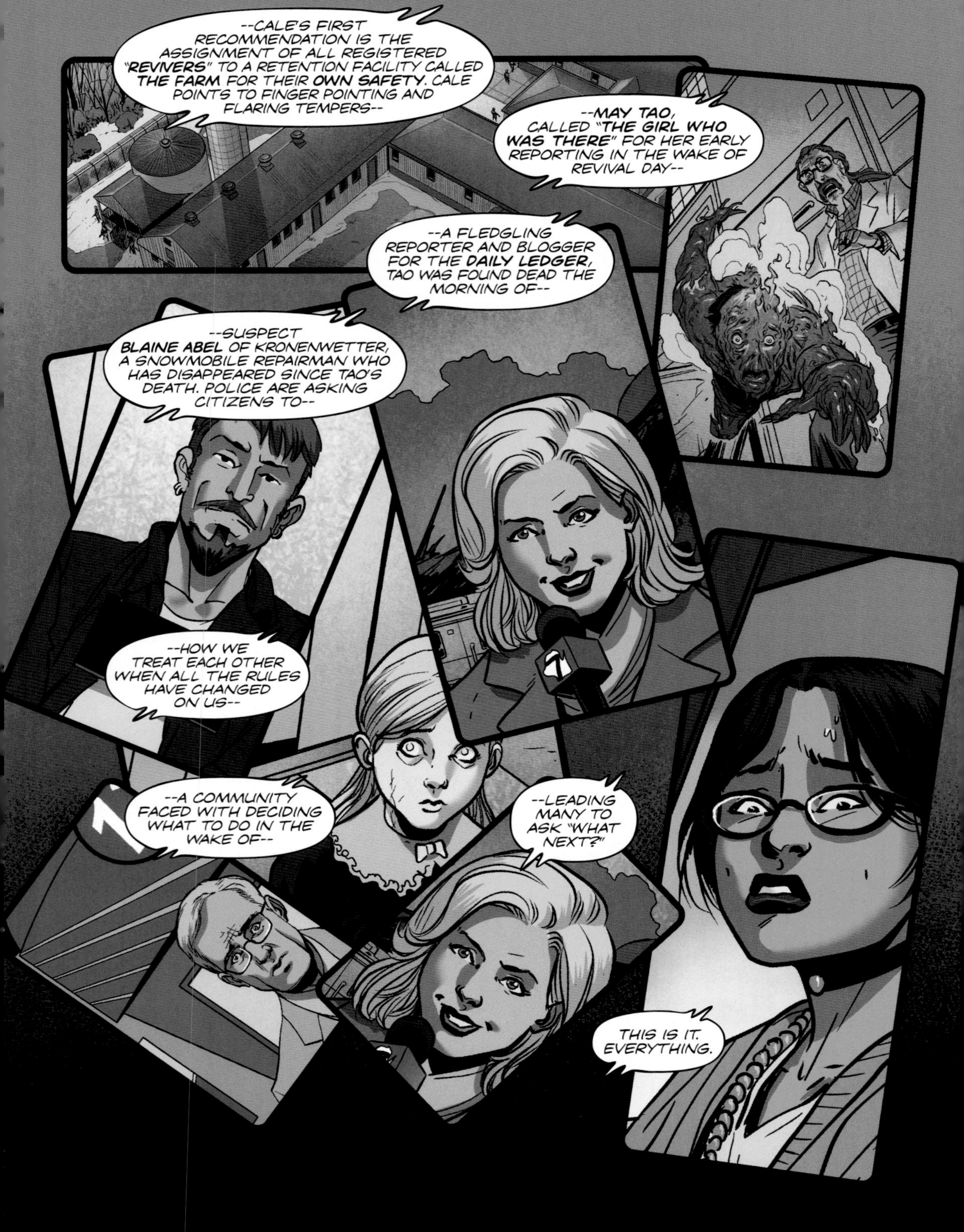

--CALE'S FIRST RECOMMENDATION IS THE ASSIGNMENT OF ALL REGISTERED "REVIVERS" TO A RETENTION FACILITY CALLED THE FARM FOR THEIR OWN SAFETY. CALE POINTS TO FINGER POINTING AND FLARING TEMPERS--
--MAY TAO, CALLED "THE GIRL WHO WAS THERE" FOR HER EARLY REPORTING IN THE WAKE OF REVIVAL DAY--
--A FLEDGLING REPORTER AND BLOGGER FOR THE DAILY LEDGER, TAO WAS FOUND DEAD THE MORNING OF--
--SUSPECT BLAINE ABEL OF KRONENWETTER, A SNOWMOBILE REPAIRMAN WHO HAS DISAPPEARED SINCE TAO'S DEATH. POLICE ARE ASKING CITIZENS TO--
--HOW WE TREAT EACH OTHER WHEN ALL THE RULES HAVE CHANGED ON US--
--A COMMUNITY FACED WITH DECIDING WHAT TO DO IN THE WAKE OF--
--LEADING MANY TO ASK "WHAT NEXT?"
THIS IS IT. EVERYTHING.
EVERYTHING IS DIFFERENT NOW.

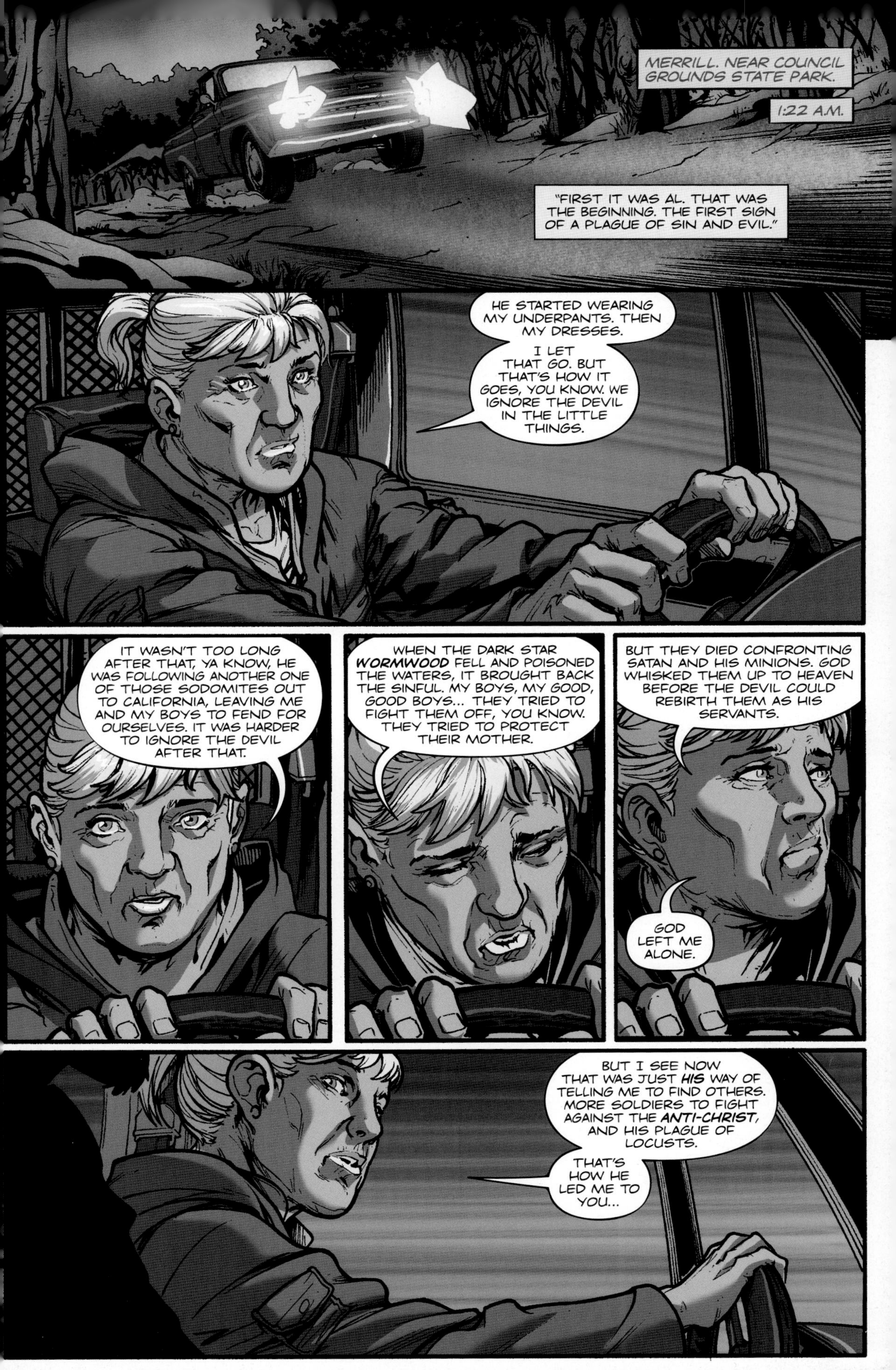
MERRILL. NEAR COUNCIL GROUNDS STATE PARK.
1:22 A.M.
"FIRST IT WAS AL. THAT WAS THE BEGINNING. THE FIRST SIGN OF A PLAGUE OF SIN AND EVIL."
HE STARTED WEARING MY UNDERPANTS. THEN MY DRESSES.
I LET THAT GO. BUT THAT'S HOW IT GOES, YOU KNOW. WE IGNORE THE DEVIL IN THE LITTLE THINGS.
IT WASN'T TOO LONG AFTER THAT, YA KNOW, HE WAS FOLLOWING ANOTHER ONE OF THOSE SODOMITES OUT TO CALIFORNIA, LEAVING ME AND MY BOYS TO FEND FOR OURSELVES. IT WAS HARDER TO IGNORE THE DEVIL AFTER THAT.
WHEN THE DARK STAR WORMWOOD FELL AND POISONED THE WATERS, IT BROUGHT BACK THE SINFUL. MY BOYS, MY GOOD, GOOD BOYS... THEY TRIED TO FIGHT THEM OFF, YOU KNOW. THEY TRIED TO PROTECT THEIR MOTHER.
BUT THEY DIED CONFRONTING SATAN AND HIS MINIONS. GOD WHISKED THEM UP TO HEAVEN BEFORE THE DEVIL COULD REBIRTH THEM AS HIS SERVANTS.
GOD LEFT ME ALONE.
BUT I SEE NOW THAT WAS JUST HIS WAY OF TELLING ME TO FIND OTHERS. MORE SOLDIERS TO FIGHT AGAINST THE ANTI-CHRIST, AND HIS PLAGUE OF LOCUSTS.
THAT'S HOW HE LED ME TO YOU...

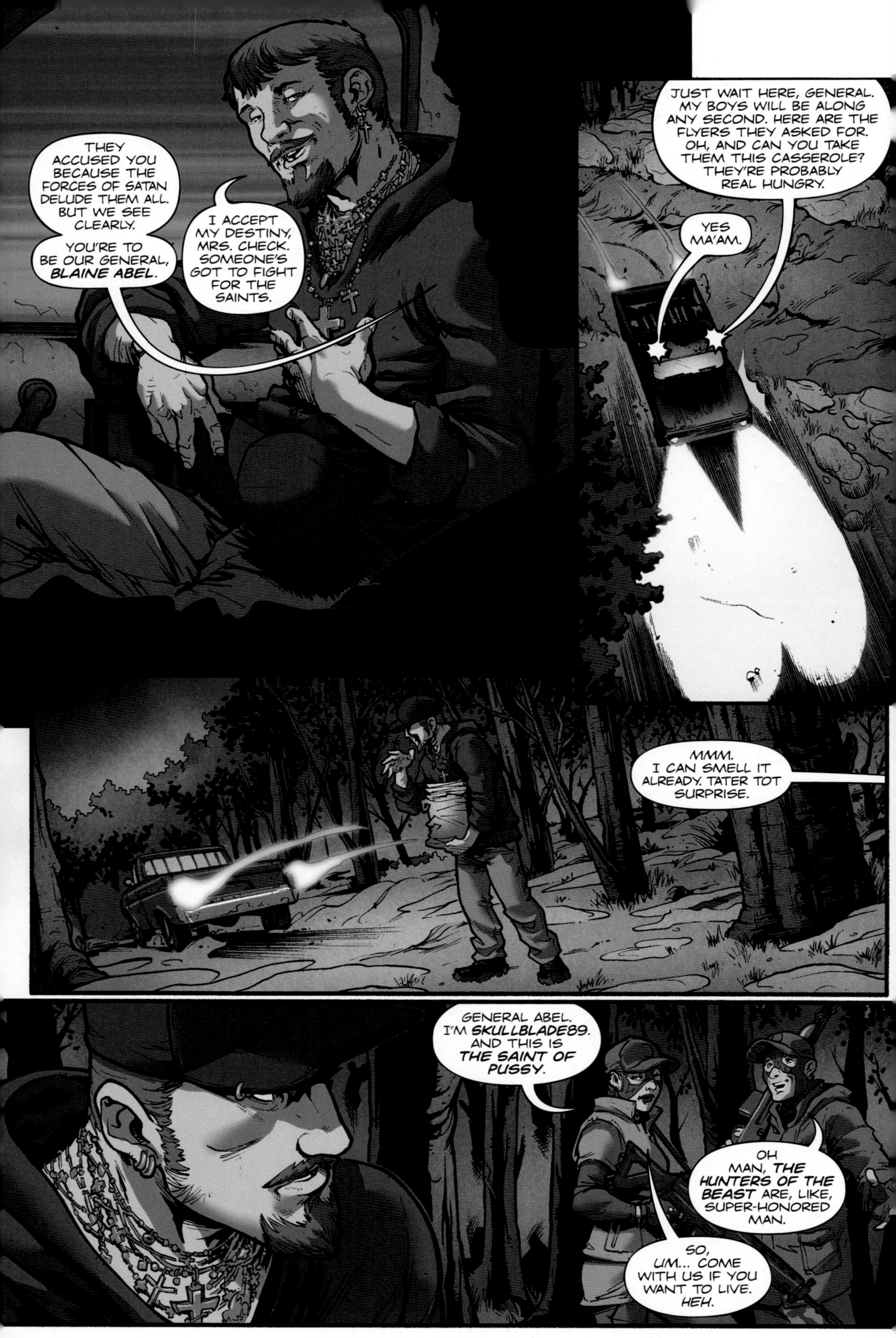

THEY ACCUSED YOU BECAUSE THE FORCES OF SATAN DELUDE THEM ALL. BUT WE SEE CLEARLY.
YOU'RE TO BE OUR GENERAL, **BLAINE ABEL**.
I ACCEPT MY DESTINY, MRS. CHECK. SOMEONE'S GOT TO FIGHT FOR THE SAINTS.
JUST WAIT HERE, GENERAL. MY BOYS WILL BE ALONG ANY SECOND. HERE ARE THE FLYERS THEY ASKED FOR. OH, AND CAN YOU TAKE THEM THIS CASSEROLE? THEY'RE PROBABLY REAL HUNGRY.
YES MA'AM.
MMM. I CAN SMELL IT ALREADY. TATER TOT SURPRISE.
GENERAL ABEL. I'M ***SKULLBLADE89***. AND THIS IS ***THE SAINT OF PUSSY***.
OH MAN, ***THE HUNTERS OF THE BEAST*** ARE, LIKE, SUPER-HONORED MAN.
SO, UM... COME WITH US IF YOU WANT TO LIVE. HEH.

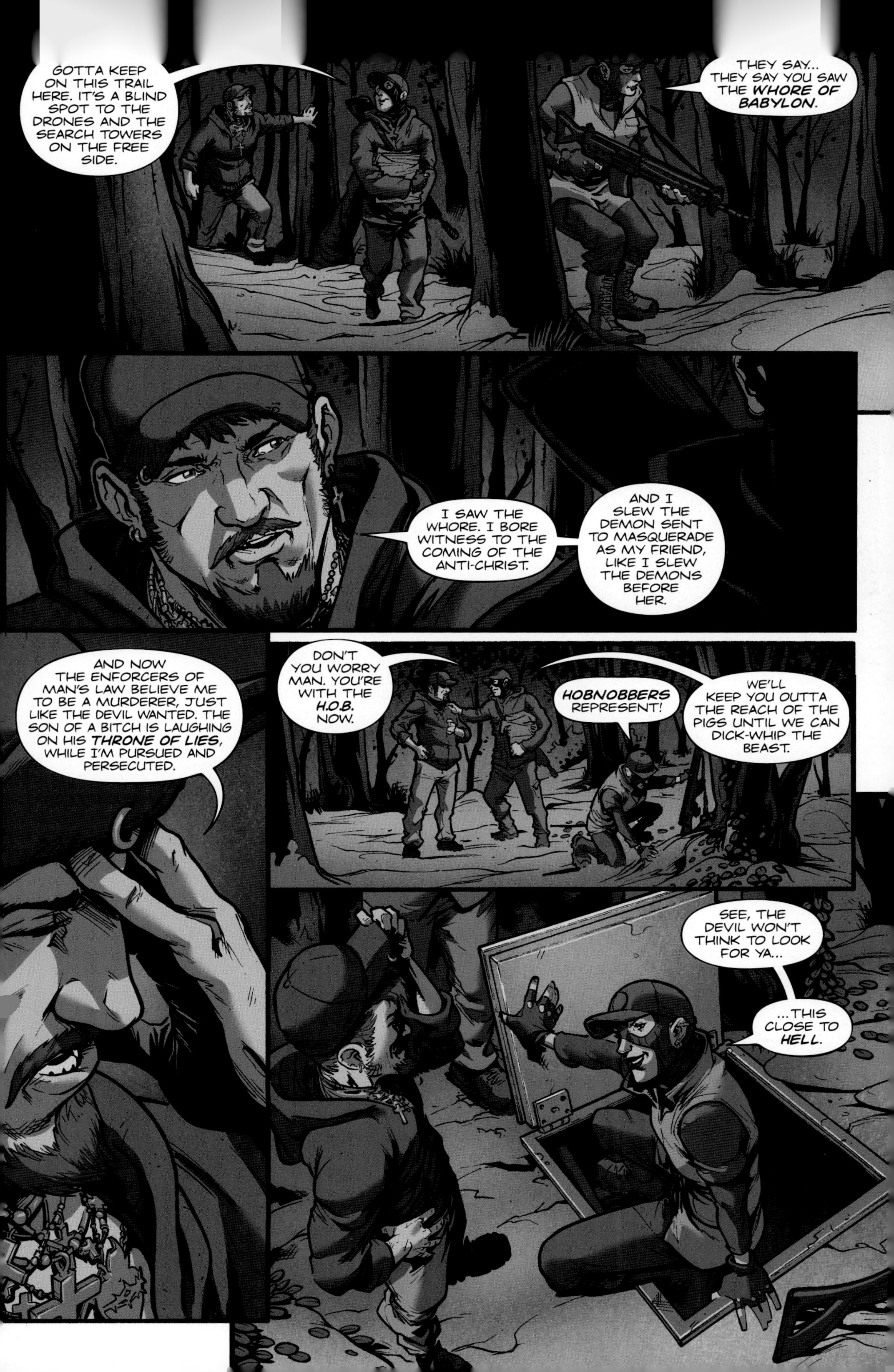
GOTTA KEEP ON THIS TRAIL HERE. IT'S A BLIND SPOT TO THE DRONES AND THE SEARCH TOWERS ON THE FREE SIDE.
THEY SAY... THEY SAY YOU SAW THE **WHORE OF BABYLON**.
I SAW THE WHORE. I BORE WITNESS TO THE COMING OF THE ANTI-CHRIST.
AND I SLEW THE DEMON SENT TO MASQUERADE AS MY FRIEND, LIKE I SLEW THE DEMONS BEFORE HER.
AND NOW THE ENFORCERS OF MAN'S LAW BELIEVE ME TO BE A MURDERER, JUST LIKE THE DEVIL WANTED. THE SON OF A BITCH IS LAUGHING ON HIS **THRONE OF LIES**, WHILE I'M PURSUED AND PERSECUTED.
DON'T YOU WORRY MAN. YOU'RE WITH THE **H.O.B.** NOW.
HOBNOBBERS REPRESENT!
WE'LL KEEP YOU OUTTA THE REACH OF THE PIGS UNTIL WE CAN DICK-WHIP THE BEAST.
SEE, THE DEVIL WON'T THINK TO LOOK FOR YA...
...THIS CLOSE TO **HELL**.

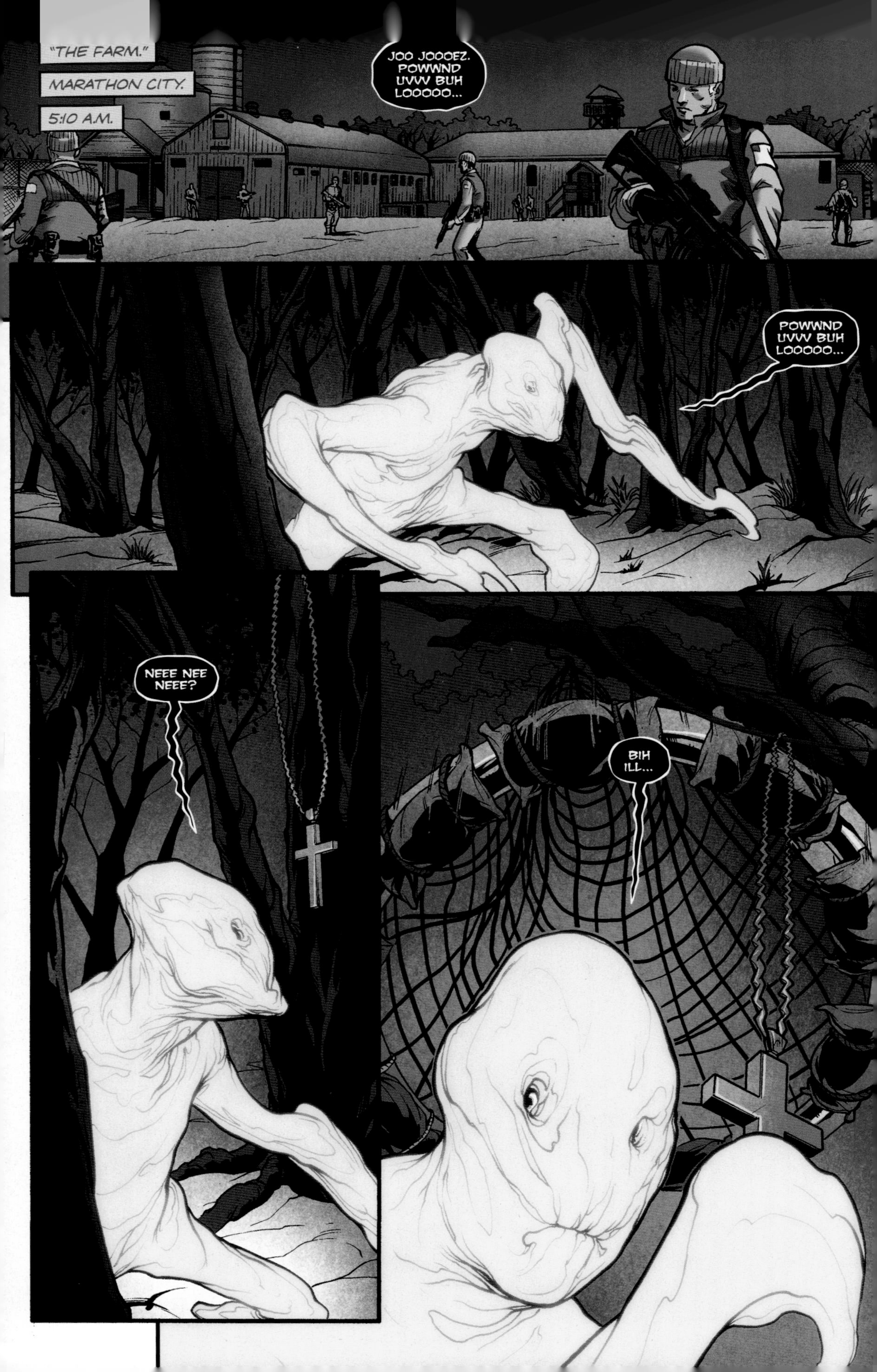
"THE FARM."
MARATHON CITY.
5:10 A.M.
JOO JOOOEZ. POWWND UVVV BUH LOOOOO...
POWWND UVVV BUH LOOOOO...
NEEE NEE NEEE?
BIH ILL...

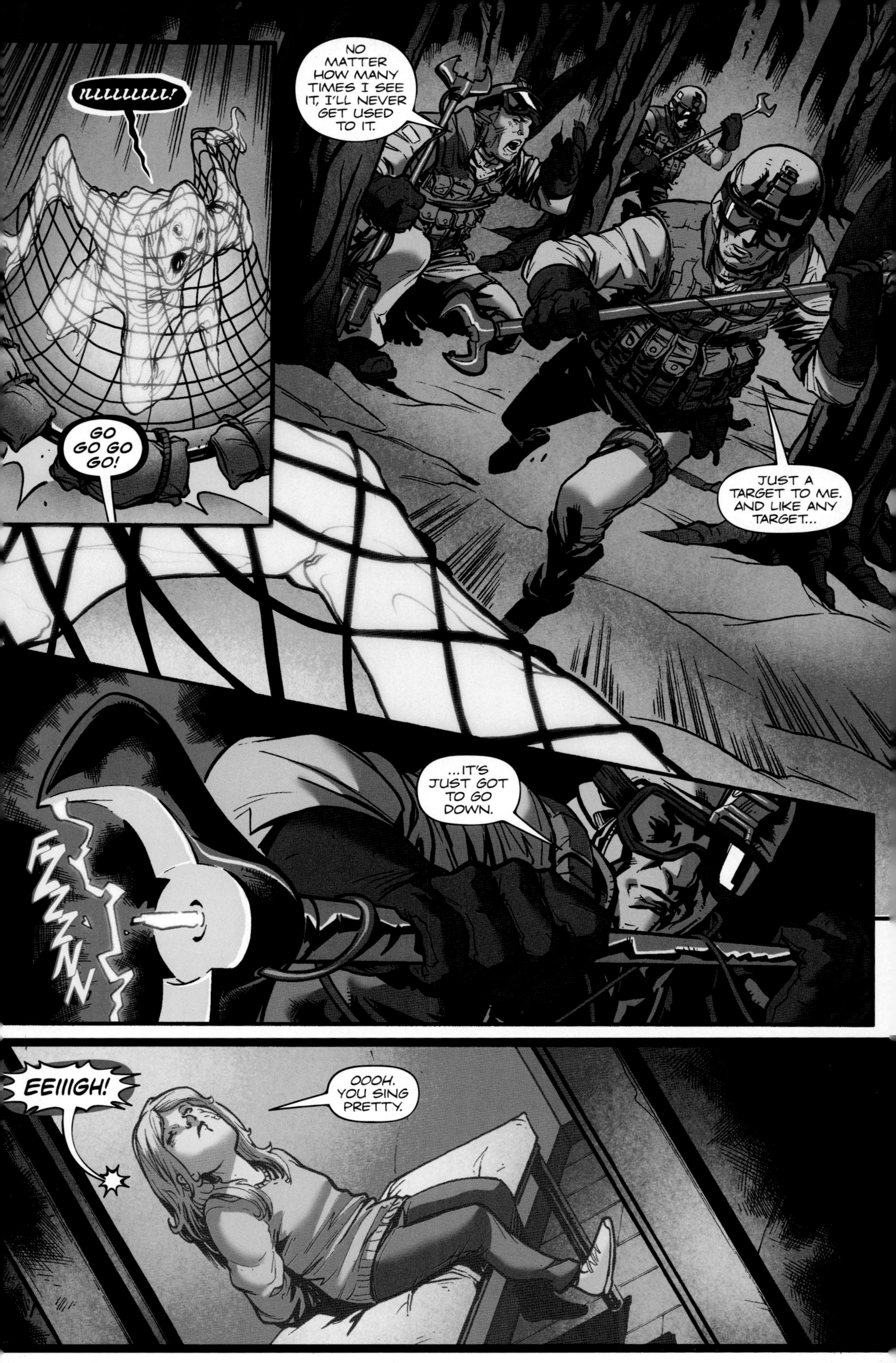
ILLLLLLLLL!
NO MATTER HOW MANY TIMES I SEE IT, I'LL NEVER GET USED TO IT.
GO GO GO GO!
JUST A TARGET TO ME. AND LIKE ANY TARGET...
...IT'S JUST GOT TO GO DOWN.
FZZZNN
EEIIIGH!
OOOH. YOU SING PRETTY.

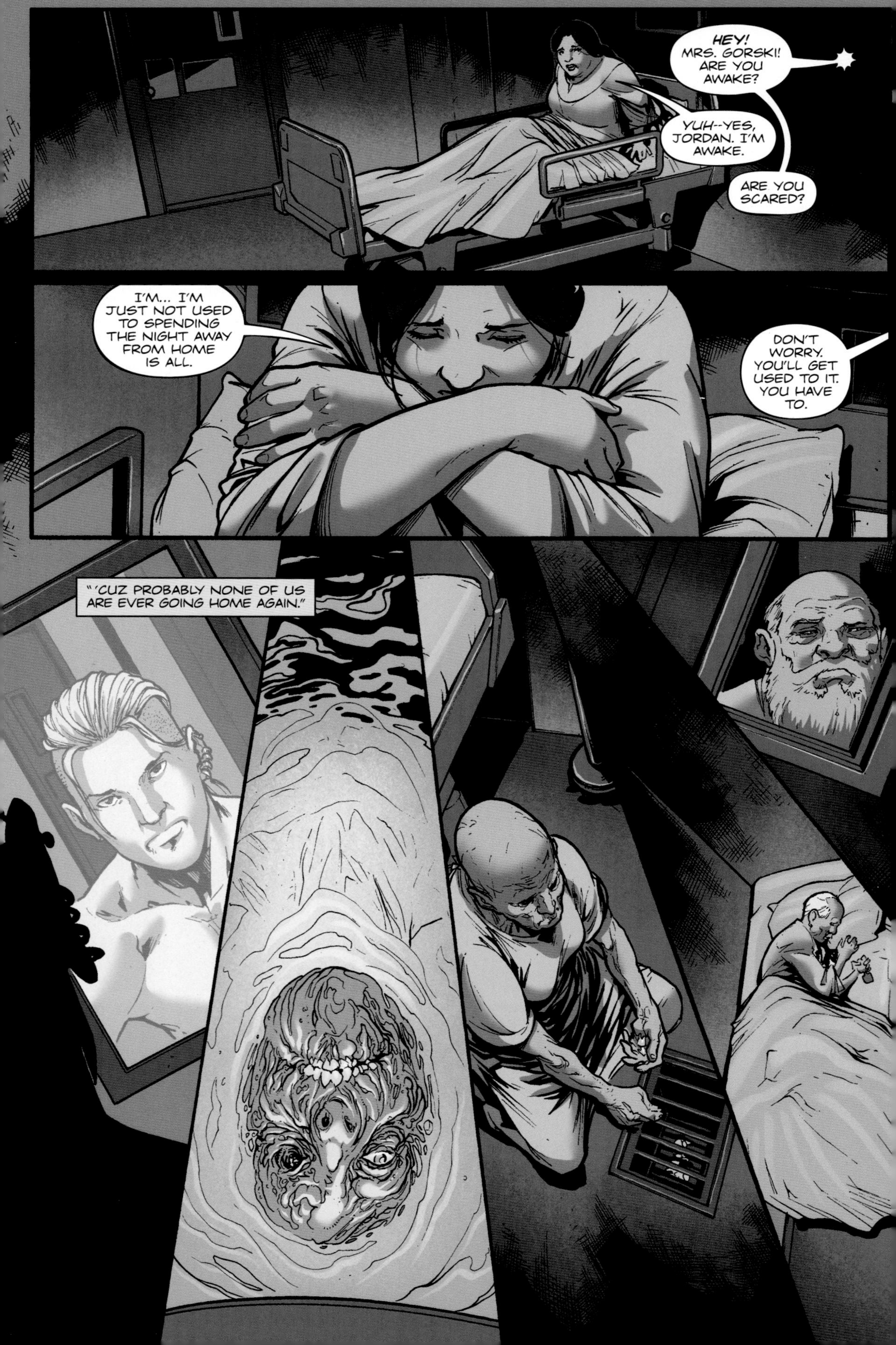
HEY! MRS. GORSKI! ARE YOU AWAKE?
YUH--YES, JORDAN. I'M AWAKE.
ARE YOU SCARED?
I'M... I'M JUST NOT USED TO SPENDING THE NIGHT AWAY FROM HOME IS ALL.
DON'T WORRY. YOU'LL GET USED TO IT. YOU HAVE TO.
"'CUZ PROBABLY NONE OF US ARE EVER GOING HOME AGAIN."

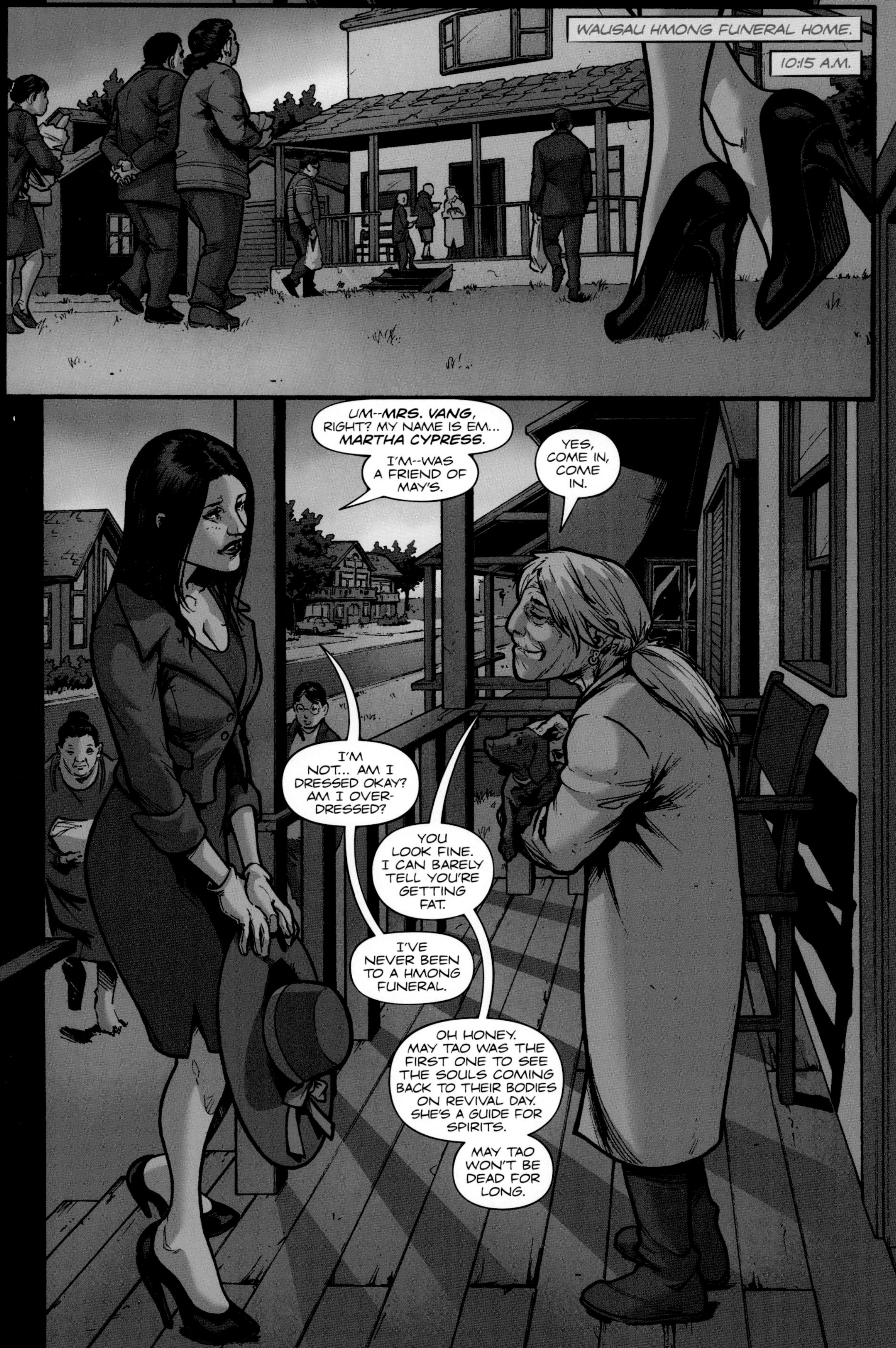
WAUSAU HMONG FUNERAL HOME.
10:15 A.M.
UM--MRS. VANG, RIGHT? MY NAME IS EM... MARTHA CYPRESS.
I'M--WAS A FRIEND OF MAY'S.
YES, COME IN, COME IN.
I'M NOT... AM I DRESSED OKAY? AM I OVER-DRESSED?
YOU LOOK FINE. I CAN BARELY TELL YOU'RE GETTING FAT.
I'VE NEVER BEEN TO A HMONG FUNERAL.
OH HONEY. MAY TAO WAS THE FIRST ONE TO SEE THE SOULS COMING BACK TO THEIR BODIES ON REVIVAL DAY. SHE'S A GUIDE FOR SPIRITS.
MAY TAO WON'T BE DEAD FOR LONG.

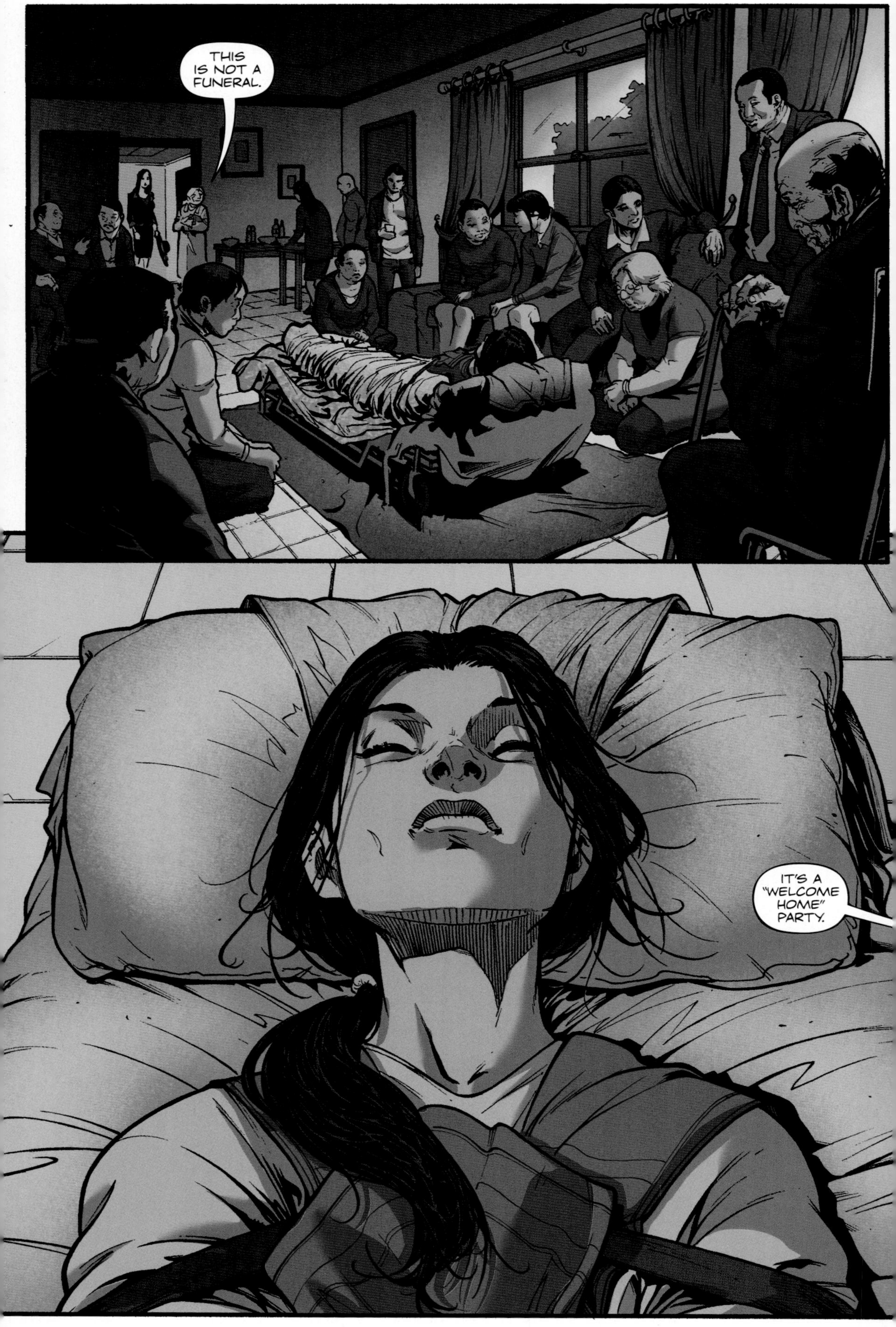
THIS IS NOT A FUNERAL.
IT'S A "WELCOME HOME" PARTY.

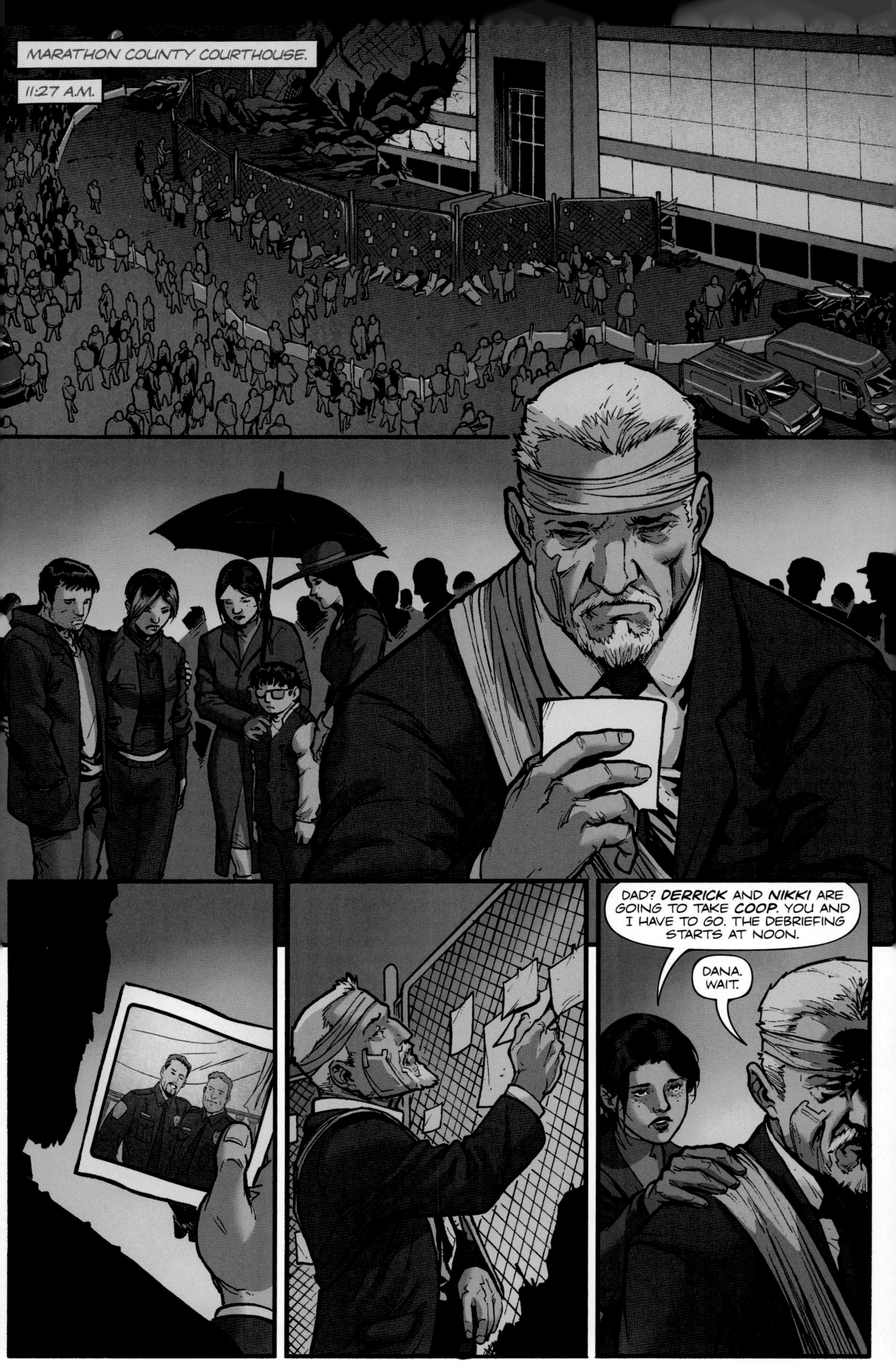
MARATHON COUNTY COURTHOUSE.
11:27 A.M.
DAD? DERRICK AND NIKKI ARE GOING TO TAKE COOP. YOU AND I HAVE TO GO. THE DEBRIEFING STARTS AT NOON.
DANA. WAIT.

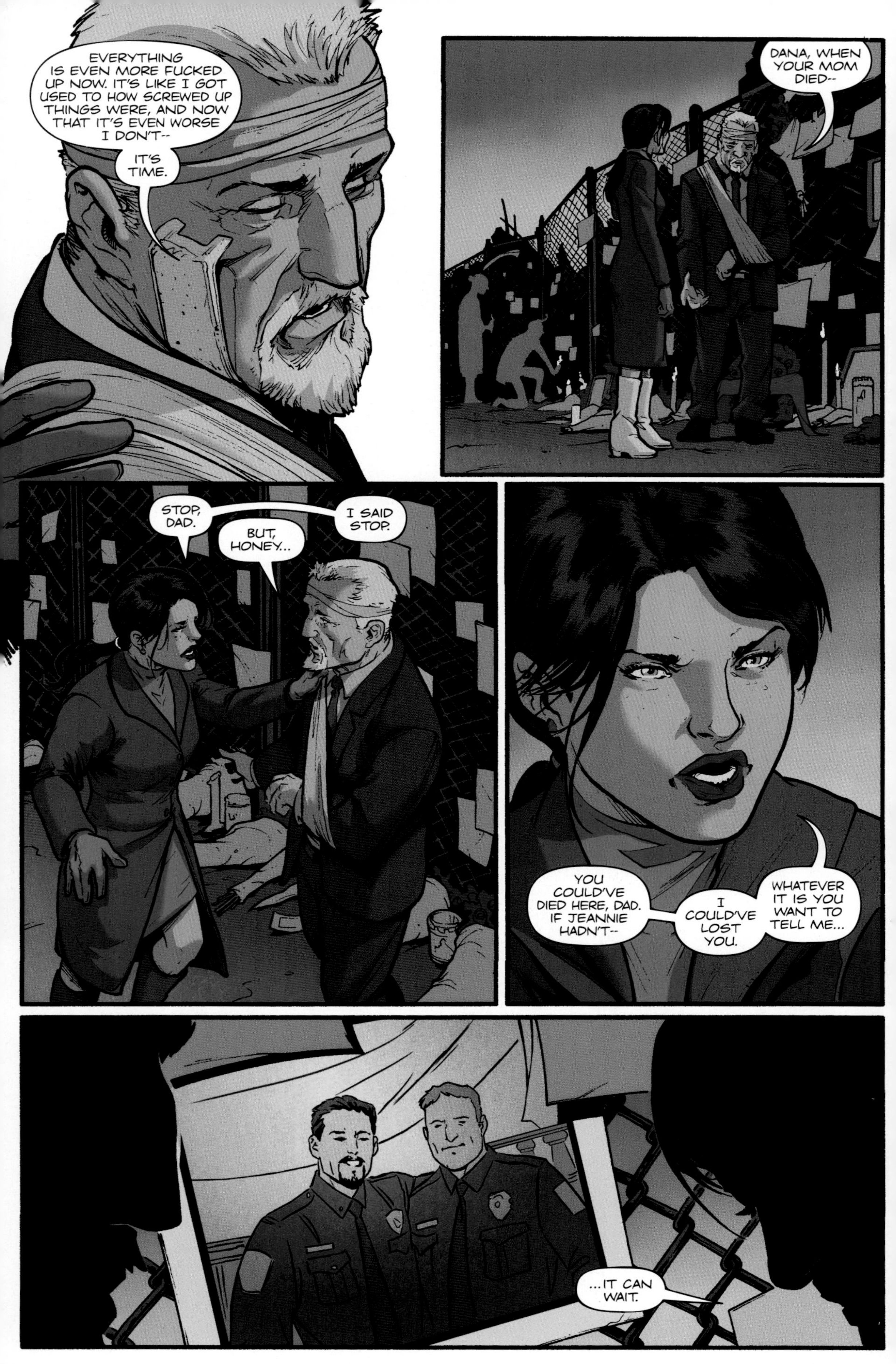
EVERYTHING IS EVEN MORE FUCKED UP NOW. IT'S LIKE I GOT USED TO HOW SCREWED UP THINGS WERE, AND NOW THAT IT'S EVEN WORSE I DON'T--
IT'S TIME.
DANA, WHEN YOUR MOM DIED--
STOP, DAD.
BUT, HONEY...
I SAID STOP.
WHATEVER IT IS YOU WANT TO TELL ME...
I COULD'VE LOST YOU.
YOU COULD'VE DIED HERE, DAD. IF JEANNIE HADN'T--
...IT CAN WAIT.

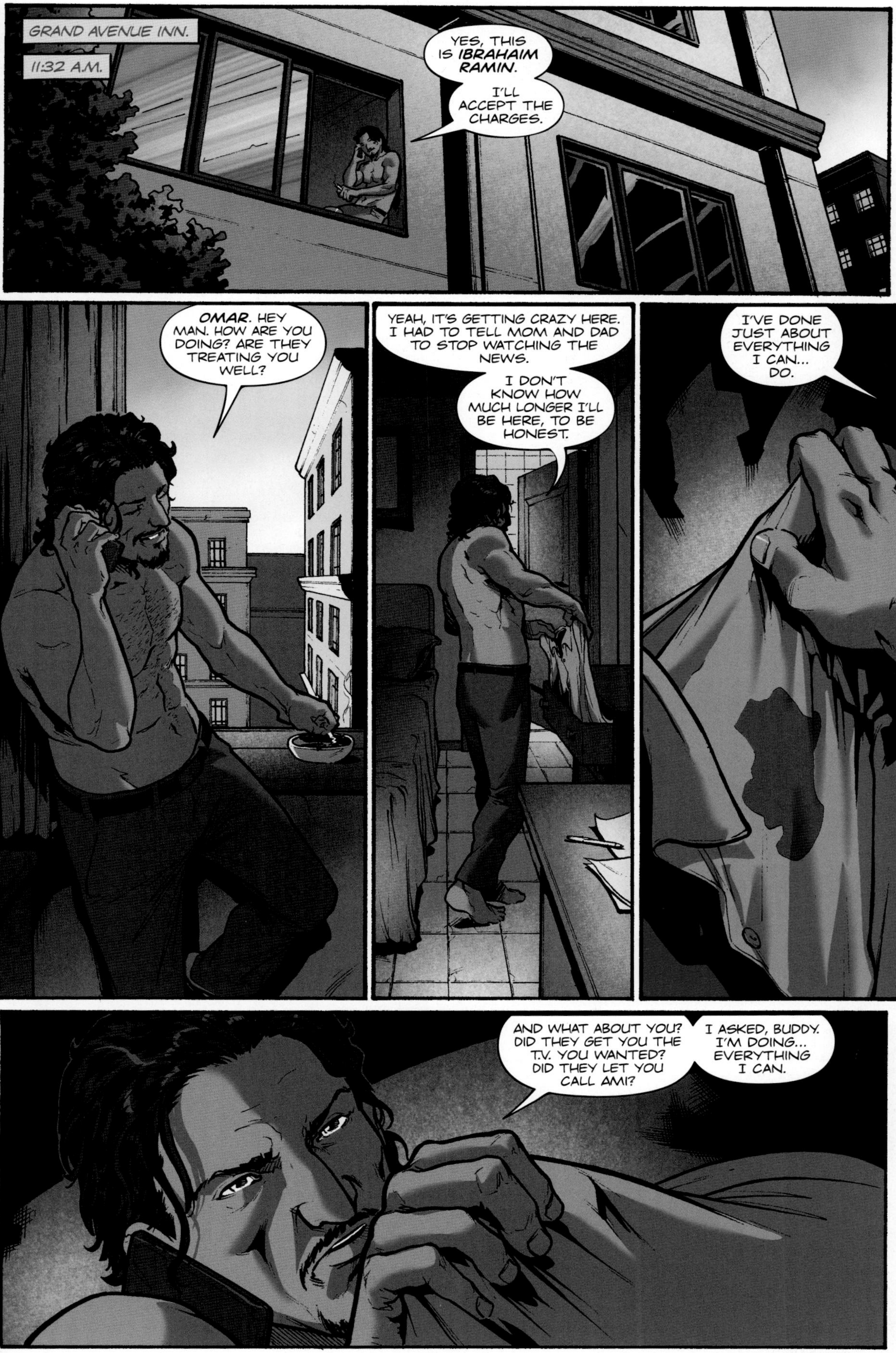
GRAND AVENUE INN.
11:32 A.M.
YES, THIS IS IBRAHAIM RAMIN.
I'LL ACCEPT THE CHARGES.
OMAR. HEY MAN. HOW ARE YOU DOING? ARE THEY TREATING YOU WELL?
YEAH, IT'S GETTING CRAZY HERE. I HAD TO TELL MOM AND DAD TO STOP WATCHING THE NEWS.
I DON'T KNOW HOW MUCH LONGER I'LL BE HERE, TO BE HONEST.
I'VE DONE JUST ABOUT EVERYTHING I CAN... DO.
AND WHAT ABOUT YOU? DID THEY GET YOU THE T.V. YOU WANTED? DID THEY LET YOU CALL AMI?
I ASKED, BUDDY. I'M DOING... EVERYTHING I CAN.

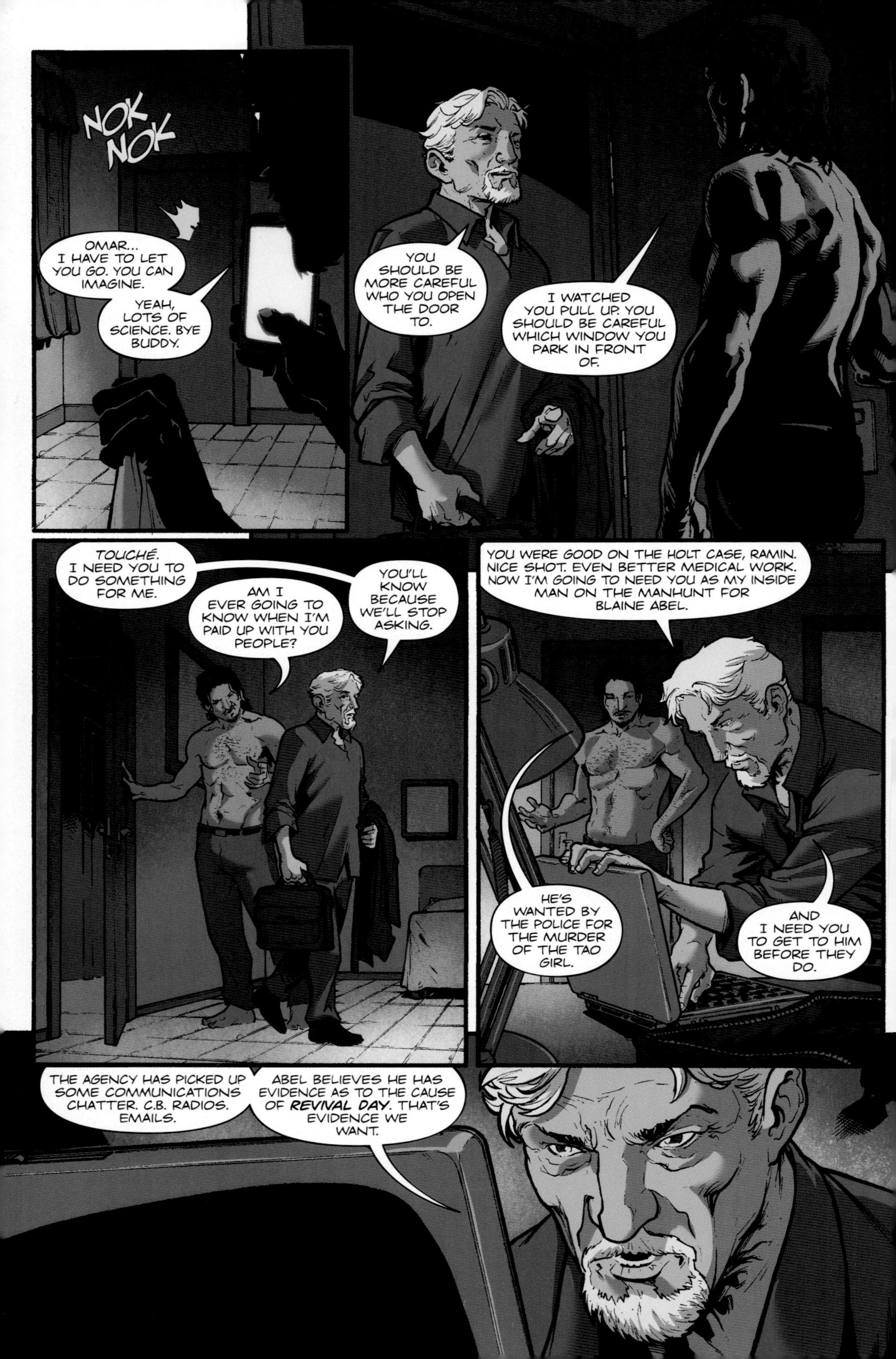
NOK NOK
OMAR... I HAVE TO LET YOU GO. YOU CAN IMAGINE.
YEAH, LOTS OF SCIENCE. BYE BUDDY.
YOU SHOULD BE MORE CAREFUL WHO YOU OPEN THE DOOR TO.
I WATCHED YOU PULL UP. YOU SHOULD BE CAREFUL WHICH WINDOW YOU PARK IN FRONT OF.
TOUCHÉ. I NEED YOU TO DO SOMETHING FOR ME.
AM I EVER GOING TO KNOW WHEN I'M PAID UP WITH YOU PEOPLE?
YOU'LL KNOW BECAUSE WE'LL STOP ASKING.
YOU WERE GOOD ON THE HOLT CASE, RAMIN. NICE SHOT. EVEN BETTER MEDICAL WORK. NOW I'M GOING TO NEED YOU AS MY INSIDE MAN ON THE MANHUNT FOR BLAINE ABEL.
HE'S WANTED BY THE POLICE FOR THE MURDER OF THE TAO GIRL.
AND I NEED YOU TO GET TO HIM BEFORE THEY DO.
THE AGENCY HAS PICKED UP SOME COMMUNICATIONS CHATTER. C.B. RADIOS. EMAILS.
ABEL BELIEVES HE HAS EVIDENCE AS TO THE CAUSE OF REVIVAL DAY. THAT'S EVIDENCE WE WANT.

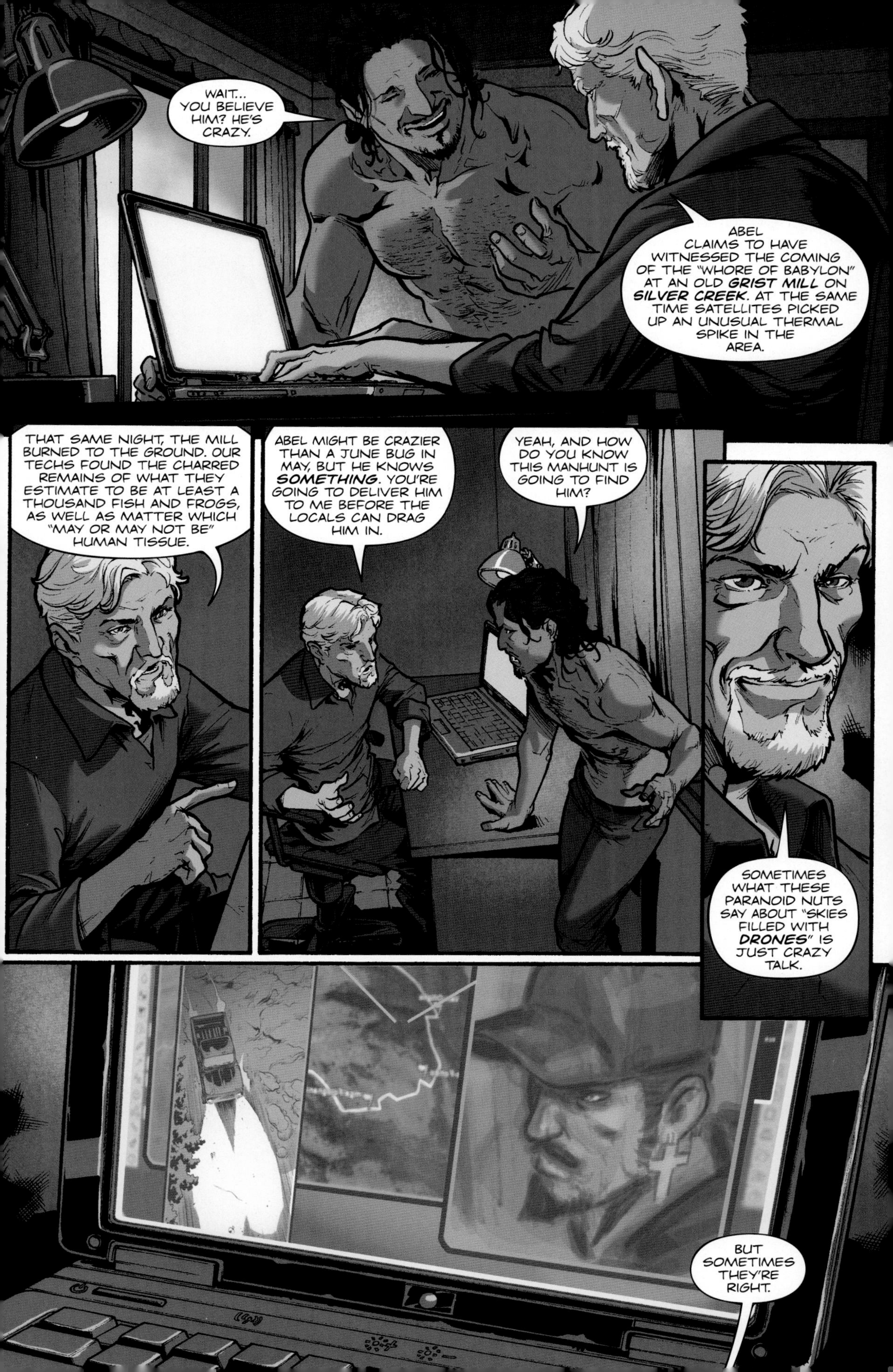
WAIT... YOU BELIEVE HIM? HE'S CRAZY.
ABEL CLAIMS TO HAVE WITNESSED THE COMING OF THE "WHORE OF BABYLON" AT AN OLD GRIST MILL ON SILVER CREEK. AT THE SAME TIME SATELLITES PICKED UP AN UNUSUAL THERMAL SPIKE IN THE AREA.
THAT SAME NIGHT, THE MILL BURNED TO THE GROUND. OUR TECHS FOUND THE CHARRED REMAINS OF WHAT THEY ESTIMATE TO BE AT LEAST A THOUSAND FISH AND FROGS, AS WELL AS MATTER WHICH "MAY OR MAY NOT BE" HUMAN TISSUE.
ABEL MIGHT BE CRAZIER THAN A JUNE BUG IN MAY, BUT HE KNOWS SOMETHING. YOU'RE GOING TO DELIVER HIM TO ME BEFORE THE LOCALS CAN DRAG HIM IN.
YEAH, AND HOW DO YOU KNOW THIS MANHUNT IS GOING TO FIND HIM?
SOMETIMES WHAT THESE PARANOID NUTS SAY ABOUT "SKIES FILLED WITH DRONES" IS JUST CRAZY TALK.
BUT SOMETIMES THEY'RE RIGHT.

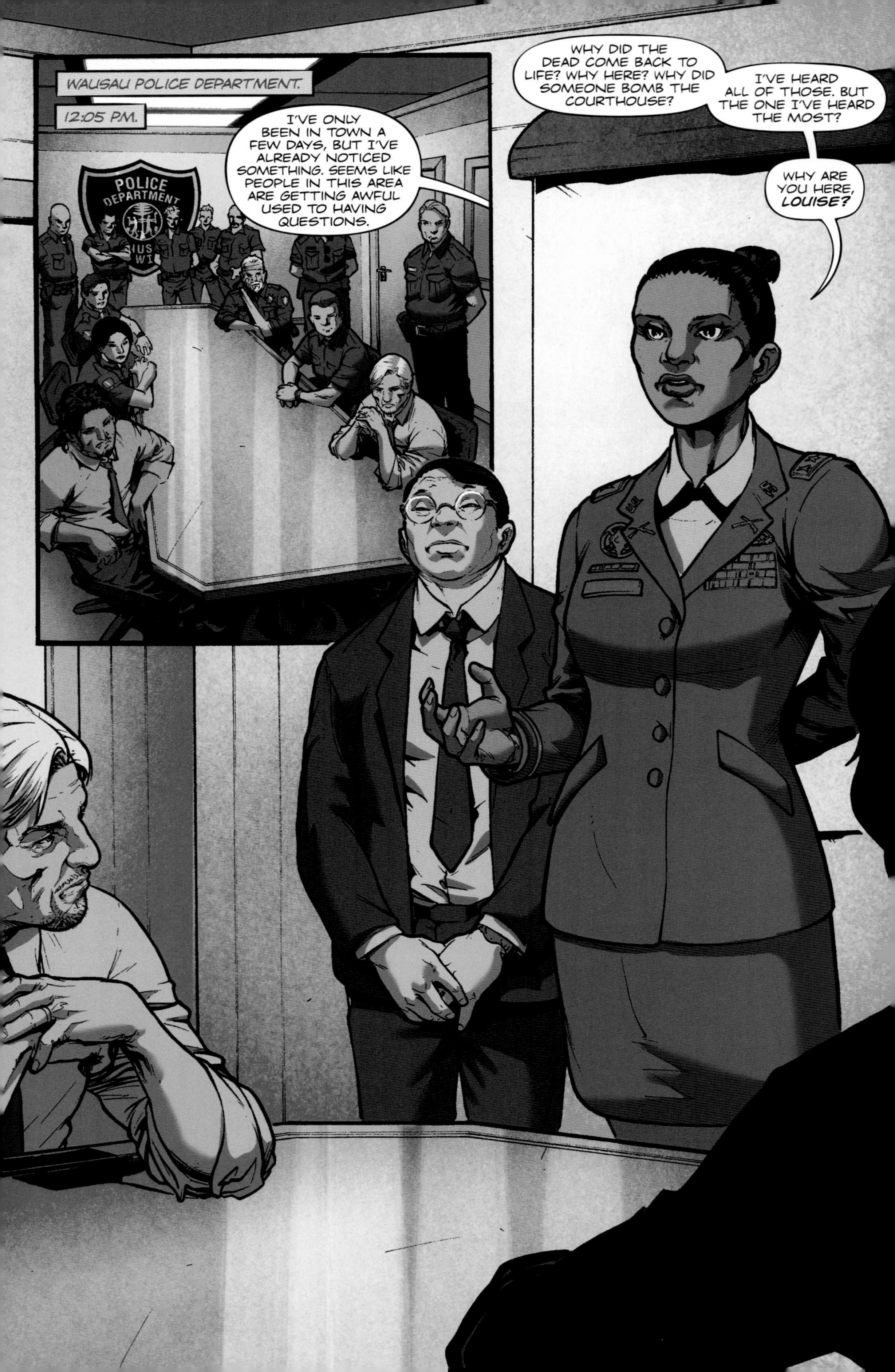
WAUSAU POLICE DEPARTMENT.
12:05 P.M.
POLICE DEPARTMENT
I'VE ONLY BEEN IN TOWN A FEW DAYS, BUT I'VE ALREADY NOTICED SOMETHING. SEEMS LIKE PEOPLE IN THIS AREA ARE GETTING AWFUL USED TO HAVING QUESTIONS.
WHY DID THE DEAD COME BACK TO LIFE? WHY HERE? WHY DID SOMEONE BOMB THE COURTHOUSE?
I'VE HEARD ALL OF THOSE. BUT THE ONE I'VE HEARD THE MOST?
WHY ARE YOU HERE, *LOUISE?*

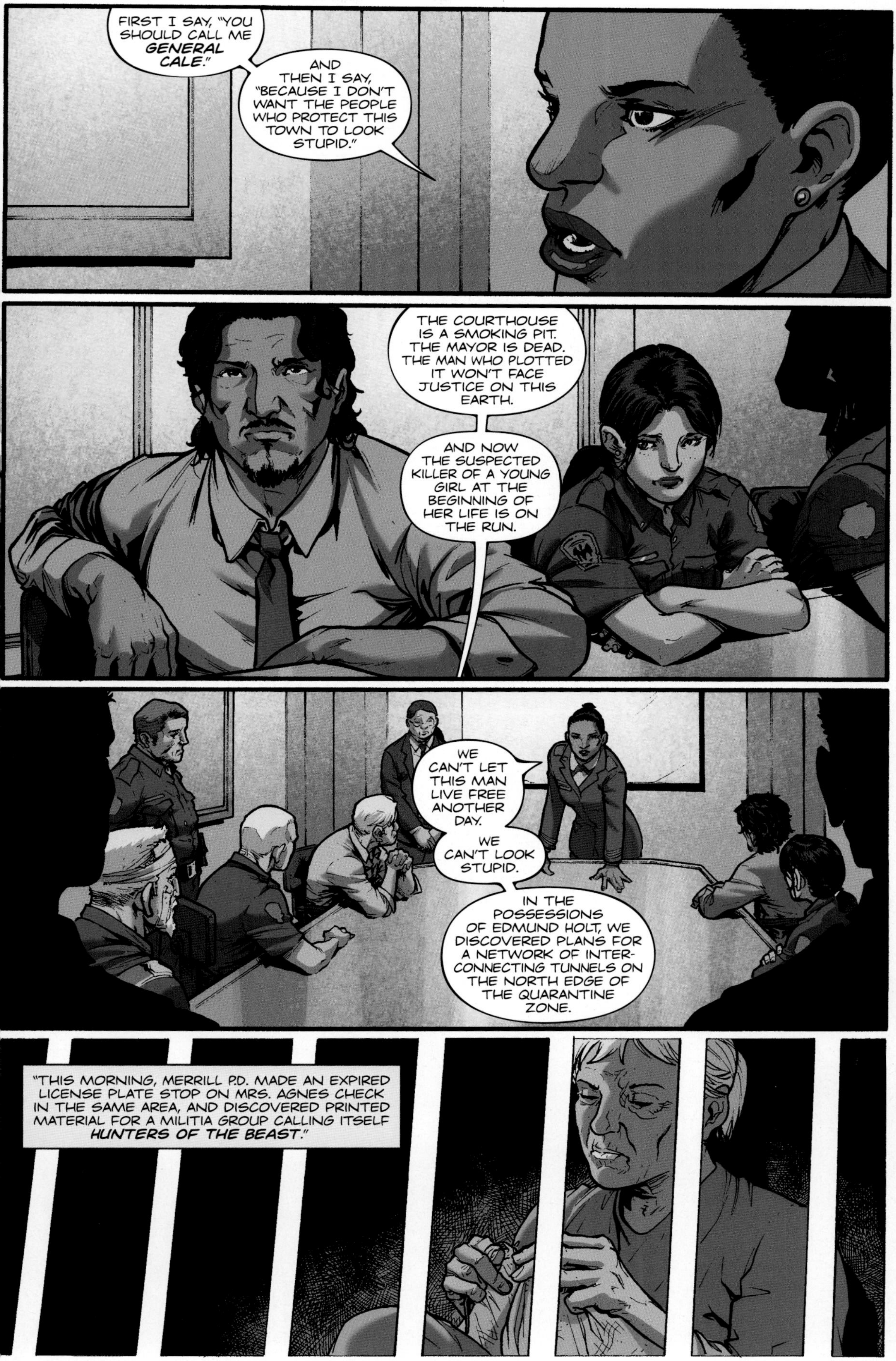
FIRST I SAY, "YOU SHOULD CALL ME GENERAL CALE."
AND THEN I SAY, "BECAUSE I DON'T WANT THE PEOPLE WHO PROTECT THIS TOWN TO LOOK STUPID."
THE COURTHOUSE IS A SMOKING PIT. THE MAYOR IS DEAD. THE MAN WHO PLOTTED IT WON'T FACE JUSTICE ON THIS EARTH.
AND NOW THE SUSPECTED KILLER OF A YOUNG GIRL AT THE BEGINNING OF HER LIFE IS ON THE RUN.
WE CAN'T LET THIS MAN LIVE FREE ANOTHER DAY.
WE CAN'T LOOK STUPID.
IN THE POSSESSIONS OF EDMUND HOLT, WE DISCOVERED PLANS FOR A NETWORK OF INTER-CONNECTING TUNNELS ON THE NORTH EDGE OF THE QUARANTINE ZONE.
"THIS MORNING, MERRILL P.D. MADE AN EXPIRED LICENSE PLATE STOP ON MRS. AGNES CHECK IN THE SAME AREA, AND DISCOVERED PRINTED MATERIAL FOR A MILITIA GROUP CALLING ITSELF HUNTERS OF THE BEAST."

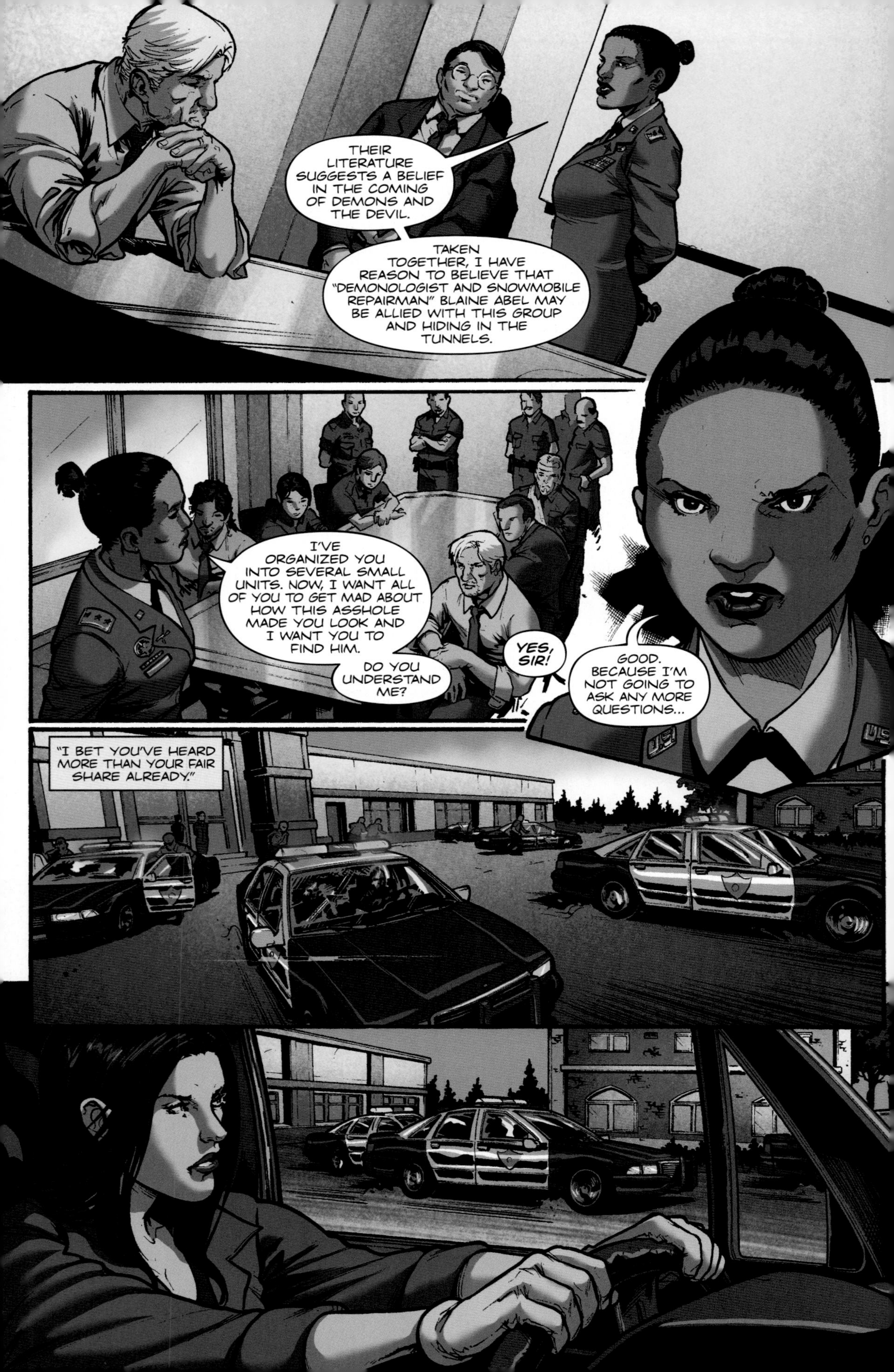

THEIR LITERATURE SUGGESTS A BELIEF IN THE COMING OF DEMONS AND THE DEVIL.
TAKEN TOGETHER, I HAVE REASON TO BELIEVE THAT "DEMONOLOGIST AND SNOWMOBILE REPAIRMAN" BLAINE ABEL MAY BE ALLIED WITH THIS GROUP AND HIDING IN THE TUNNELS.
I'VE ORGANIZED YOU INTO SEVERAL SMALL UNITS. NOW, I WANT ALL OF YOU TO GET MAD ABOUT HOW THIS ASSHOLE MADE YOU LOOK AND I WANT YOU TO FIND HIM.
DO YOU UNDERSTAND ME?
YES, SIR!
GOOD. BECAUSE I'M NOT GOING TO ASK ANY MORE QUESTIONS...
"I BET YOU'VE HEARD MORE THAN YOUR FAIR SHARE ALREADY."

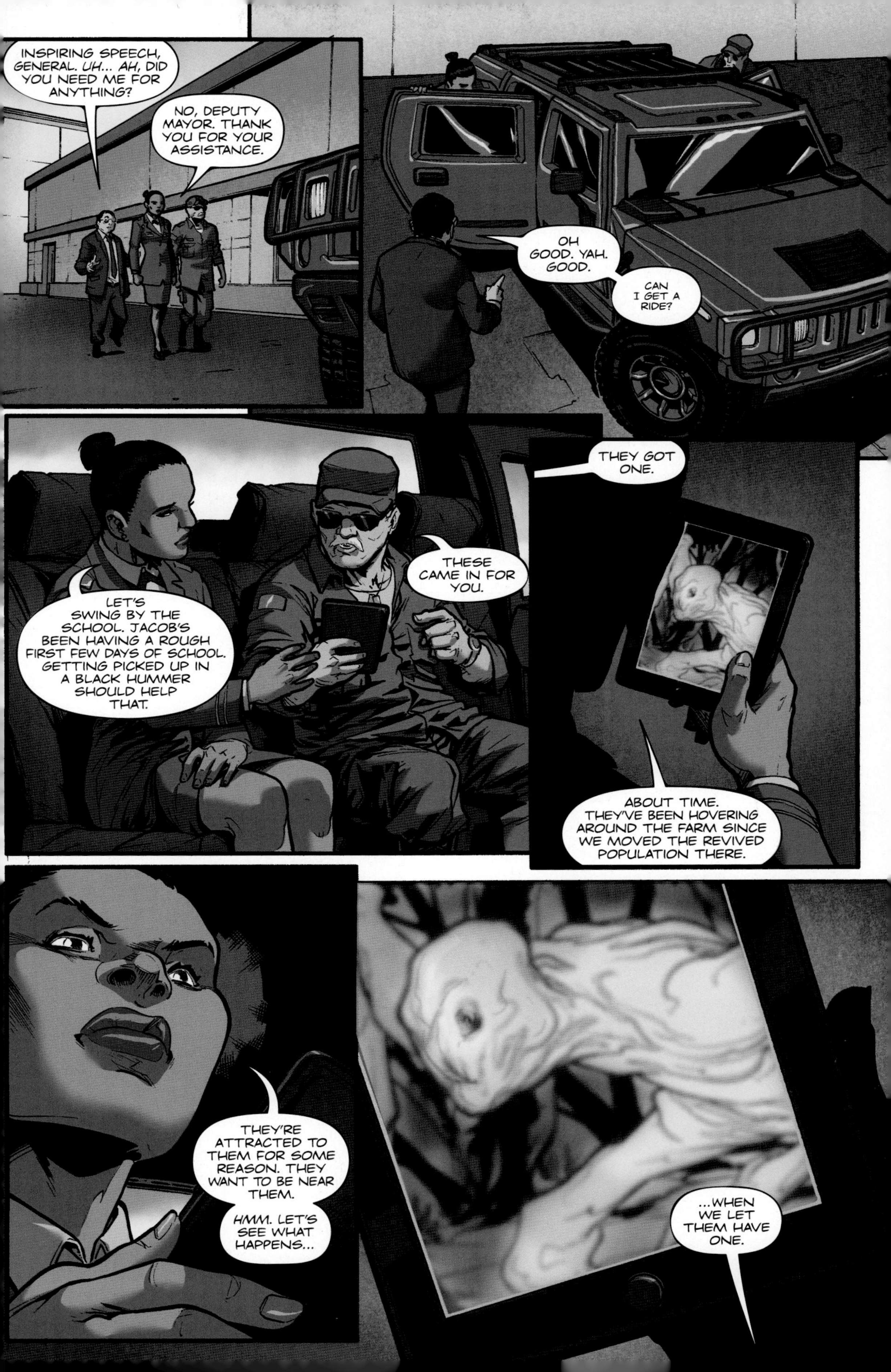
INSPIRING SPEECH, GENERAL. UH... AH, DID YOU NEED ME FOR ANYTHING?
NO, DEPUTY MAYOR. THANK YOU FOR YOUR ASSISTANCE.
OH GOOD. YAH. GOOD.
CAN I GET A RIDE?
THESE CAME IN FOR YOU.
LET'S SWING BY THE SCHOOL. JACOB'S BEEN HAVING A ROUGH FIRST FEW DAYS OF SCHOOL. GETTING PICKED UP IN A BLACK HUMMER SHOULD HELP THAT.
THEY GOT ONE.
ABOUT TIME. THEY'VE BEEN HOVERING AROUND THE FARM SINCE WE MOVED THE REVIVED POPULATION THERE.
THEY'RE ATTRACTED TO THEM FOR SOME REASON. THEY WANT TO BE NEAR THEM.
HMM. LET'S SEE WHAT HAPPENS...
...WHEN WE LET THEM HAVE ONE.

BEEEEP
BEEEP
BEEEP

12:45 PERIMETER CHECK.

WEST CLEAR. SOUTH--

OH MOTHER-FUCKER.

TUMP TUMP

WHAT THE--?!

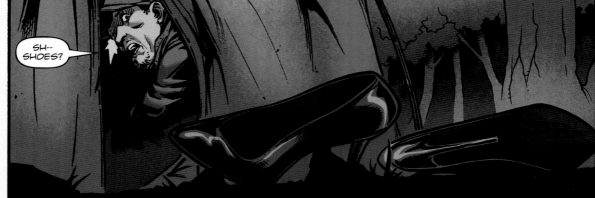

SH--SHOES?

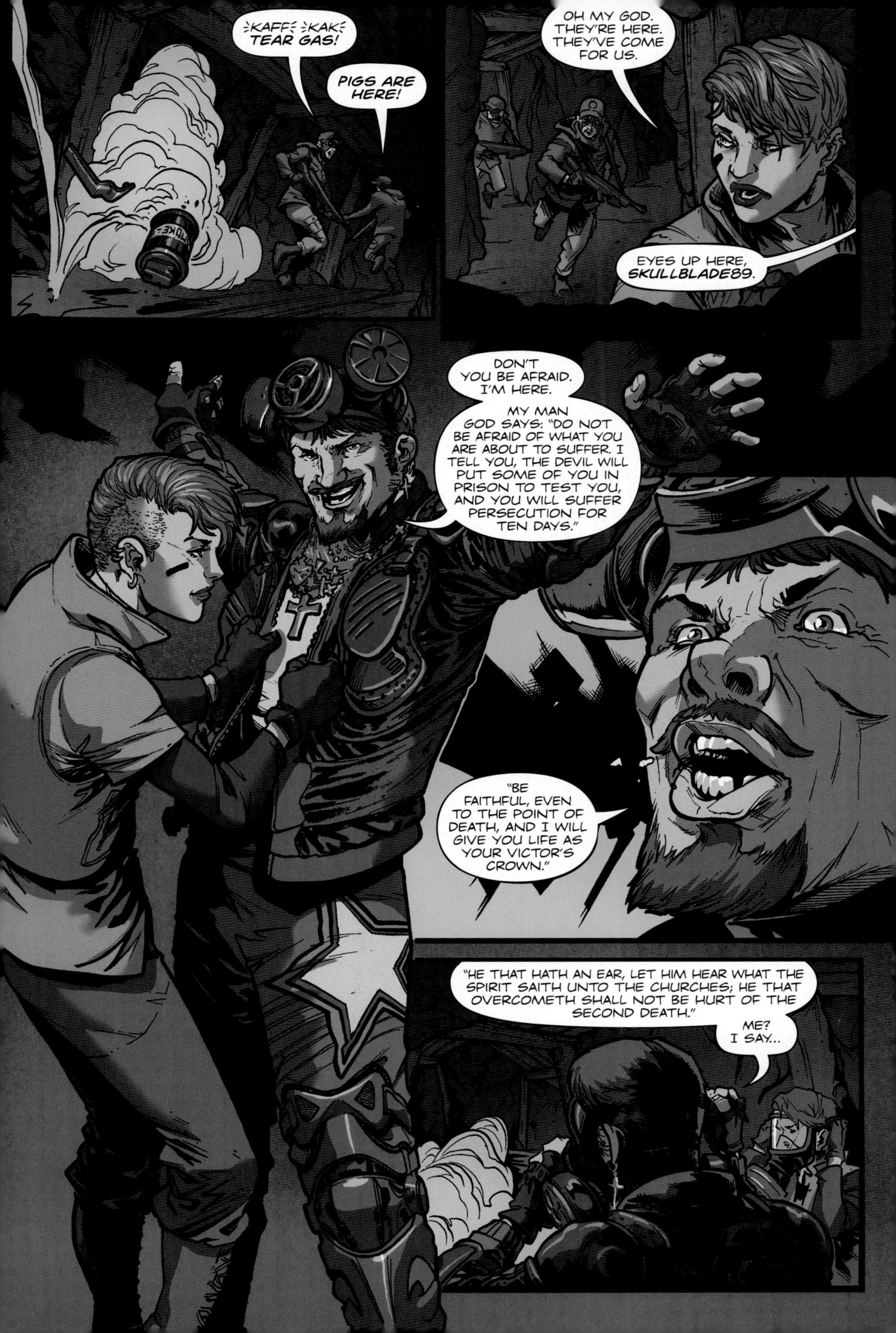

KAFF KAK TEAR GAS!
PIGS ARE HERE!
SMOKE
OH MY GOD. THEY'RE HERE. THEY'VE COME FOR US.
EYES UP HERE, SKULLBLADE89.
DON'T YOU BE AFRAID. I'M HERE.
MY MAN GOD SAYS: "DO NOT BE AFRAID OF WHAT YOU ARE ABOUT TO SUFFER. I TELL YOU, THE DEVIL WILL PUT SOME OF YOU IN PRISON TO TEST YOU, AND YOU WILL SUFFER PERSECUTION FOR TEN DAYS."
"BE FAITHFUL, EVEN TO THE POINT OF DEATH, AND I WILL GIVE YOU LIFE AS YOUR VICTOR'S CROWN."
"HE THAT HATH AN EAR, LET HIM HEAR WHAT THE SPIRIT SAITH UNTO THE CHURCHES; HE THAT OVERCOMETH SHALL NOT BE HURT OF THE SECOND DEATH."
ME? I SAY...

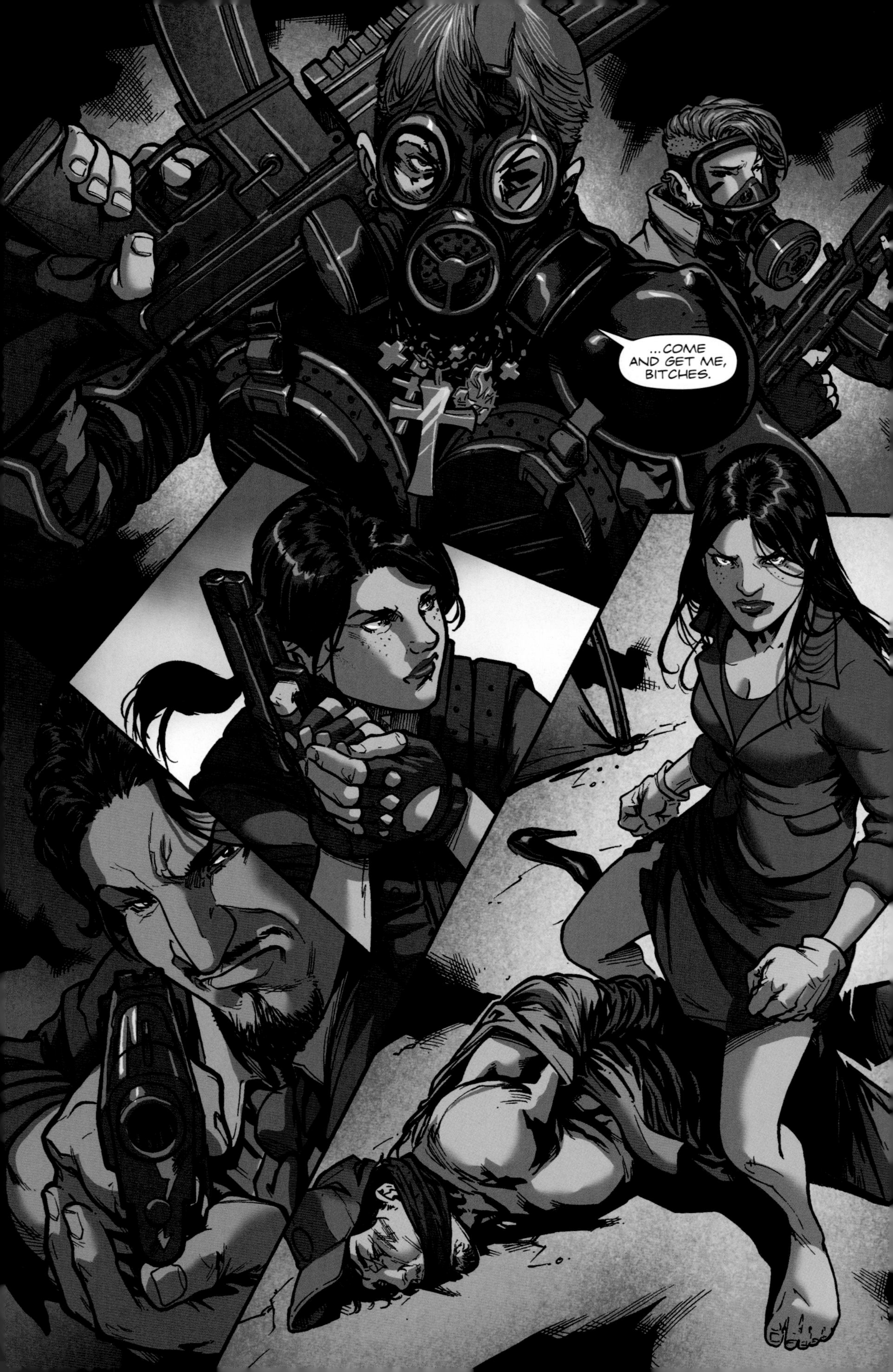
...COME AND GET ME, BITCHES.

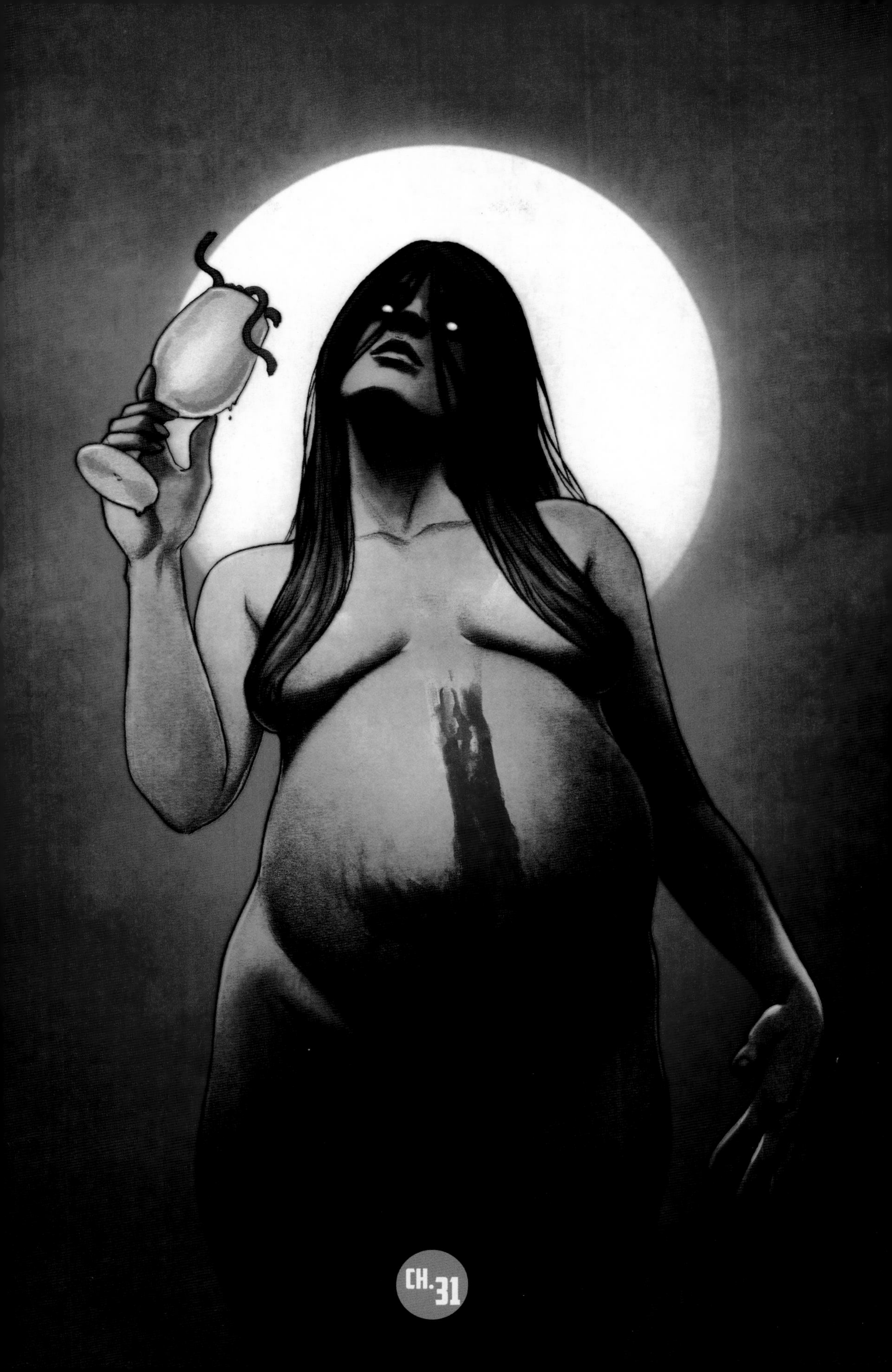
CH. 31

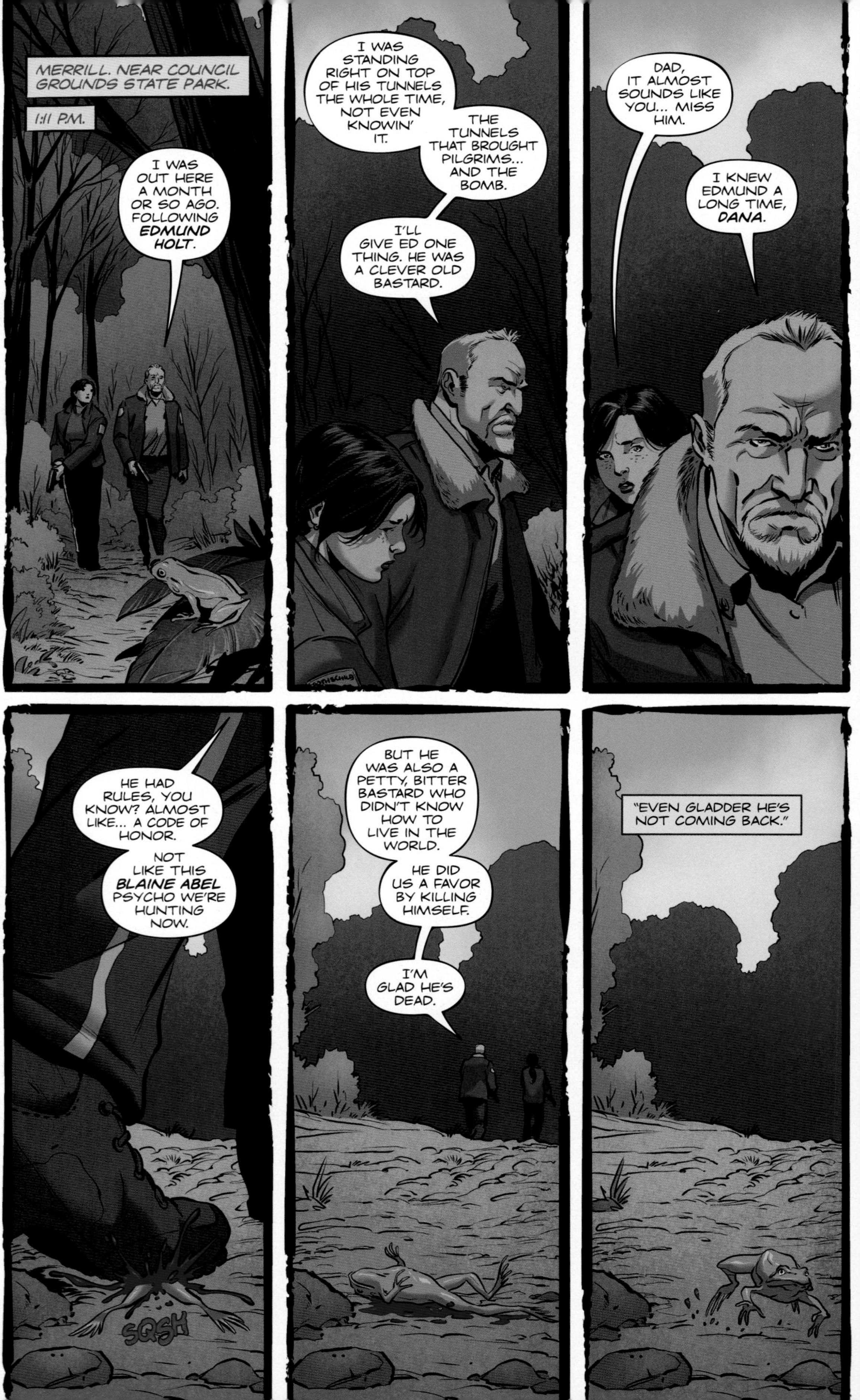
MERRILL. NEAR COUNCIL GROUNDS STATE PARK.
1:11 P.M.
I WAS OUT HERE A MONTH OR SO AGO. FOLLOWING **EDMUND HOLT**.
I WAS STANDING RIGHT ON TOP OF HIS TUNNELS THE WHOLE TIME, NOT EVEN KNOWIN' IT.
THE TUNNELS THAT BROUGHT PILGRIMS... AND THE BOMB.
I'LL GIVE ED ONE THING. HE WAS A CLEVER OLD BASTARD.
DAD, IT ALMOST SOUNDS LIKE YOU... MISS HIM.
I KNEW EDMUND A LONG TIME, **DANA**.
HE HAD RULES, YOU KNOW? ALMOST LIKE... A CODE OF HONOR.
NOT LIKE THIS ***BLAINE ABEL*** PSYCHO WE'RE HUNTING NOW.
SQSH
BUT HE WAS ALSO A PETTY, BITTER BASTARD WHO DIDN'T KNOW HOW TO LIVE IN THE WORLD.
HE DID US A FAVOR BY KILLING HIMSELF.
I'M GLAD HE'S DEAD.
"EVEN GLADDER HE'S NOT COMING BACK."

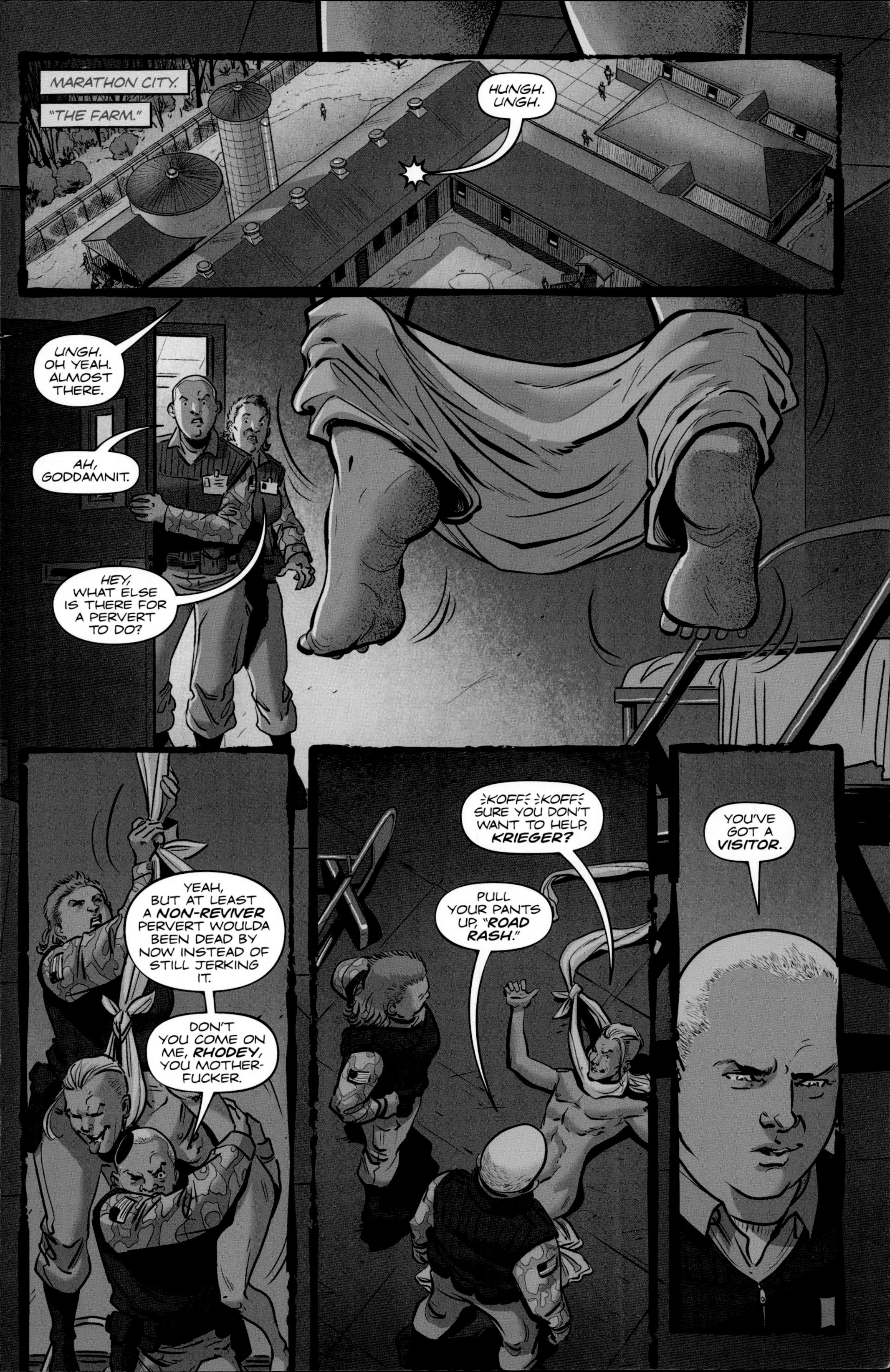
MARATHON CITY.
"THE FARM."
HUNGH. UNGH.
UNGH. OH YEAH. ALMOST THERE.
AH, GODDAMNIT.
HEY, WHAT ELSE IS THERE FOR A PERVERT TO DO?
YEAH, BUT AT LEAST A NON-REVIVER PERVERT WOULDA BEEN DEAD BY NOW INSTEAD OF STILL JERKING IT.
DON'T YOU COME ON ME, RHODEY, YOU MOTHER-FUCKER.
KOFF KOFF SURE YOU DON'T WANT TO HELP, KRIEGER?
PULL YOUR PANTS UP, "ROAD RASH."
YOU'VE GOT A VISITOR.

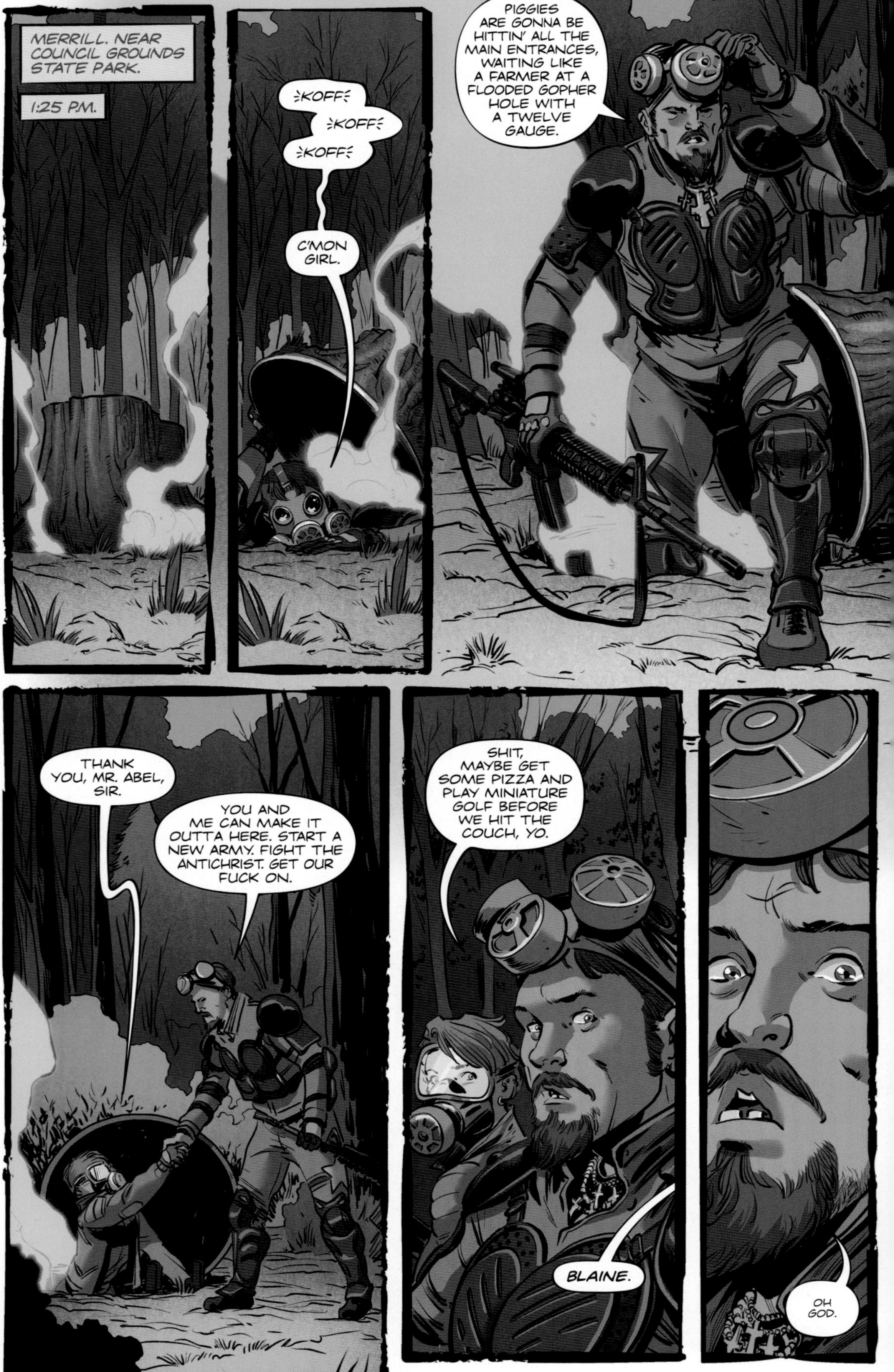
MERRILL. NEAR COUNCIL GROUNDS STATE PARK.
1:25 P.M.
KOFF
KOFF
KOFF
C'MON GIRL.
PIGGIES ARE GONNA BE HITTIN' ALL THE MAIN ENTRANCES, WAITING LIKE A FARMER AT A FLOODED GOPHER HOLE WITH A TWELVE GAUGE.
THANK YOU, MR. ABEL, SIR.
YOU AND ME CAN MAKE IT OUTTA HERE. START A NEW ARMY. FIGHT THE ANTICHRIST. GET OUR FUCK ON.
SHIT, MAYBE GET SOME PIZZA AND PLAY MINIATURE GOLF BEFORE WE HIT THE COUCH, YO.
BLAINE.
OH GOD.

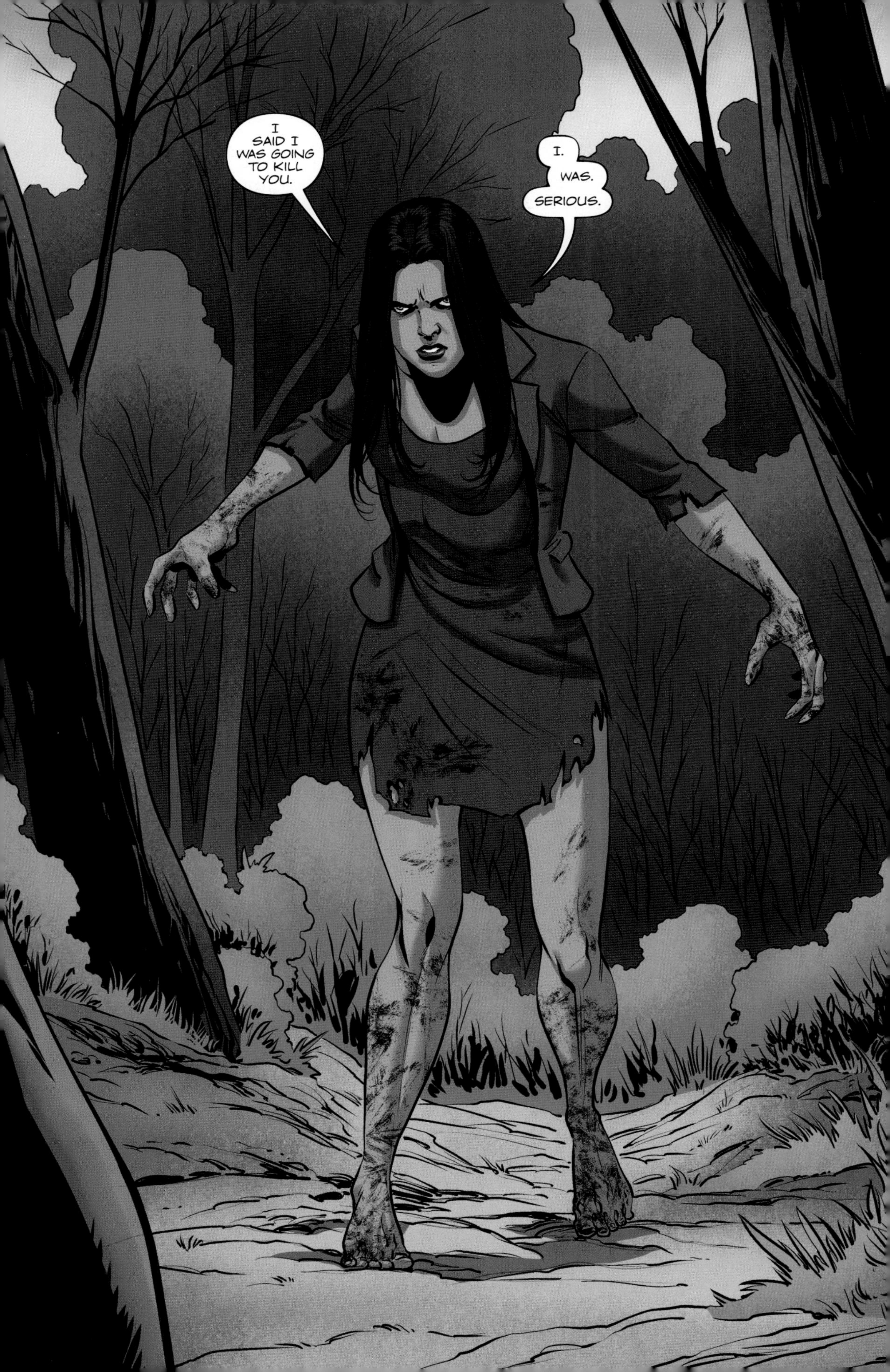
I SAID I WAS GOING TO KILL YOU.
I.
WAS.
SERIOUS.

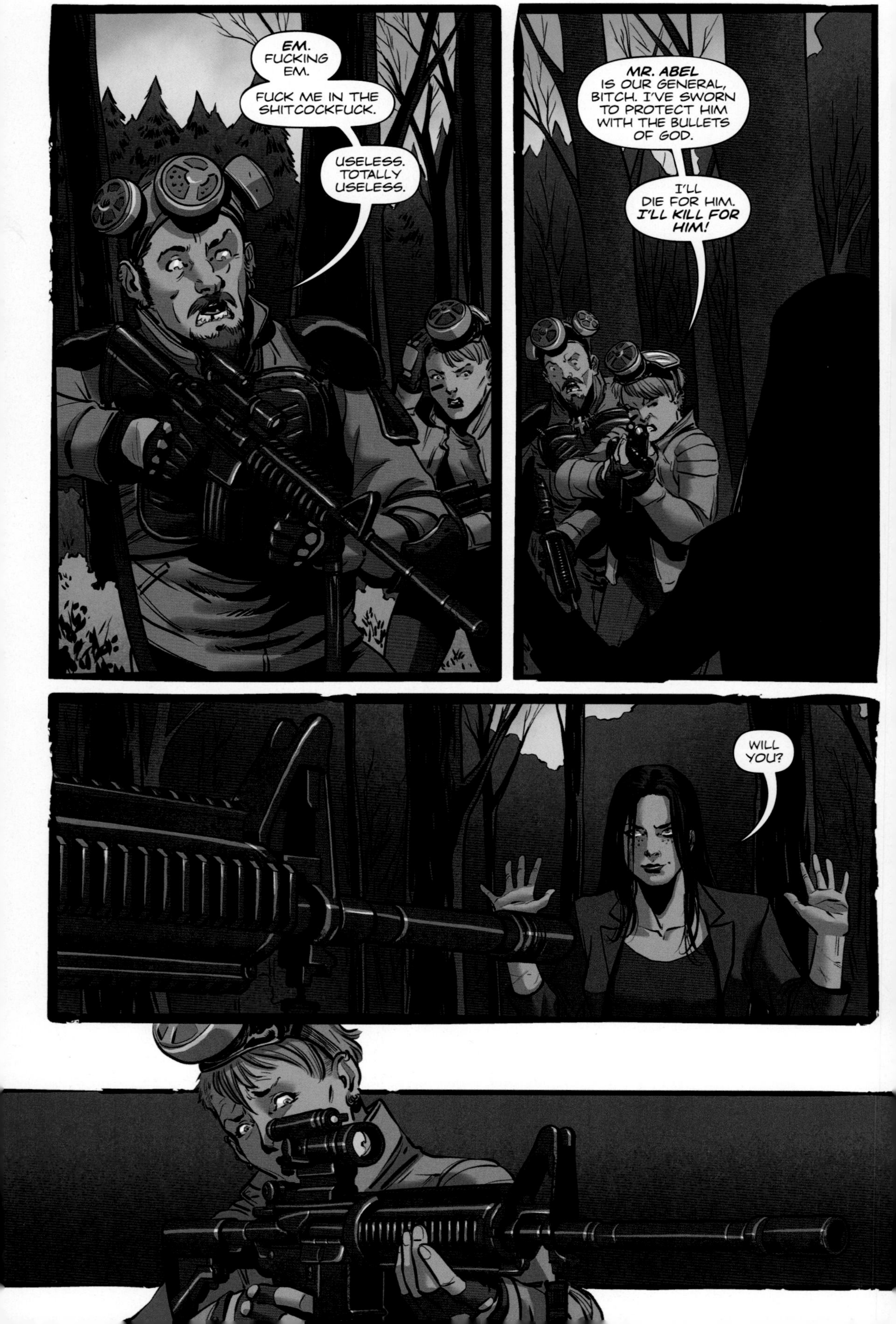
EM. FUCKING EM.
FUCK ME IN THE SHITCOCKFUCK.
USELESS. TOTALLY USELESS.
MR. ABEL IS OUR GENERAL, BITCH. I'VE SWORN TO PROTECT HIM WITH THE BULLETS OF GOD.
I'LL DIE FOR HIM. I'LL KILL FOR HIM!
WILL YOU?

GRAAAAHH!!

AHHHHH!

KRAK

MIINNH...

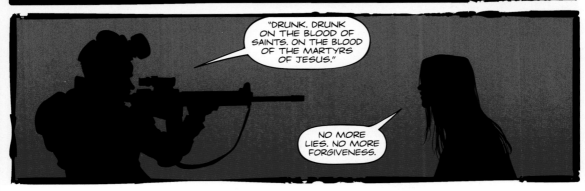

"DRUNK. DRUNK ON THE BLOOD OF SAINTS. ON THE BLOOD OF THE MARTYRS OF JESUS."

NO MORE LIES. NO MORE FORGIVENESS.

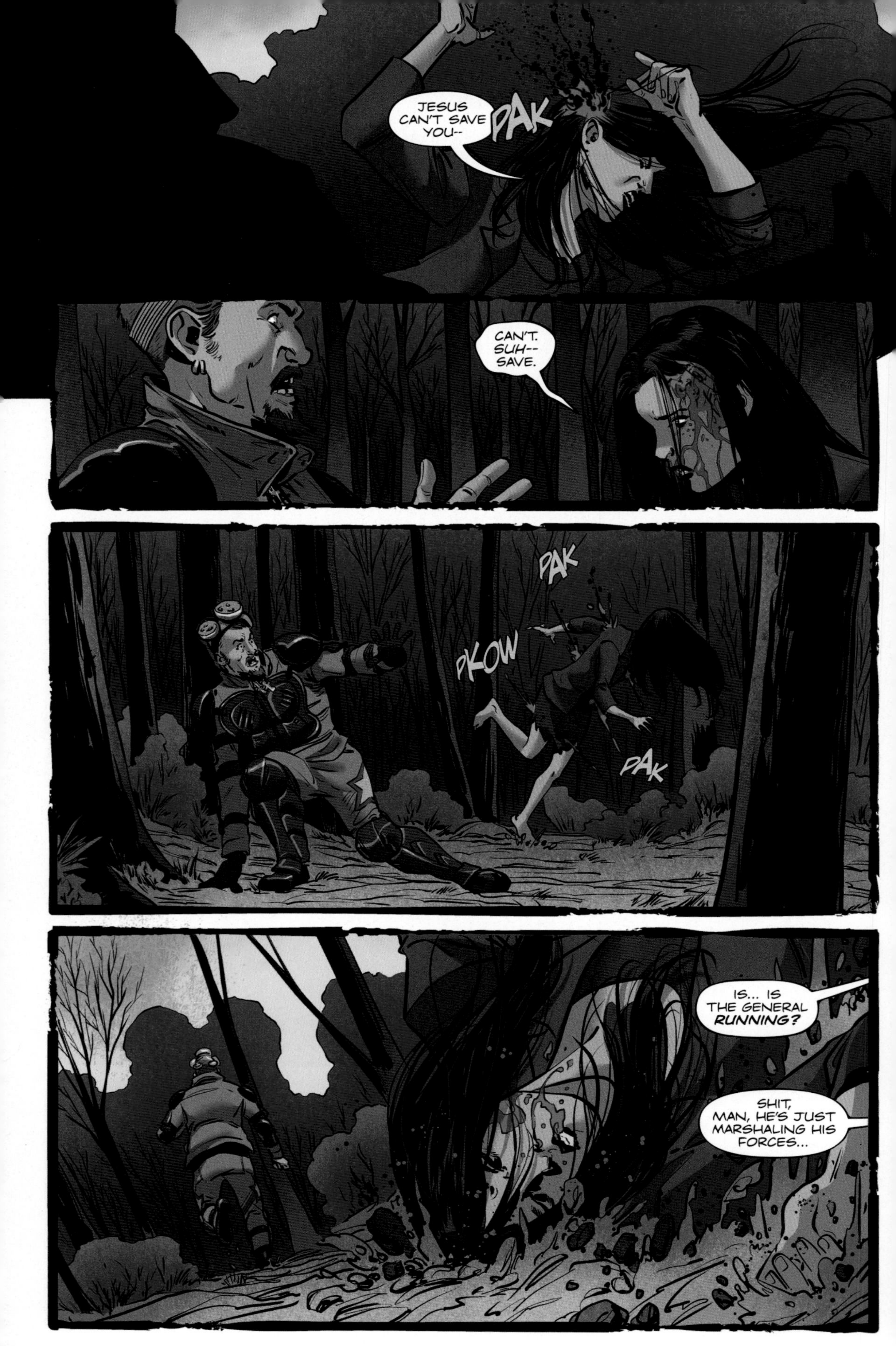
JESUS CAN'T SAVE YOU--
PAK
CAN'T. SUH-- SAVE.
PAK
PKOW
PAK
IS... IS THE GENERAL *RUNNING?*
SHIT, MAN, HE'S JUST MARSHALING HIS FORCES...

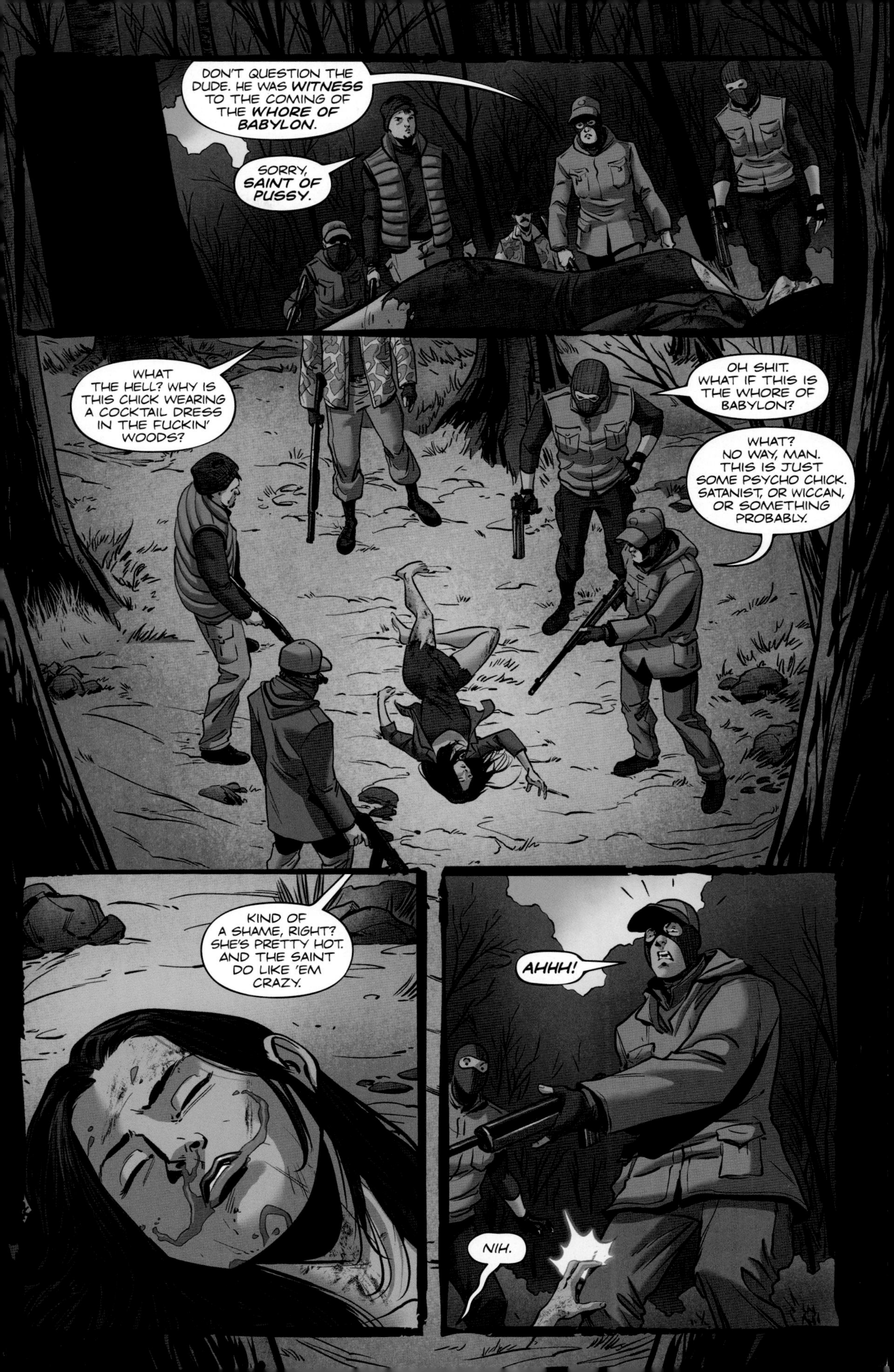
DON'T QUESTION THE DUDE. HE WAS WITNESS TO THE COMING OF THE WHORE OF BABYLON.
SORRY, SAINT OF PUSSY.
WHAT THE HELL? WHY IS THIS CHICK WEARING A COCKTAIL DRESS IN THE FUCKIN' WOODS?
OH SHIT. WHAT IF THIS IS THE WHORE OF BABYLON?
WHAT? NO WAY, MAN. THIS IS JUST SOME PSYCHO CHICK. SATANIST, OR WICCAN, OR SOMETHING PROBABLY.
KIND OF A SHAME, RIGHT? SHE'S PRETTY HOT. AND THE SAINT DO LIKE 'EM CRAZY.
AHHH!
NIH.

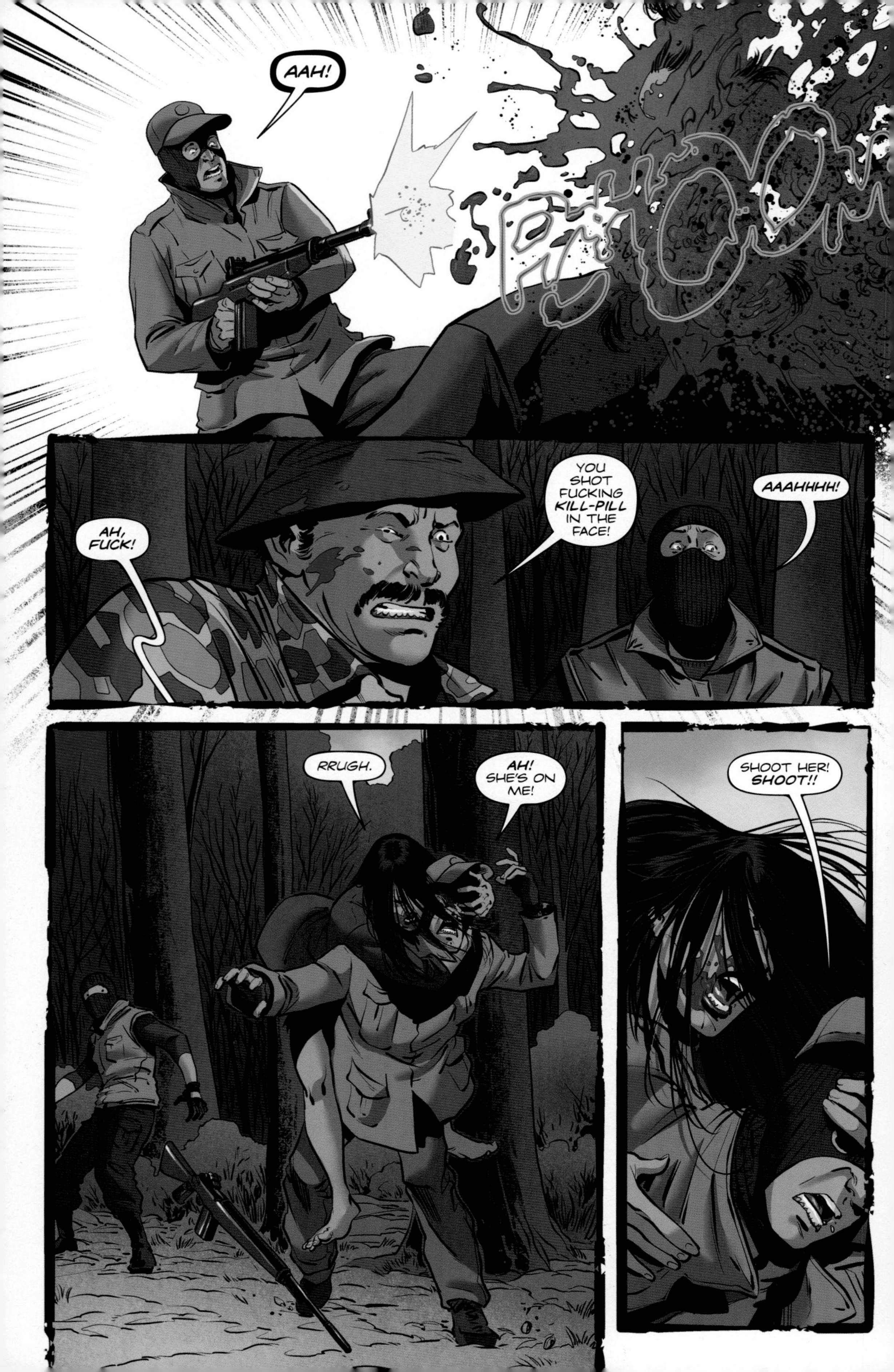
AAH!
AH, FUCK!
YOU SHOT FUCKING KILL-PILL IN THE FACE!
AAAHHHH!
RRUGH.
AH! SHE'S ON ME!
SHOOT HER! SHOOT!!

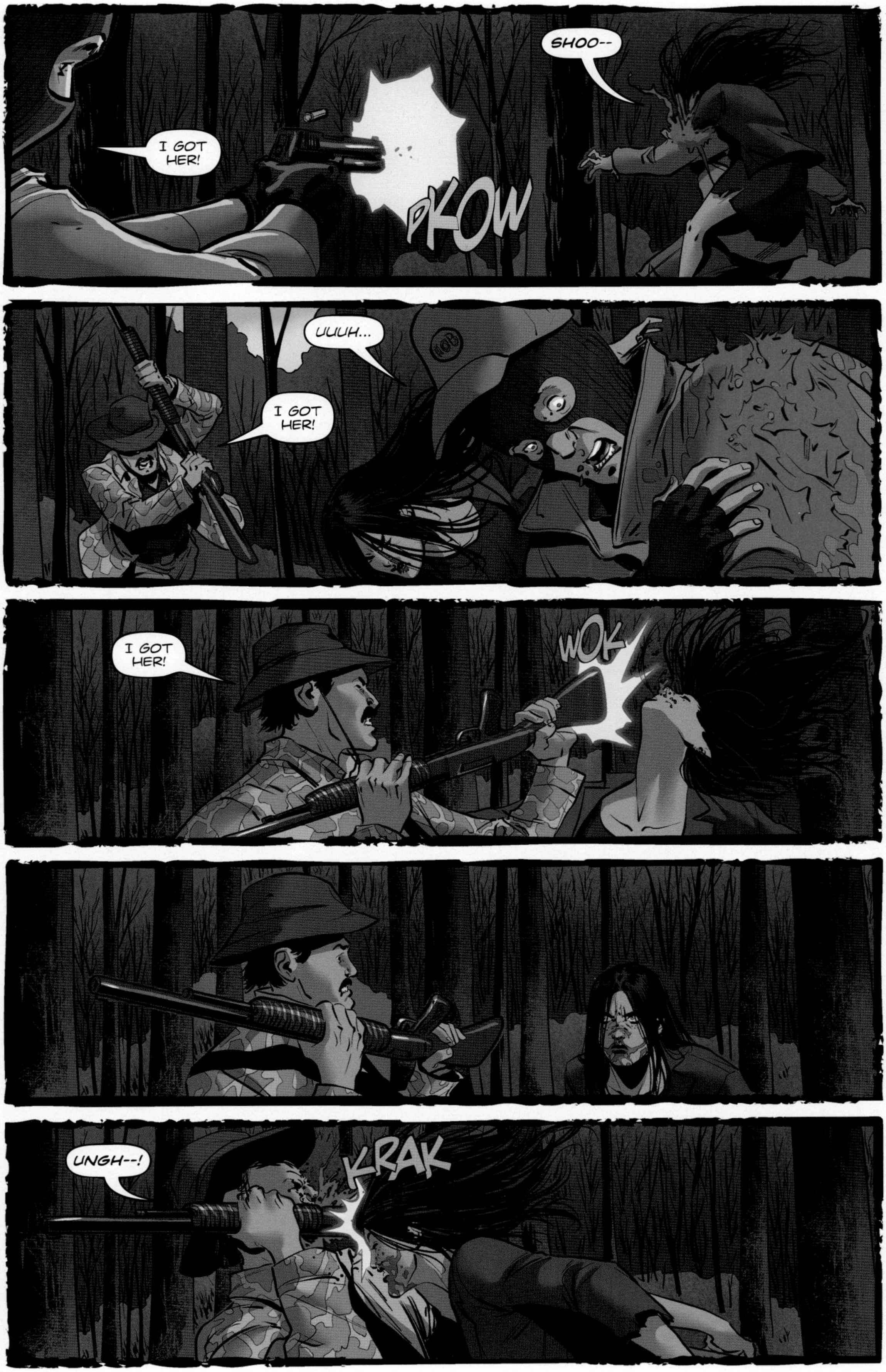
I GOT HER!
PKOW
SHOO--
UUUH...
I GOT HER!
I GOT HER!
WOK
UNGH--!
KRAK

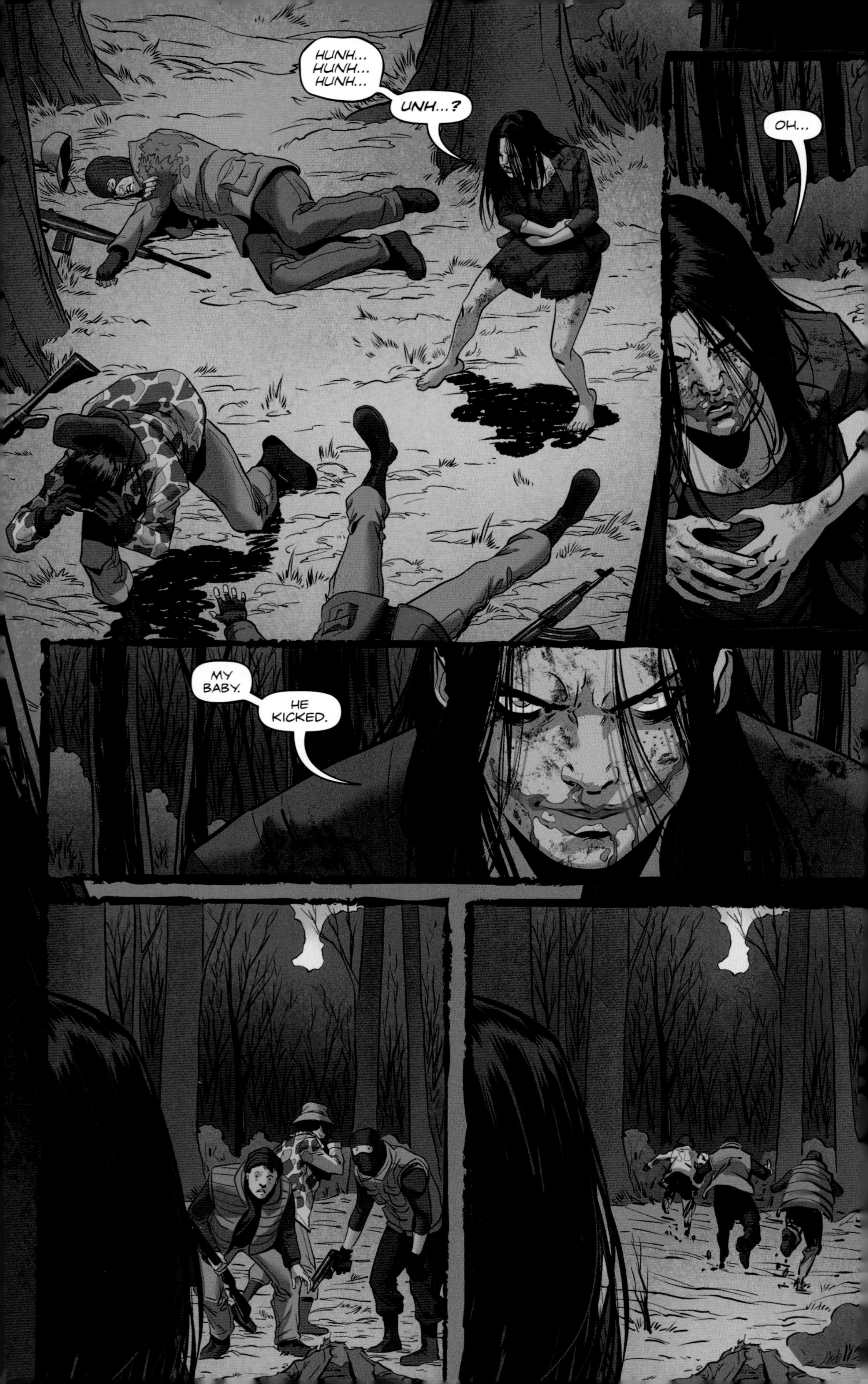
HUNH... HUNH... HUNH...
UNH...?
OH...
MY BABY.
HE KICKED.

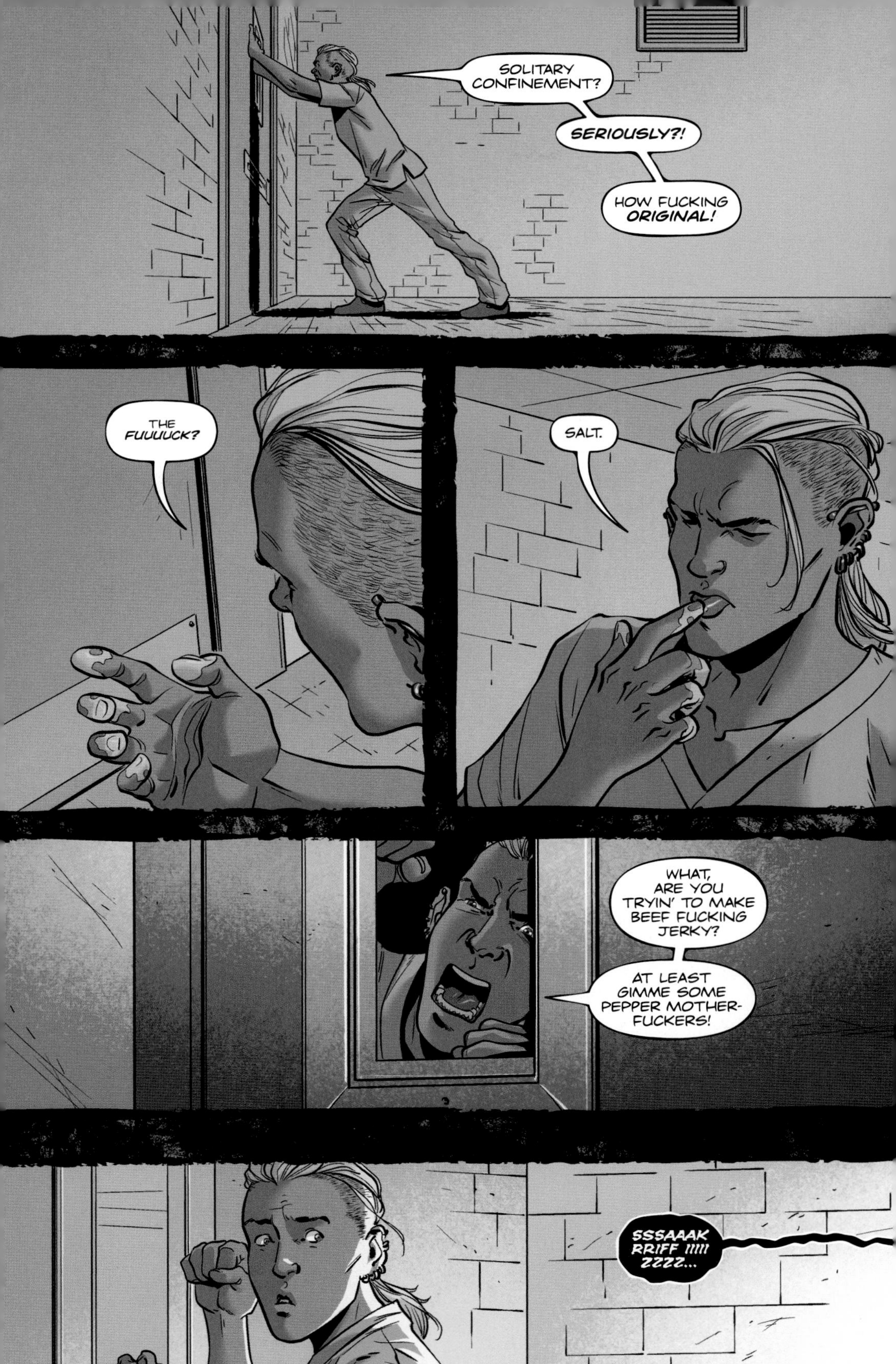
SOLITARY CONFINEMENT?
SERIOUSLY?!
HOW FUCKING ORIGINAL!
THE FUUUUCK?
SALT.
WHAT, ARE YOU TRYIN' TO MAKE BEEF FUCKING JERKY?
AT LEAST GIMME SOME PEPPER MOTHER-FUCKERS!
SSSAAAK RRIFF !!!!! ZZZZ...

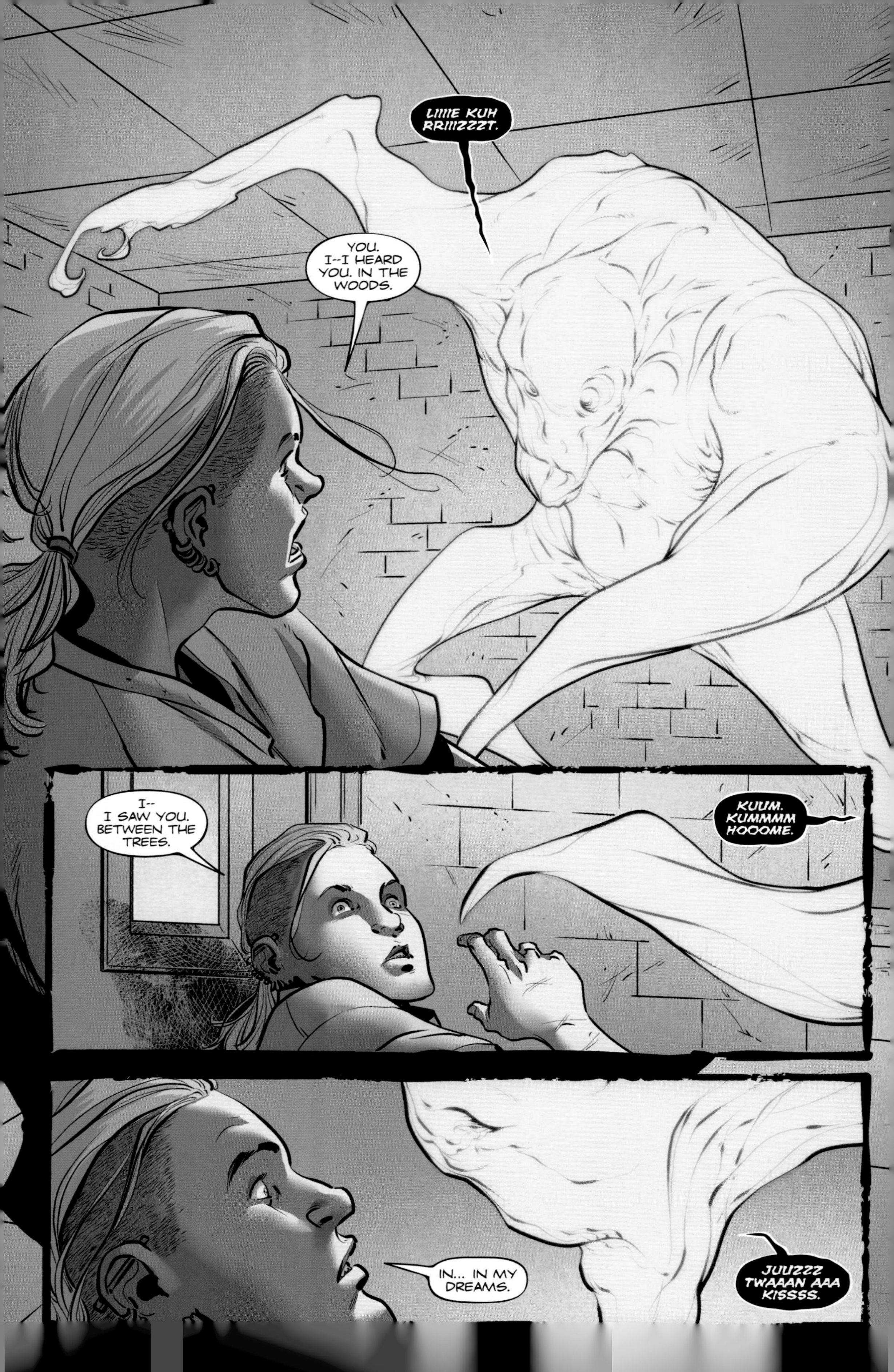
LIIIIE KUH RRIIIZZZT.
YOU. I--I HEARD YOU. IN THE WOODS.
I-- I SAW YOU. BETWEEN THE TREES.
KUUM. KUMMMM HOOOME.
IN... IN MY DREAMS.
JUUZZZ TWAAAN AAA KISSSS.

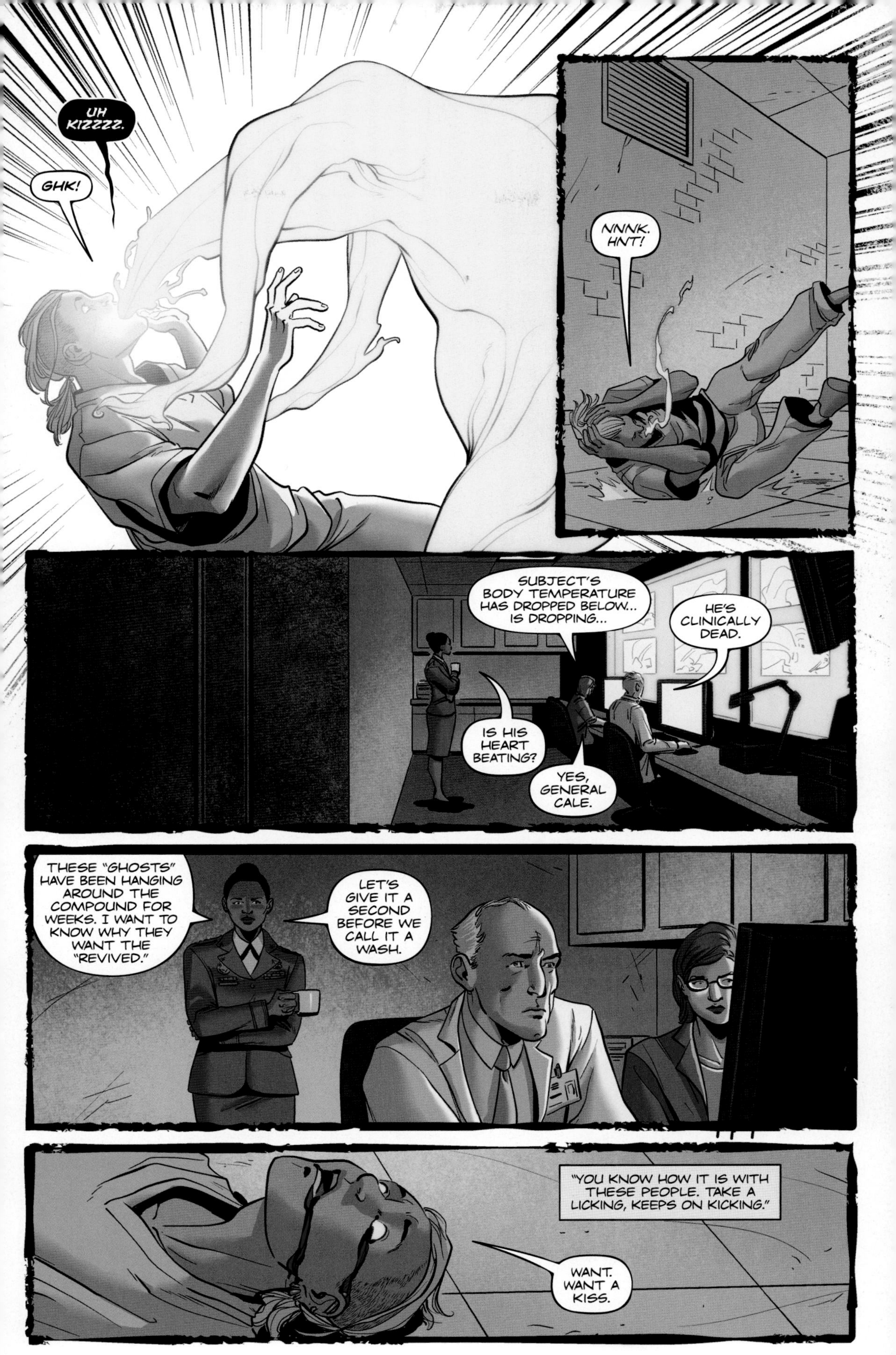
UH KIZZZZ.
GHK!
NNNK. HNT!
SUBJECT'S BODY TEMPERATURE HAS DROPPED BELOW... IS DROPPING...
HE'S CLINICALLY DEAD.
IS HIS HEART BEATING?
YES, GENERAL CALE.
THESE "GHOSTS" HAVE BEEN HANGING AROUND THE COMPOUND FOR WEEKS. I WANT TO KNOW WHY THEY WANT THE "REVIVED."
LET'S GIVE IT A SECOND BEFORE WE CALL IT A WASH.
"YOU KNOW HOW IT IS WITH THESE PEOPLE. TAKE A LICKING, KEEPS ON KICKING."
WANT. WANT A KISS.

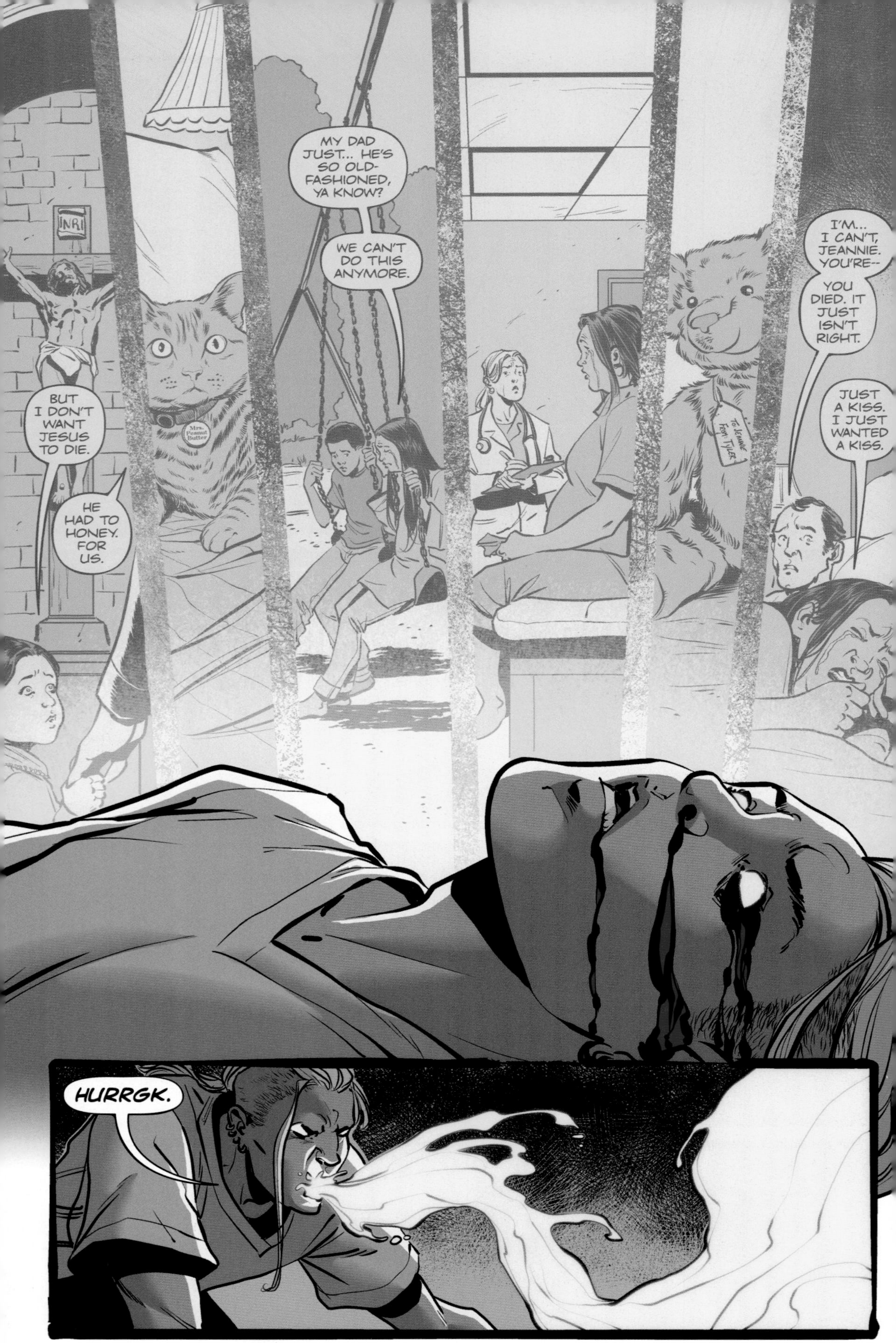
INRI
BUT I DON'T WANT JESUS TO DIE.
HE HAD TO HONEY. FOR US.
Mrs. Peanut Butter
MY DAD JUST... HE'S SO OLD-FASHIONED, YA KNOW?
WE CAN'T DO THIS ANYMORE.
To Jeannie From Tyler
I'M... I CAN'T, JEANNIE. YOU'RE--
YOU DIED. IT JUST ISN'T RIGHT.
JUST A KISS. I JUST WANTED A KISS.
HURRGK.

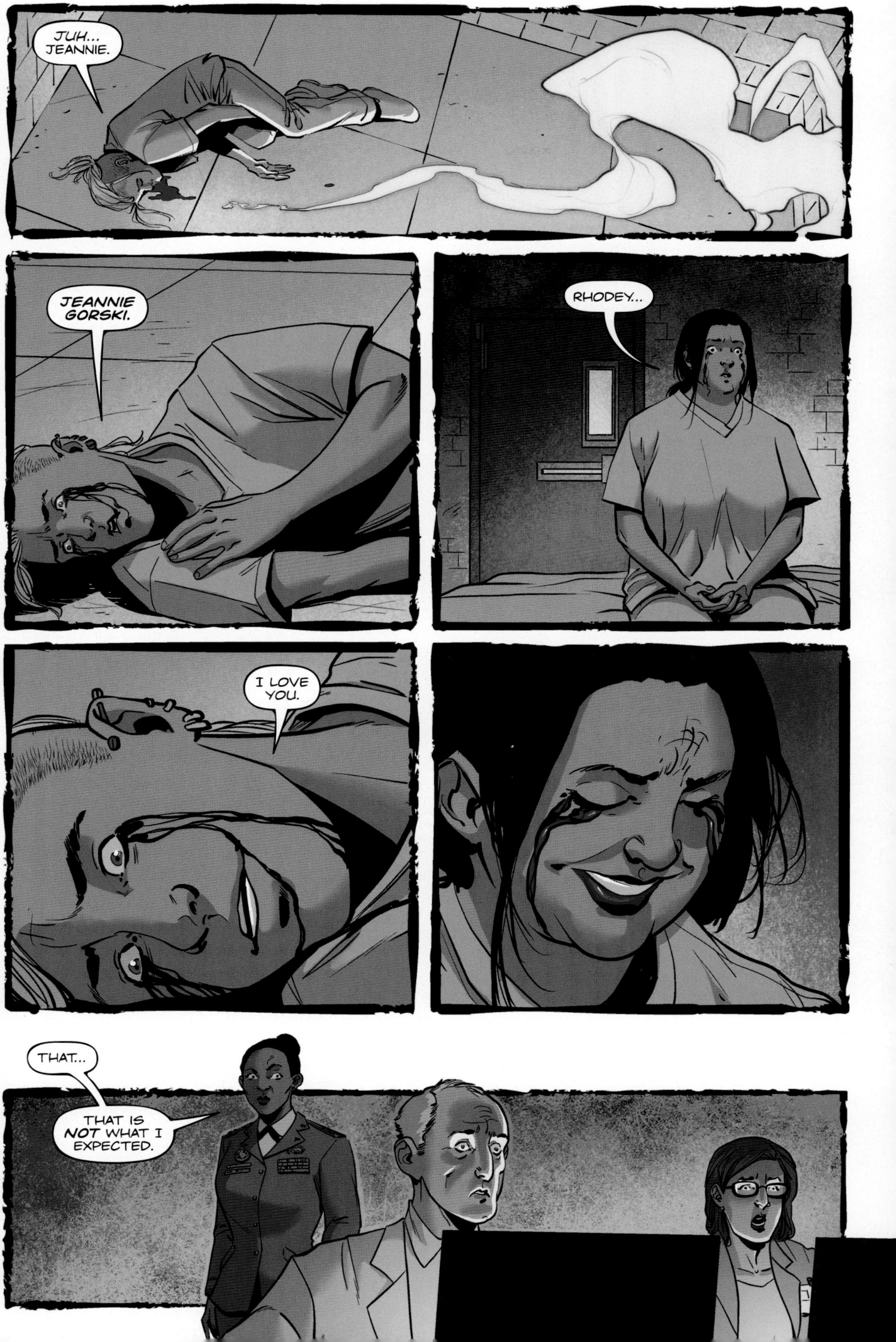
JUH... JEANNIE.
JEANNIE GORSKI.
RHODEY...
I LOVE YOU.
THAT...
THAT IS NOT WHAT I EXPECTED.

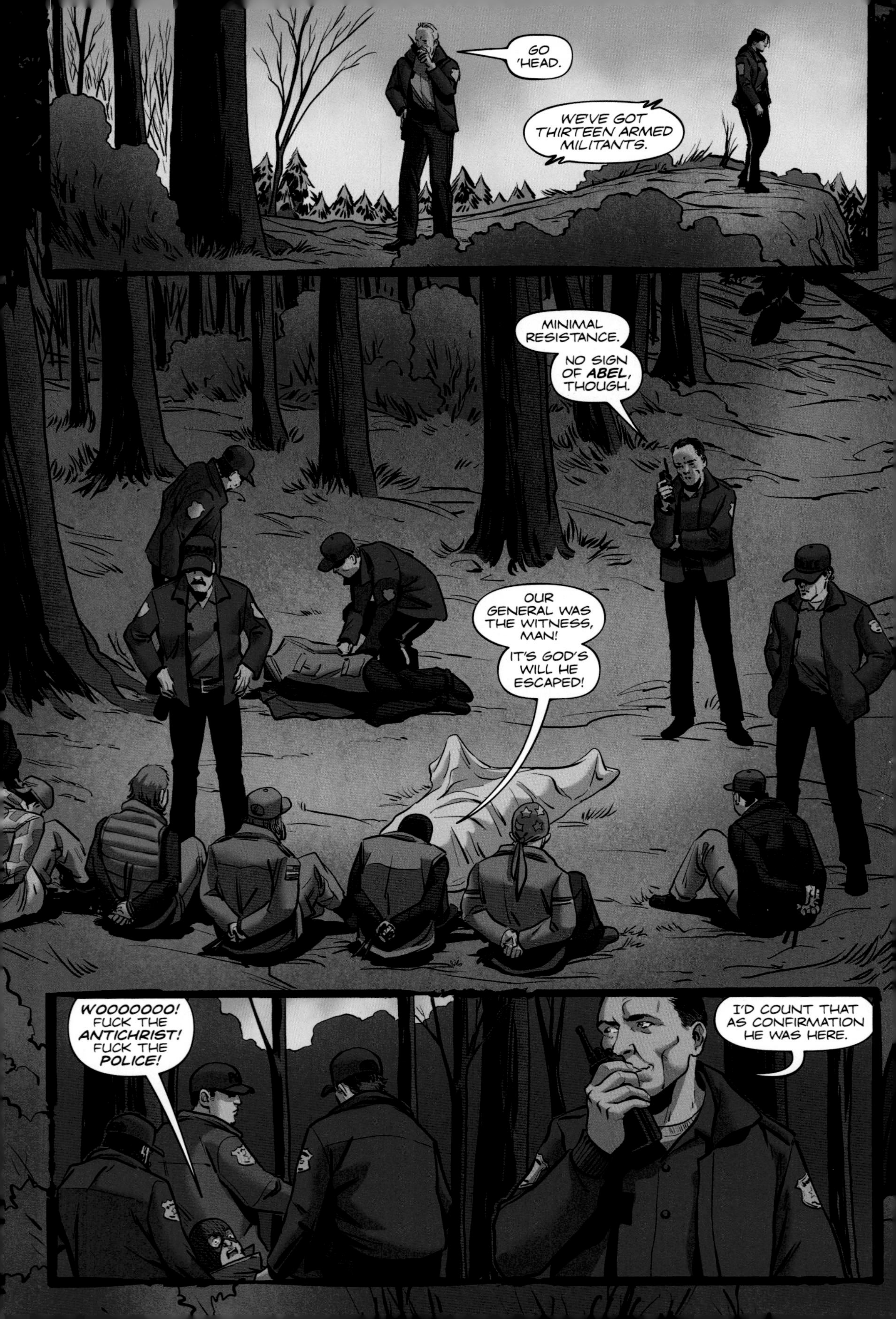
GO 'HEAD.
WE'VE GOT THIRTEEN ARMED MILITANTS.
MINIMAL RESISTANCE.
NO SIGN OF **ABEL**, THOUGH.
OUR GENERAL WAS THE WITNESS, MAN!
IT'S GOD'S WILL HE ESCAPED!
WOOOOOOO! FUCK THE **ANTICHRIST!** FUCK THE **POLICE!**
I'D COUNT THAT AS CONFIRMATION HE WAS HERE.

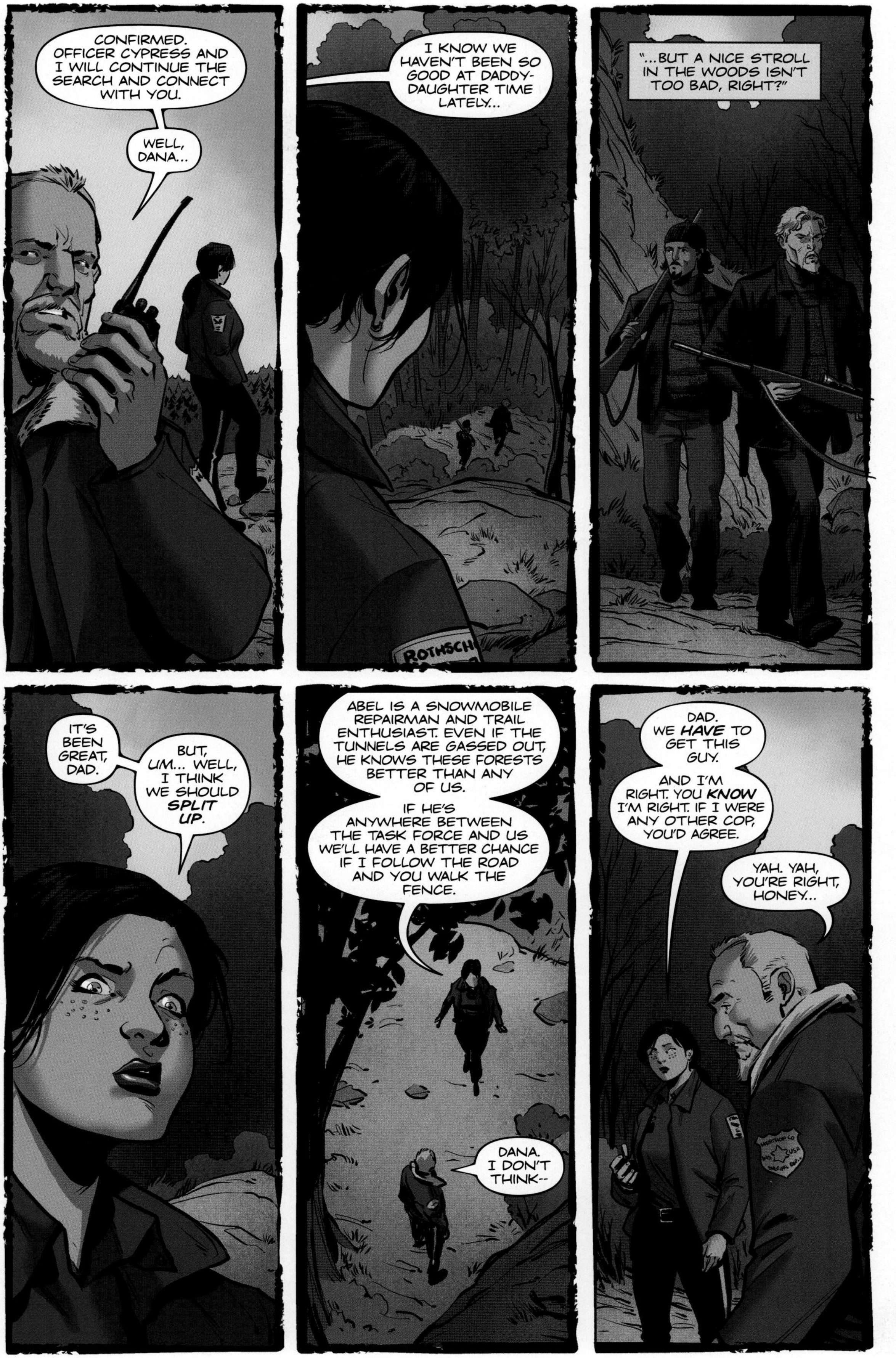
CONFIRMED. OFFICER CYPRESS AND I WILL CONTINUE THE SEARCH AND CONNECT WITH YOU.
WELL, DANA...
I KNOW WE HAVEN'T BEEN SO GOOD AT DADDY-DAUGHTER TIME LATELY...
ROTHSCH
"...BUT A NICE STROLL IN THE WOODS ISN'T TOO BAD, RIGHT?"
IT'S BEEN GREAT, DAD.
BUT, UM... WELL, I THINK WE SHOULD SPLIT UP.
ABEL IS A SNOWMOBILE REPAIRMAN AND TRAIL ENTHUSIAST. EVEN IF THE TUNNELS ARE GASSED OUT, HE KNOWS THESE FORESTS BETTER THAN ANY OF US.
IF HE'S ANYWHERE BETWEEN THE TASK FORCE AND US WE'LL HAVE A BETTER CHANCE IF I FOLLOW THE ROAD AND YOU WALK THE FENCE.
DANA. I DON'T THINK--
DAD. WE HAVE TO GET THIS GUY.
AND I'M RIGHT. YOU KNOW I'M RIGHT. IF I WERE ANY OTHER COP, YOU'D AGREE.
YAH. YAH, YOU'RE RIGHT, HONEY...

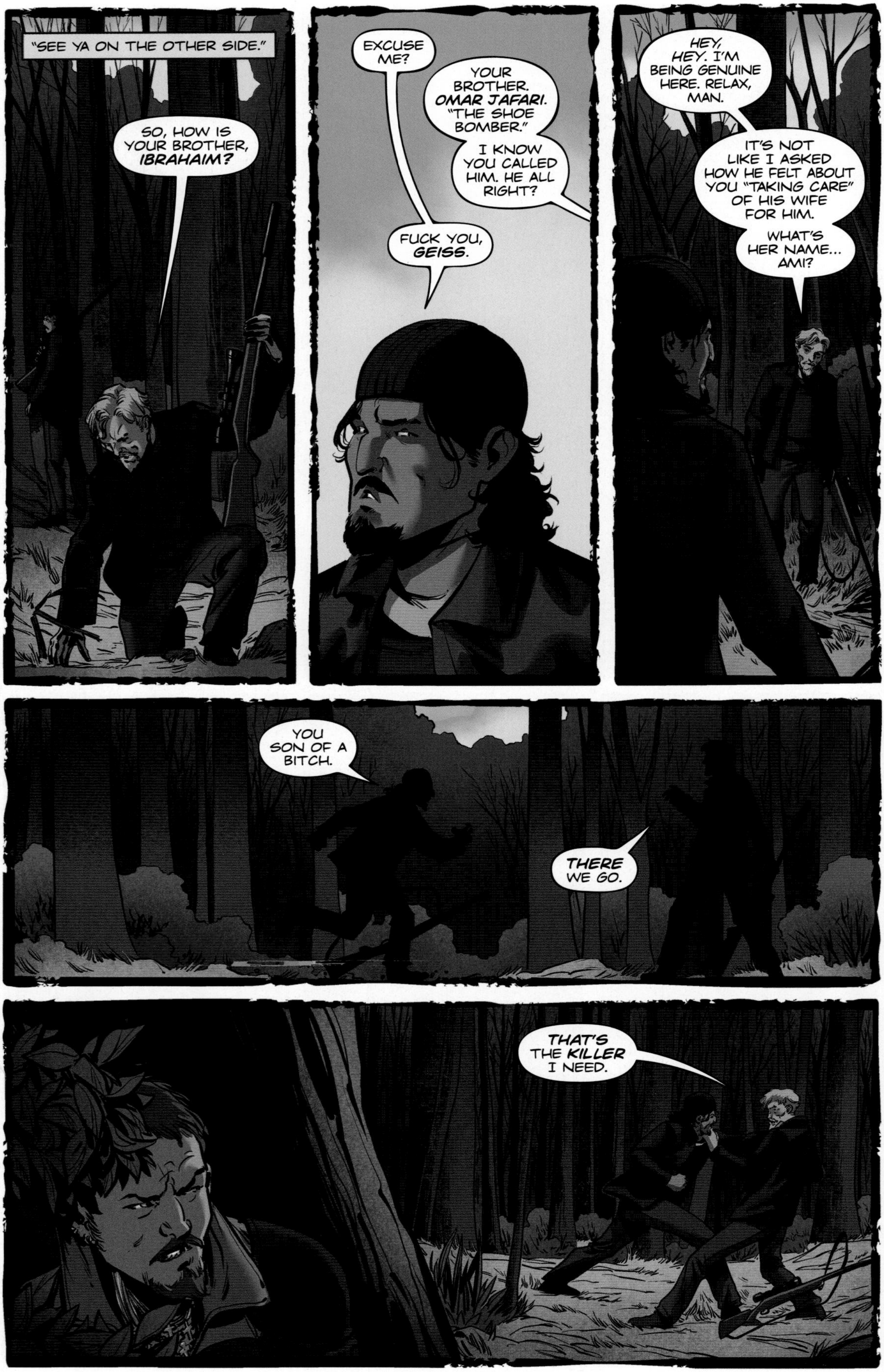
"SEE YA ON THE OTHER SIDE."
SO, HOW IS YOUR BROTHER, IBRAHAIM?
EXCUSE ME?
YOUR BROTHER. OMAR JAFARI. "THE SHOE BOMBER."
I KNOW YOU CALLED HIM. HE ALL RIGHT?
FUCK YOU, GEISS.
HEY, HEY. I'M BEING GENUINE HERE. RELAX, MAN.
IT'S NOT LIKE I ASKED HOW HE FELT ABOUT YOU "TAKING CARE" OF HIS WIFE FOR HIM.
WHAT'S HER NAME... AMI?
YOU SON OF A BITCH.
THERE WE GO.
THAT'S THE KILLER I NEED.

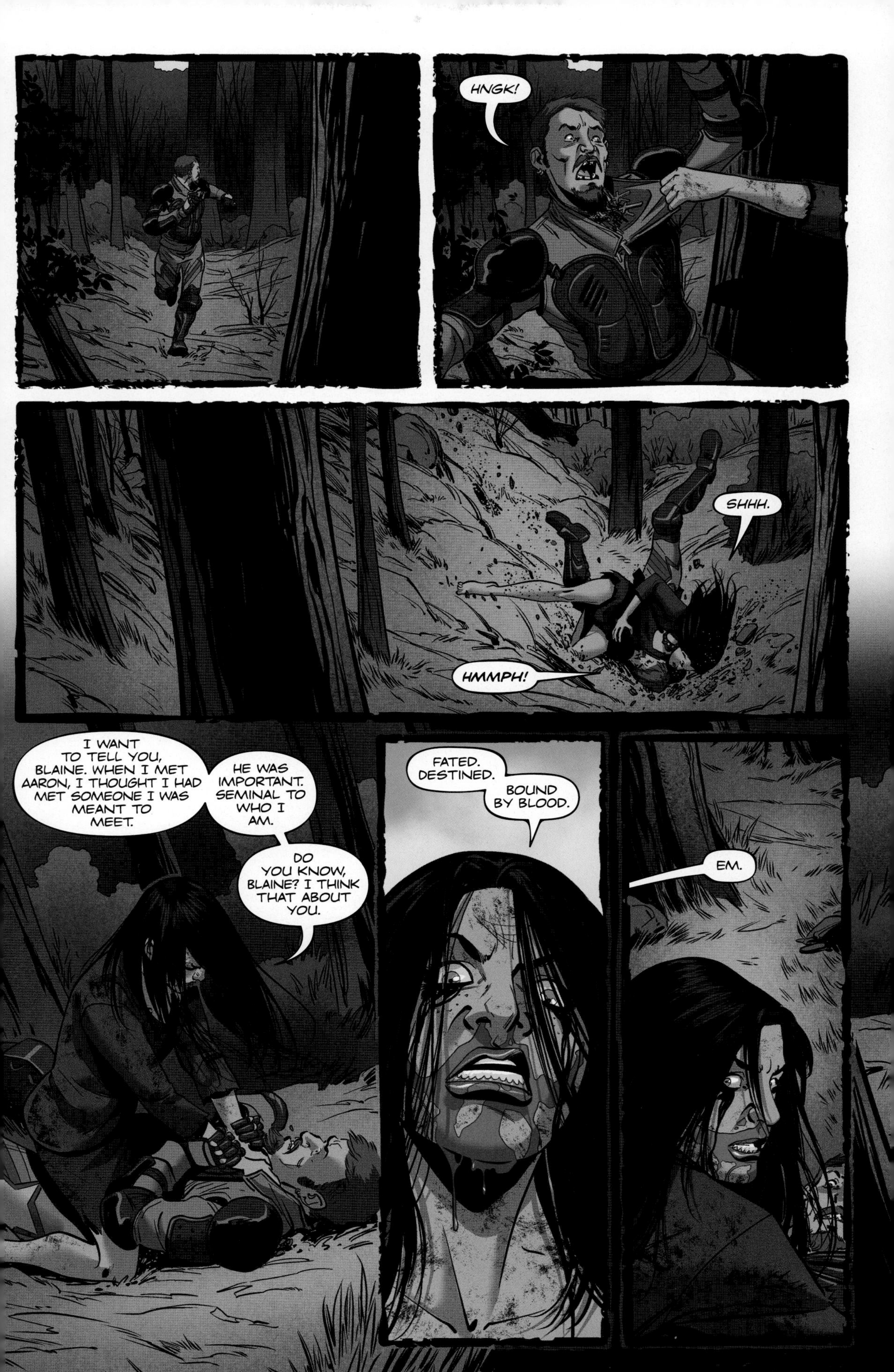
HNGK!
SHHH.
HMMPH!
I WANT TO TELL YOU, BLAINE. WHEN I MET AARON, I THOUGHT I HAD MET SOMEONE I WAS MEANT TO MEET.
HE WAS IMPORTANT. SEMINAL TO WHO I AM.
DO YOU KNOW, BLAINE? I THINK THAT ABOUT YOU.
FATED. DESTINED.
BOUND BY BLOOD.
EM.

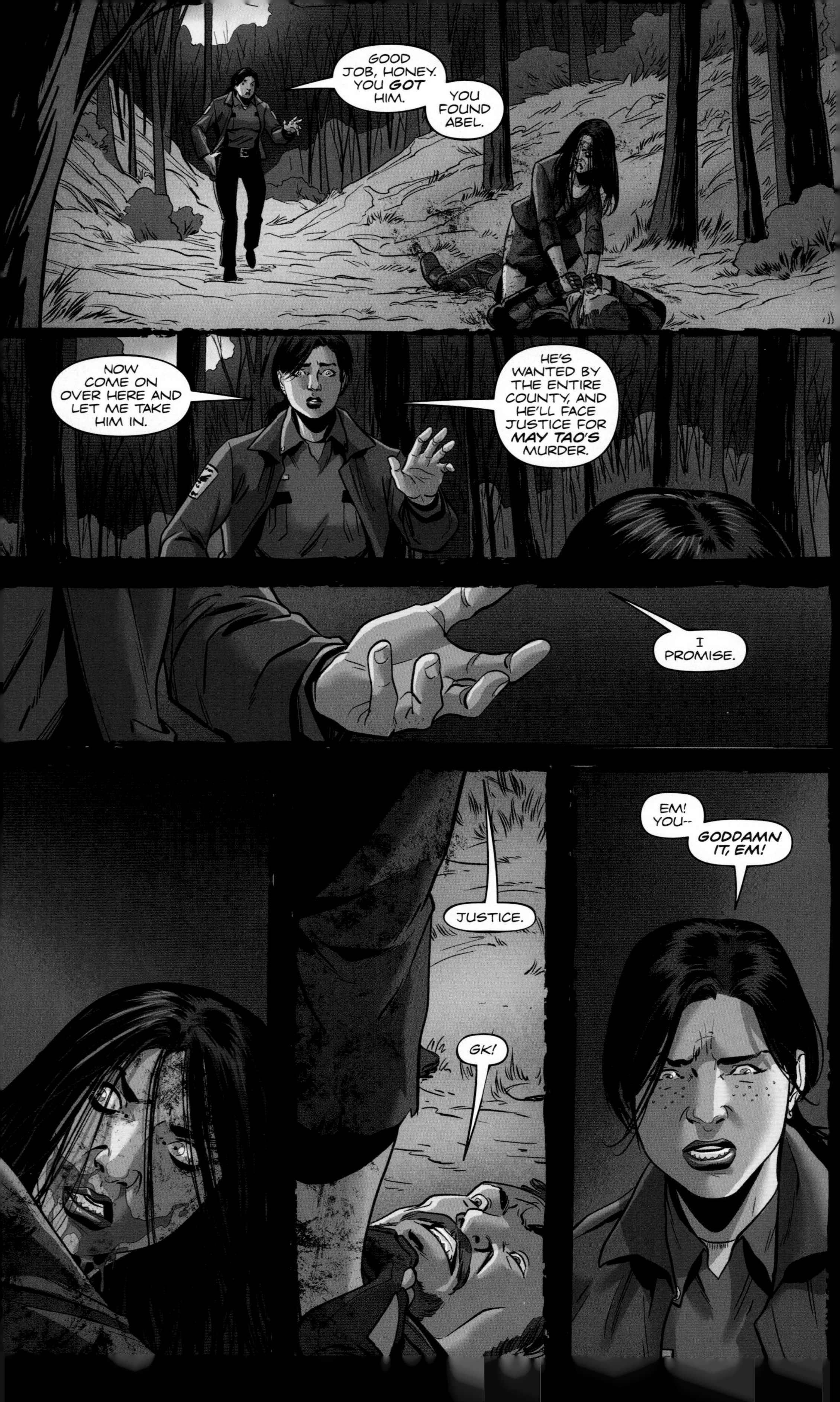
GOOD JOB, HONEY. YOU **GOT** HIM.
YOU FOUND ABEL.
NOW COME ON OVER HERE AND LET ME TAKE HIM IN.
HE'S WANTED BY THE ENTIRE COUNTY, AND HE'LL FACE JUSTICE FOR ***MAY TAO'S*** MURDER.
I PROMISE.
JUSTICE.
GK!
EM! YOU--
GODDAMN IT, EM!

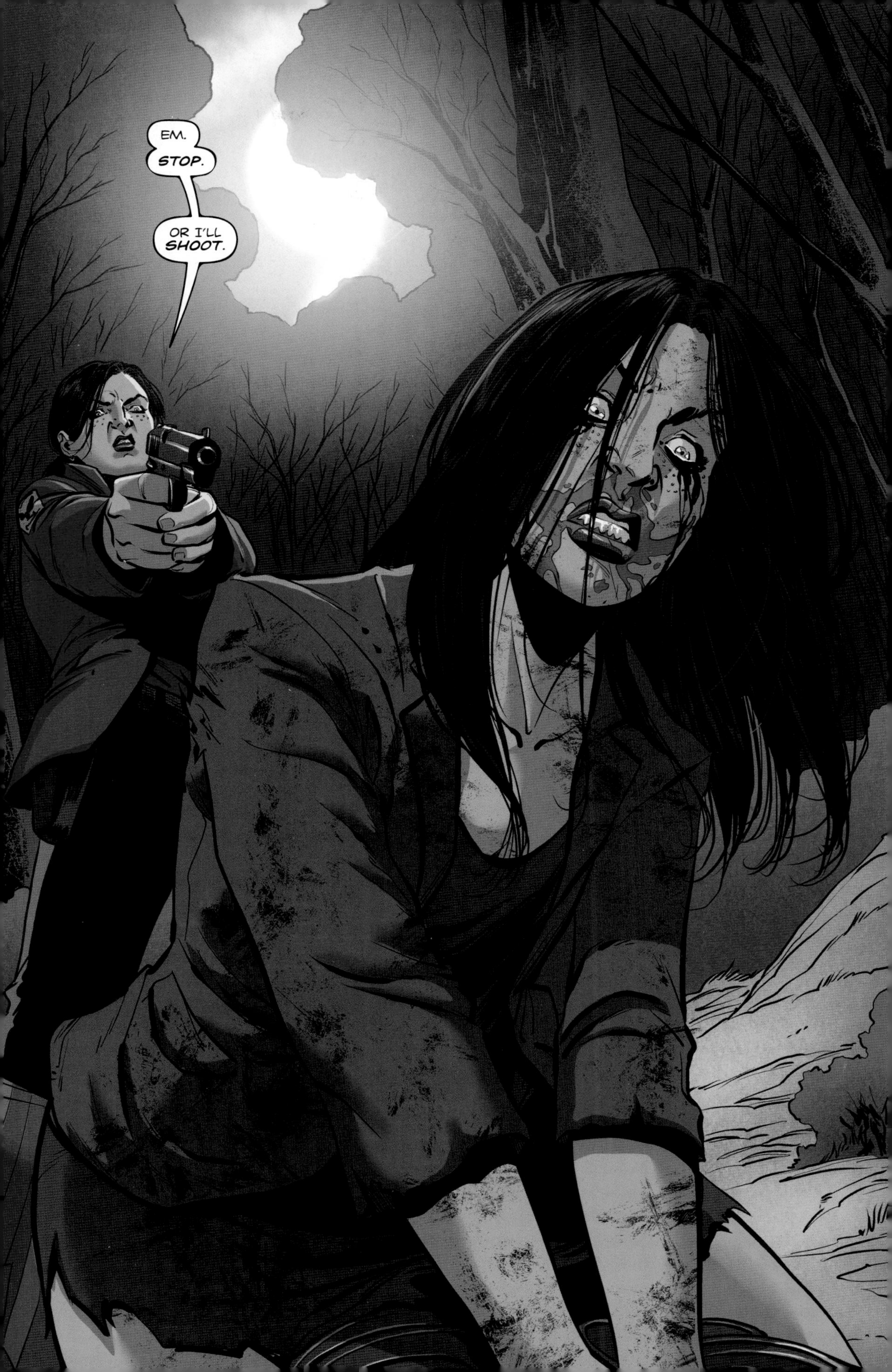
EM.
STOP.
OR I'LL SHOOT.

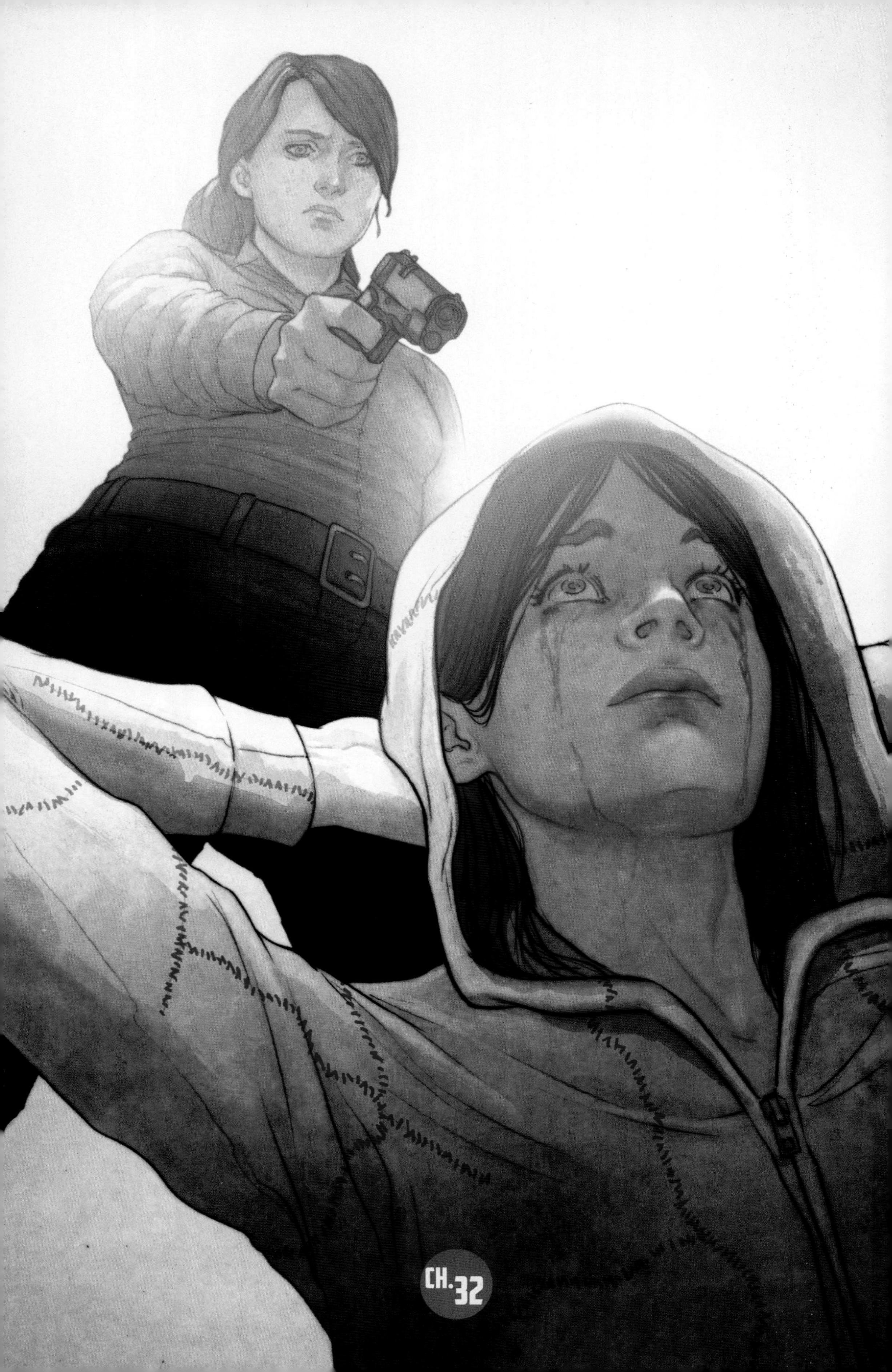
CH. 32

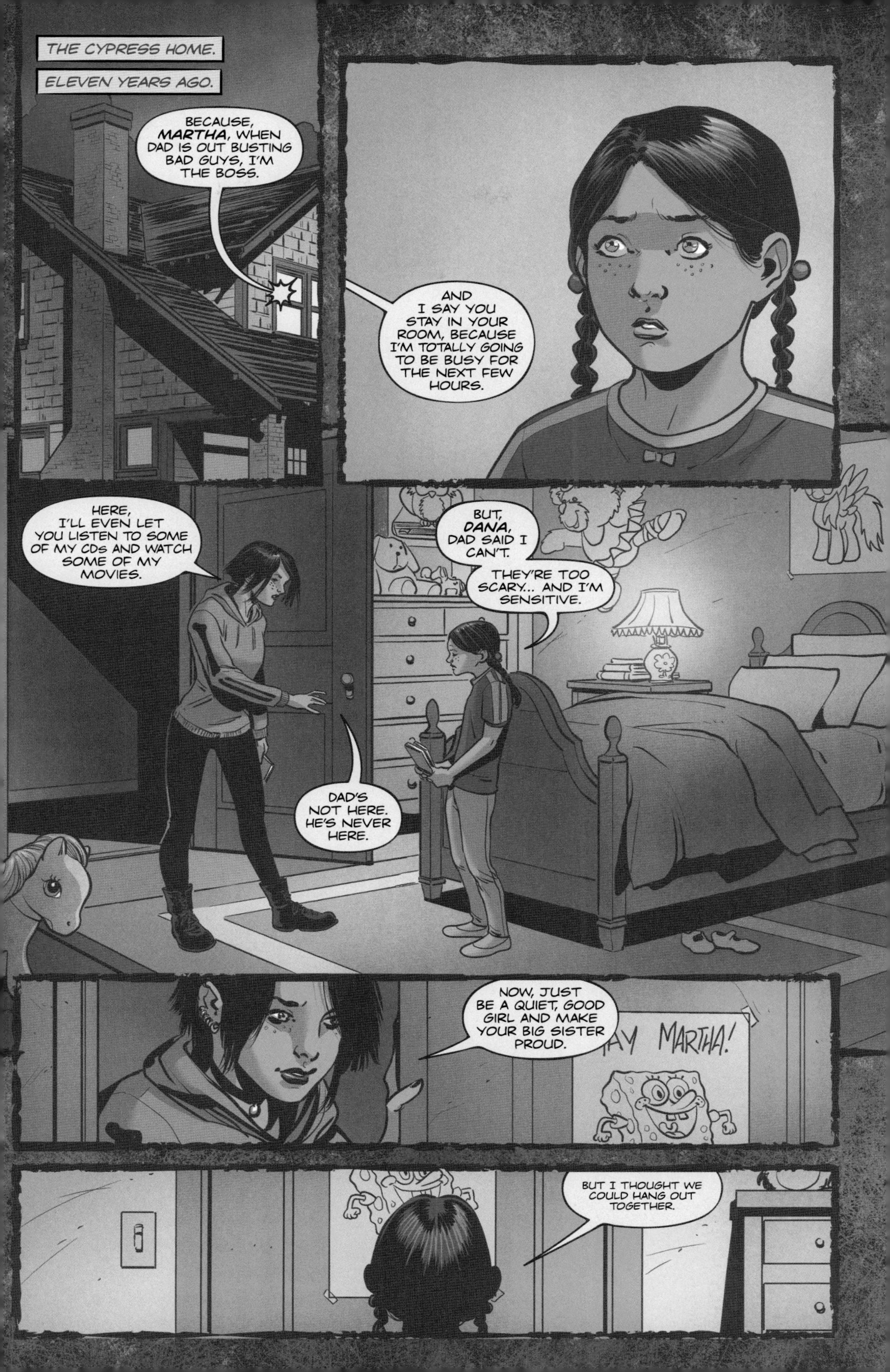
THE CYPRESS HOME.
ELEVEN YEARS AGO.
BECAUSE, MARTHA, WHEN DAD IS OUT BUSTING BAD GUYS, I'M THE BOSS.
AND I SAY YOU STAY IN YOUR ROOM, BECAUSE I'M TOTALLY GOING TO BE BUSY FOR THE NEXT FEW HOURS.
HERE, I'LL EVEN LET YOU LISTEN TO SOME OF MY CDs AND WATCH SOME OF MY MOVIES.
BUT, DANA, DAD SAID I CAN'T.
THEY'RE TOO SCARY... AND I'M SENSITIVE.
DAD'S NOT HERE. HE'S NEVER HERE.
NOW, JUST BE A QUIET, GOOD GIRL AND MAKE YOUR BIG SISTER PROUD.
...AY MARTHA!
BUT I THOUGHT WE COULD HANG OUT TOGETHER.

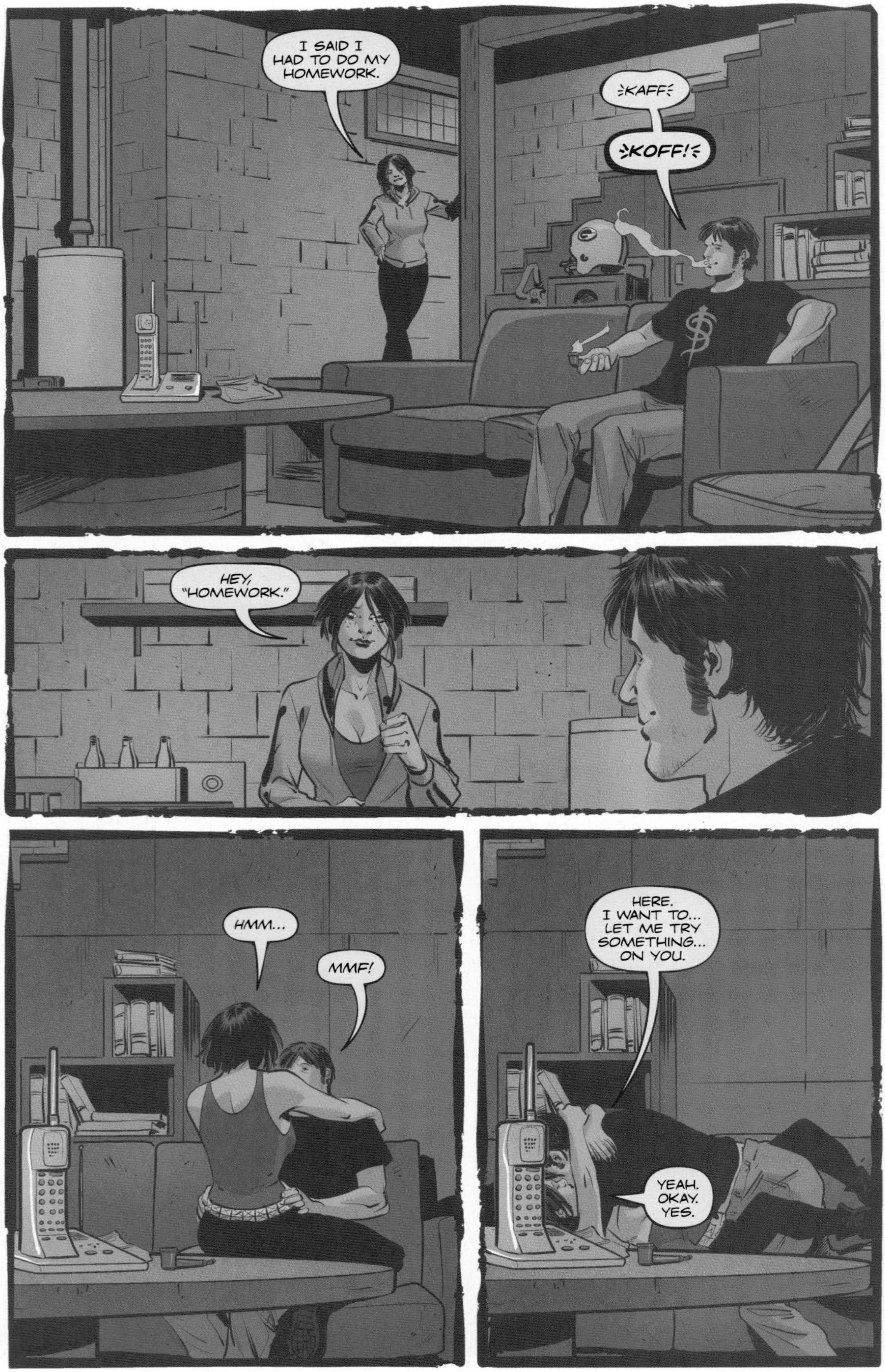
I SAID I HAD TO DO MY HOMEWORK.
KAFF
KOFF!
HEY, "HOMEWORK."
HMM...
MMF!
HERE. I WANT TO... LET ME TRY SOMETHING... ON YOU.
YEAH. OKAY. YES.

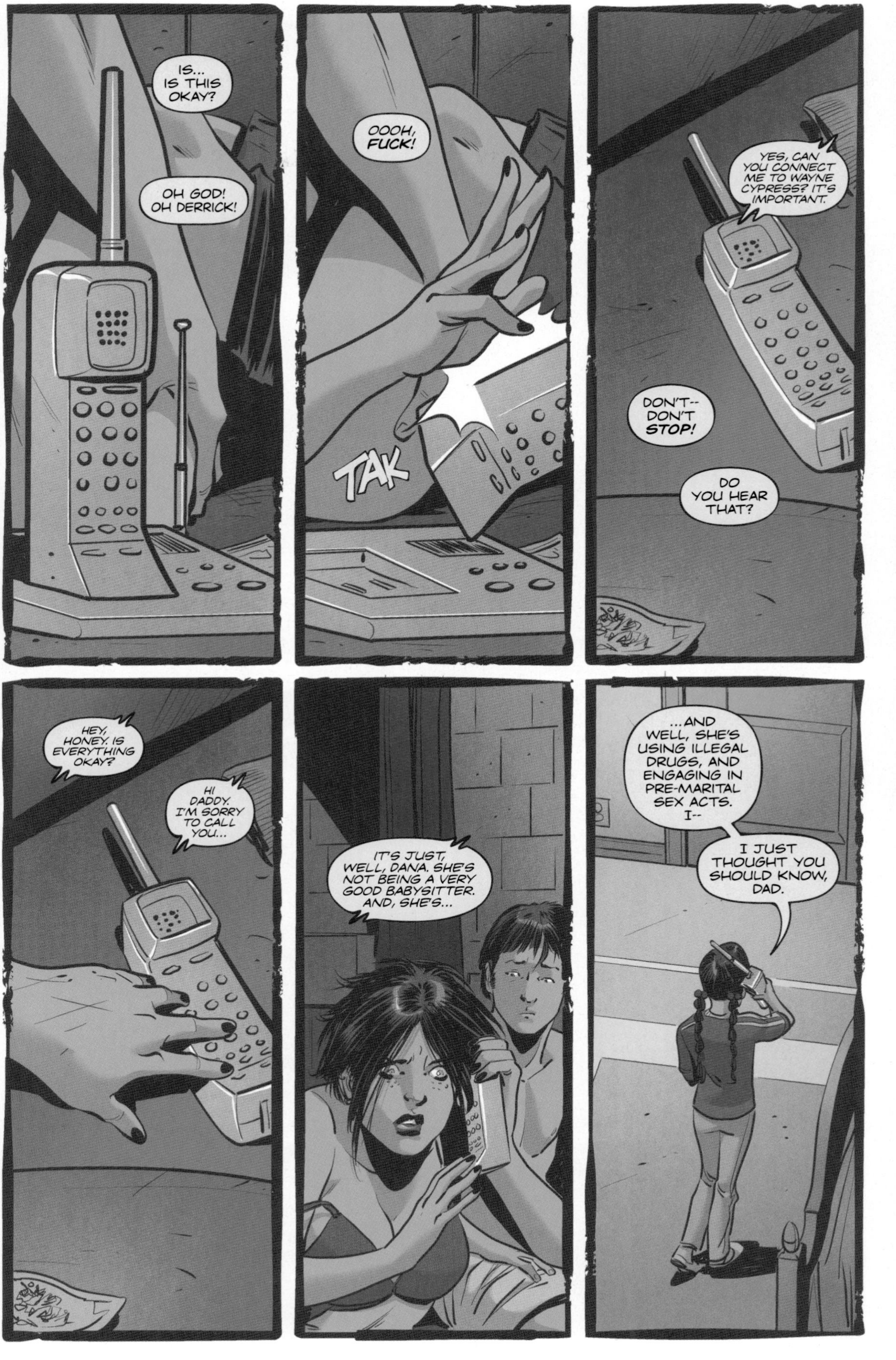
IS... IS THIS OKAY?
OH GOD! OH DERRICK!
OOOH, FUCK!
TAK
YES, CAN YOU CONNECT ME TO WAYNE CYPRESS? IT'S IMPORTANT.
DON'T-- DON'T STOP!
DO YOU HEAR THAT?
HEY, HONEY. IS EVERYTHING OKAY?
HI DADDY. I'M SORRY TO CALL YOU...
IT'S JUST, WELL, DANA. SHE'S NOT BEING A VERY GOOD BABYSITTER. AND, SHE'S...
...AND WELL, SHE'S USING ILLEGAL DRUGS, AND ENGAGING IN PRE-MARITAL SEX ACTS. I--
I JUST THOUGHT YOU SHOULD KNOW, DAD.

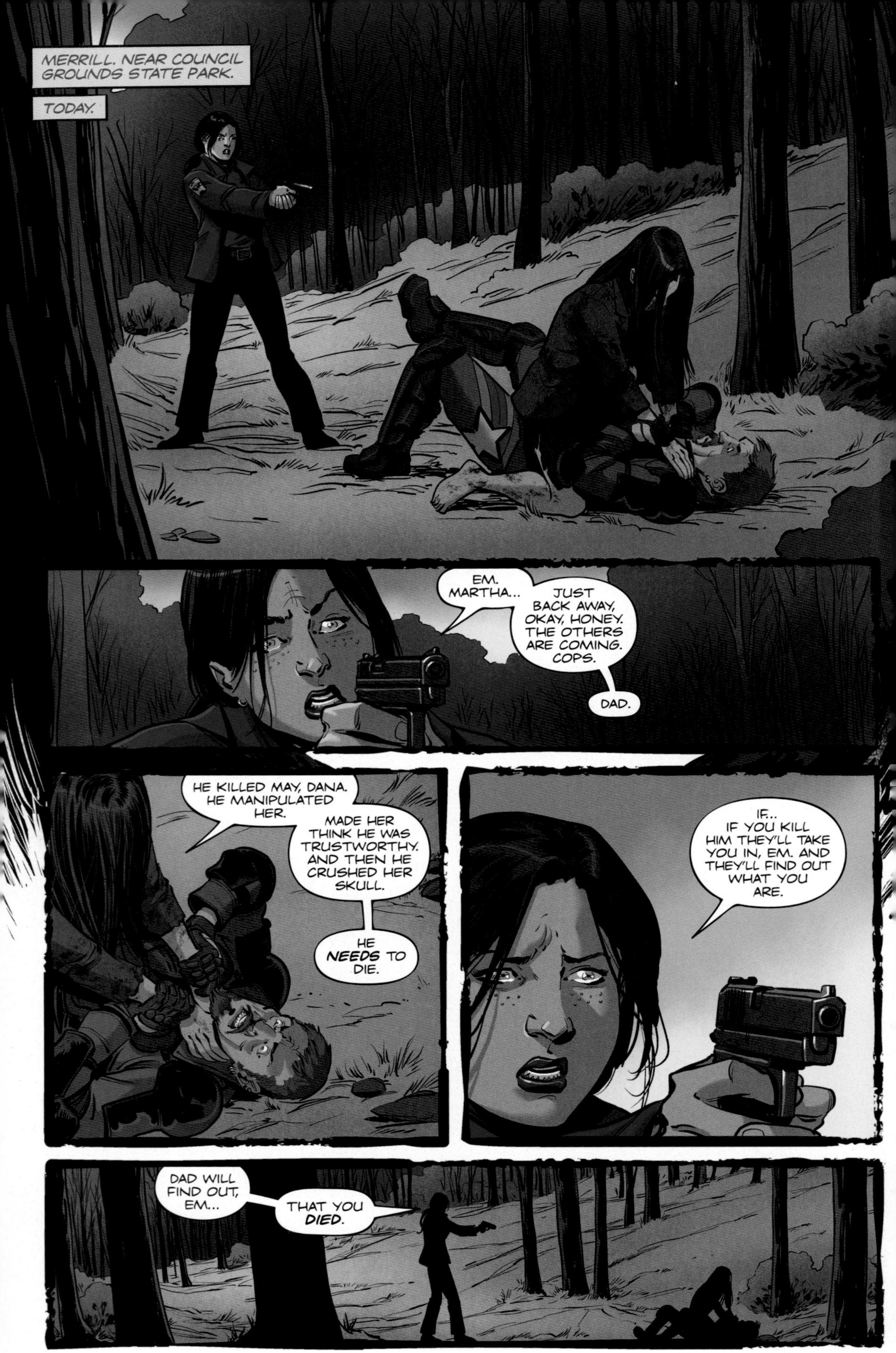
MERRILL. NEAR COUNCIL GROUNDS STATE PARK.
TODAY.
EM. MARTHA...
JUST BACK AWAY, OKAY, HONEY. THE OTHERS ARE COMING. COPS.
DAD.
HE KILLED MAY, DANA. HE MANIPULATED HER.
MADE HER THINK HE WAS TRUSTWORTHY. AND THEN HE CRUSHED HER SKULL.
HE NEEDS TO DIE.
IF... IF YOU KILL HIM THEY'LL TAKE YOU IN, EM. AND THEY'LL FIND OUT WHAT YOU ARE.
DAD WILL FIND OUT, EM...
THAT YOU DIED.

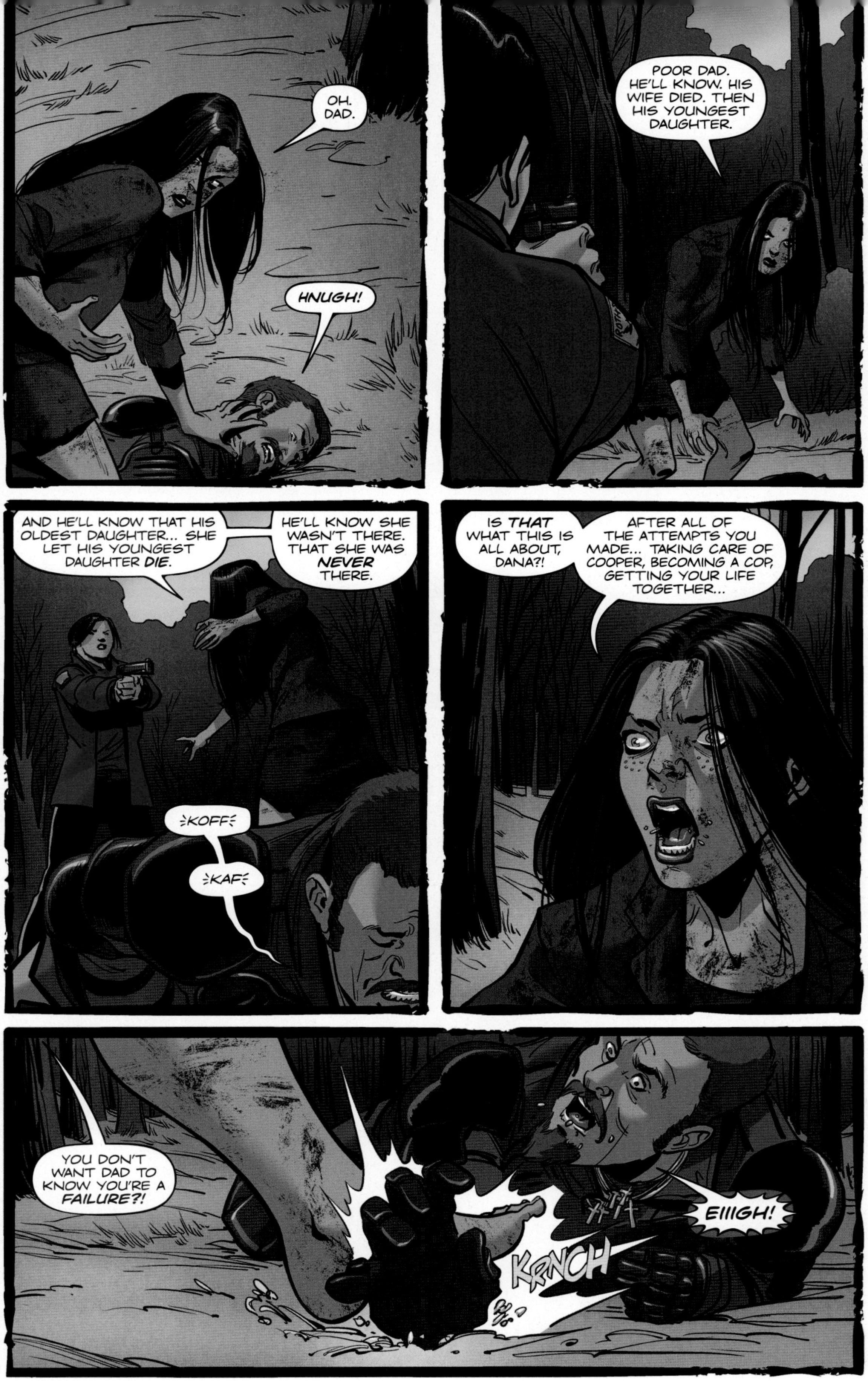

OH. DAD.
HNUGH!
POOR DAD. HE'LL KNOW. HIS WIFE DIED. THEN HIS YOUNGEST DAUGHTER.
AND HE'LL KNOW THAT HIS OLDEST DAUGHTER... SHE LET HIS YOUNGEST DAUGHTER *DIE*.
HE'LL KNOW SHE WASN'T THERE. THAT SHE WAS *NEVER* THERE.
KOFF
KAF
IS *THAT* WHAT THIS IS ALL ABOUT, DANA?!
AFTER ALL OF THE ATTEMPTS YOU MADE... TAKING CARE OF COOPER, BECOMING A COP, GETTING YOUR LIFE TOGETHER...
YOU DON'T WANT DAD TO KNOW YOU'RE A *FAILURE?!*
EIIIGH!
KRNCH

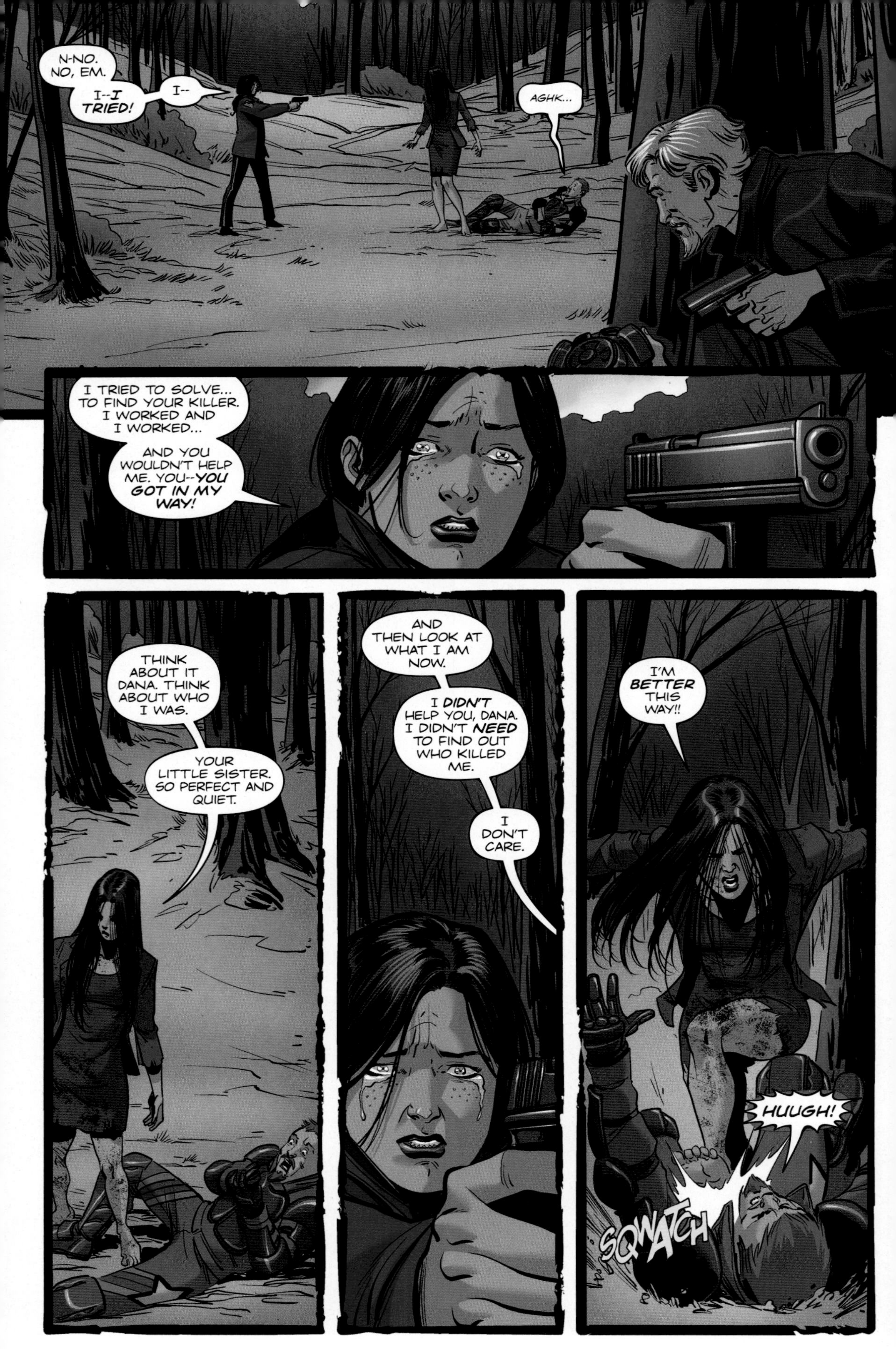

N-NO. NO, EM.
I--I TRIED!
I--
AGHK...
I TRIED TO SOLVE... TO FIND YOUR KILLER. I WORKED AND I WORKED...
AND YOU WOULDN'T HELP ME. YOU--YOU GOT IN MY WAY!
THINK ABOUT IT DANA. THINK ABOUT WHO I WAS.
YOUR LITTLE SISTER. SO PERFECT AND QUIET.
AND THEN LOOK AT WHAT I AM NOW.
I DIDN'T HELP YOU, DANA. I DIDN'T NEED TO FIND OUT WHO KILLED ME.
I DON'T CARE.
I'M BETTER THIS WAY!!
HUUGH!
SQWATCH

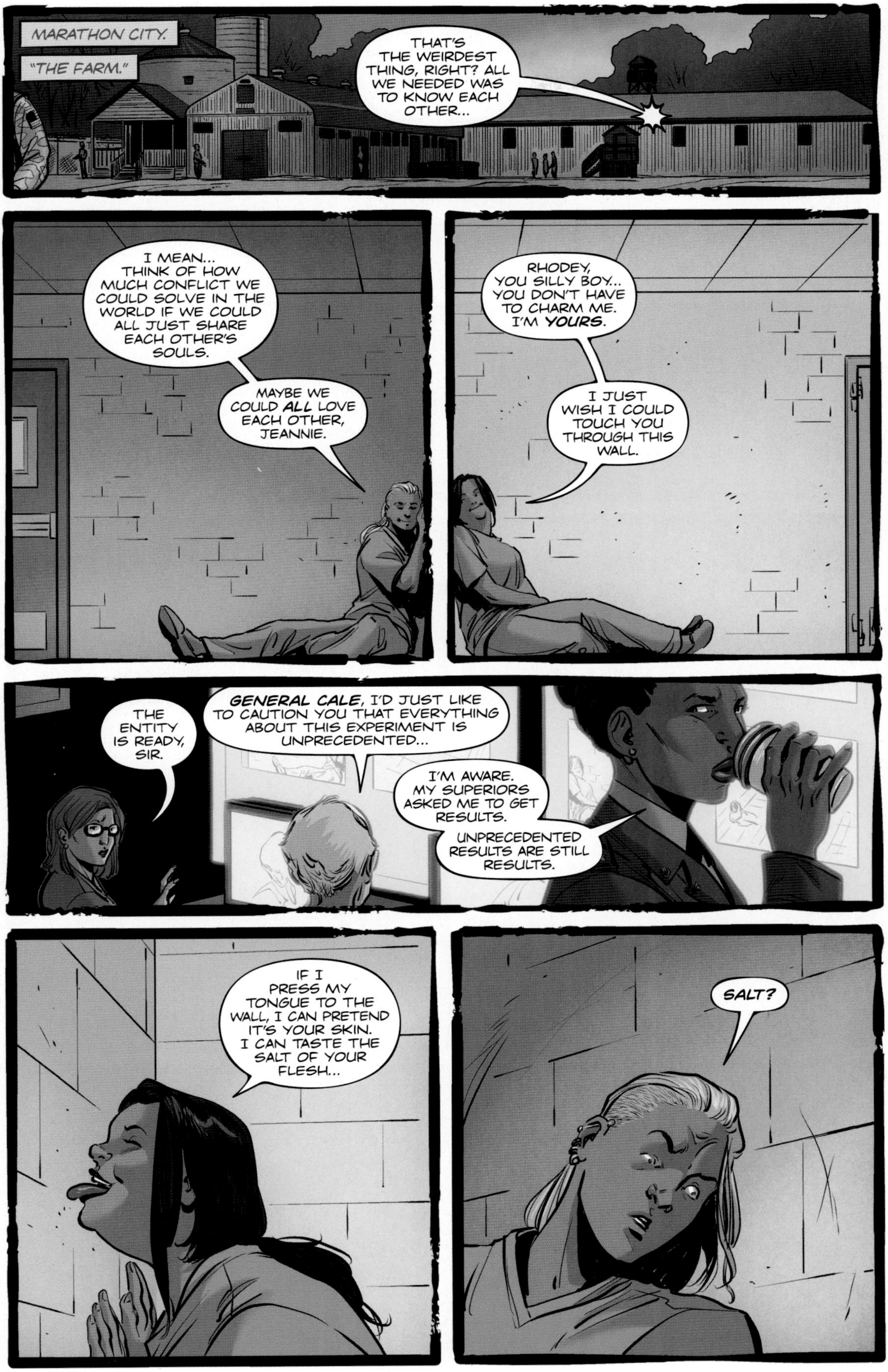
MARATHON CITY.
"THE FARM."
THAT'S THE WEIRDEST THING, RIGHT? ALL WE NEEDED WAS TO KNOW EACH OTHER...
I MEAN... THINK OF HOW MUCH CONFLICT WE COULD SOLVE IN THE WORLD IF WE COULD ALL JUST SHARE EACH OTHER'S SOULS.
MAYBE WE COULD ALL LOVE EACH OTHER, JEANNIE.
RHODEY, YOU SILLY BOY... YOU DON'T HAVE TO CHARM ME. I'M YOURS.
I JUST WISH I COULD TOUCH YOU THROUGH THIS WALL.
THE ENTITY IS READY, SIR.
GENERAL CALE, I'D JUST LIKE TO CAUTION YOU THAT EVERYTHING ABOUT THIS EXPERIMENT IS UNPRECEDENTED...
I'M AWARE. MY SUPERIORS ASKED ME TO GET RESULTS.
UNPRECEDENTED RESULTS ARE STILL RESULTS.
IF I PRESS MY TONGUE TO THE WALL, I CAN PRETEND IT'S YOUR SKIN. I CAN TASTE THE SALT OF YOUR FLESH...
SALT?

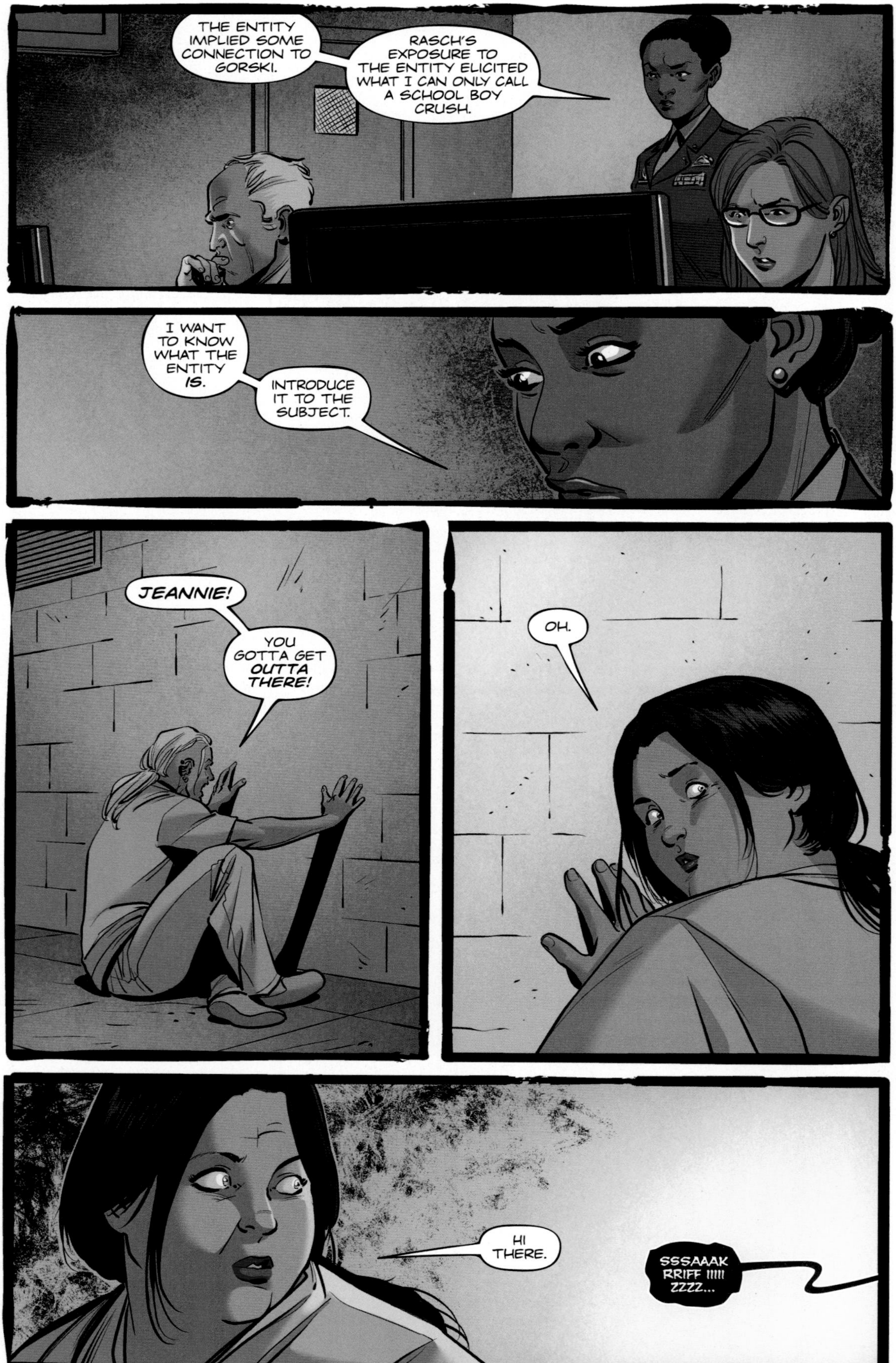

THE ENTITY IMPLIED SOME CONNECTION TO GORSKI.
RASCH'S EXPOSURE TO THE ENTITY ELICITED WHAT I CAN ONLY CALL A SCHOOL BOY CRUSH.
I WANT TO KNOW WHAT THE ENTITY *IS.*
INTRODUCE IT TO THE SUBJECT.
JEANNIE!
YOU GOTTA GET *OUTTA THERE!*
OH.
HI THERE.
SSSAAAK RRIFF !!!!! ZZZZ...

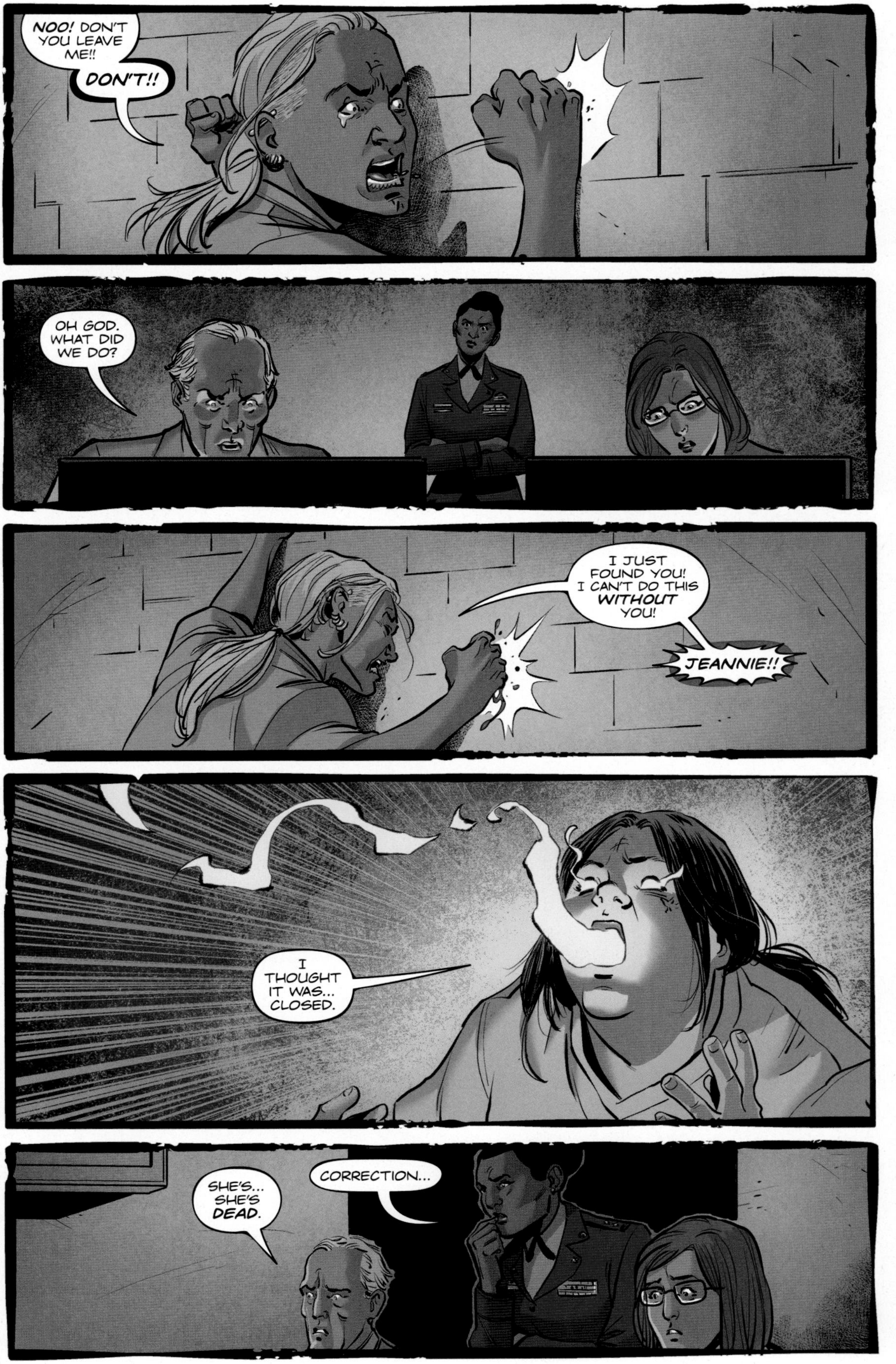
NOO! DON'T YOU LEAVE ME!!
DON'T!!
OH GOD. WHAT DID WE DO?
I JUST FOUND YOU! I CAN'T DO THIS WITHOUT YOU!
JEANNIE!!
I THOUGHT IT WAS... CLOSED.
SHE'S... SHE'S DEAD.
CORRECTION...

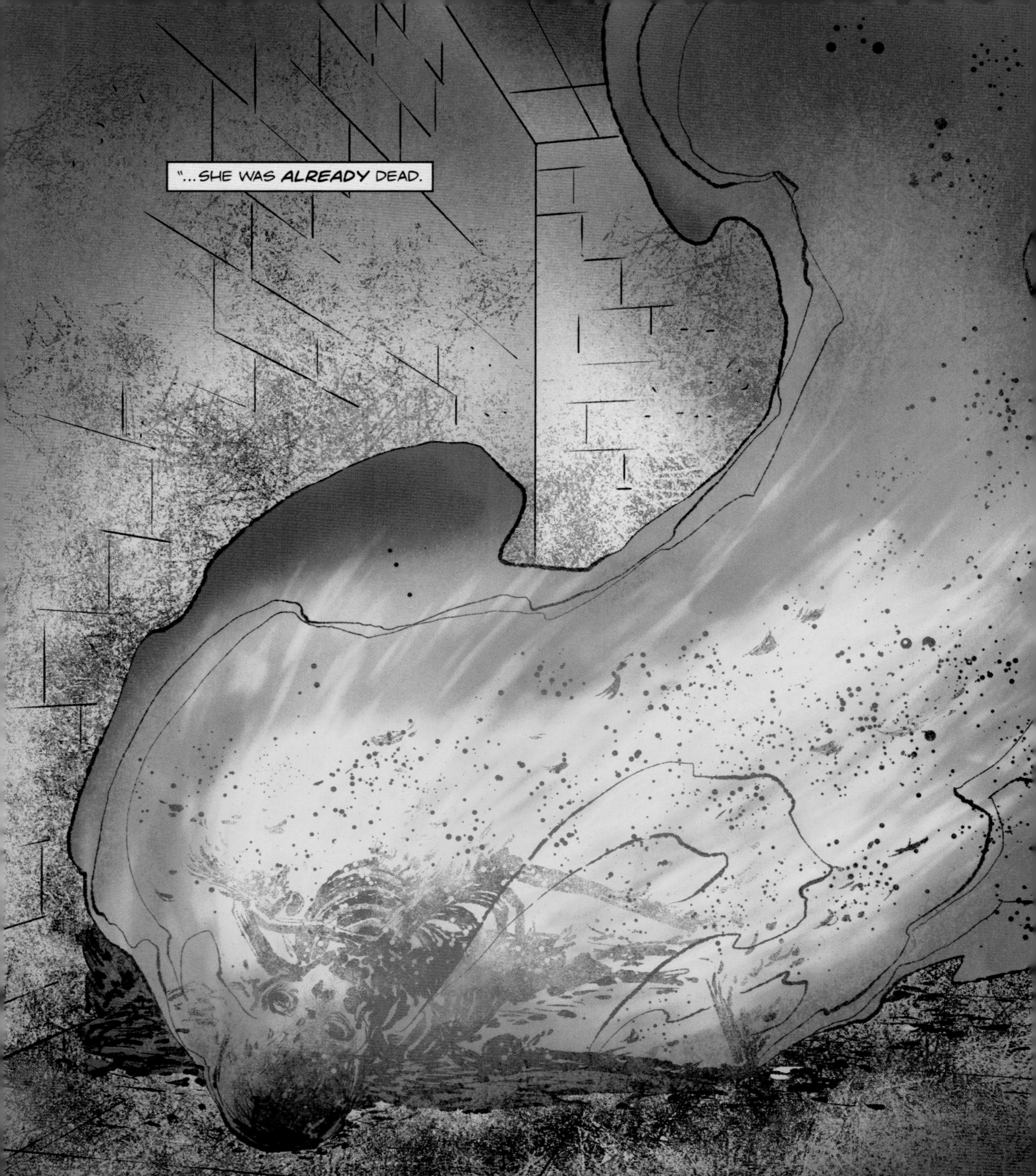
"...SHE WAS ALREADY DEAD.

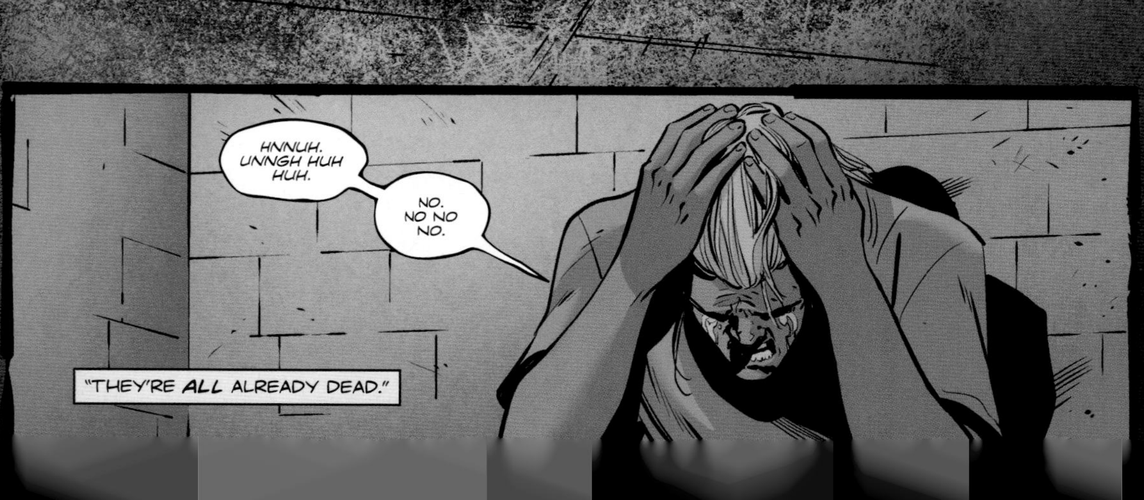
HNNUH. UNNGH HUH HUH.
NO. NO NO NO.
"THEY'RE ALL ALREADY DEAD."

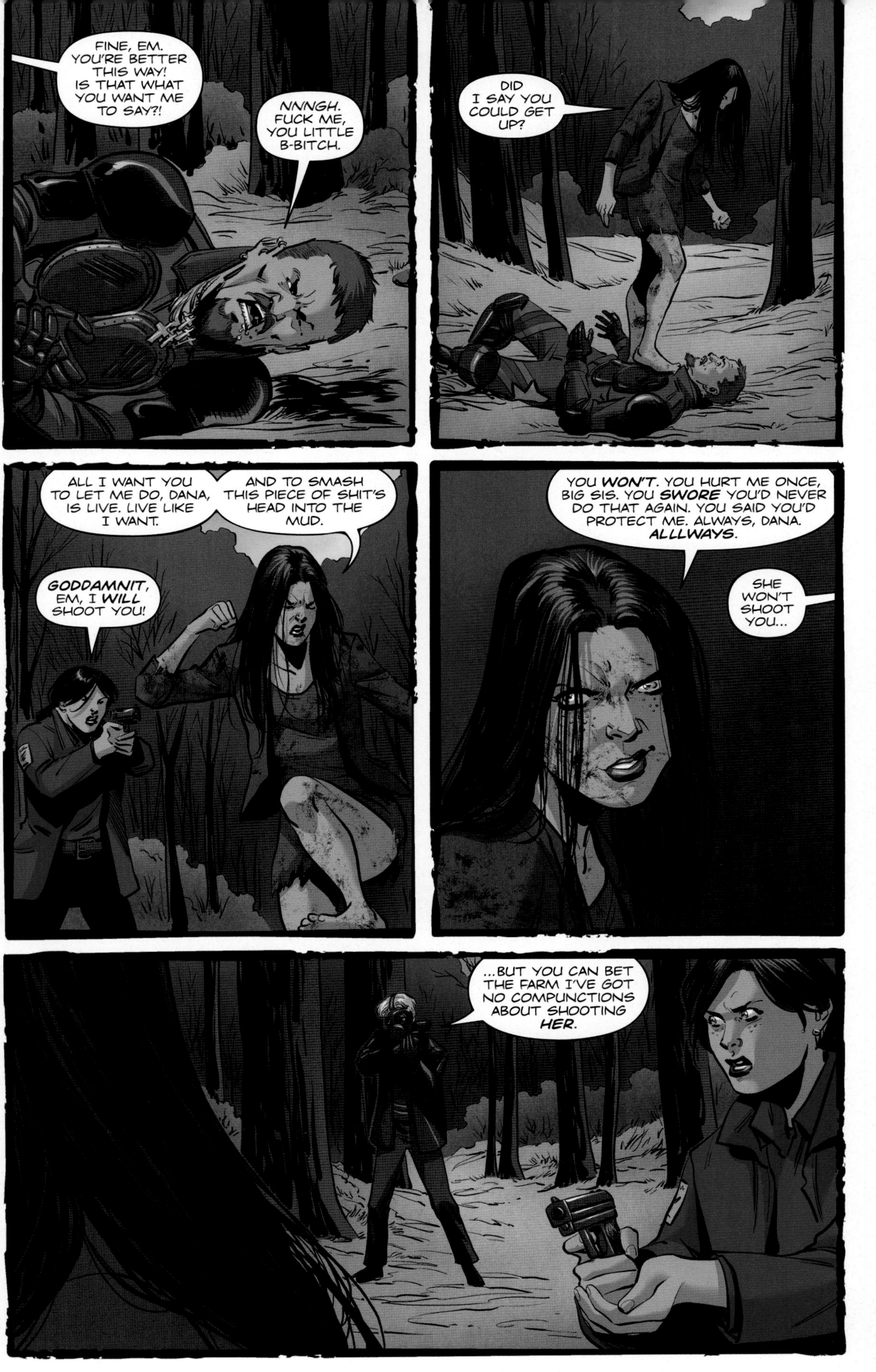
FINE, EM. YOU'RE BETTER THIS WAY! IS THAT WHAT YOU WANT ME TO SAY?!
NNNGH. FUCK ME, YOU LITTLE B-BITCH.
DID I SAY YOU COULD GET UP?
ALL I WANT YOU TO LET ME DO, DANA, IS LIVE. LIVE LIKE I WANT.
AND TO SMASH THIS PIECE OF SHIT'S HEAD INTO THE MUD.
GODDAMNIT, EM, I WILL SHOOT YOU!
YOU WON'T. YOU HURT ME ONCE, BIG SIS. YOU SWORE YOU'D NEVER DO THAT AGAIN. YOU SAID YOU'D PROTECT ME. ALWAYS, DANA. ALLLWAYS.
SHE WON'T SHOOT YOU...
...BUT YOU CAN BET THE FARM I'VE GOT NO COMPUNCTIONS ABOUT SHOOTING HER.

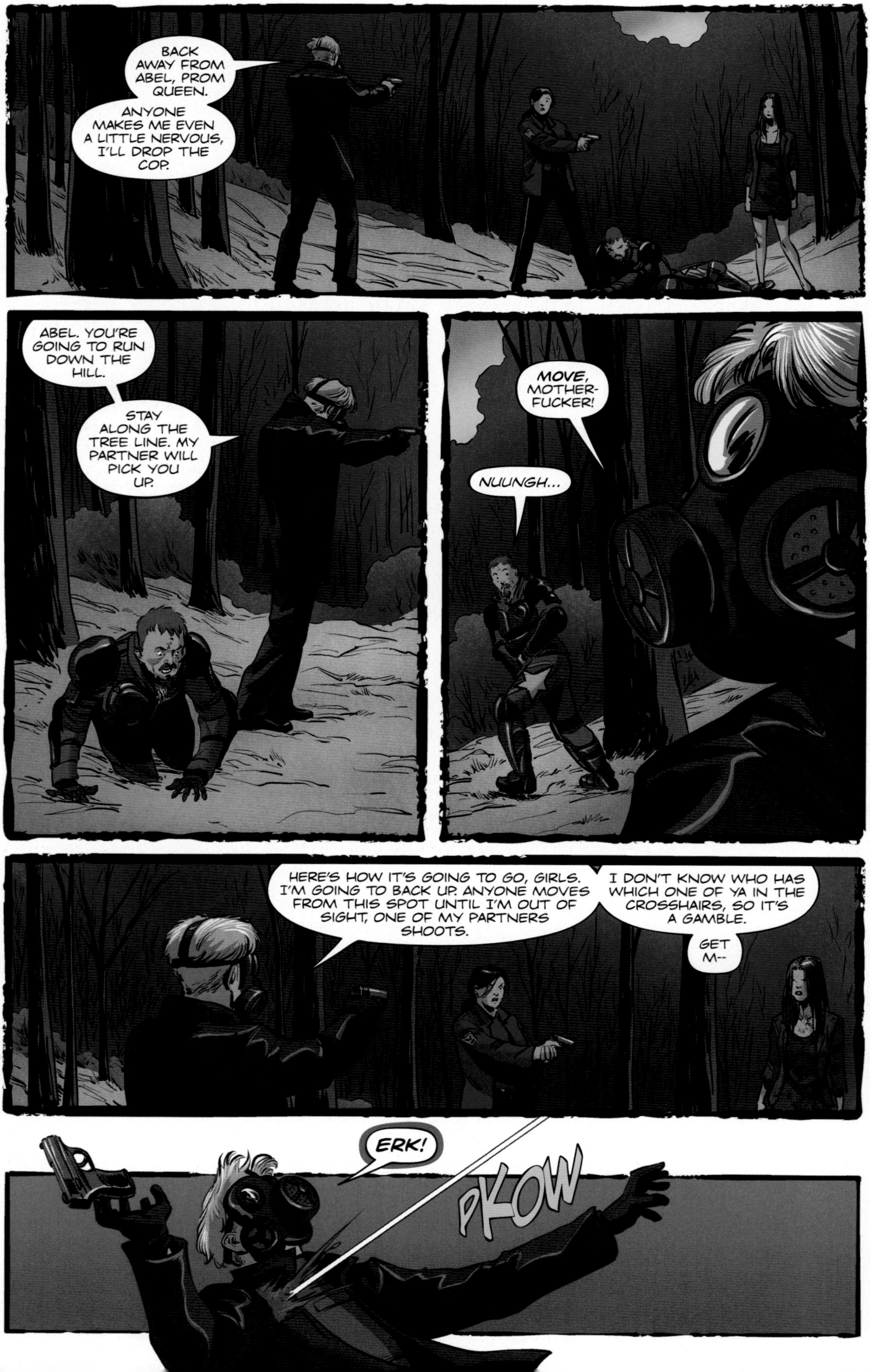
BACK AWAY FROM ABEL, PROM QUEEN.
ANYONE MAKES ME EVEN A LITTLE NERVOUS, I'LL DROP THE COP.
ABEL. YOU'RE GOING TO RUN DOWN THE HILL.
STAY ALONG THE TREE LINE. MY PARTNER WILL PICK YOU UP.
MOVE, MOTHER-FUCKER!
NUUNGH...
HERE'S HOW IT'S GOING TO GO, GIRLS. I'M GOING TO BACK UP. ANYONE MOVES FROM THIS SPOT UNTIL I'M OUT OF SIGHT, ONE OF MY PARTNERS SHOOTS.
I DON'T KNOW WHO HAS WHICH ONE OF YA IN THE CROSSHAIRS, SO IT'S A GAMBLE.
GET M--
ERK!
PKOW

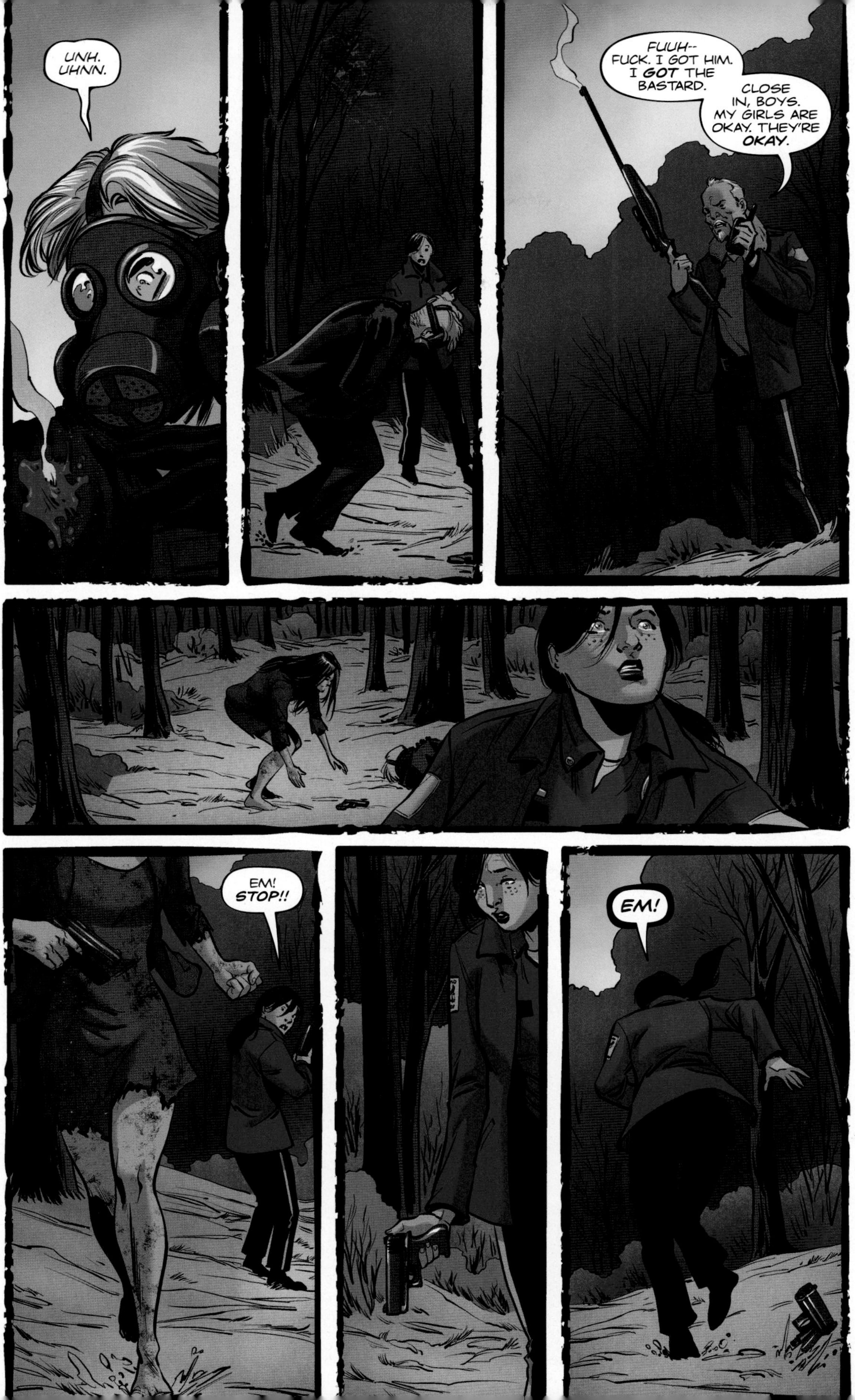
UNH. UHNN.
FUUH-- FUCK. I GOT HIM. I GOT THE BASTARD.
CLOSE IN, BOYS. MY GIRLS ARE OKAY. THEY'RE OKAY.
EM! STOP!!
EM!

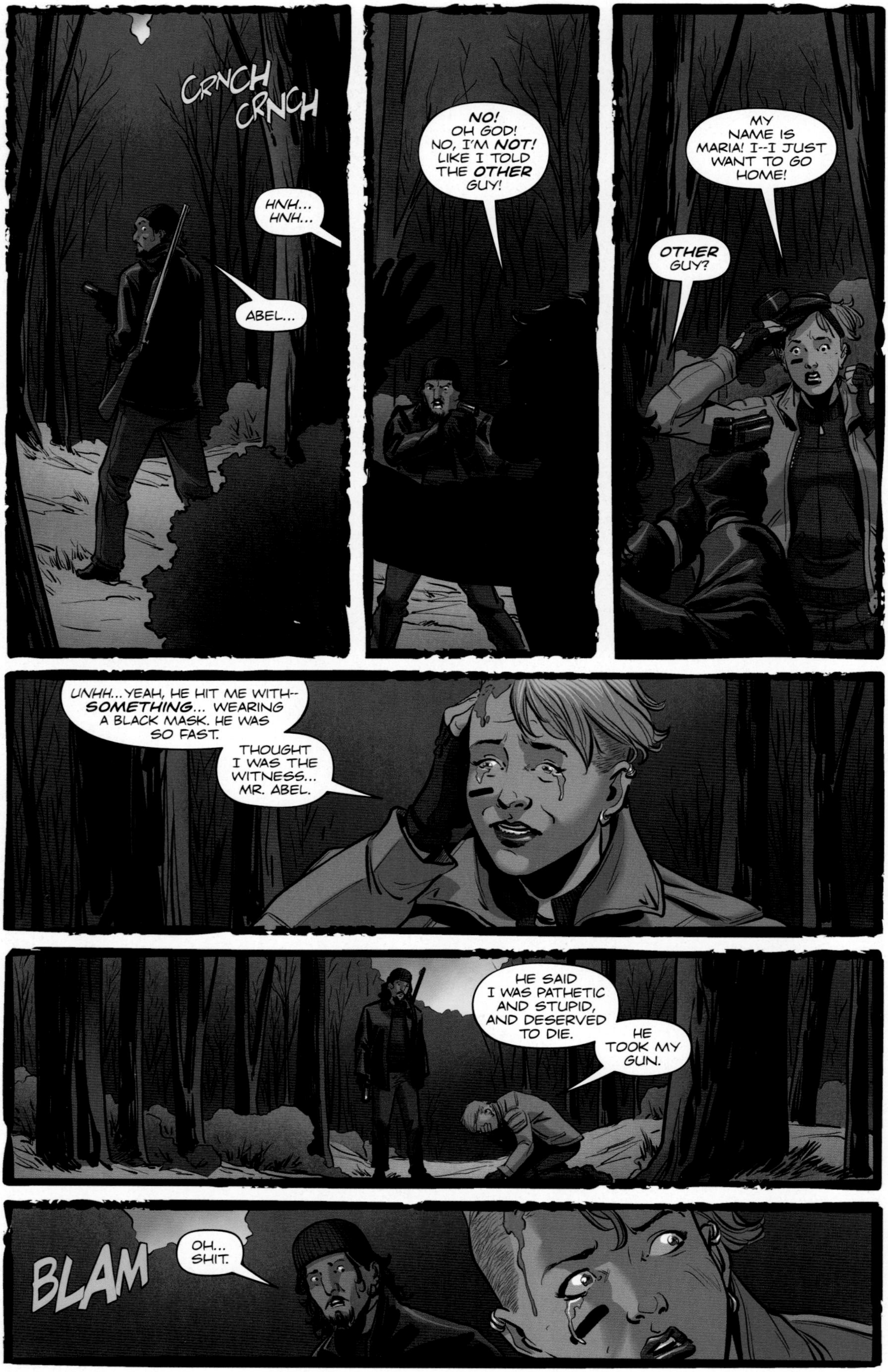
CRNCH CRNCH
HNH... HNH...
ABEL...
NO! OH GOD! NO, I'M NOT! LIKE I TOLD THE OTHER GUY!
MY NAME IS MARIA! I--I JUST WANT TO GO HOME!
OTHER GUY?
UNHH...YEAH, HE HIT ME WITH-- SOMETHING... WEARING A BLACK MASK. HE WAS SO FAST.
THOUGHT I WAS THE WITNESS... MR. ABEL.
HE SAID I WAS PATHETIC AND STUPID, AND DESERVED TO DIE.
HE TOOK MY GUN.
BLAM
OH... SHIT.

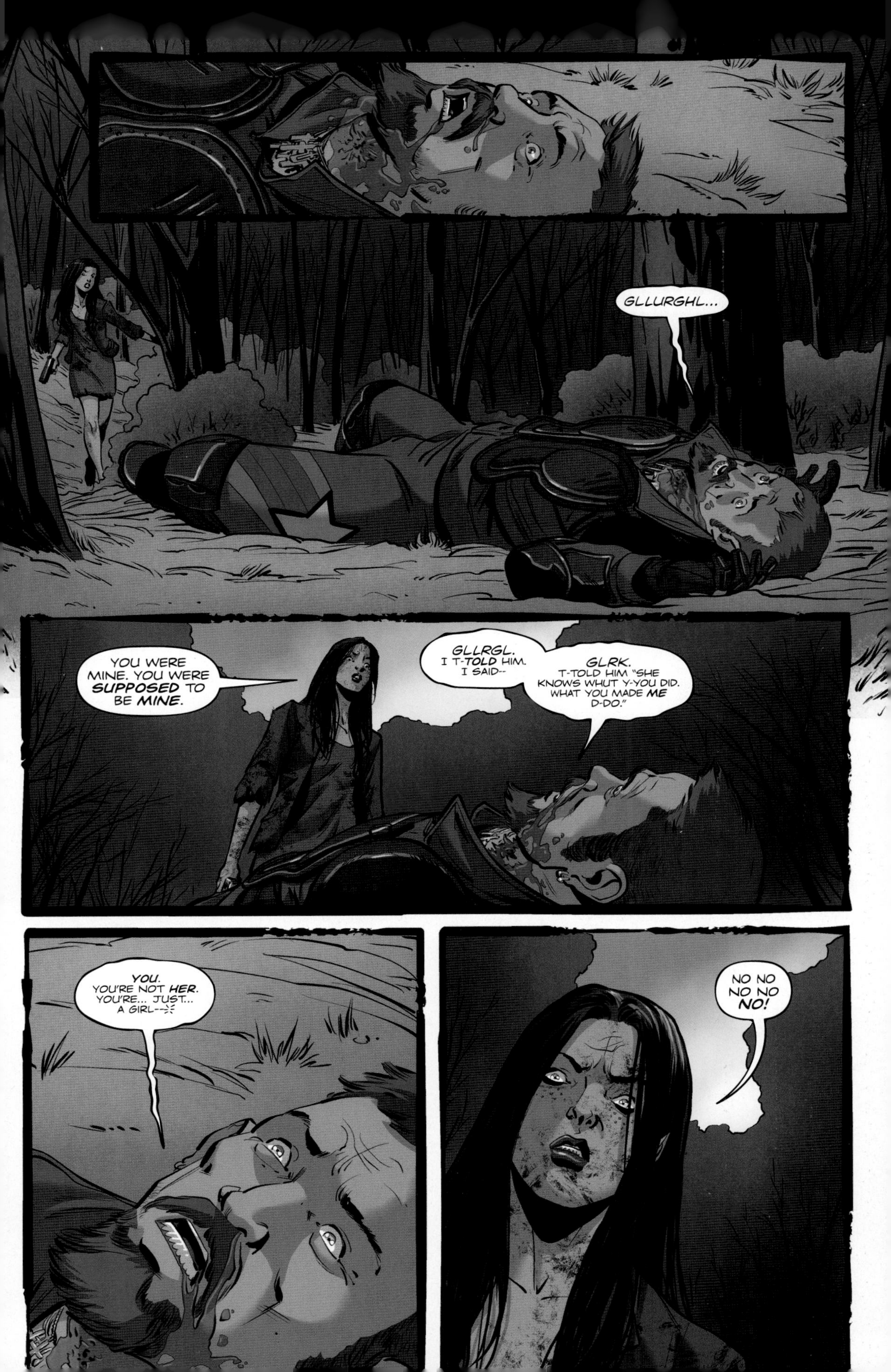
GLLURGHL...
YOU WERE MINE. YOU WERE SUPPOSED TO BE MINE.
GLLRGL. I T-TOLD HIM. I SAID--
GLRK. T-TOLD HIM "SHE KNOWS WHUT Y-YOU DID. WHAT YOU MADE ME D-DO."
YOU. YOU'RE NOT HER. YOU'RE... JUST... A GIRL--
...
NO NO NO NO NO!

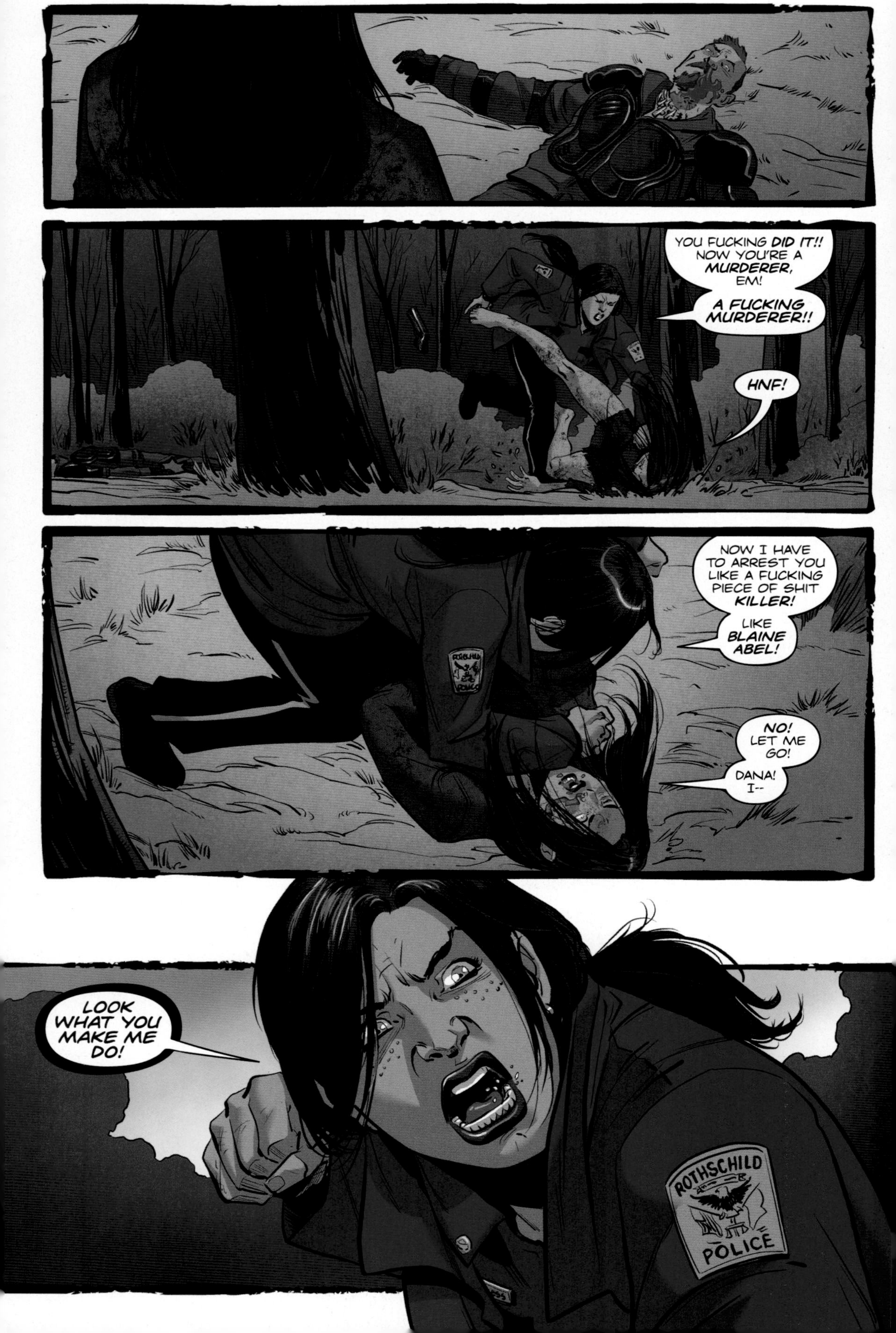
YOU FUCKING DID IT!! NOW YOU'RE A MURDERER, EM!
A FUCKING MURDERER!!
HNF!
NOW I HAVE TO ARREST YOU LIKE A FUCKING PIECE OF SHIT KILLER!
LIKE BLAINE ABEL!
NO! LET ME GO!
DANA! I--
LOOK WHAT YOU MAKE ME DO!
ROTHSCHILD
POLICE

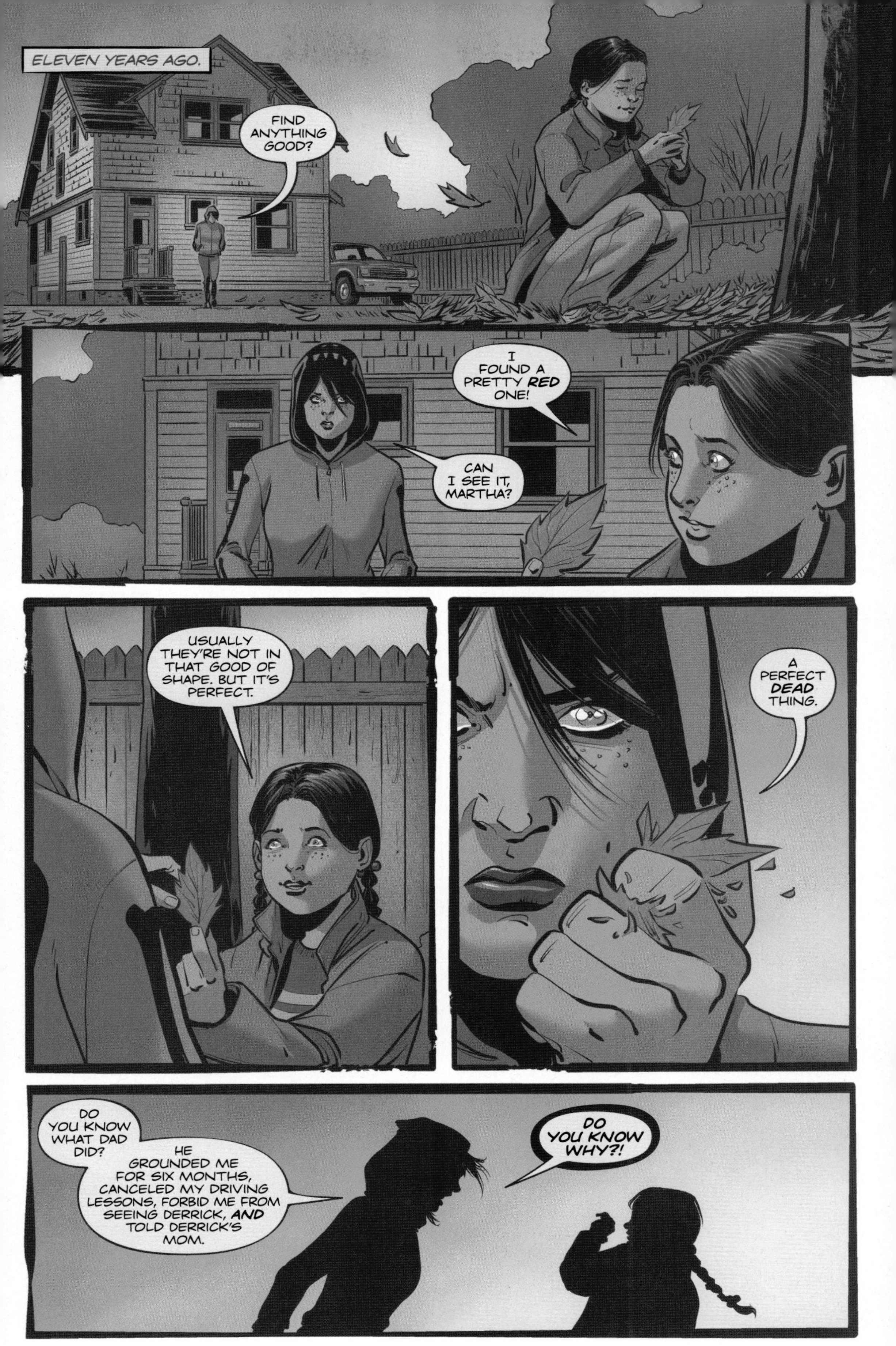
ELEVEN YEARS AGO.
FIND ANYTHING GOOD?
I FOUND A PRETTY RED ONE!
CAN I SEE IT, MARTHA?
USUALLY THEY'RE NOT IN THAT GOOD OF SHAPE. BUT IT'S PERFECT.
A PERFECT DEAD THING.
DO YOU KNOW WHAT DAD DID?
HE GROUNDED ME FOR SIX MONTHS, CANCELED MY DRIVING LESSONS, FORBID ME FROM SEEING DERRICK, AND TOLD DERRICK'S MOM.
DO YOU KNOW WHY?!

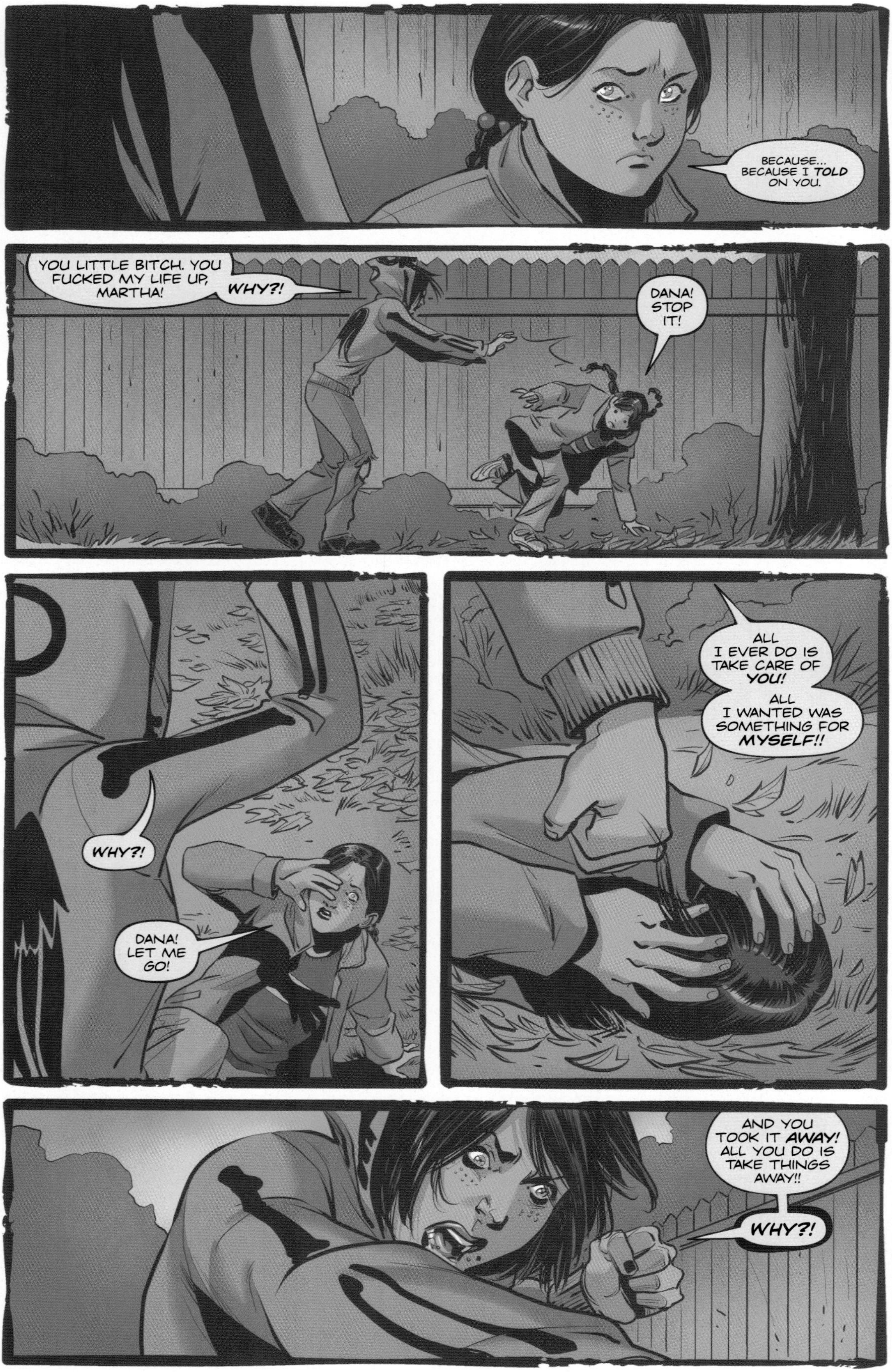
BECAUSE... BECAUSE I TOLD ON YOU.
YOU LITTLE BITCH. YOU FUCKED MY LIFE UP, MARTHA!
WHY?!
DANA! STOP IT!
WHY?!
DANA! LET ME GO!
ALL I EVER DO IS TAKE CARE OF YOU!
ALL I WANTED WAS SOMETHING FOR MYSELF!!
AND YOU TOOK IT AWAY! ALL YOU DO IS TAKE THINGS AWAY!!
WHY?!

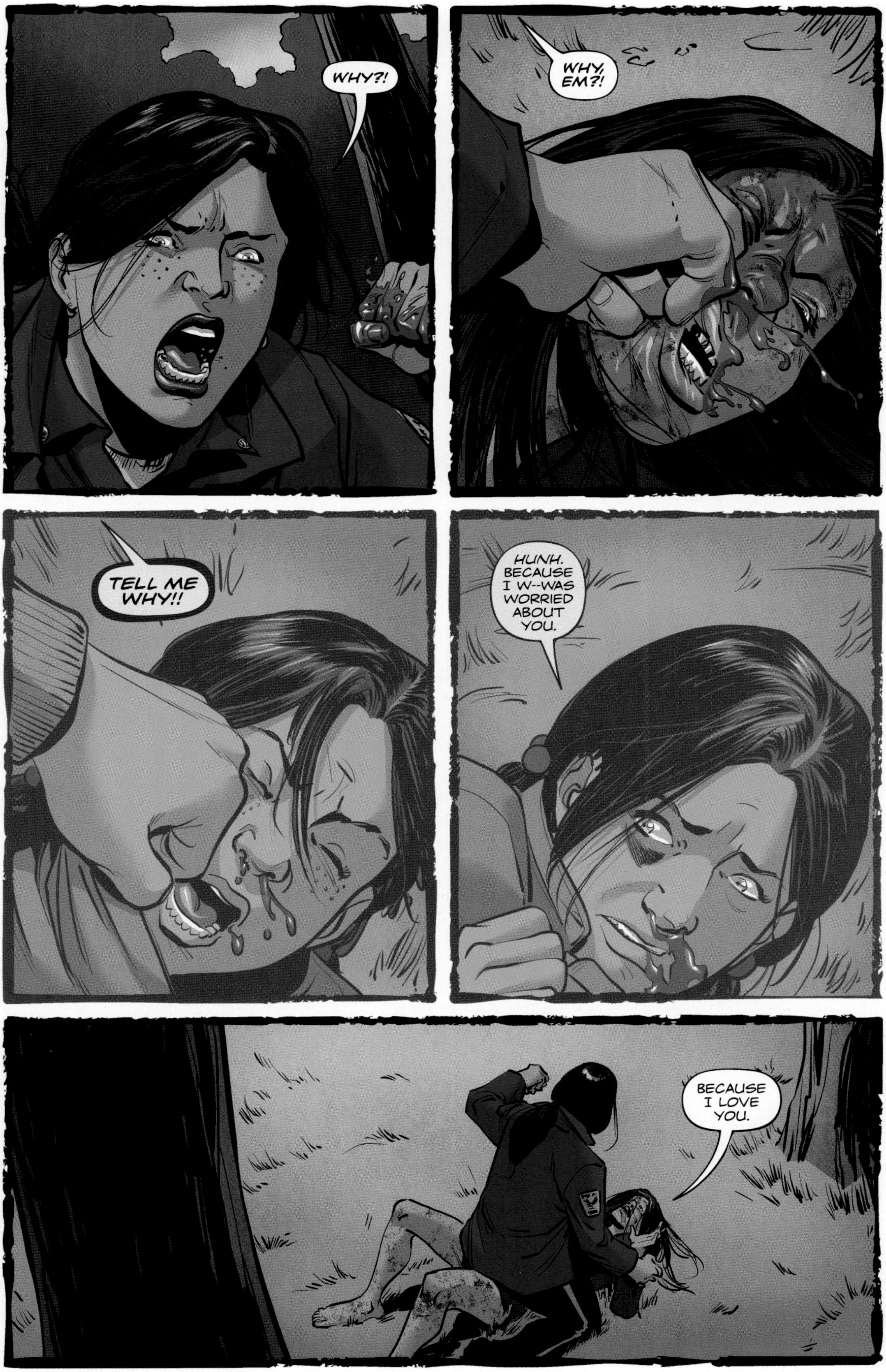
WHY?!
WHY, EM?!
TELL ME WHY!!
HUNH. BECAUSE I W--WAS WORRIED ABOUT YOU.
BECAUSE I LOVE YOU.

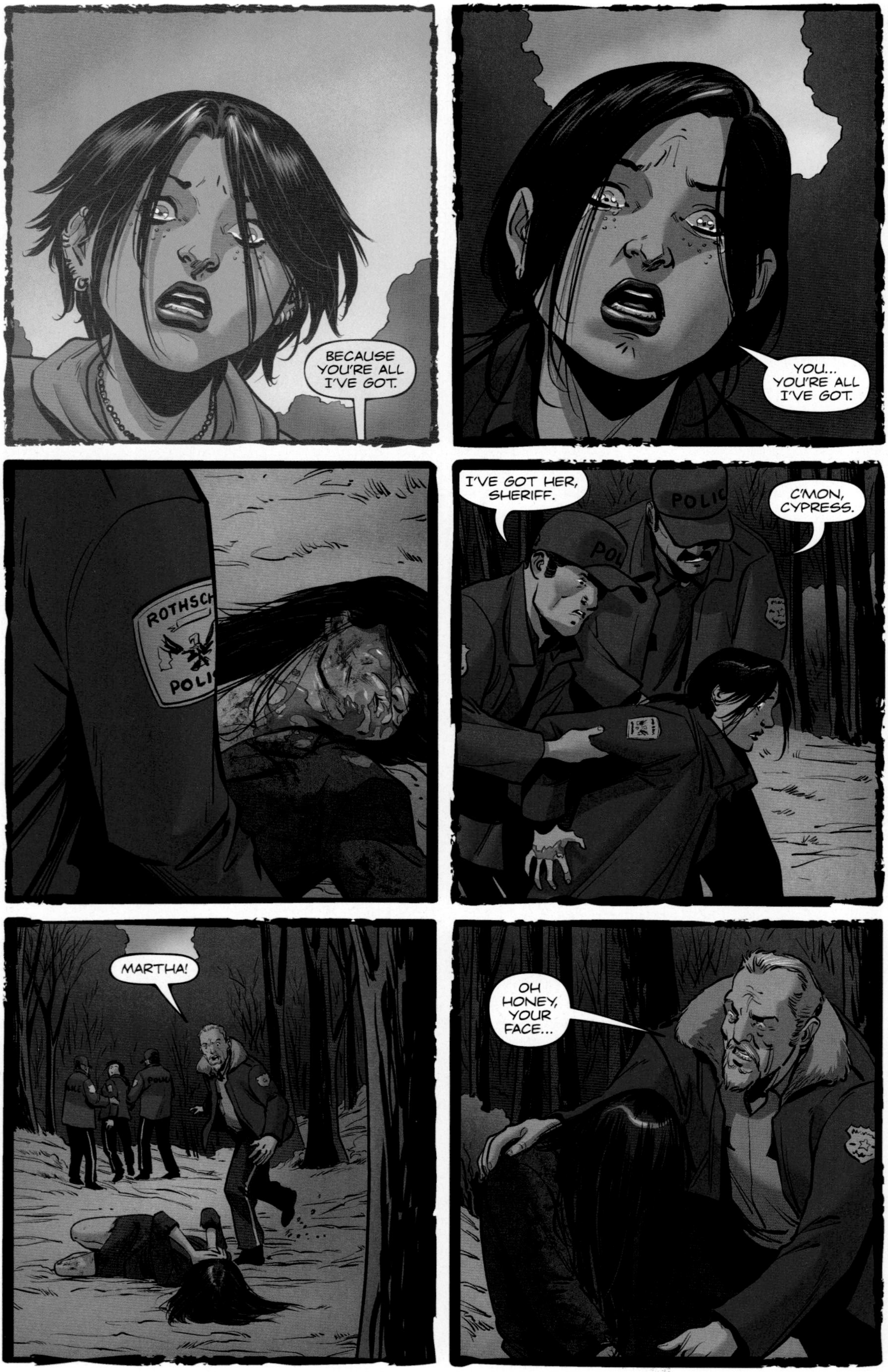
BECAUSE YOU'RE ALL I'VE GOT.
YOU... YOU'RE ALL I'VE GOT.
ROTHSCH
POLIC
I'VE GOT HER, SHERIFF.
C'MON, CYPRESS.
POLIC
MARTHA!
OH HONEY, YOUR FACE...

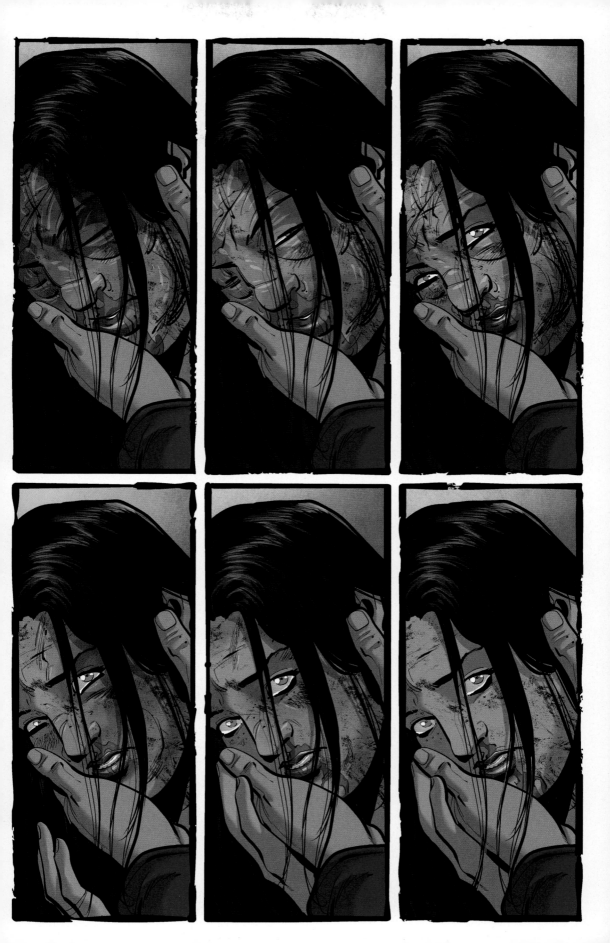

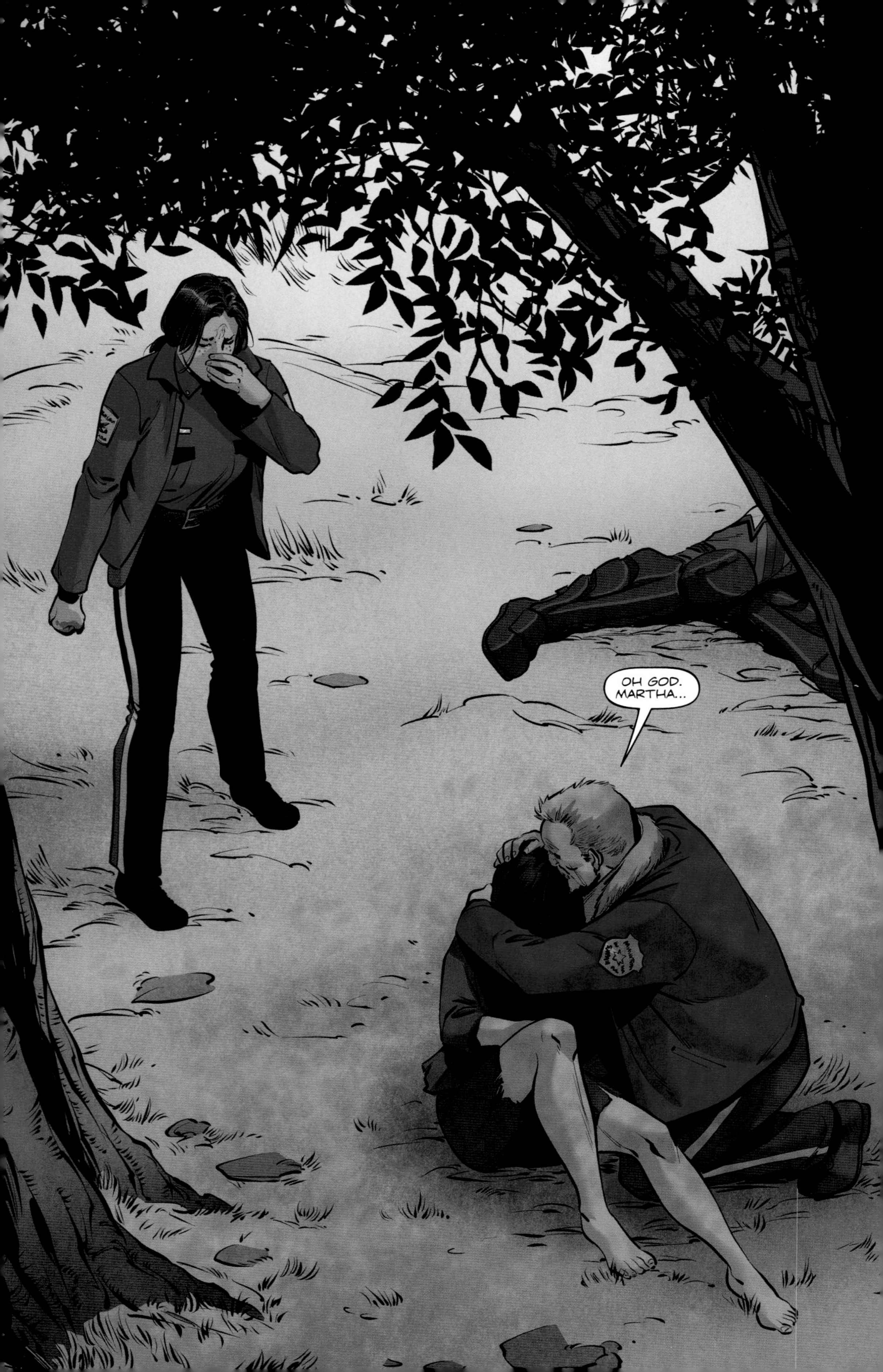
OH GOD. MARTHA...

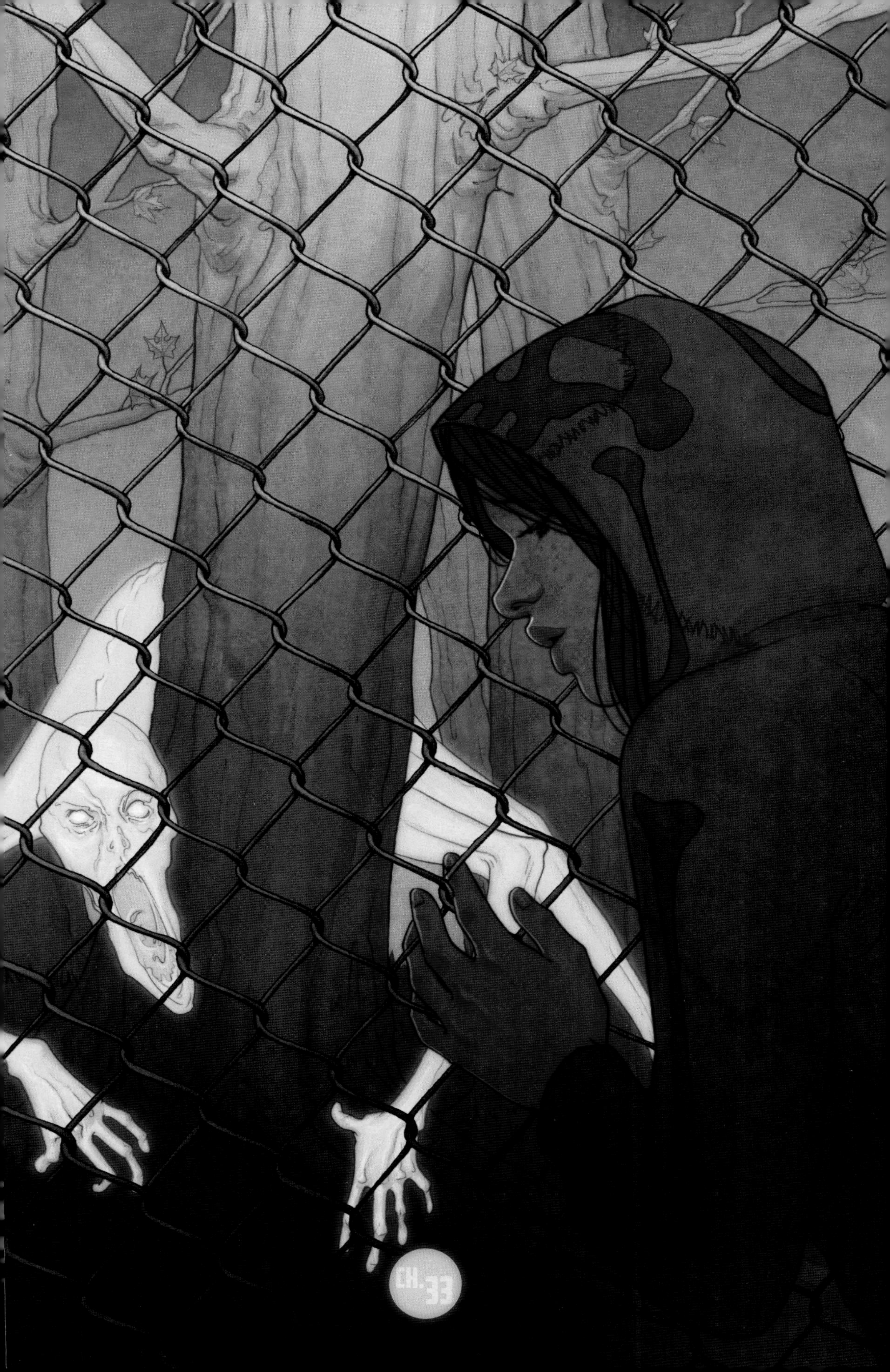
CH. 33

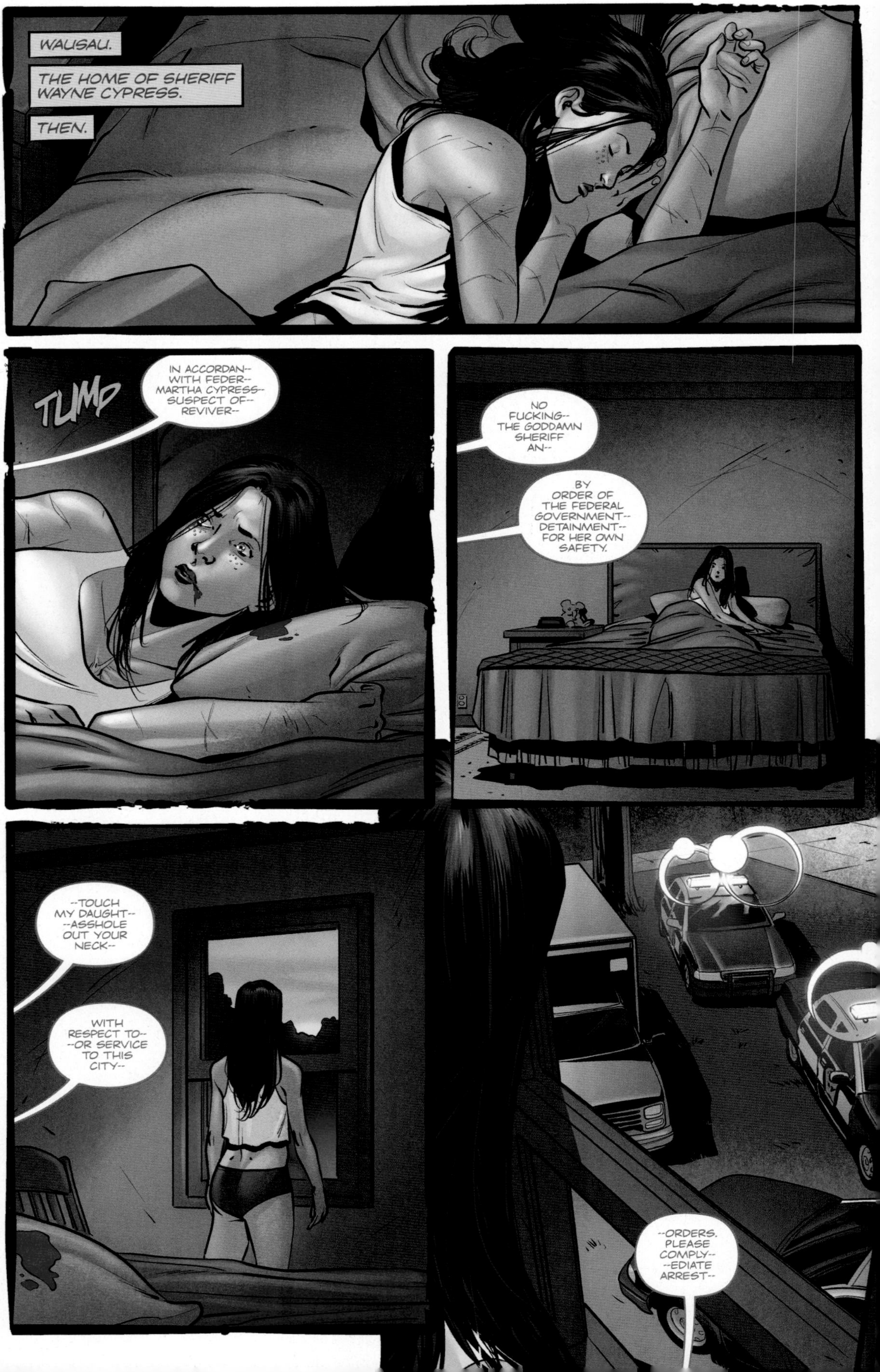
WAUSAU.
THE HOME OF SHERIFF WAYNE CYPRESS.
THEN.
TUMP
IN ACCORDAN-- WITH FEDER-- MARTHA CYPRESS-- SUSPECT OF-- REVIVER--
NO FUCKING-- THE GODDAMN SHERIFF AN--
BY ORDER OF THE FEDERAL GOVERNMENT-- DETAINMENT-- FOR HER OWN SAFETY.
--TOUCH MY DAUGHT-- --ASSHOLE OUT YOUR NECK--
WITH RESPECT TO-- --OR SERVICE TO THIS CITY--
--ORDERS. PLEASE COMPLY-- --EDIATE ARREST--

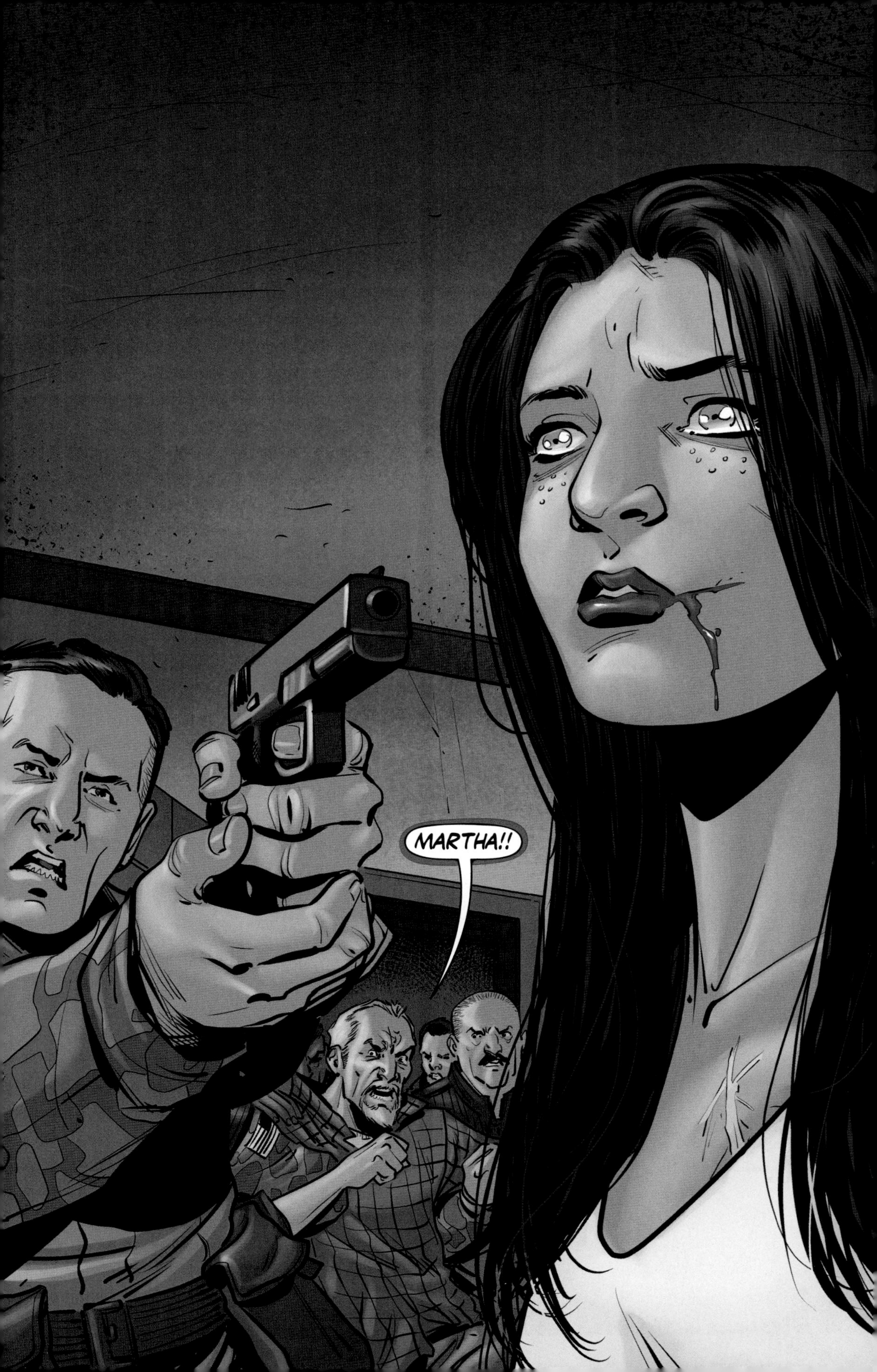
MARTHA!!

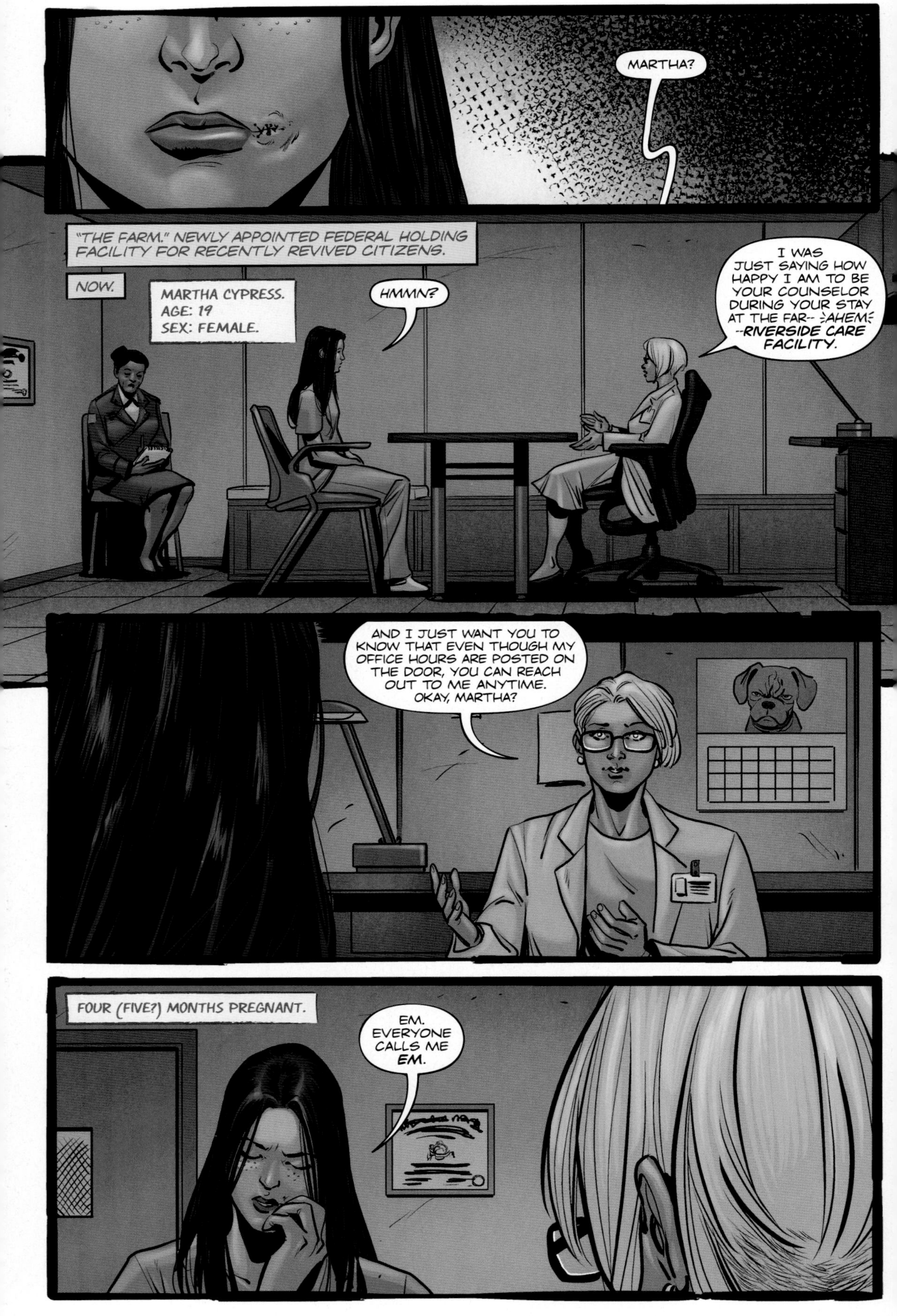
MARTHA?
"THE FARM." NEWLY APPOINTED FEDERAL HOLDING FACILITY FOR RECENTLY REVIVED CITIZENS.
NOW.
MARTHA CYPRESS.
AGE: 19
SEX: FEMALE.
HMMN?
I WAS JUST SAYING HOW HAPPY I AM TO BE YOUR COUNSELOR DURING YOUR STAY AT THE FAR-- AHEM --RIVERSIDE CARE FACILITY.
AND I JUST WANT YOU TO KNOW THAT EVEN THOUGH MY OFFICE HOURS ARE POSTED ON THE DOOR, YOU CAN REACH OUT TO ME ANYTIME. OKAY, MARTHA?
FOUR (FIVE?) MONTHS PREGNANT.
EM. EVERYONE CALLS ME EM.

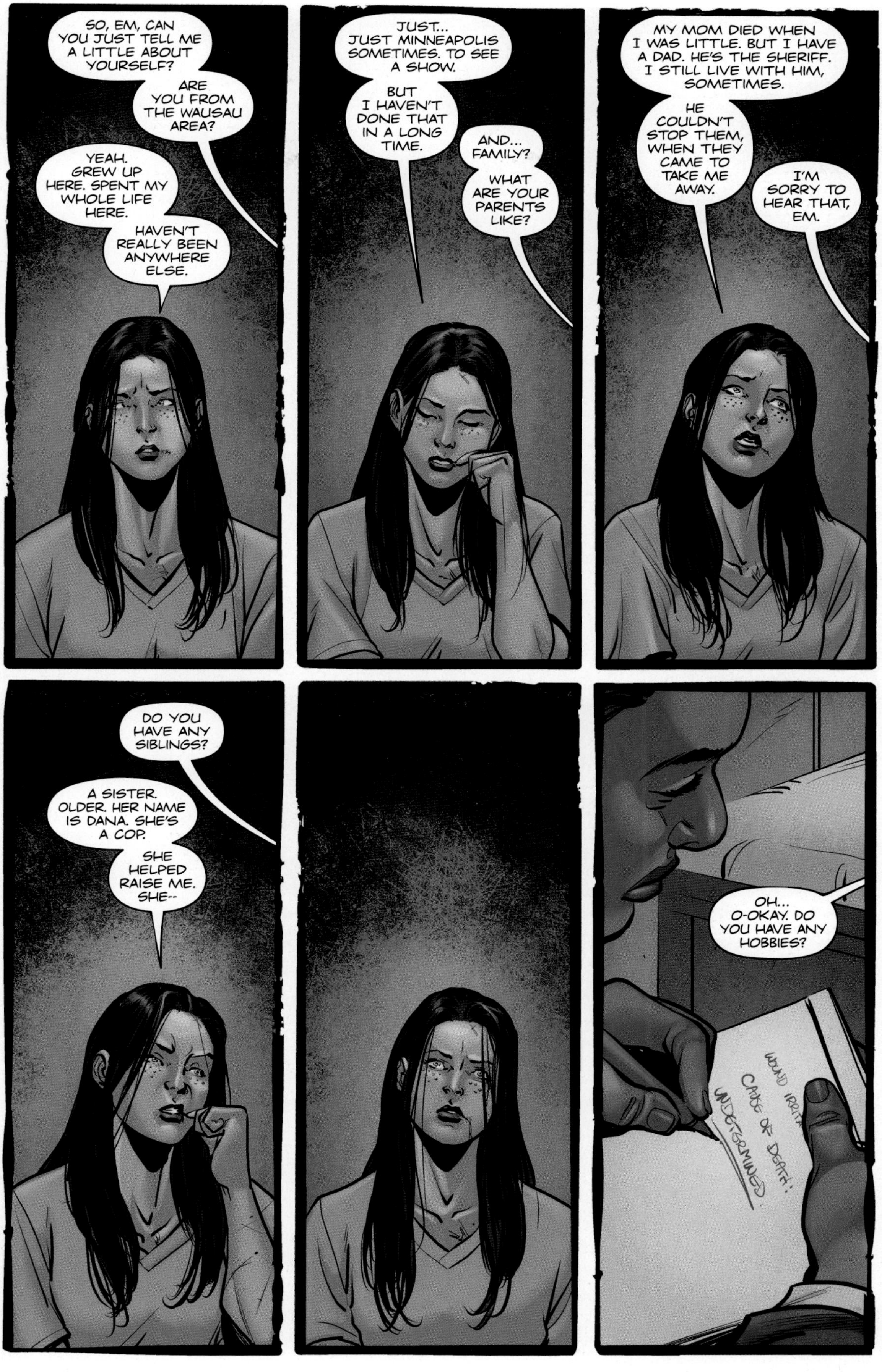
SO, EM, CAN YOU JUST TELL ME A LITTLE ABOUT YOURSELF?
ARE YOU FROM THE WAUSAU AREA?
YEAH. GREW UP HERE. SPENT MY WHOLE LIFE HERE.
HAVEN'T REALLY BEEN ANYWHERE ELSE.
JUST... JUST MINNEAPOLIS SOMETIMES. TO SEE A SHOW.
BUT I HAVEN'T DONE THAT IN A LONG TIME.
AND... FAMILY?
WHAT ARE YOUR PARENTS LIKE?
MY MOM DIED WHEN I WAS LITTLE. BUT I HAVE A DAD. HE'S THE SHERIFF. I STILL LIVE WITH HIM, SOMETIMES.
HE COULDN'T STOP THEM, WHEN THEY CAME TO TAKE ME AWAY.
I'M SORRY TO HEAR THAT, EM.
DO YOU HAVE ANY SIBLINGS?
A SISTER. OLDER. HER NAME IS DANA. SHE'S A COP.
SHE HELPED RAISE ME. SHE--
OH... O-OKAY. DO YOU HAVE ANY HOBBIES?
CAUSE OF DEATH:
UNDETERMINED

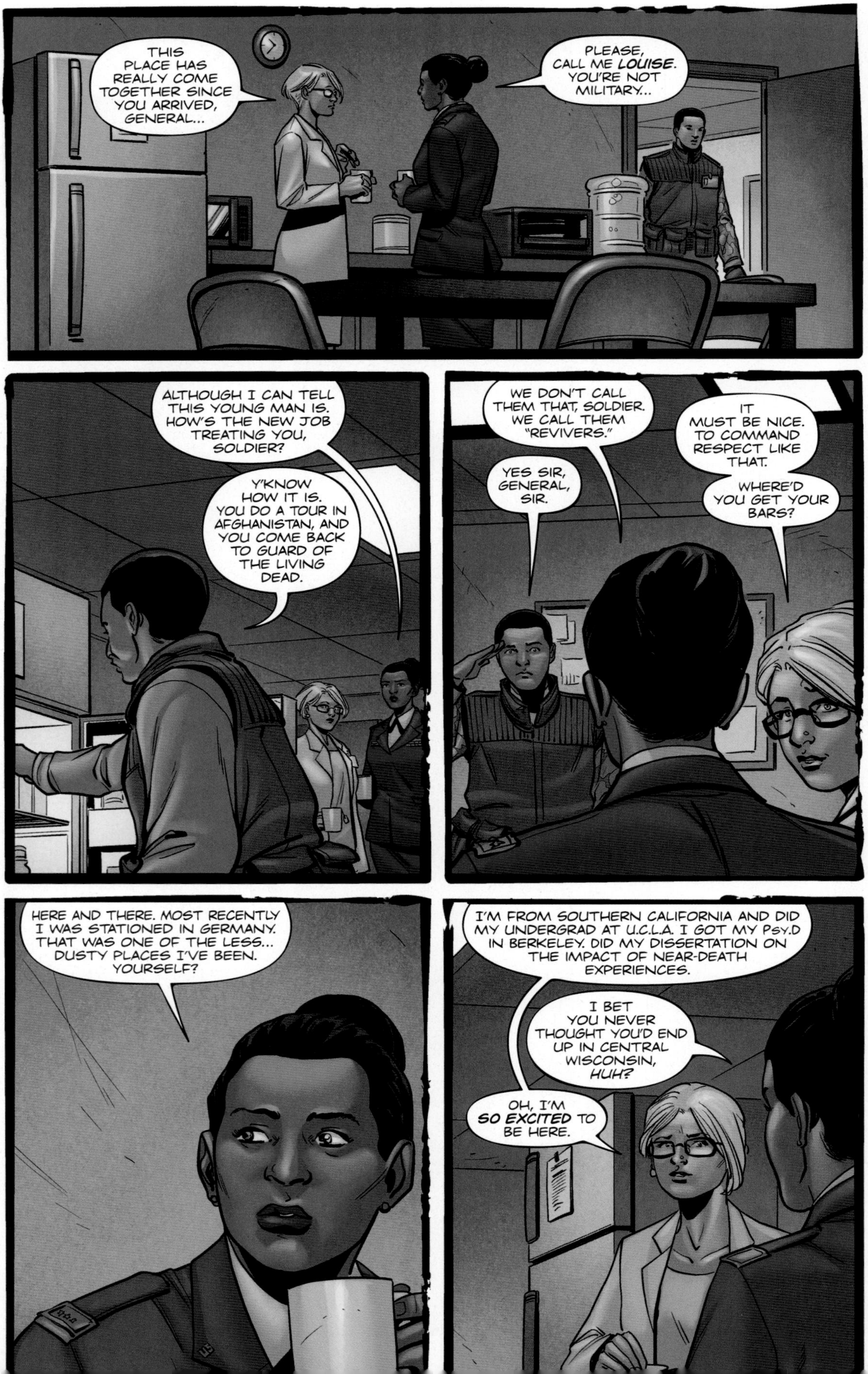
THIS PLACE HAS REALLY COME TOGETHER SINCE YOU ARRIVED, GENERAL...
PLEASE, CALL ME *LOUISE*. YOU'RE NOT MILITARY...
ALTHOUGH I CAN TELL THIS YOUNG MAN IS. HOW'S THE NEW JOB TREATING YOU, SOLDIER?
Y'KNOW HOW IT IS. YOU DO A TOUR IN AFGHANISTAN, AND YOU COME BACK TO GUARD OF THE LIVING DEAD.
WE DON'T CALL THEM THAT, SOLDIER. WE CALL THEM "REVIVERS."
YES SIR, GENERAL, SIR.
IT MUST BE NICE. TO COMMAND RESPECT LIKE THAT.
WHERE'D YOU GET YOUR BARS?
HERE AND THERE. MOST RECENTLY I WAS STATIONED IN GERMANY. THAT WAS ONE OF THE LESS... DUSTY PLACES I'VE BEEN. YOURSELF?
I'M FROM SOUTHERN CALIFORNIA AND DID MY UNDERGRAD AT U.C.L.A. I GOT MY Psy.D IN BERKELEY. DID MY DISSERTATION ON THE IMPACT OF NEAR-DEATH EXPERIENCES.
I BET YOU NEVER THOUGHT YOU'D END UP IN CENTRAL WISCONSIN, *HUH?*
OH, I'M ***SO EXCITED*** TO BE HERE.

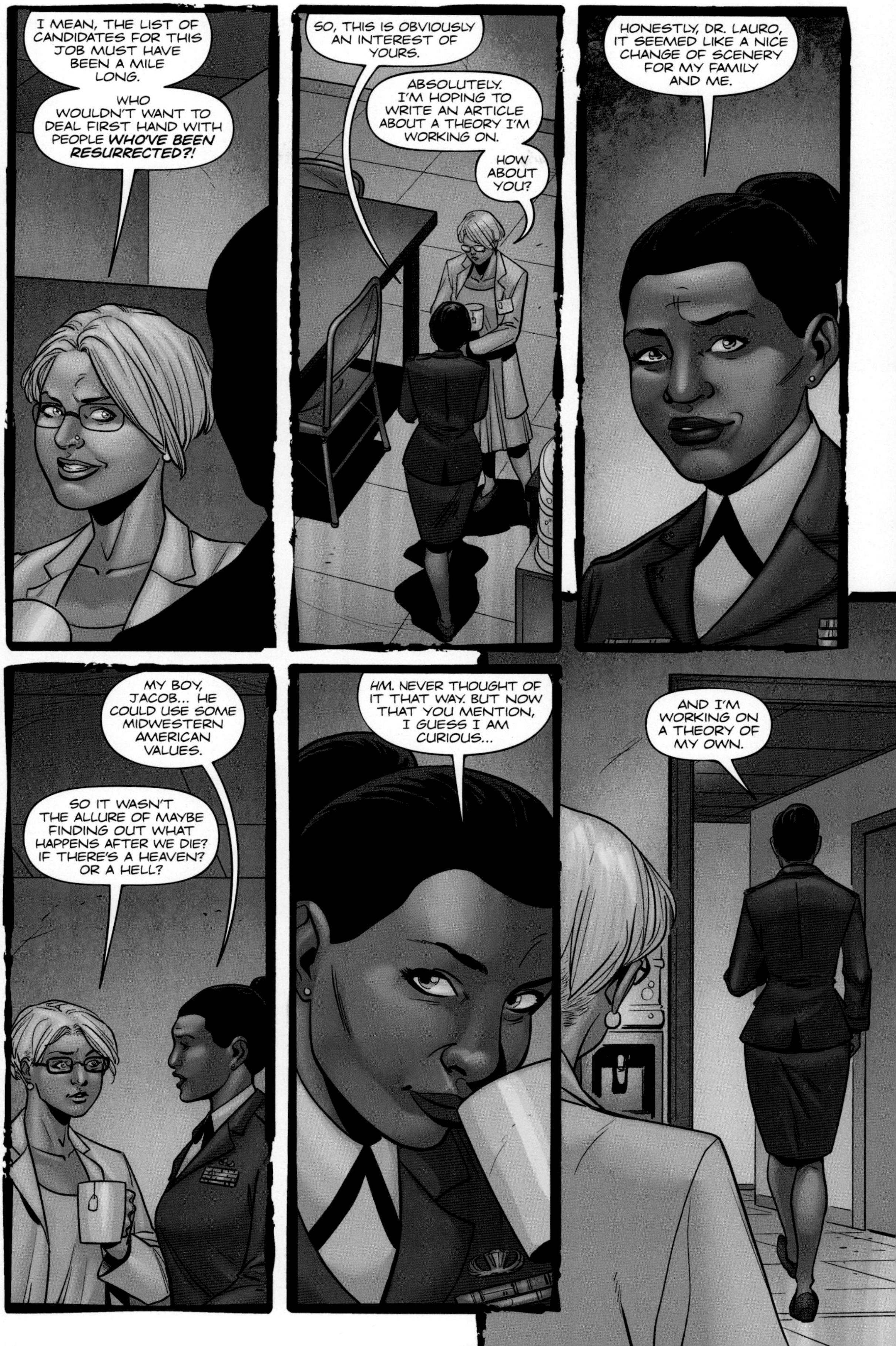
I MEAN, THE LIST OF CANDIDATES FOR THIS JOB MUST HAVE BEEN A MILE LONG.
WHO WOULDN'T WANT TO DEAL FIRST HAND WITH PEOPLE ***WHO'VE BEEN RESURRECTED?!***
SO, THIS IS OBVIOUSLY AN INTEREST OF YOURS.
ABSOLUTELY. I'M HOPING TO WRITE AN ARTICLE ABOUT A THEORY I'M WORKING ON.
HOW ABOUT YOU?
HONESTLY, DR. LAURO, IT SEEMED LIKE A NICE CHANGE OF SCENERY FOR MY FAMILY AND ME.
MY BOY, JACOB... HE COULD USE SOME MIDWESTERN AMERICAN VALUES.
SO IT WASN'T THE ALLURE OF MAYBE FINDING OUT WHAT HAPPENS AFTER WE DIE? IF THERE'S A HEAVEN? OR A HELL?
HM. NEVER THOUGHT OF IT THAT WAY. BUT NOW THAT YOU MENTION, I GUESS I AM CURIOUS...
AND I'M WORKING ON A THEORY OF MY OWN.

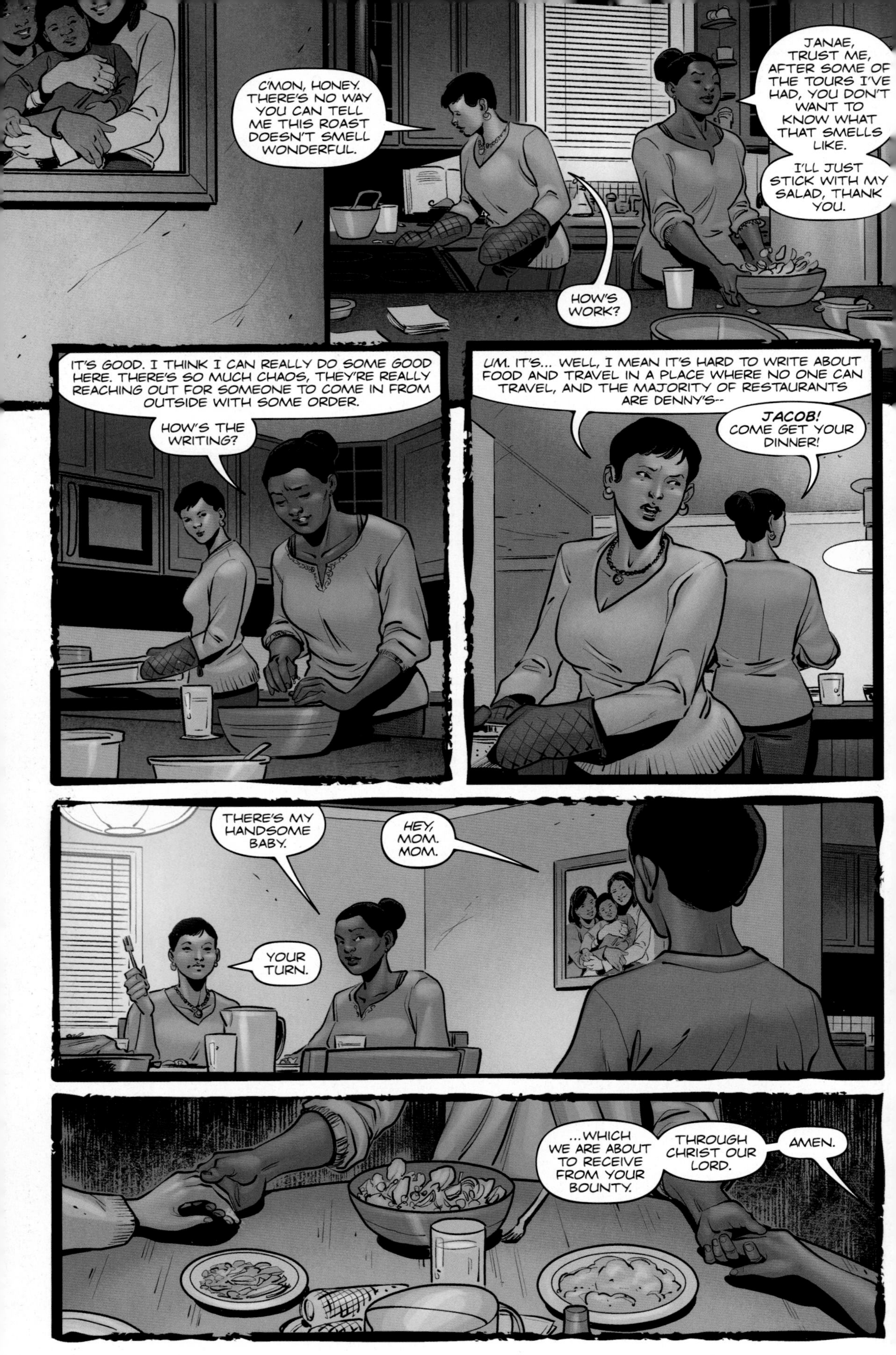
C'MON, HONEY. THERE'S NO WAY YOU CAN TELL ME THIS ROAST DOESN'T SMELL WONDERFUL.
JANAE, TRUST ME, AFTER SOME OF THE TOURS I'VE HAD, YOU DON'T WANT TO KNOW WHAT THAT SMELLS LIKE.
I'LL JUST STICK WITH MY SALAD, THANK YOU.
HOW'S WORK?
IT'S GOOD. I THINK I CAN REALLY DO SOME GOOD HERE. THERE'S SO MUCH CHAOS, THEY'RE REALLY REACHING OUT FOR SOMEONE TO COME IN FROM OUTSIDE WITH SOME ORDER.
HOW'S THE WRITING?
UM. IT'S... WELL, I MEAN IT'S HARD TO WRITE ABOUT FOOD AND TRAVEL IN A PLACE WHERE NO ONE CAN TRAVEL, AND THE MAJORITY OF RESTAURANTS ARE DENNY'S--
JACOB! COME GET YOUR DINNER!
THERE'S MY HANDSOME BABY.
HEY, MOM. MOM.
YOUR TURN.
...WHICH WE ARE ABOUT TO RECEIVE FROM YOUR BOUNTY.
THROUGH CHRIST OUR LORD.
AMEN.

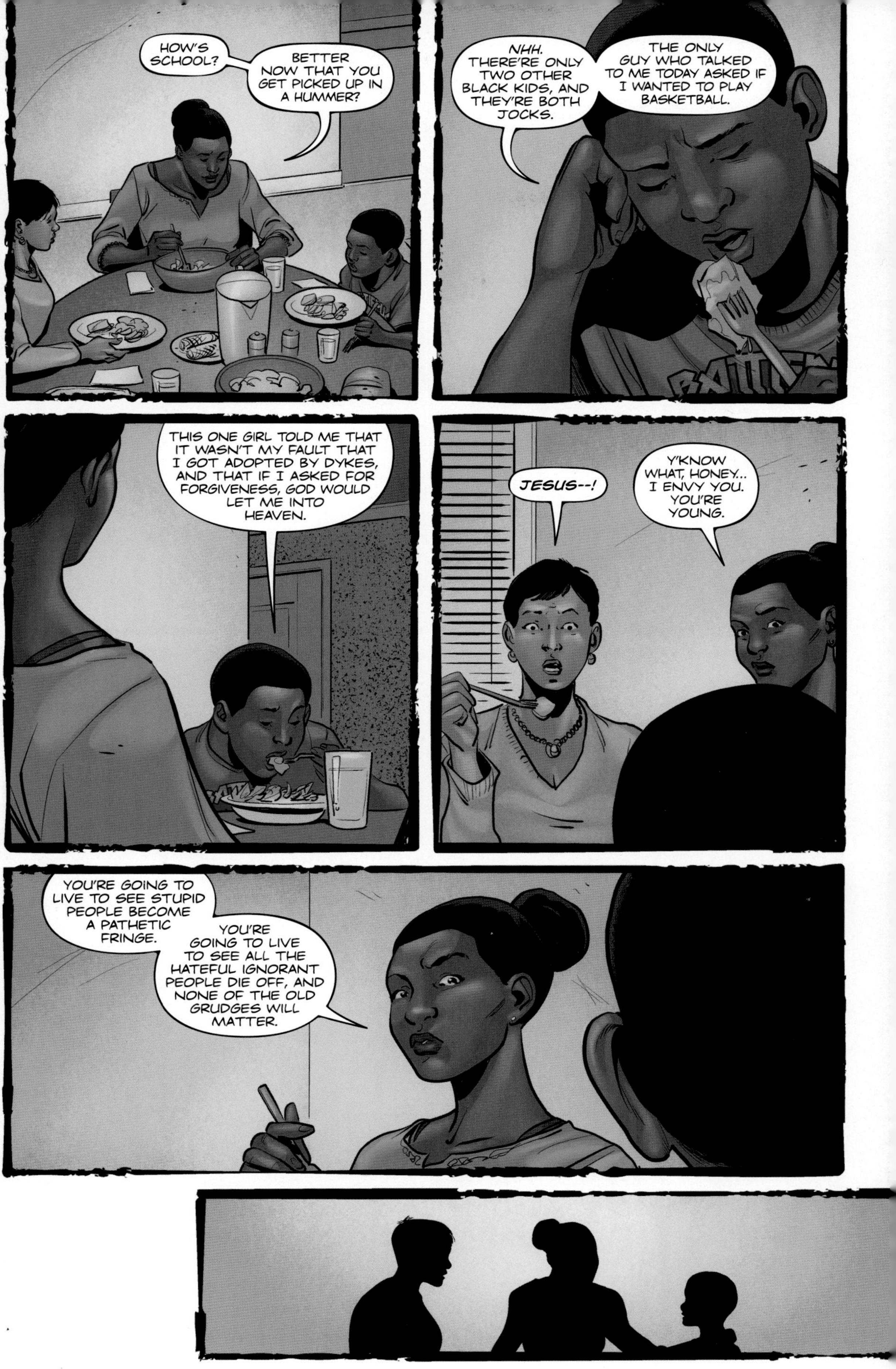
HOW'S SCHOOL?
BETTER NOW THAT YOU GET PICKED UP IN A HUMMER?
NHH. THERE'RE ONLY TWO OTHER BLACK KIDS, AND THEY'RE BOTH JOCKS.
THE ONLY GUY WHO TALKED TO ME TODAY ASKED IF I WANTED TO PLAY BASKETBALL.
THIS ONE GIRL TOLD ME THAT IT WASN'T MY FAULT THAT I GOT ADOPTED BY DYKES, AND THAT IF I ASKED FOR FORGIVENESS, GOD WOULD LET ME INTO HEAVEN.
JESUS--!
Y'KNOW WHAT, HONEY... I ENVY YOU. YOU'RE YOUNG.
YOU'RE GOING TO LIVE TO SEE STUPID PEOPLE BECOME A PATHETIC FRINGE.
YOU'RE GOING TO LIVE TO SEE ALL THE HATEFUL IGNORANT PEOPLE DIE OFF, AND NONE OF THE OLD GRUDGES WILL MATTER.

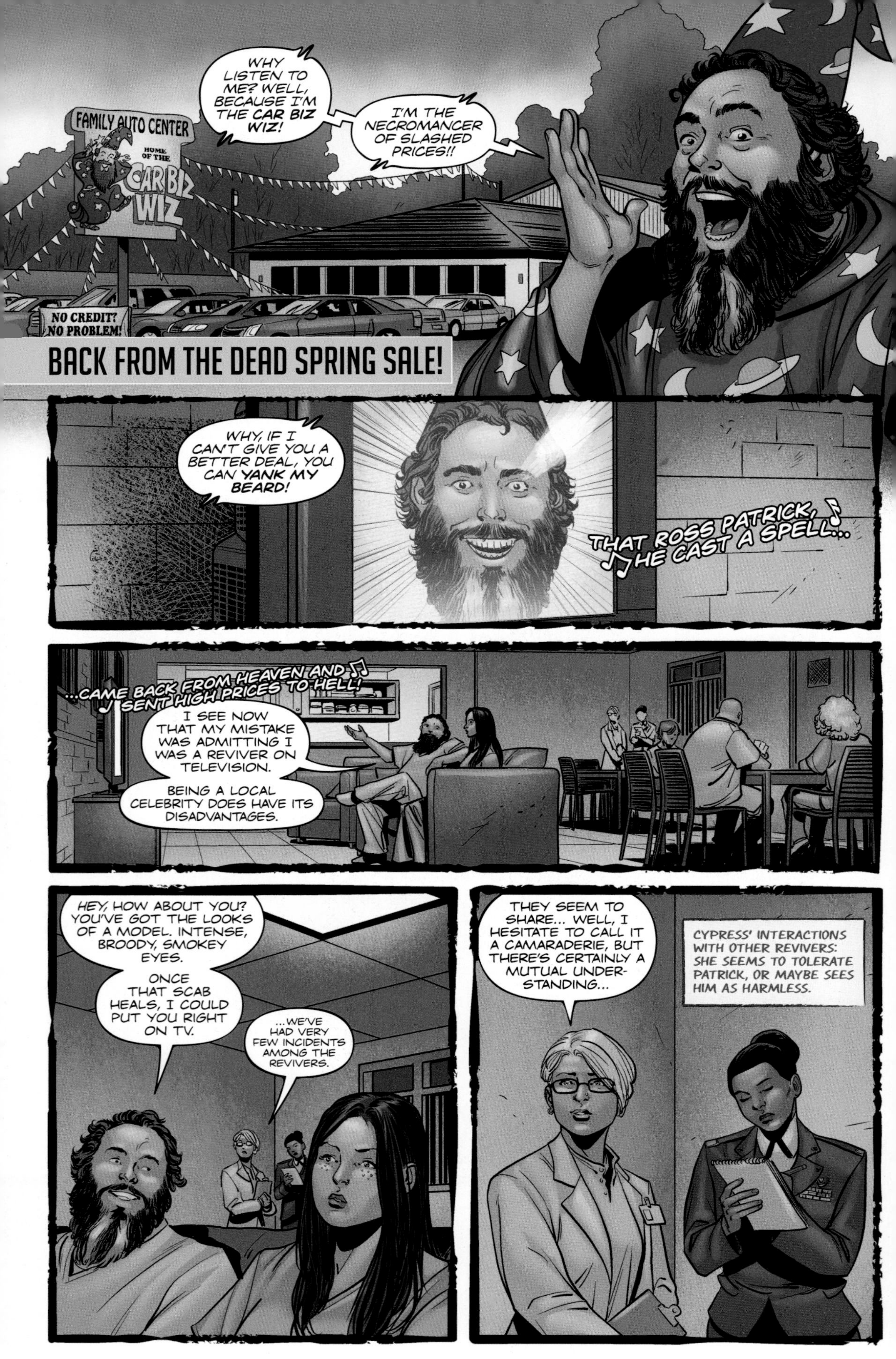
WHY LISTEN TO ME? WELL, BECAUSE I'M THE CAR BIZ WIZ!
I'M THE NECROMANCER OF SLASHED PRICES!!
FAMILY AUTO CENTER
HOME OF THE
CAR BIZ WIZ
NO CREDIT? NO PROBLEM!
BACK FROM THE DEAD SPRING SALE!
WHY, IF I CAN'T GIVE YOU A BETTER DEAL, YOU CAN YANK MY BEARD!
THAT ROSS PATRICK, HE CAST A SPELL...
...CAME BACK FROM HEAVEN AND SENT HIGH PRICES TO HELL!
I SEE NOW THAT MY MISTAKE WAS ADMITTING I WAS A REVIVER ON TELEVISION.
BEING A LOCAL CELEBRITY DOES HAVE ITS DISADVANTAGES.
HEY, HOW ABOUT YOU? YOU'VE GOT THE LOOKS OF A MODEL. INTENSE, BROODY, SMOKEY EYES.
ONCE THAT SCAB HEALS, I COULD PUT YOU RIGHT ON TV.
...WE'VE HAD VERY FEW INCIDENTS AMONG THE REVIVERS.
THEY SEEM TO SHARE... WELL, I HESITATE TO CALL IT A CAMARADERIE, BUT THERE'S CERTAINLY A MUTUAL UNDER-STANDING...
CYPRESS' INTERACTIONS WITH OTHER REVIVERS: SHE SEEMS TO TOLERATE PATRICK, OR MAYBE SEES HIM AS HARMLESS.

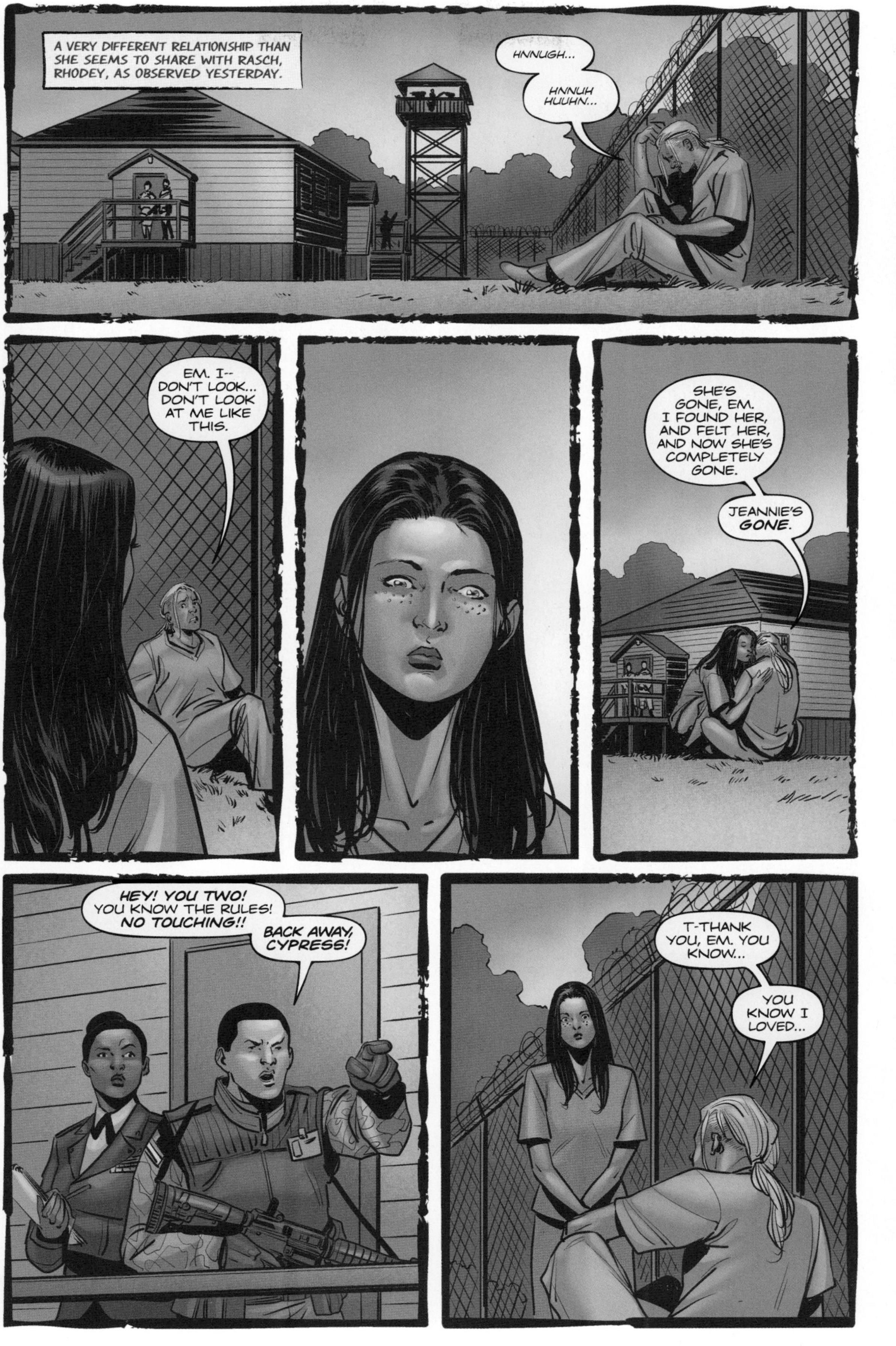
A VERY DIFFERENT RELATIONSHIP THAN SHE SEEMS TO SHARE WITH RASCH, RHODEY, AS OBSERVED YESTERDAY.
HNNUGH...
HNNUH HUUHN...
EM. I-- DON'T LOOK... DON'T LOOK AT ME LIKE THIS.
SHE'S GONE, EM. I FOUND HER, AND FELT HER, AND NOW SHE'S COMPLETELY GONE.
JEANNIE'S GONE.
HEY! YOU TWO! YOU KNOW THE RULES! NO TOUCHING!!
BACK AWAY, CYPRESS!
T-THANK YOU, EM. YOU KNOW...
YOU KNOW I LOVED...

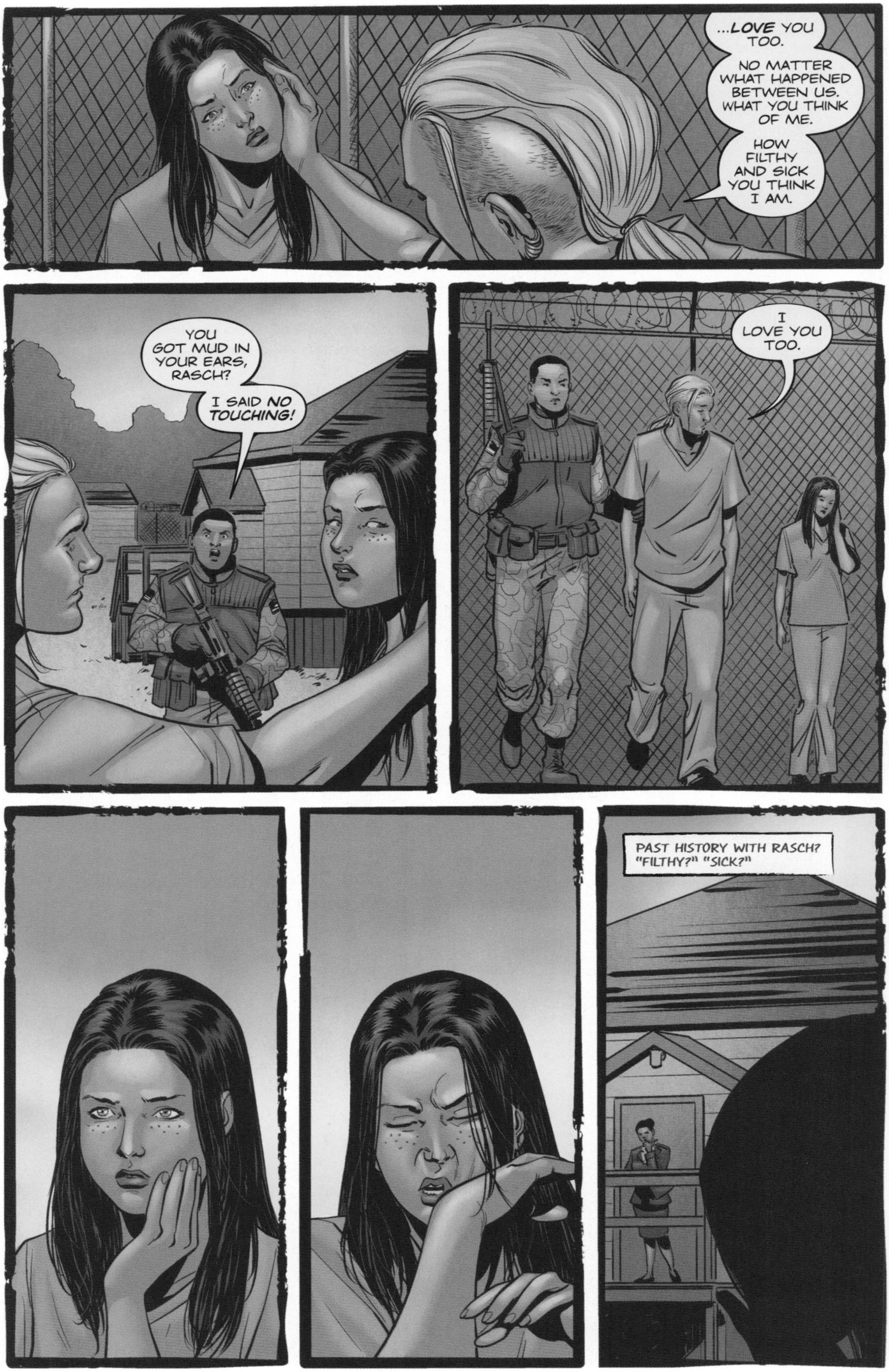
...LOVE YOU TOO.
NO MATTER WHAT HAPPENED BETWEEN US. WHAT YOU THINK OF ME.
HOW FILTHY AND SICK YOU THINK I AM.
YOU GOT MUD IN YOUR EARS, RASCH?
I SAID NO TOUCHING!
I LOVE YOU TOO.
PAST HISTORY WITH RASCH? "FILTHY?" "SICK?"

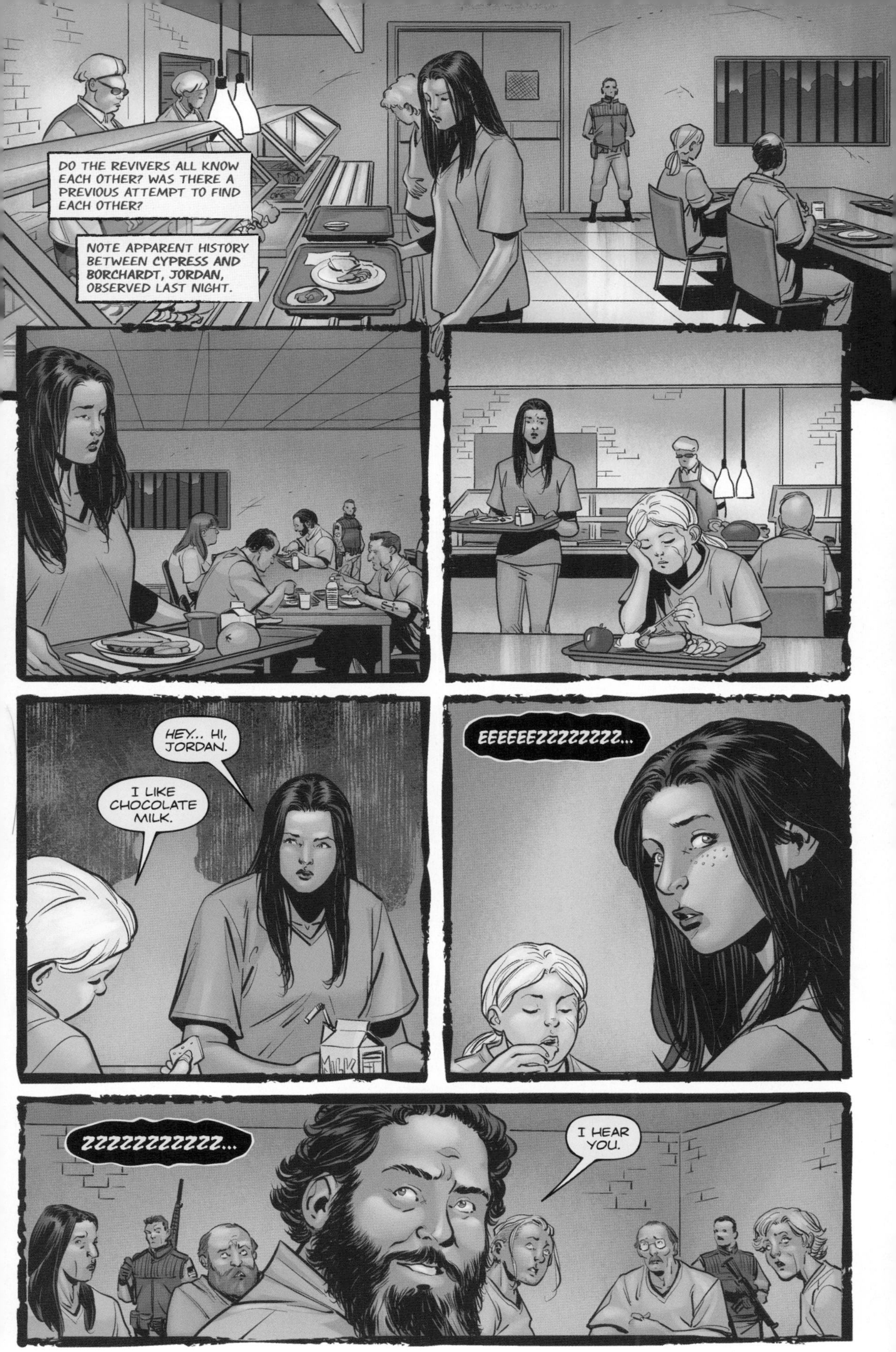
DO THE REVIVERS ALL KNOW EACH OTHER? WAS THERE A PREVIOUS ATTEMPT TO FIND EACH OTHER?
NOTE APPARENT HISTORY BETWEEN CYPRESS AND BORCHARDT, JORDAN, OBSERVED LAST NIGHT.
HEY... HI, JORDAN.
I LIKE CHOCOLATE MILK.
MILK
EEEEEEZZZZZZZZ...
ZZZZZZZZZZZ...
I HEAR YOU.

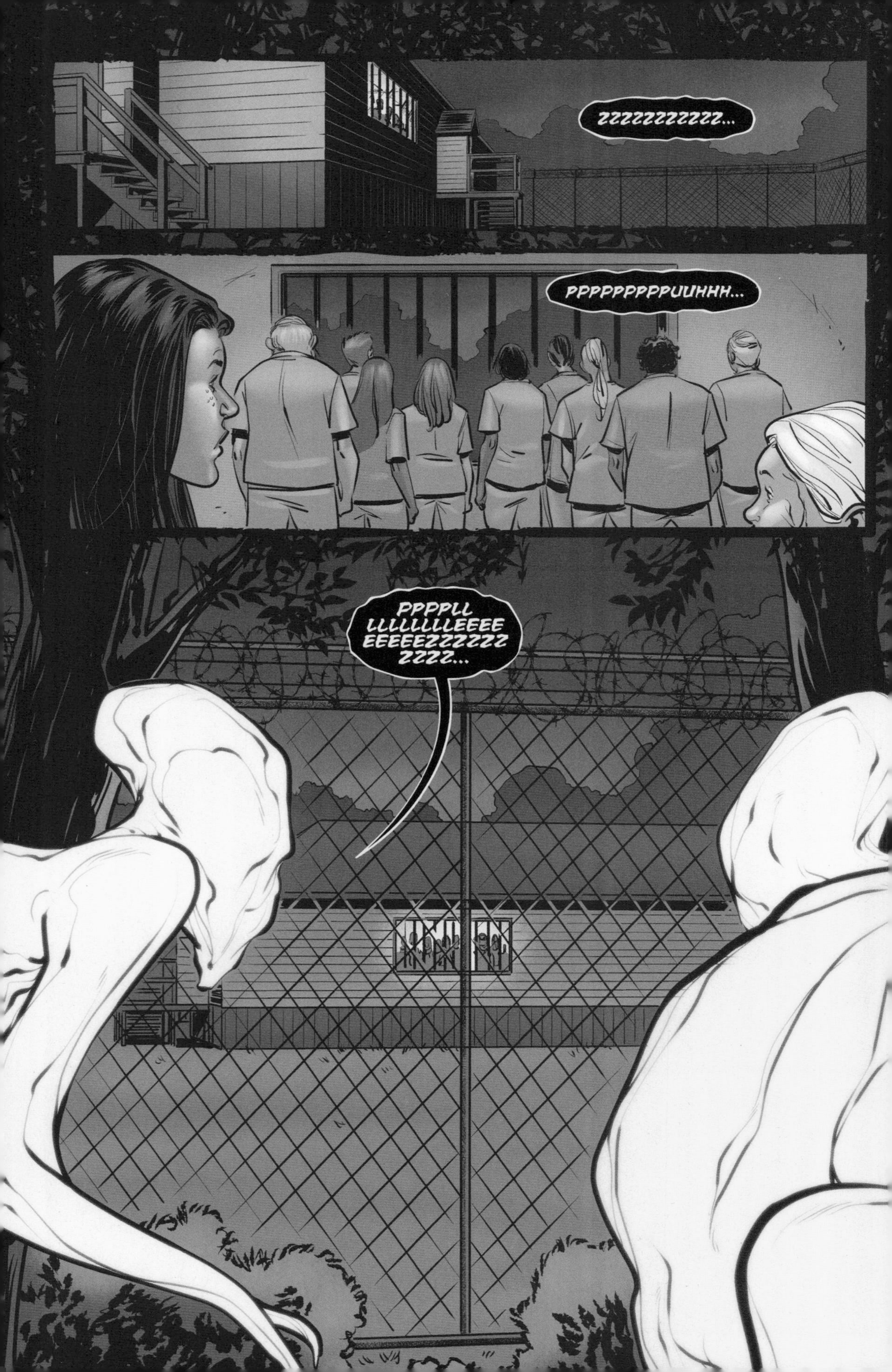
ZZZZZZZZZZZ...
PPPPPPPPPUUHHH...
PPPPLL LLLLLLLLEEEE EEEEEZZZZZZ ZZZZ...

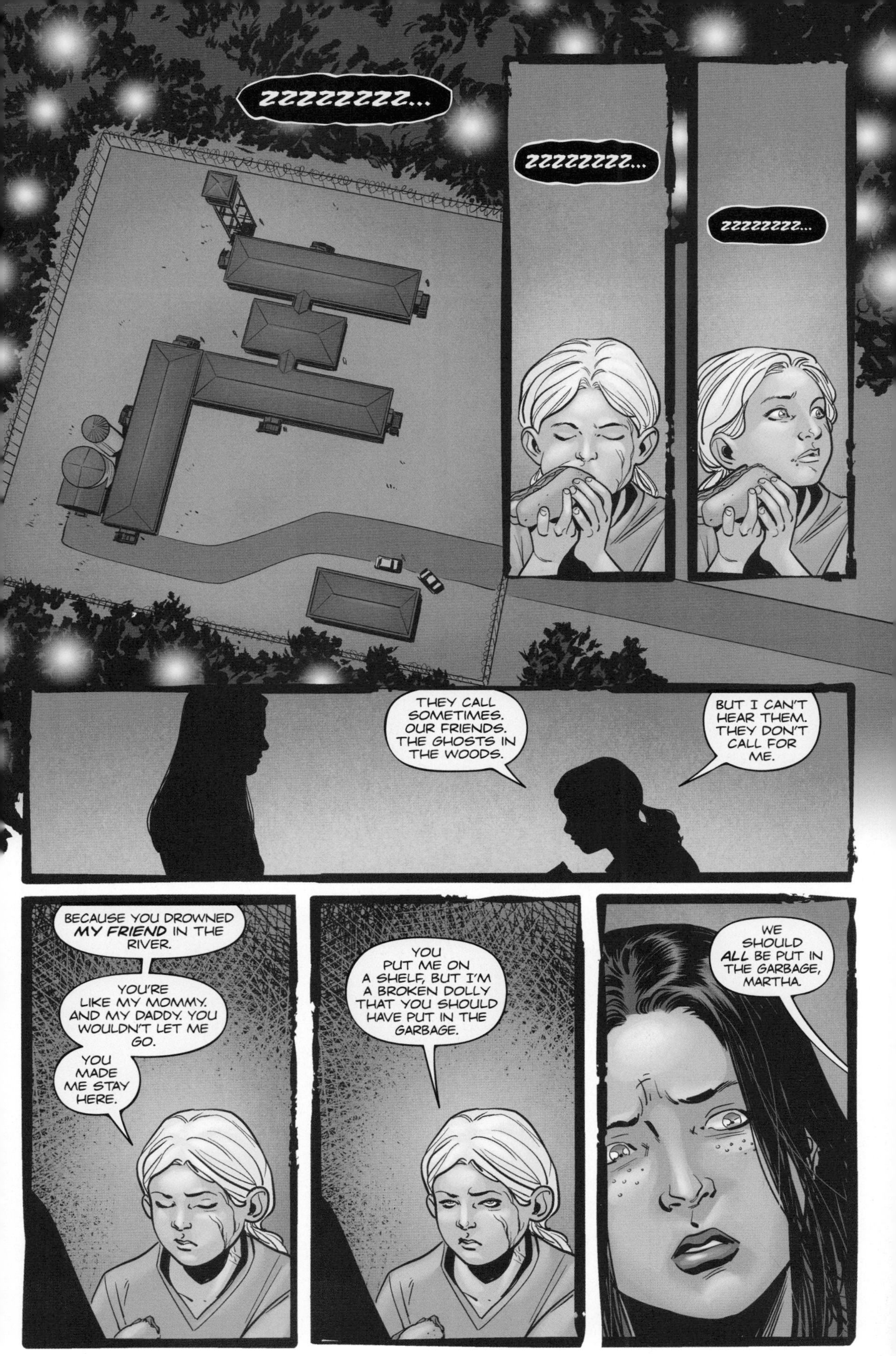
ZZZZZZZZ...
ZZZZZZZZ...
ZZZZZZZZ...
THEY CALL SOMETIMES. OUR FRIENDS. THE GHOSTS IN THE WOODS.
BUT I CAN'T HEAR THEM. THEY DON'T CALL FOR ME.
BECAUSE YOU DROWNED MY FRIEND IN THE RIVER.
YOU'RE LIKE MY MOMMY. AND MY DADDY. YOU WOULDN'T LET ME GO.
YOU MADE ME STAY HERE.
YOU PUT ME ON A SHELF, BUT I'M A BROKEN DOLLY THAT YOU SHOULD HAVE PUT IN THE GARBAGE.
WE SHOULD ALL BE PUT IN THE GARBAGE, MARTHA.

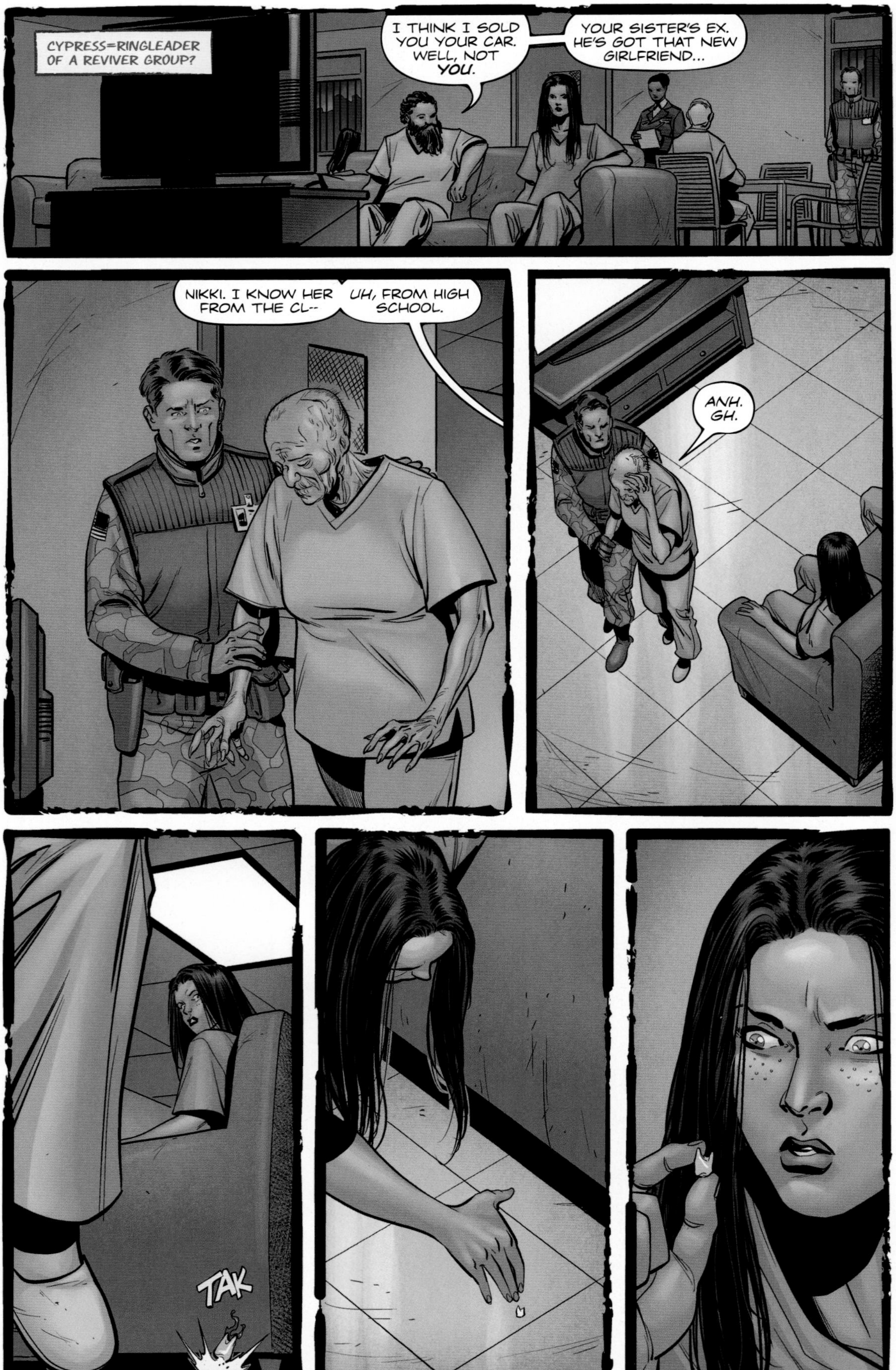
CYPRESS=RINGLEADER OF A REVIVER GROUP?
I THINK I SOLD YOU YOUR CAR. WELL, NOT YOU.
YOUR SISTER'S EX. HE'S GOT THAT NEW GIRLFRIEND...
NIKKI. I KNOW HER FROM THE CL--
UH, FROM HIGH SCHOOL.
ANH. GH.
TAK

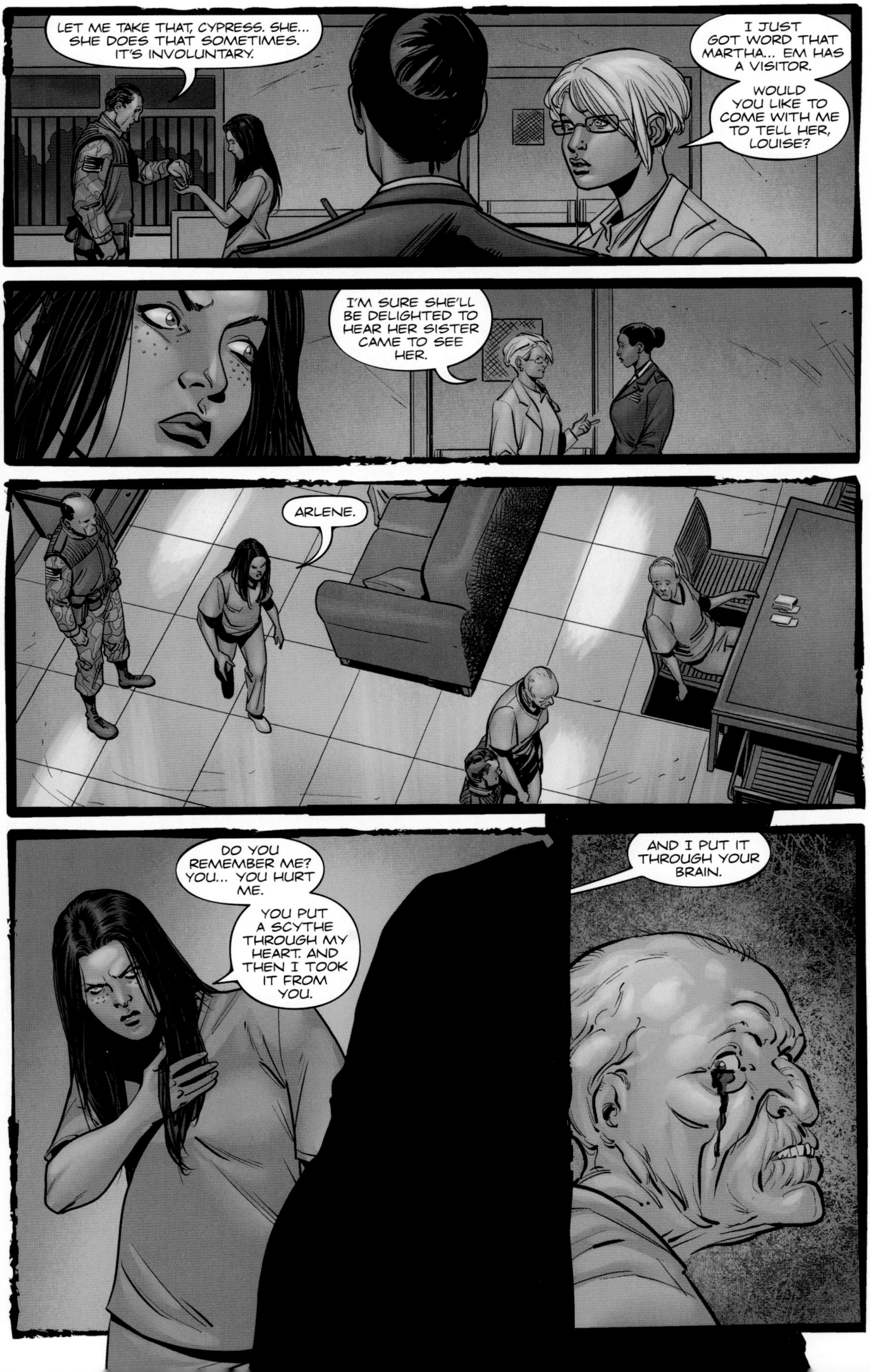
LET ME TAKE THAT, CYPRESS. SHE... SHE DOES THAT SOMETIMES. IT'S INVOLUNTARY.
I JUST GOT WORD THAT MARTHA... EM HAS A VISITOR.
WOULD YOU LIKE TO COME WITH ME TO TELL HER, LOUISE?
I'M SURE SHE'LL BE DELIGHTED TO HEAR HER SISTER CAME TO SEE HER.
ARLENE.
DO YOU REMEMBER ME? YOU... YOU HURT ME.
YOU PUT A SCYTHE THROUGH MY HEART. AND THEN I TOOK IT FROM YOU.
AND I PUT IT THROUGH YOUR BRAIN.

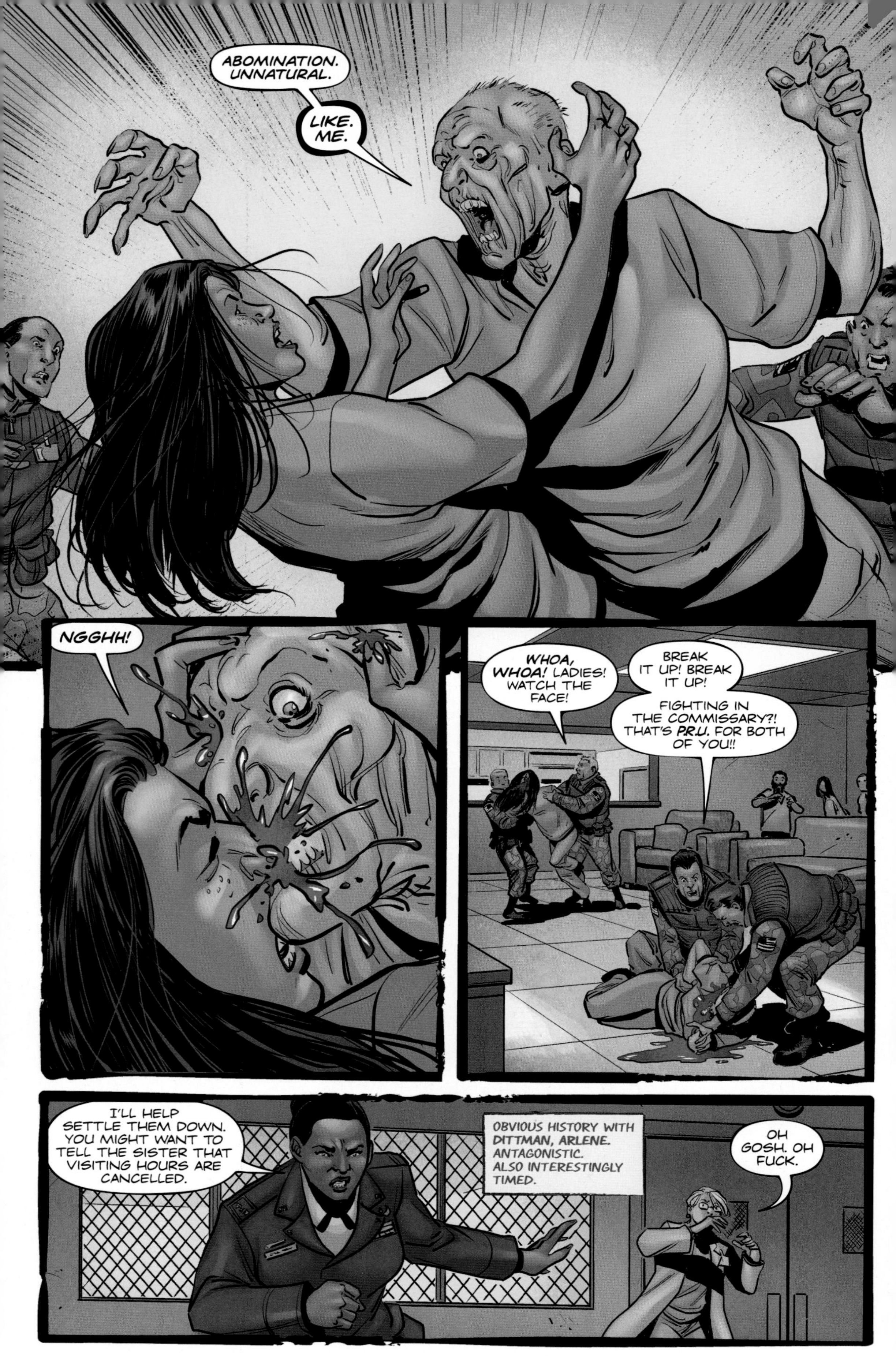
ABOMINATION. UNNATURAL.
LIKE. ME.
NGGHH!
WHOA, WHOA! LADIES! WATCH THE FACE!
BREAK IT UP! BREAK IT UP!
FIGHTING IN THE COMMISSARY?! THAT'S P.R.U. FOR BOTH OF YOU!!
I'LL HELP SETTLE THEM DOWN. YOU MIGHT WANT TO TELL THE SISTER THAT VISITING HOURS ARE CANCELLED.
OBVIOUS HISTORY WITH DITTMAN, ARLENE. ANTAGONISTIC. ALSO INTERESTINGLY TIMED.
OH GOSH. OH FUCK.

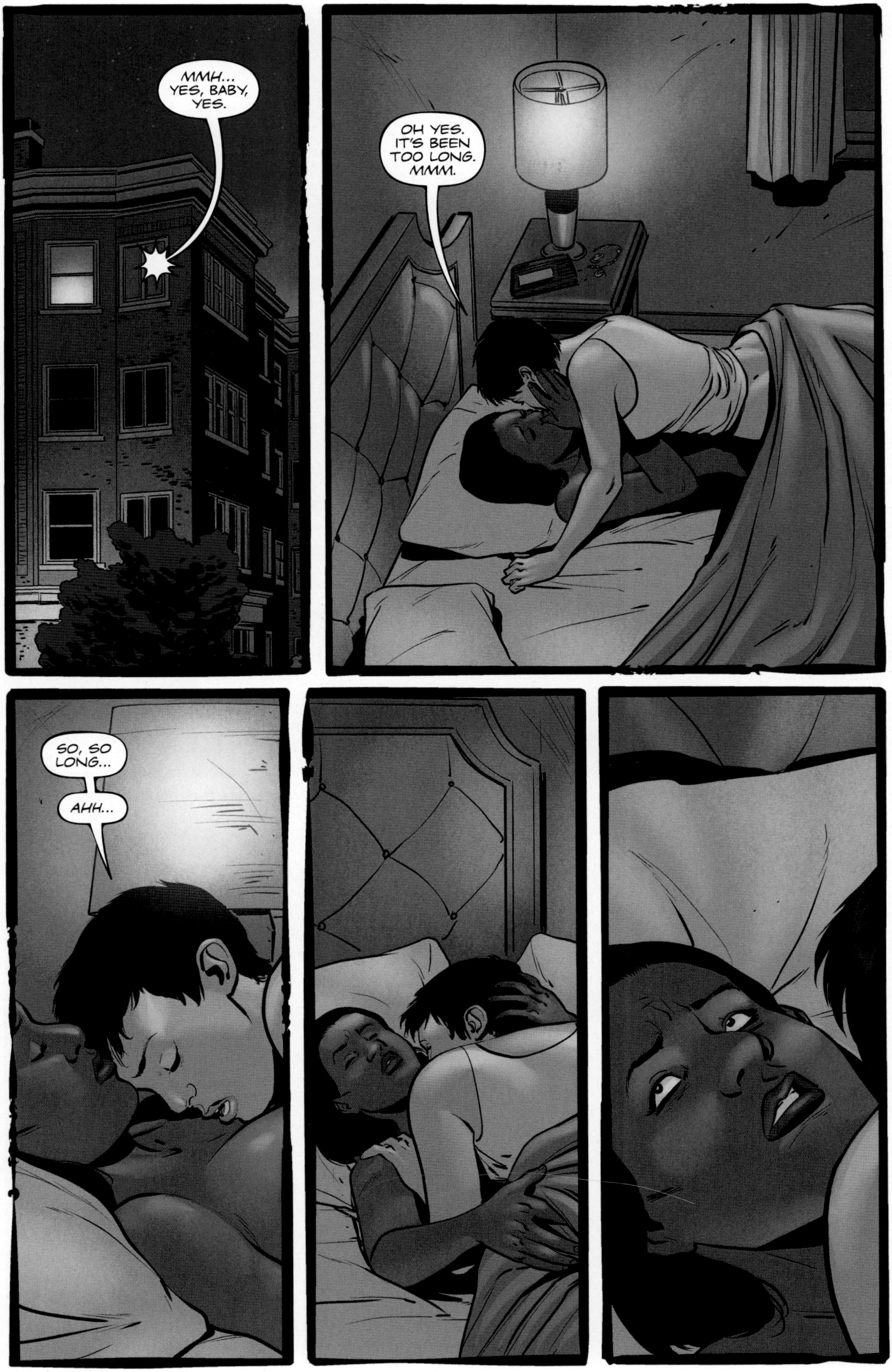
MMH... YES, BABY, YES.
OH YES. IT'S BEEN TOO LONG. MMM.
SO, SO LONG...
AHH...

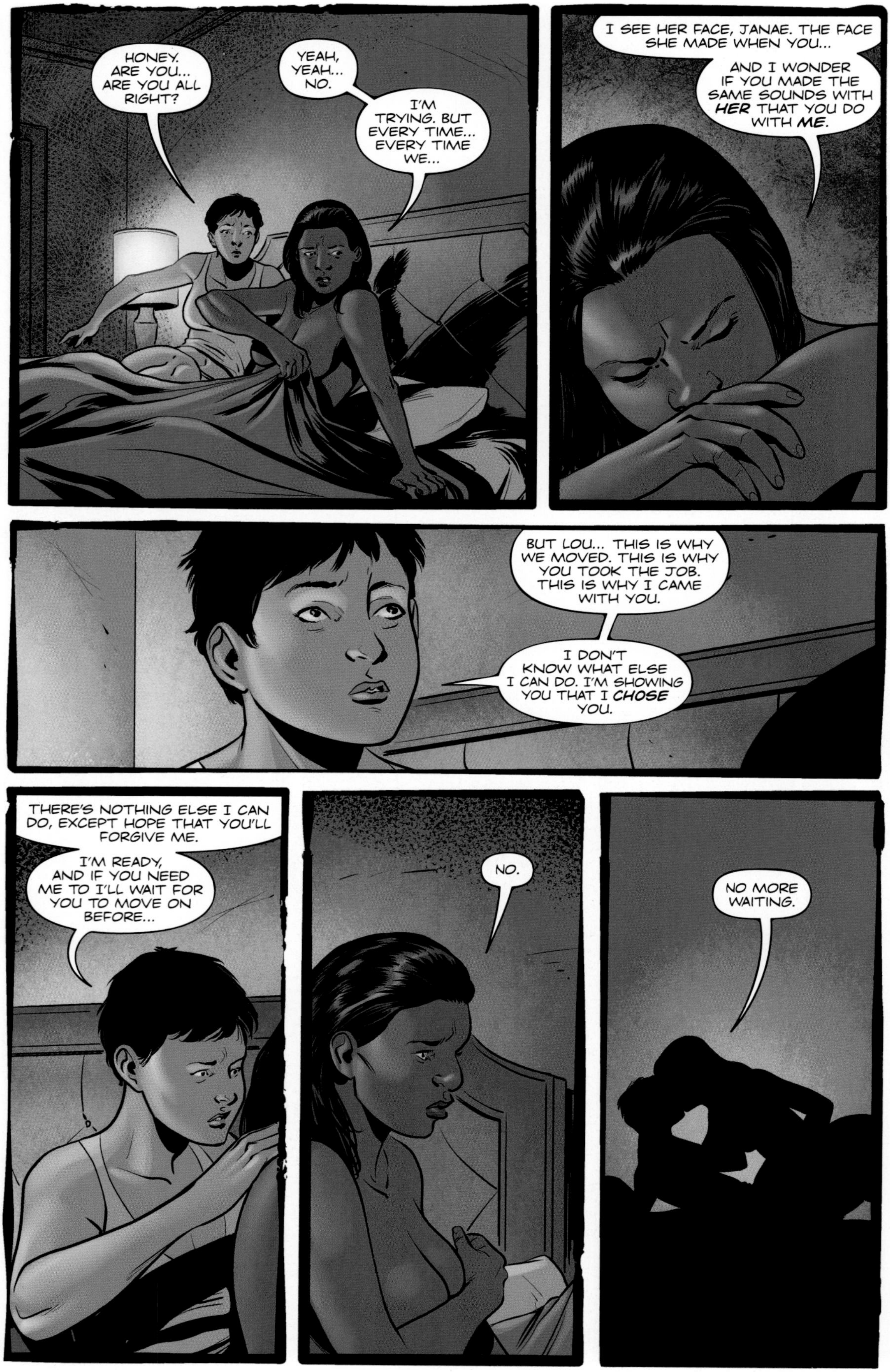
HONEY. ARE YOU... ARE YOU ALL RIGHT?
YEAH, YEAH... NO.
I'M TRYING. BUT EVERY TIME... EVERY TIME WE...
I SEE HER FACE, JANAE. THE FACE SHE MADE WHEN YOU...
AND I WONDER IF YOU MADE THE SAME SOUNDS WITH HER THAT YOU DO WITH ME.
BUT LOU... THIS IS WHY WE MOVED. THIS IS WHY YOU TOOK THE JOB. THIS IS WHY I CAME WITH YOU.
I DON'T KNOW WHAT ELSE I CAN DO. I'M SHOWING YOU THAT I CHOSE YOU.
THERE'S NOTHING ELSE I CAN DO, EXCEPT HOPE THAT YOU'LL FORGIVE ME.
I'M READY, AND IF YOU NEED ME TO I'LL WAIT FOR YOU TO MOVE ON BEFORE...
NO.
NO MORE WAITING.

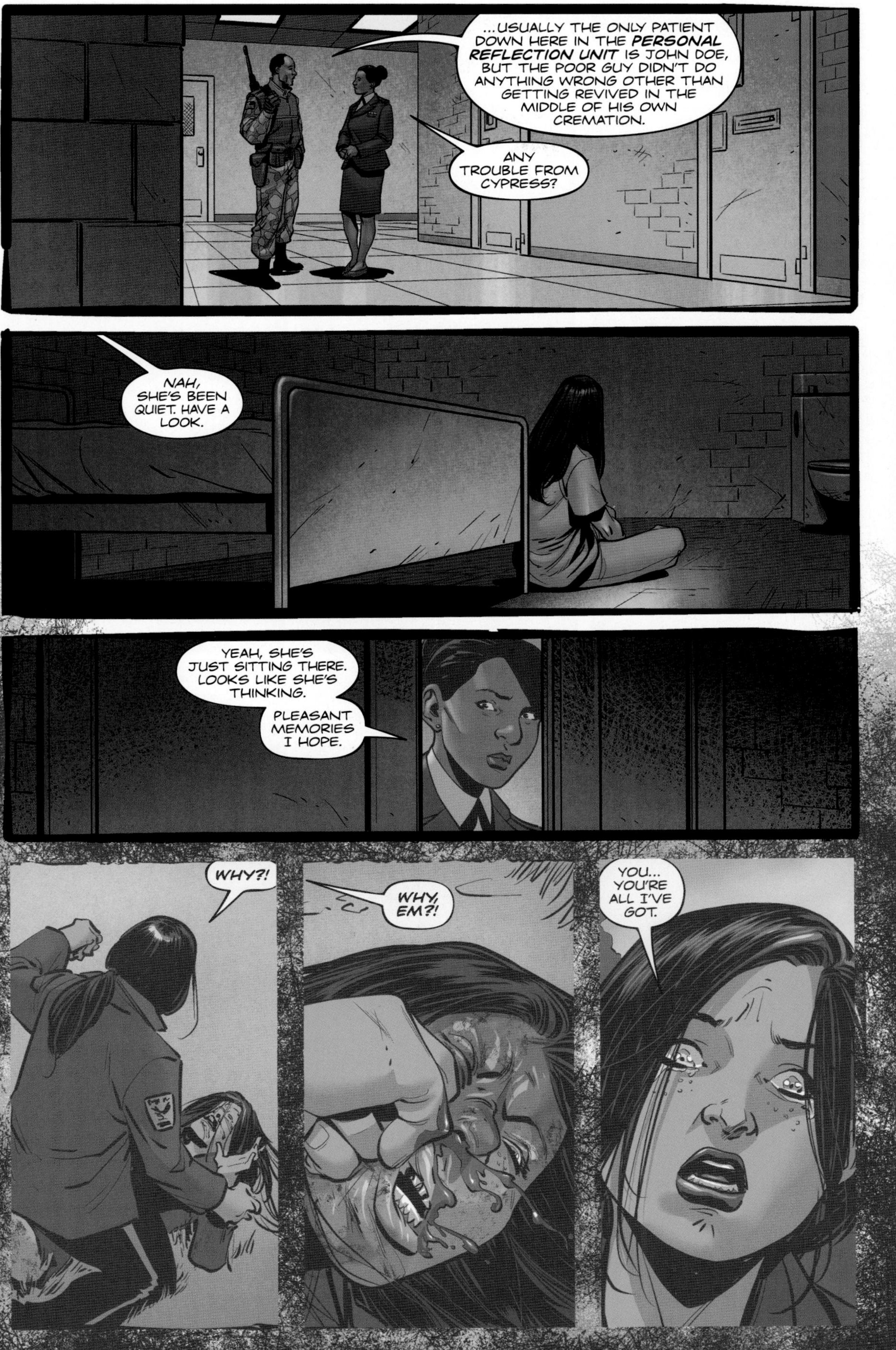
...USUALLY THE ONLY PATIENT DOWN HERE IN THE **PERSONAL REFLECTION UNIT** IS JOHN DOE, BUT THE POOR GUY DIDN'T DO ANYTHING WRONG OTHER THAN GETTING REVIVED IN THE MIDDLE OF HIS OWN CREMATION.
ANY TROUBLE FROM CYPRESS?
NAH, SHE'S BEEN QUIET. HAVE A LOOK.
YEAH, SHE'S JUST SITTING THERE. LOOKS LIKE SHE'S THINKING.
PLEASANT MEMORIES I HOPE.
WHY?!
WHY, EM?!
YOU... YOU'RE ALL I'VE GOT.

WELL, HAVE A GOOD SHIFT, SOLDIER. I'VE GOT PAPERWORK TO DO.

SOUNDS FUN.

TRUST ME, THERE ARE DAYS I WISH I WAS STILL STANDING GUARD OVER THE LIVING DE-- REVIVERS...

WHERE'D I PUT MY PEN?

LET'S CALL THAT A SENIOR MOMENT. DON'T TELL ANYONE.

YOUR SECRET IS SAFE WITH ME, GENERAL, SIR.

THEORY ON THE REVIVERS, AS OBSERVED IN THE ACTIONS OF CYPRESS, MARTHA, AND OTHER PATIENTS.

THE REVIVERS ARE TRAPPED IN A MOMENT. THE MOMENT JUST BEFORE THEY DIED THAT FIRST TIME.

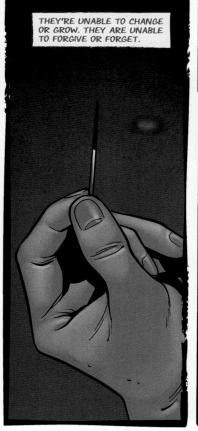

THEY'RE UNABLE TO CHANGE OR GROW. THEY ARE UNABLE TO FORGIVE OR FORGET.

THE ONE THING THAT BINDS ALL OF HUMANITY TOGETHER, AS DEEPLY HIDDEN AS IT CAN SOMETIMES BE... THAT ACUTE AWARENESS THAT WE ARE MORTAL BEINGS WHO EXPERIENCE LIFE FOR BUT A BRIEF MOMENT, IS LOST IN THEM.

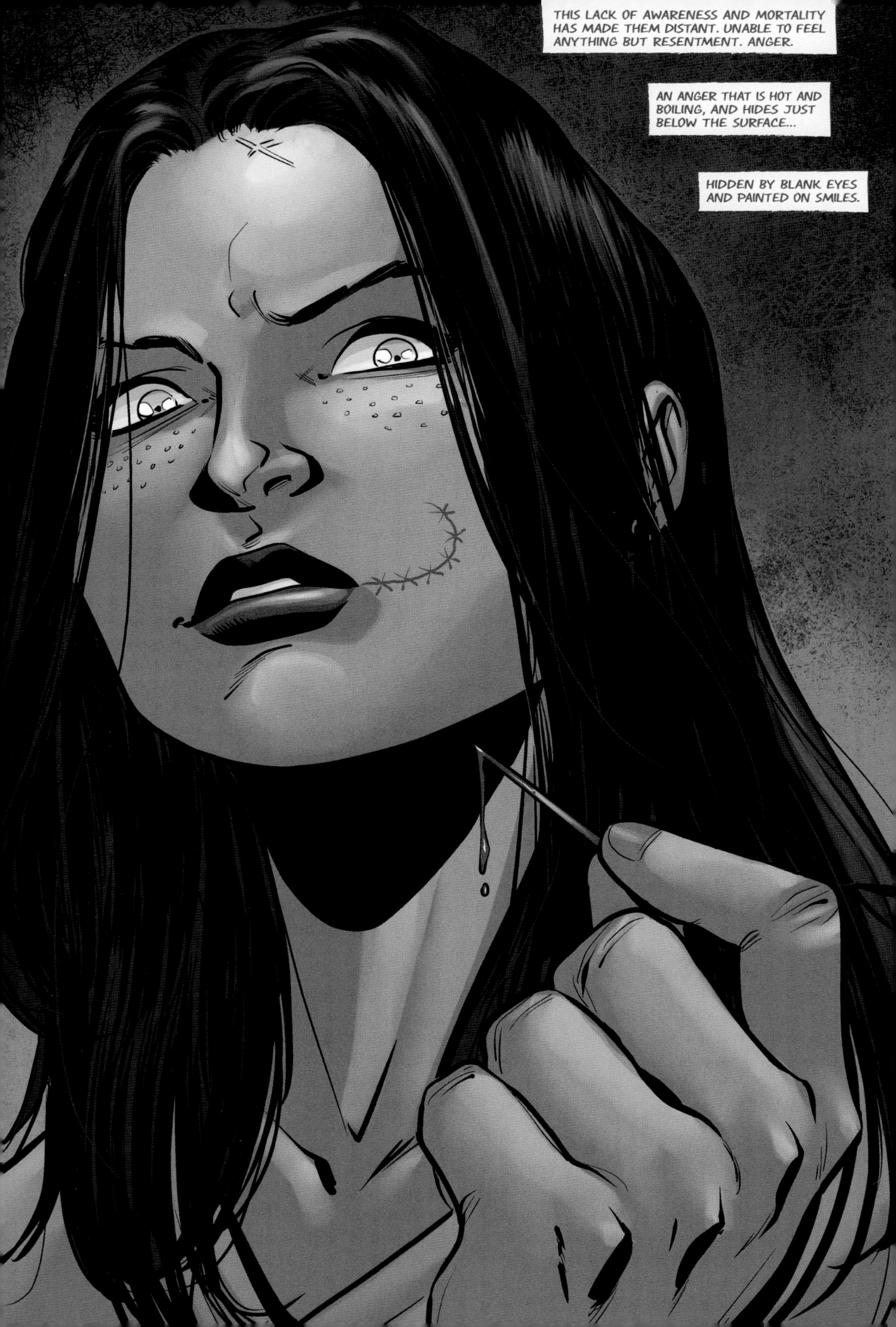
THIS LACK OF AWARENESS AND MORTALITY HAS MADE THEM DISTANT. UNABLE TO FEEL ANYTHING BUT RESENTMENT. ANGER.
AN ANGER THAT IS HOT AND BOILING, AND HIDES JUST BELOW THE SURFACE...
HIDDEN BY BLANK EYES AND PAINTED ON SMILES.

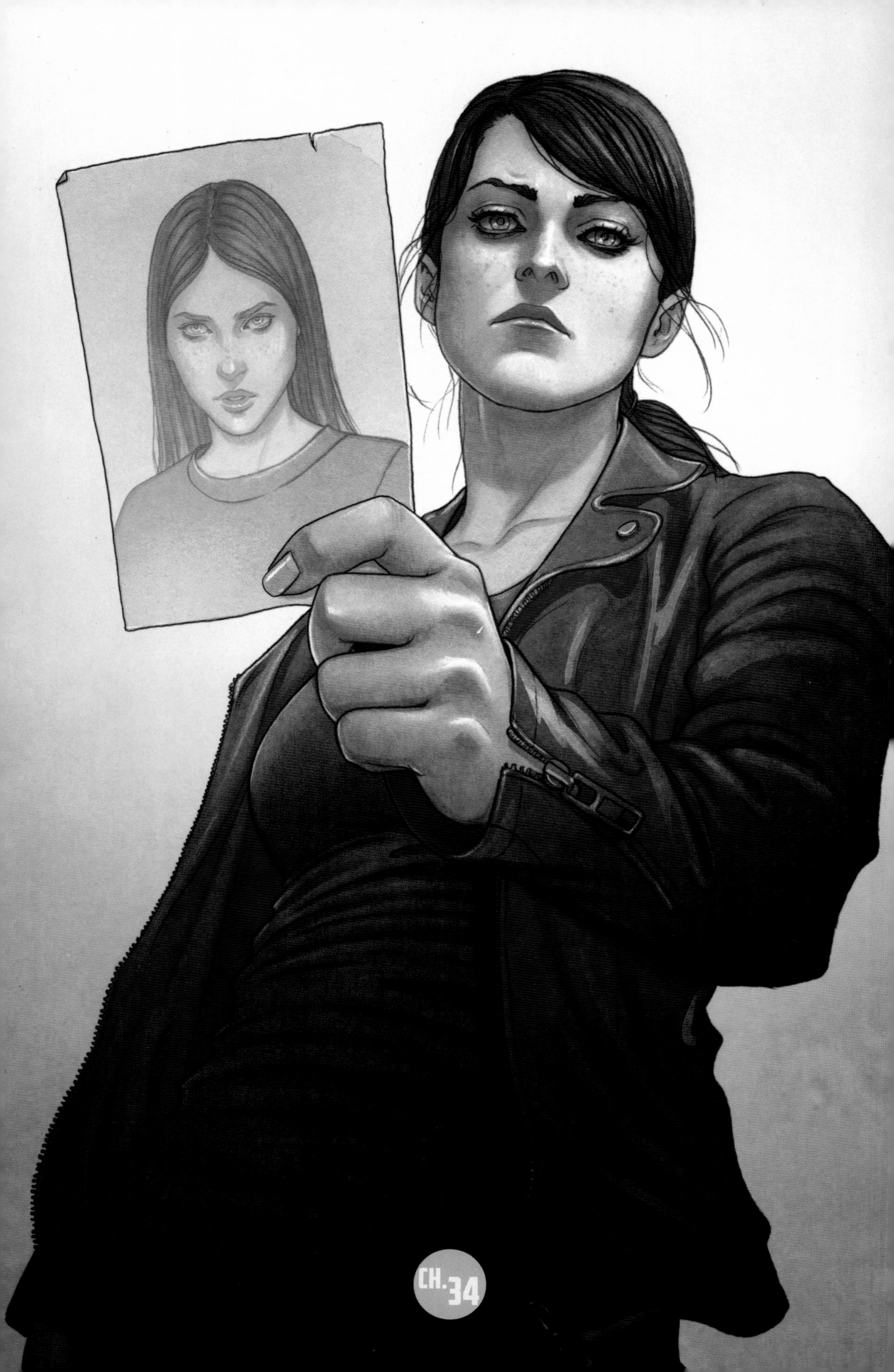
CH. 34

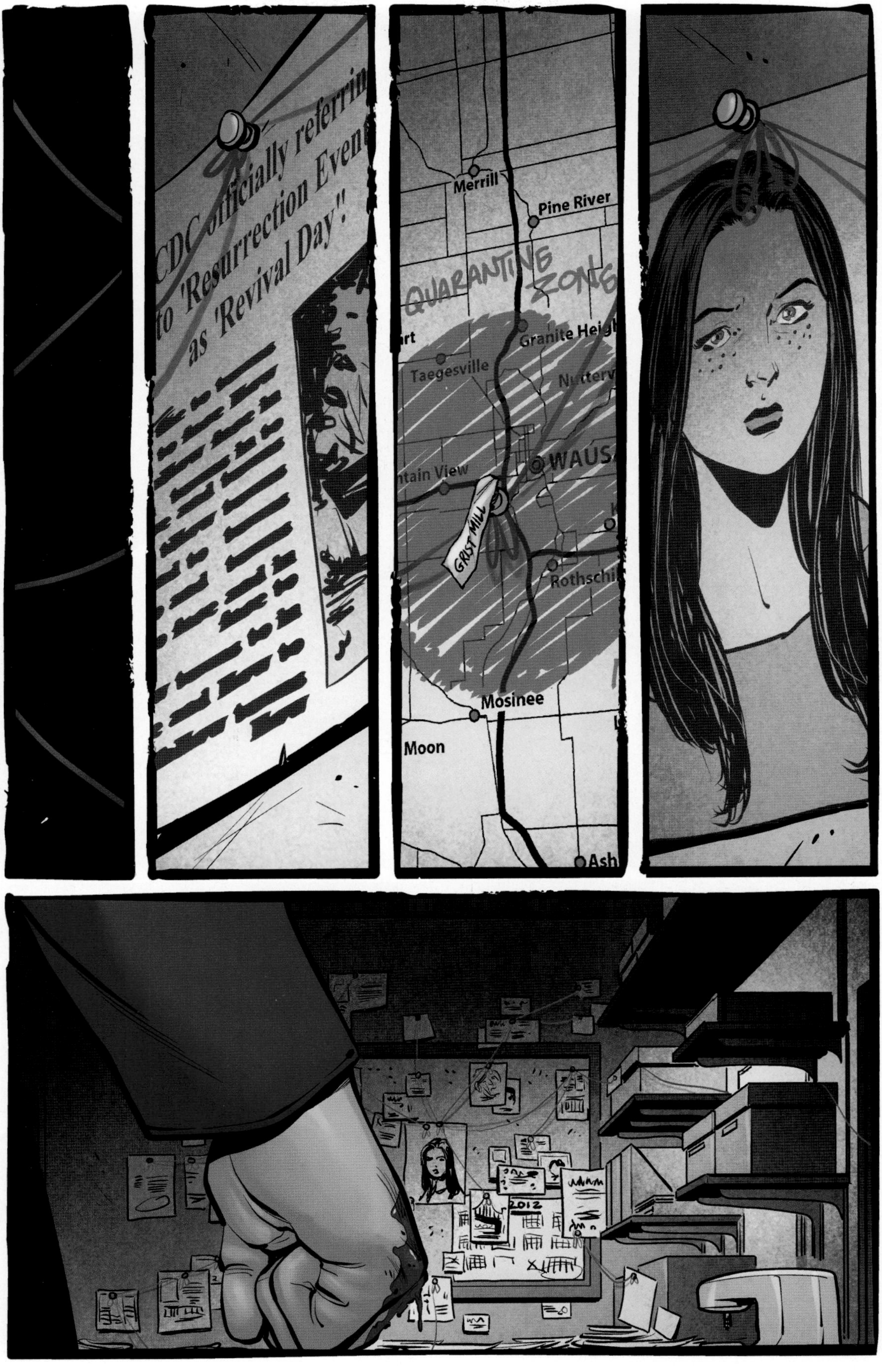
CDC officially referrin
to 'Resurrection Event
as 'Revival Day'!
Merrill
Pine River
QUARANTINE ZONE
Granite Heig
Taegesville
WAUS
tain View
GRIST MILL
Rothschi
Mosinee
Moon
Ash
2012

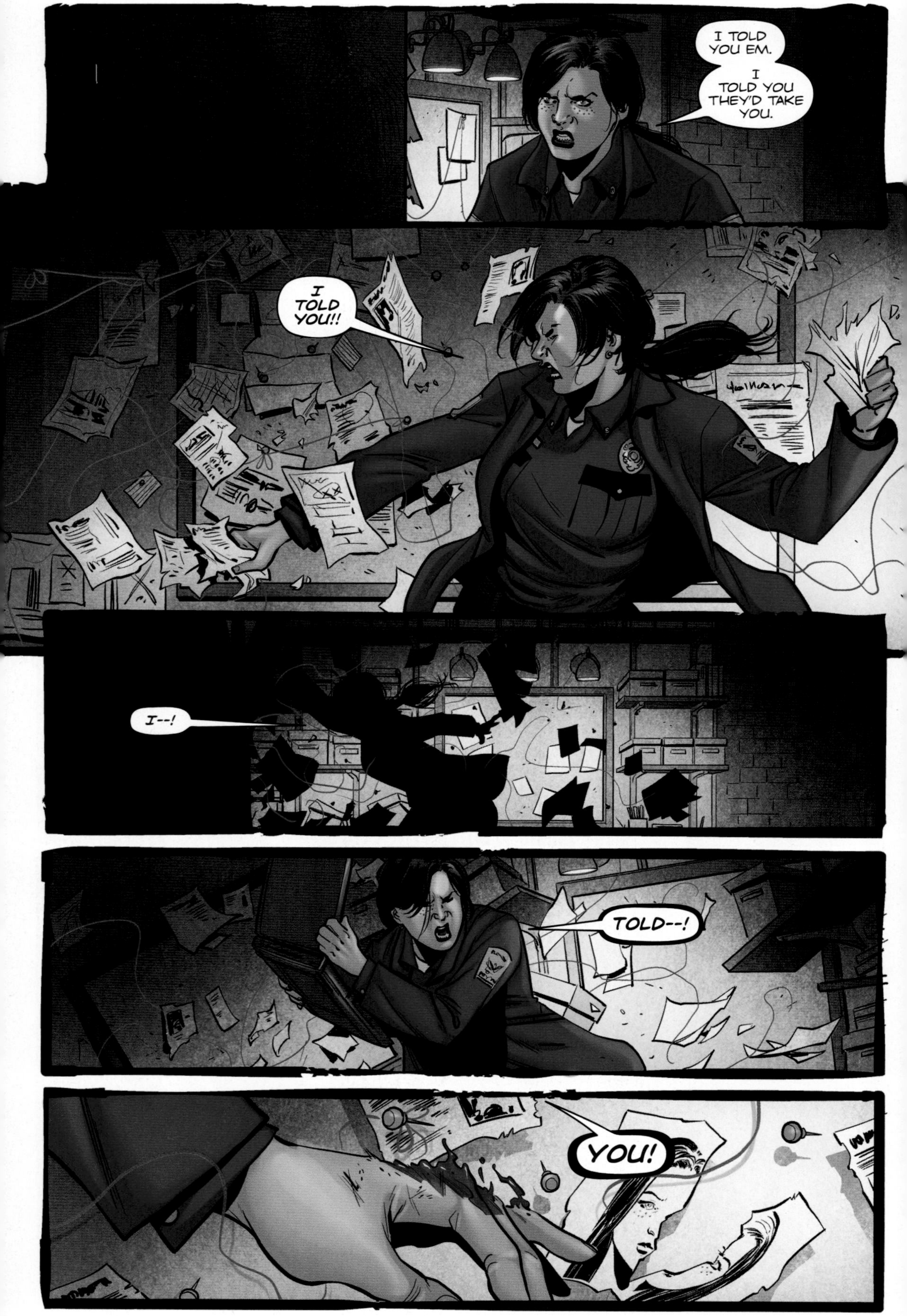
I TOLD YOU EM.
I TOLD YOU THEY'D TAKE YOU.
I TOLD YOU!!
I--!
TOLD--!
YOU!

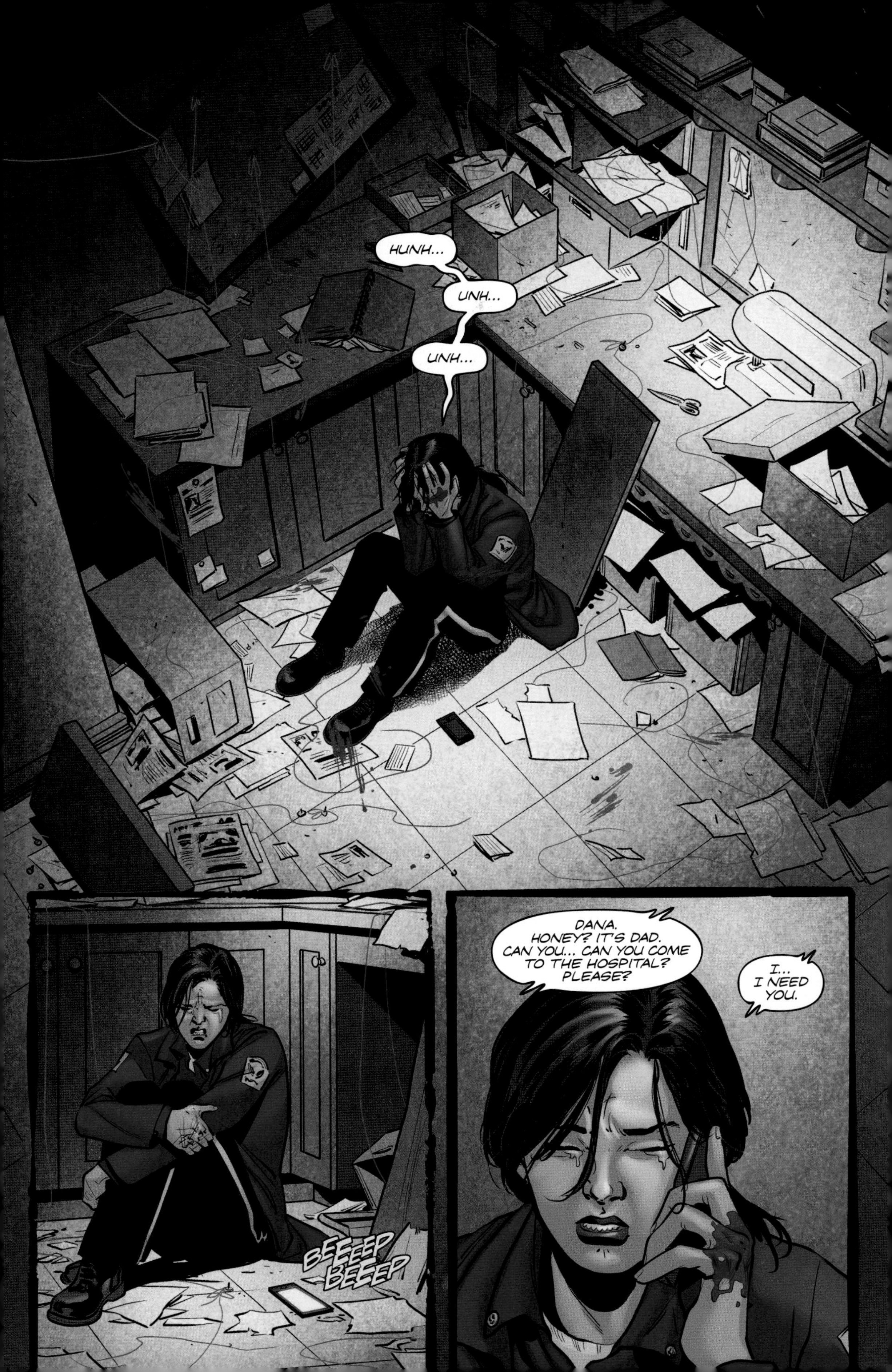
HUNH...
UNH...
UNH...
BEEEEP BEEEEP
DANA. HONEY? IT'S DAD. CAN YOU... CAN YOU COME TO THE HOSPITAL? PLEASE?
I... I NEED YOU.

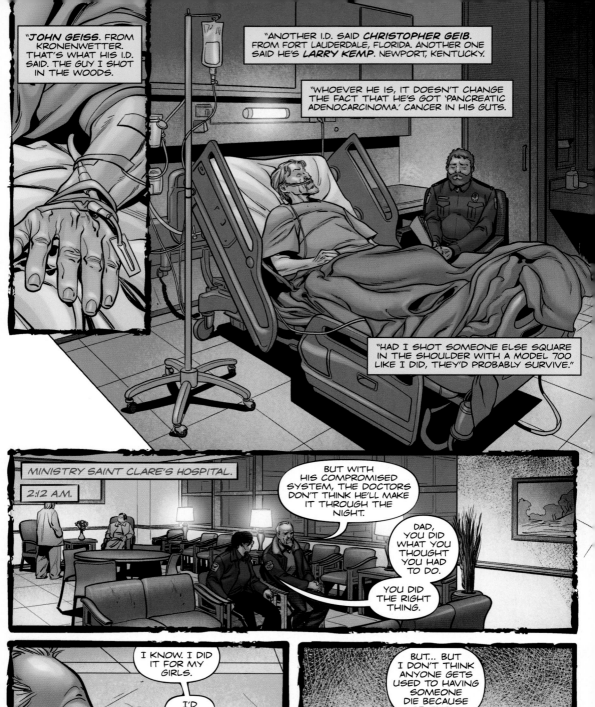

"JOHN GEISS. FROM KRONENWETTER. THAT'S WHAT HIS I.D. SAID. THE GUY I SHOT IN THE WOODS.

"ANOTHER I.D. SAID CHRISTOPHER GEIB. FROM FORT LAUDERDALE, FLORIDA. ANOTHER ONE SAID HE'S LARRY KEMP. NEWPORT, KENTUCKY.

"WHOEVER HE IS, IT DOESN'T CHANGE THE FACT THAT HE'S GOT 'PANCREATIC ADENOCARCINOMA.' CANCER IN HIS GUTS.

"HAD I SHOT SOMEONE ELSE SQUARE IN THE SHOULDER WITH A MODEL 700 LIKE I DID, THEY'D PROBABLY SURVIVE."

MINISTRY SAINT CLARE'S HOSPITAL.

2:12 A.M.

BUT WITH HIS COMPROMISED SYSTEM, THE DOCTORS DON'T THINK HE'LL MAKE IT THROUGH THE NIGHT.

DAD, YOU DID WHAT YOU THOUGHT YOU HAD TO DO.

YOU DID THE RIGHT THING.

I KNOW. I DID IT FOR MY GIRLS.

I'D DO IT AGAIN.

BUT... BUT I DON'T THINK ANYONE GETS USED TO HAVING SOMEONE DIE BECAUSE OF THEM.

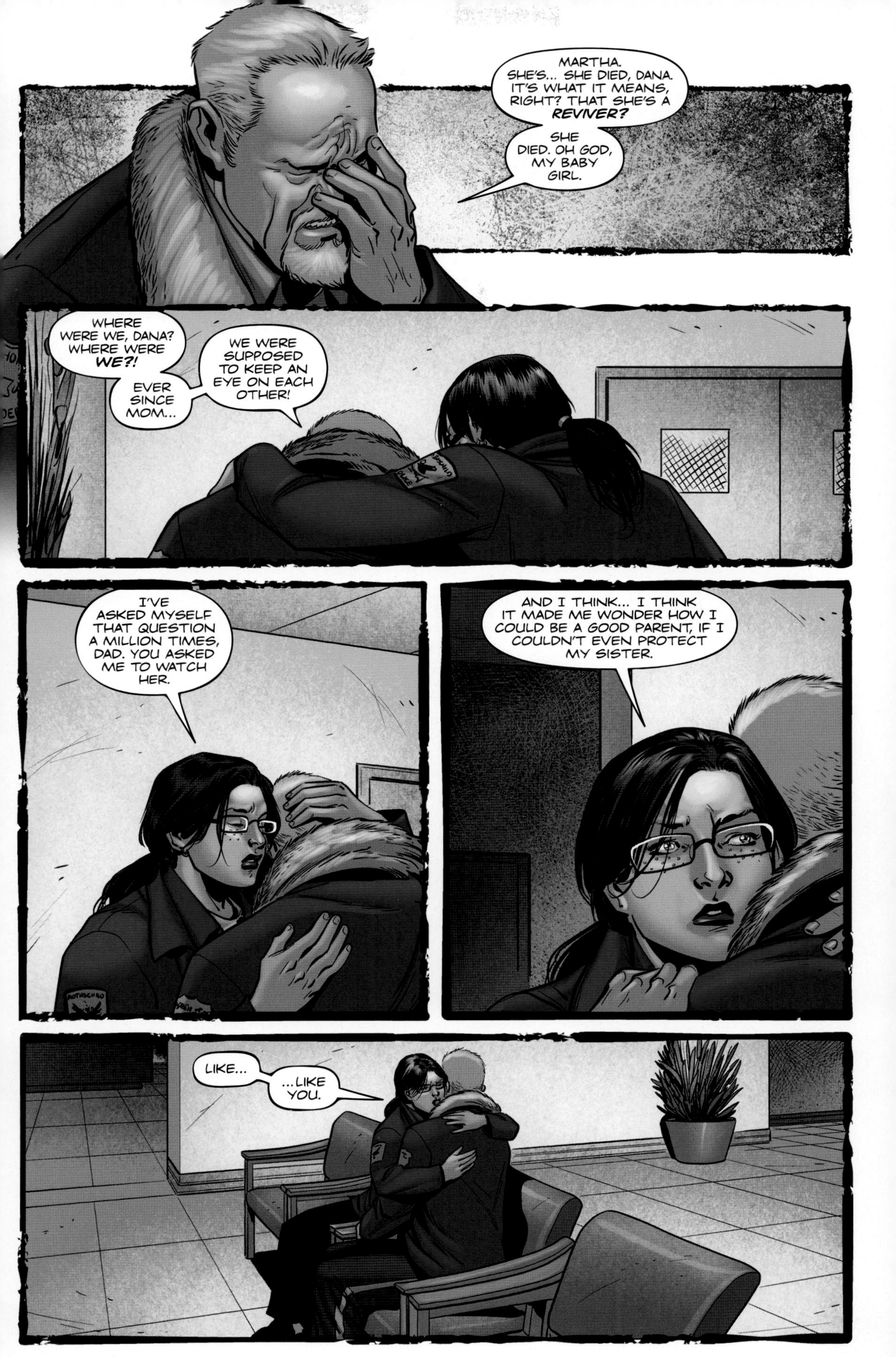
MARTHA. SHE'S... SHE DIED, DANA. IT'S WHAT IT MEANS, RIGHT? THAT SHE'S A REVIVER?
SHE DIED. OH GOD, MY BABY GIRL.
WHERE WERE WE, DANA? WHERE WERE WE?!
EVER SINCE MOM...
WE WERE SUPPOSED TO KEEP AN EYE ON EACH OTHER!
I'VE ASKED MYSELF THAT QUESTION A MILLION TIMES, DAD. YOU ASKED ME TO WATCH HER.
AND I THINK... I THINK IT MADE ME WONDER HOW I COULD BE A GOOD PARENT, IF I COULDN'T EVEN PROTECT MY SISTER.
LIKE...
...LIKE YOU.

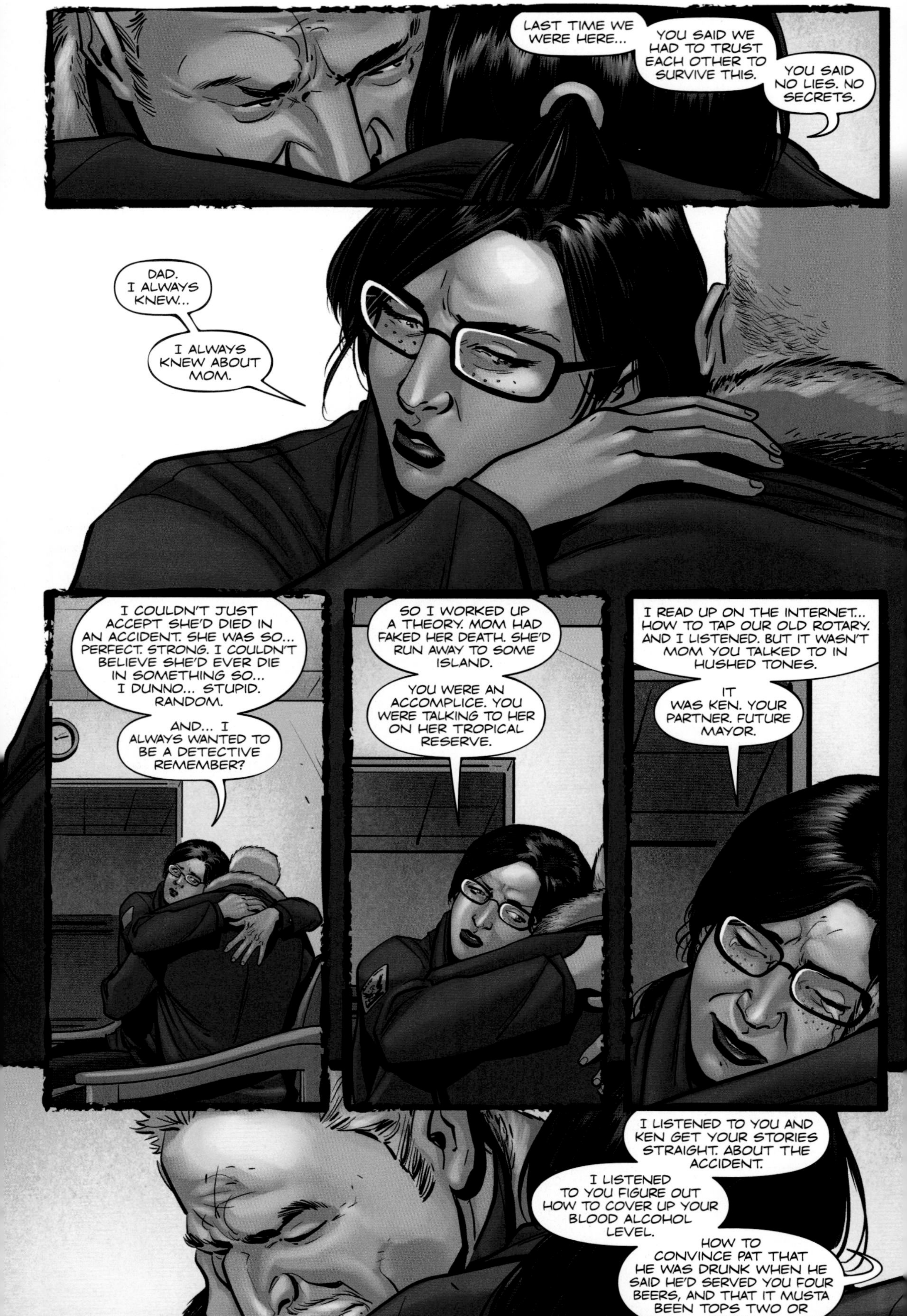
LAST TIME WE WERE HERE...
YOU SAID WE HAD TO TRUST EACH OTHER TO SURVIVE THIS.
YOU SAID NO LIES. NO SECRETS.
DAD. I ALWAYS KNEW...
I ALWAYS KNEW ABOUT MOM.
I COULDN'T JUST ACCEPT SHE'D DIED IN AN ACCIDENT. SHE WAS SO... PERFECT. STRONG. I COULDN'T BELIEVE SHE'D EVER DIE IN SOMETHING SO... I DUNNO... STUPID. RANDOM.
AND... I ALWAYS WANTED TO BE A DETECTIVE REMEMBER?
SO I WORKED UP A THEORY. MOM HAD FAKED HER DEATH. SHE'D RUN AWAY TO SOME ISLAND.
YOU WERE AN ACCOMPLICE. YOU WERE TALKING TO HER ON HER TROPICAL RESERVE.
I READ UP ON THE INTERNET... HOW TO TAP OUR OLD ROTARY. AND I LISTENED. BUT IT WASN'T MOM YOU TALKED TO IN HUSHED TONES.
IT WAS KEN. YOUR PARTNER. FUTURE MAYOR.
I LISTENED TO YOU AND KEN GET YOUR STORIES STRAIGHT. ABOUT THE ACCIDENT.
I LISTENED TO YOU FIGURE OUT HOW TO COVER UP YOUR BLOOD ALCOHOL LEVEL.
HOW TO CONVINCE PAT THAT HE WAS DRUNK WHEN HE SAID HE'D SERVED YOU FOUR BEERS, AND THAT IT MUSTA BEEN TOPS TWO OR THREE.

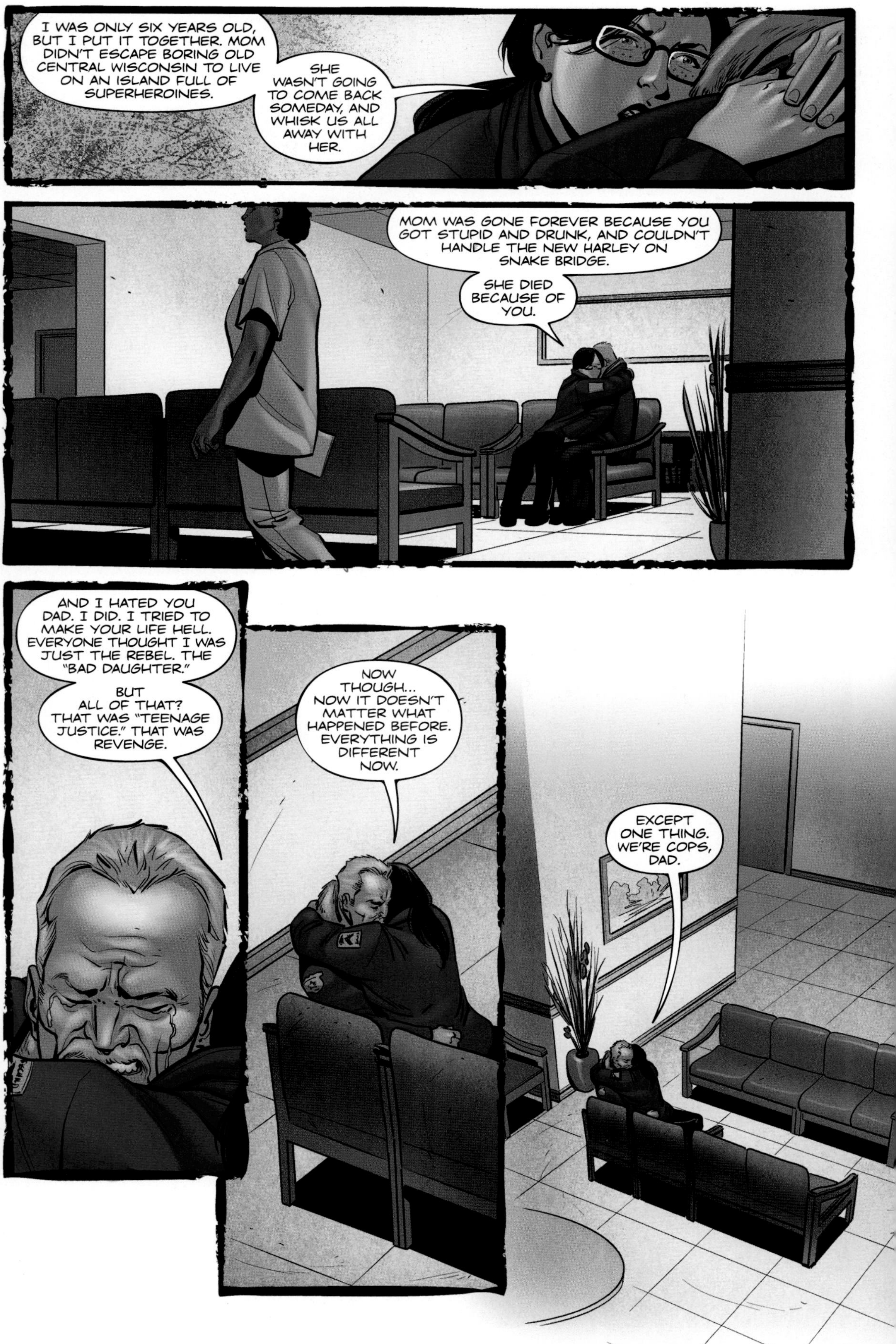
I WAS ONLY SIX YEARS OLD, BUT I PUT IT TOGETHER. MOM DIDN'T ESCAPE BORING OLD CENTRAL WISCONSIN TO LIVE ON AN ISLAND FULL OF SUPERHEROINES.
SHE WASN'T GOING TO COME BACK SOMEDAY, AND WHISK US ALL AWAY WITH HER.
MOM WAS GONE FOREVER BECAUSE YOU GOT STUPID AND DRUNK, AND COULDN'T HANDLE THE NEW HARLEY ON SNAKE BRIDGE.
SHE DIED BECAUSE OF YOU.
AND I HATED YOU DAD. I DID. I TRIED TO MAKE YOUR LIFE HELL. EVERYONE THOUGHT I WAS JUST THE REBEL. THE "BAD DAUGHTER."
BUT ALL OF THAT? THAT WAS "TEENAGE JUSTICE." THAT WAS REVENGE.
NOW THOUGH... NOW IT DOESN'T MATTER WHAT HAPPENED BEFORE. EVERYTHING IS DIFFERENT NOW.
EXCEPT ONE THING. WE'RE COPS, DAD.

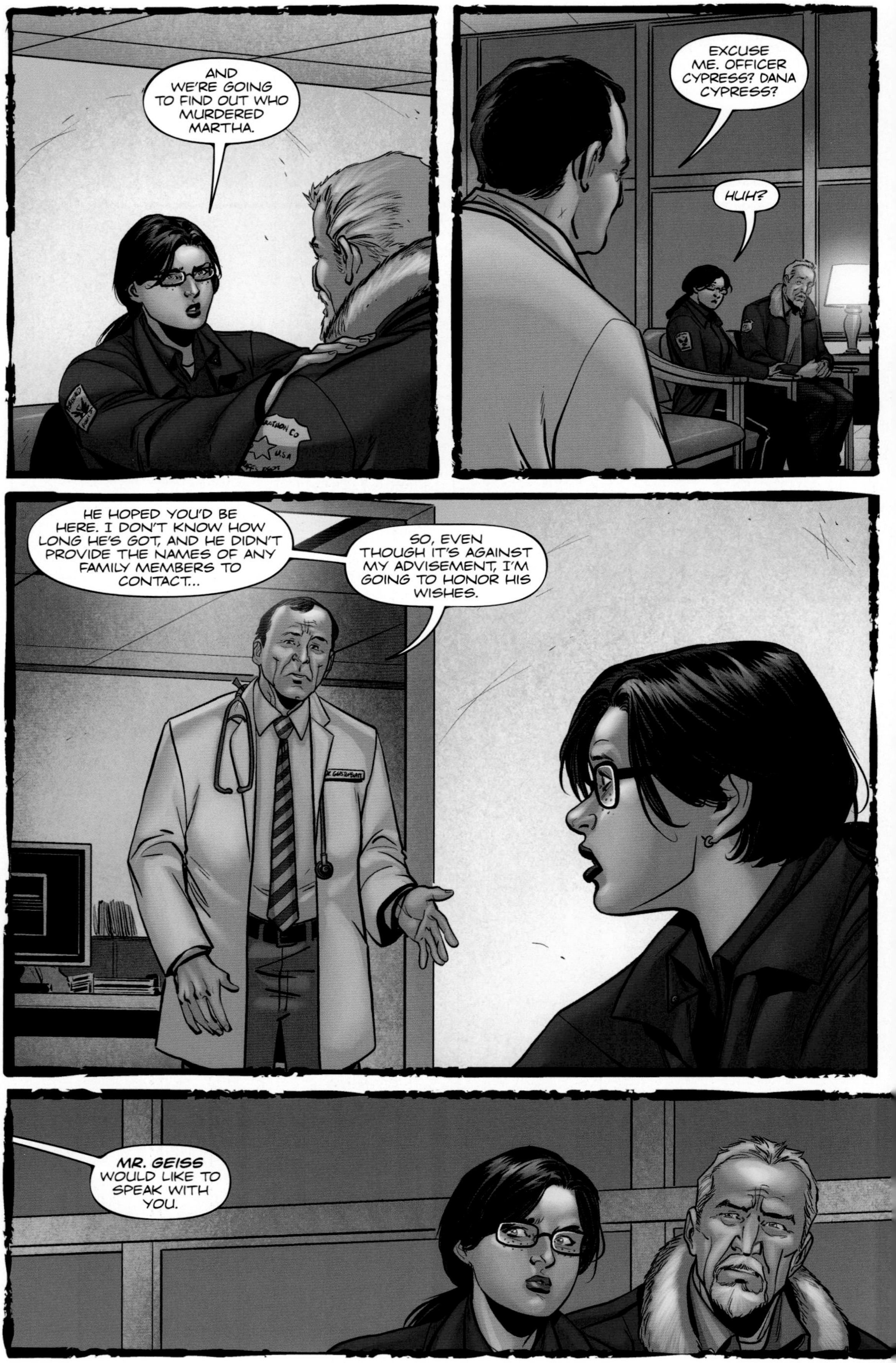

AND WE'RE GOING TO FIND OUT WHO MURDERED MARTHA.
EXCUSE ME. OFFICER CYPRESS? DANA CYPRESS?
HUH?
HE HOPED YOU'D BE HERE. I DON'T KNOW HOW LONG HE'S GOT, AND HE DIDN'T PROVIDE THE NAMES OF ANY FAMILY MEMBERS TO CONTACT...
SO, EVEN THOUGH IT'S AGAINST MY ADVISEMENT, I'M GOING TO HONOR HIS WISHES.
MR. GEISS WOULD LIKE TO SPEAK WITH YOU.

YOU CAN GO, BRENT.

YOU SURE?

I GOT THIS.

HEY. DANA, RIGHT?

DON'T WORRY. I'M NOT GONNA PULL A GUN ON YOU. THIS TIME.

YOU REMEMBER ME, RIGHT? WITHOUT THE GAS MASK?

YEAH. FROM THE NIGHT *EDMUND HOLT*... DIED.

HOLT. WHAT A PIECE OF WORK THAT GUY WAS. ANOTHER LONE NUT THAT THINKS HE'S GOT WHAT IT TAKES TO CURE THE "ILLS" OF THIS COUNTRY.

ASSHOLE. HE DESERVED WHAT HE GOT.

WHAT DO YOU WANT?

YOU ARE "NO BULLSHIT" AREN'T YOU? WELL, I DON'T KNOW WHO I'M FOOLING. IT'S NOT LIKE I'VE GOT A LOT OF TIME TO GET CHATTY.

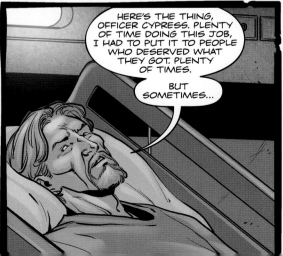

HERE'S THE THING, OFFICER CYPRESS. PLENTY OF TIME DOING THIS JOB, I HAD TO PUT IT TO PEOPLE WHO DESERVED WHAT THEY GOT. PLENTY OF TIMES.

BUT SOMETIMES...

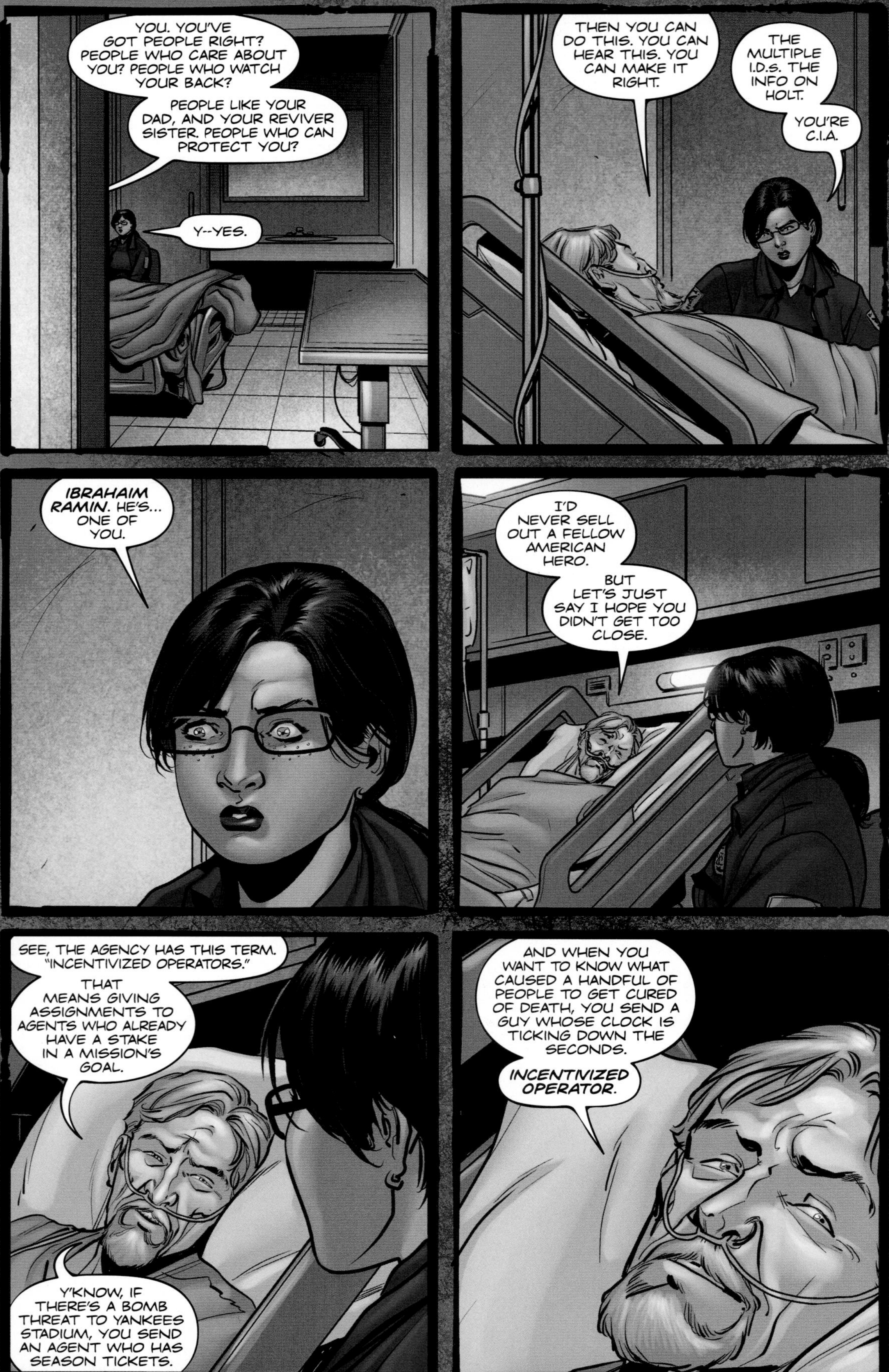
YOU. YOU'VE GOT PEOPLE RIGHT? PEOPLE WHO CARE ABOUT YOU? PEOPLE WHO WATCH YOUR BACK?
PEOPLE LIKE YOUR DAD, AND YOUR REVIVER SISTER. PEOPLE WHO CAN PROTECT YOU?
Y--YES.
THEN YOU CAN DO THIS. YOU CAN HEAR THIS. YOU CAN MAKE IT RIGHT.
THE MULTIPLE I.D.S. THE INFO ON HOLT.
YOU'RE C.I.A.
IBRAHAIM RAMIN. HE'S... ONE OF YOU.
I'D NEVER SELL OUT A FELLOW AMERICAN HERO.
BUT LET'S JUST SAY I HOPE YOU DIDN'T GET TOO CLOSE.
SEE, THE AGENCY HAS THIS TERM. "INCENTIVIZED OPERATORS."
THAT MEANS GIVING ASSIGNMENTS TO AGENTS WHO ALREADY HAVE A STAKE IN A MISSION'S GOAL.
Y'KNOW, IF THERE'S A BOMB THREAT TO YANKEES STADIUM, YOU SEND AN AGENT WHO HAS SEASON TICKETS.
AND WHEN YOU WANT TO KNOW WHAT CAUSED A HANDFUL OF PEOPLE TO GET CURED OF DEATH, YOU SEND A GUY WHOSE CLOCK IS TICKING DOWN THE SECONDS.
INCENTIVIZED OPERATOR.

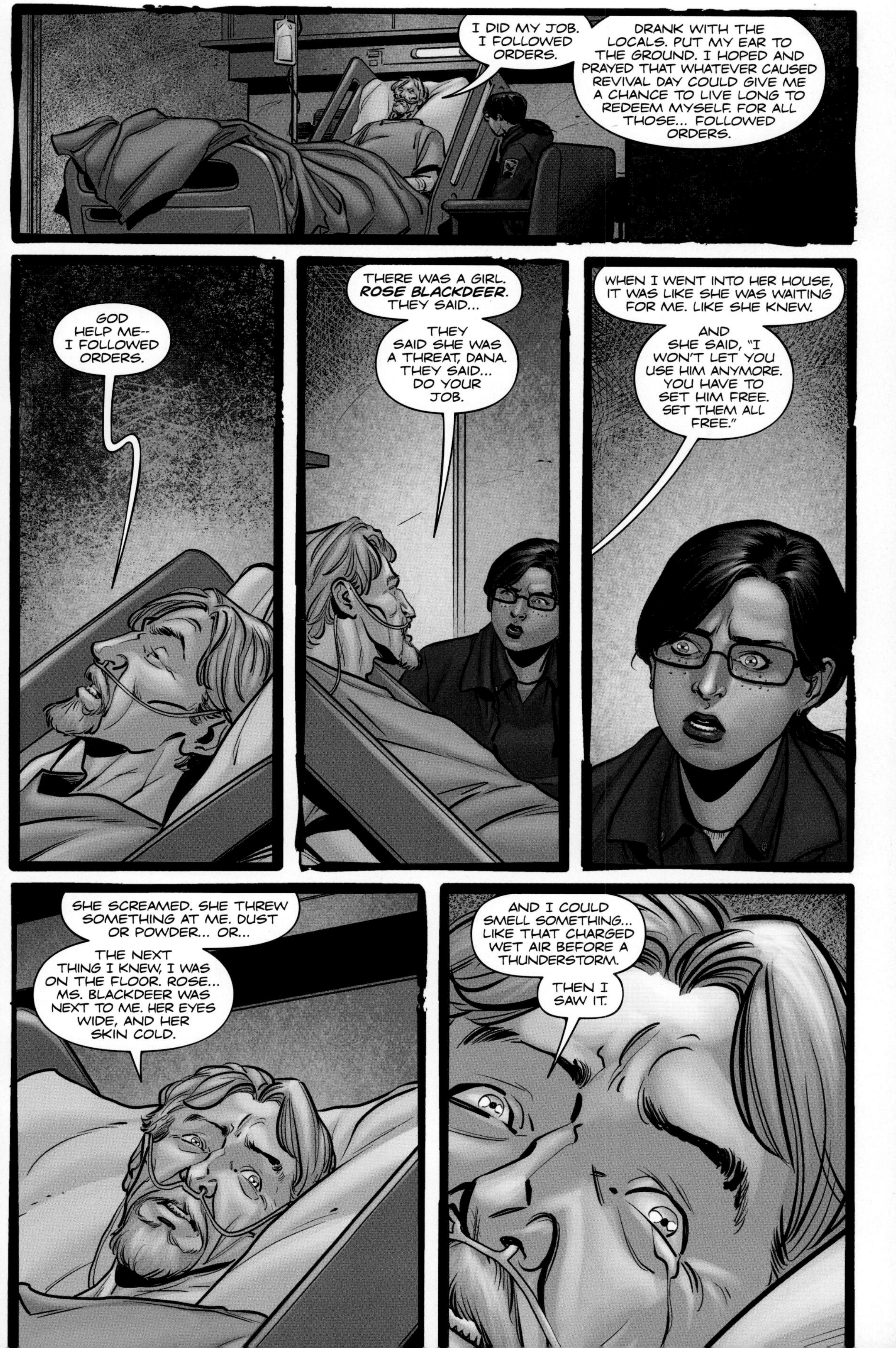
I DID MY JOB. I FOLLOWED ORDERS.
DRANK WITH THE LOCALS. PUT MY EAR TO THE GROUND. I HOPED AND PRAYED THAT WHATEVER CAUSED REVIVAL DAY COULD GIVE ME A CHANCE TO LIVE LONG TO REDEEM MYSELF. FOR ALL THOSE... FOLLOWED ORDERS.
GOD HELP ME-- I FOLLOWED ORDERS.
THERE WAS A GIRL. ***ROSE BLACKDEER***. THEY SAID...
THEY SAID SHE WAS A THREAT, DANA. THEY SAID... DO YOUR JOB.
WHEN I WENT INTO HER HOUSE, IT WAS LIKE SHE WAS WAITING FOR ME. LIKE SHE KNEW.
AND SHE SAID, "I WON'T LET YOU USE HIM ANYMORE. YOU HAVE TO SET HIM FREE. SET THEM ALL FREE."
SHE SCREAMED. SHE THREW SOMETHING AT ME. DUST OR POWDER... OR...
THE NEXT THING I KNEW, I WAS ON THE FLOOR. ROSE... MS. BLACKDEER WAS NEXT TO ME. HER EYES WIDE, AND HER SKIN COLD.
AND I COULD SMELL SOMETHING... LIKE THAT CHARGED WET AIR BEFORE A THUNDERSTORM.
THEN I SAW IT.

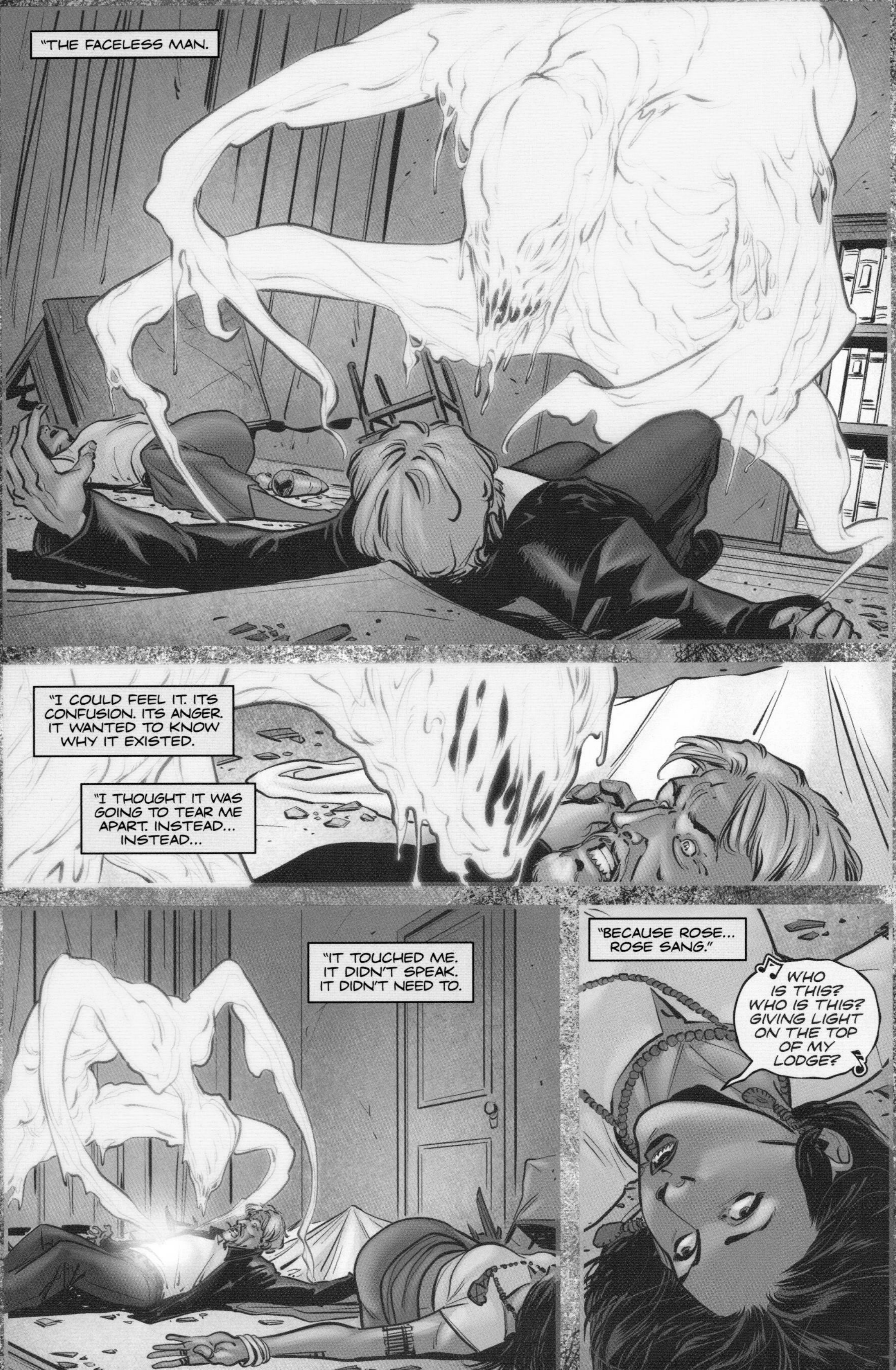
"THE FACELESS MAN.
"I COULD FEEL IT. ITS CONFUSION. ITS ANGER. IT WANTED TO KNOW WHY IT EXISTED.
"I THOUGHT IT WAS GOING TO TEAR ME APART. INSTEAD... INSTEAD...
"IT TOUCHED ME. IT DIDN'T SPEAK. IT DIDN'T NEED TO.
"BECAUSE ROSE... ROSE SANG."
WHO IS THIS? WHO IS THIS? GIVING LIGHT ON THE TOP OF MY LODGE?

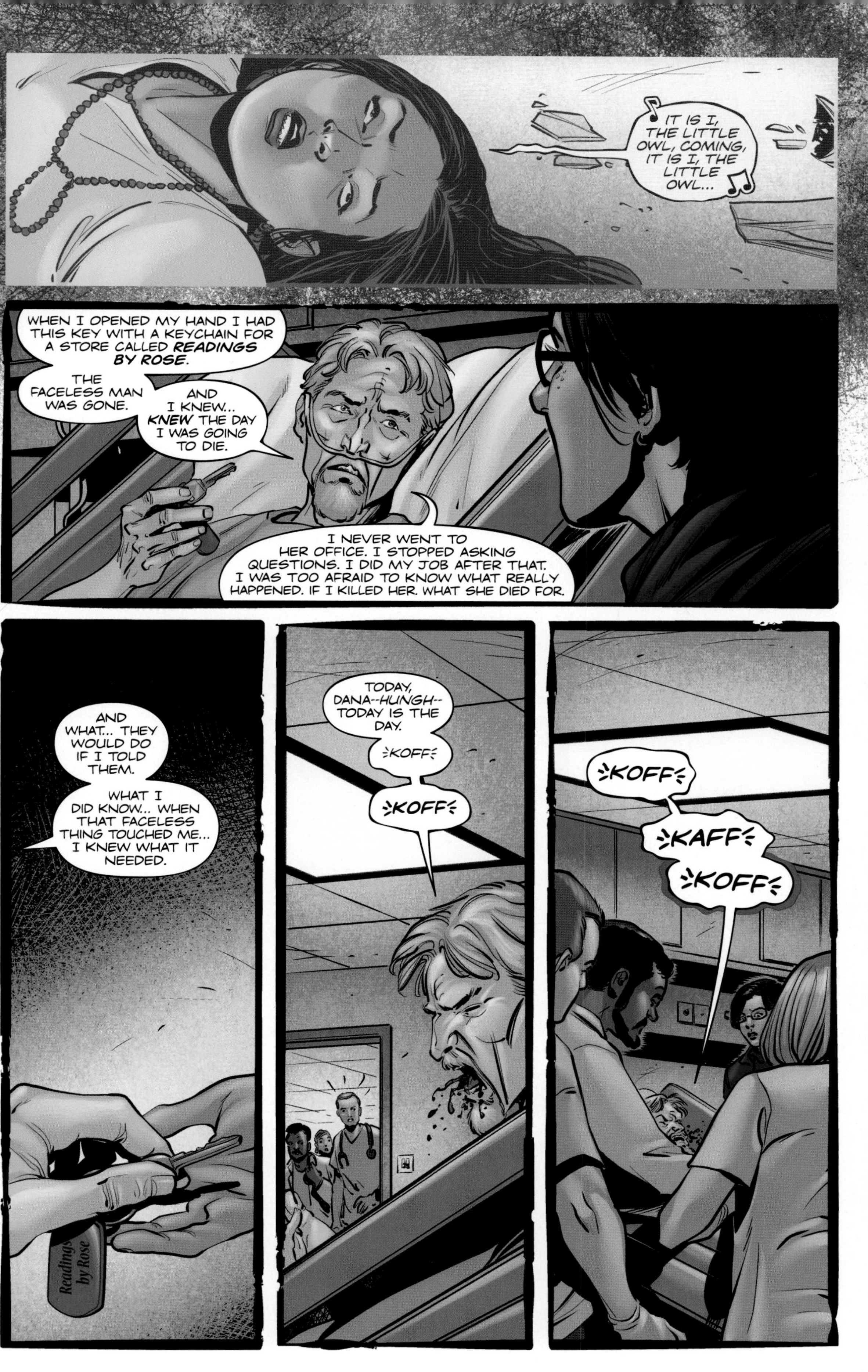
IT IS I, THE LITTLE OWL, COMING, IT IS I, THE LITTLE OWL...
WHEN I OPENED MY HAND I HAD THIS KEY WITH A KEYCHAIN FOR A STORE CALLED READINGS BY ROSE.
THE FACELESS MAN WAS GONE.
AND I KNEW... KNEW THE DAY I WAS GOING TO DIE.
I NEVER WENT TO HER OFFICE. I STOPPED ASKING QUESTIONS. I DID MY JOB AFTER THAT. I WAS TOO AFRAID TO KNOW WHAT REALLY HAPPENED. IF I KILLED HER. WHAT SHE DIED FOR.
AND WHAT... THEY WOULD DO IF I TOLD THEM.
WHAT I DID KNOW... WHEN THAT FACELESS THING TOUCHED ME... I KNEW WHAT IT NEEDED.
Readings by Rose
TODAY, DANA--HUNGH-- TODAY IS THE DAY.
KOFF
KOFF
KOFF
KAFF
KOFF

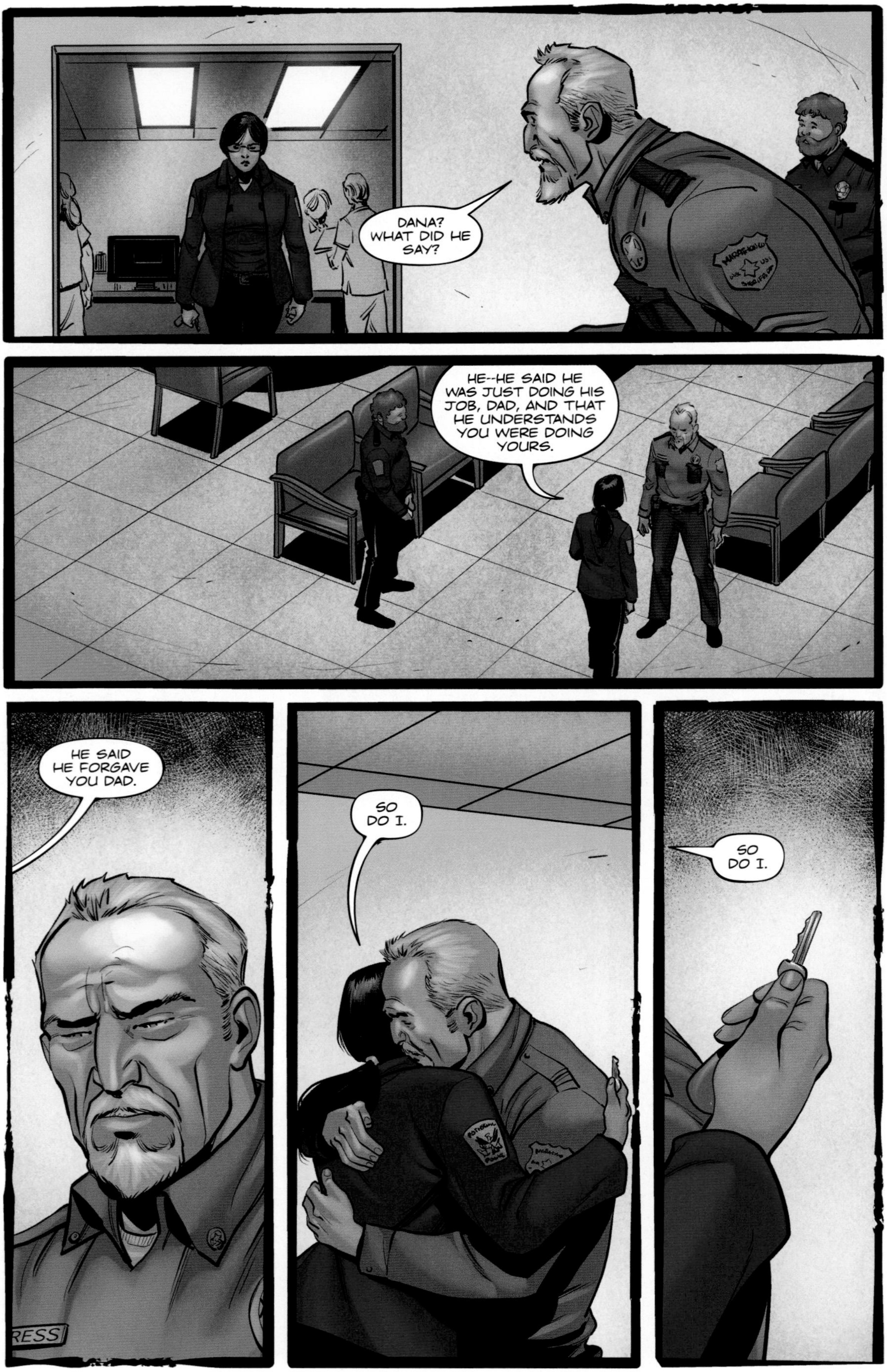
DANA? WHAT DID HE SAY?
HE--HE SAID HE WAS JUST DOING HIS JOB, DAD, AND THAT HE UNDERSTANDS YOU WERE DOING YOURS.
HE SAID HE FORGAVE YOU DAD.
RESS
SO DO I.
SO DO I.

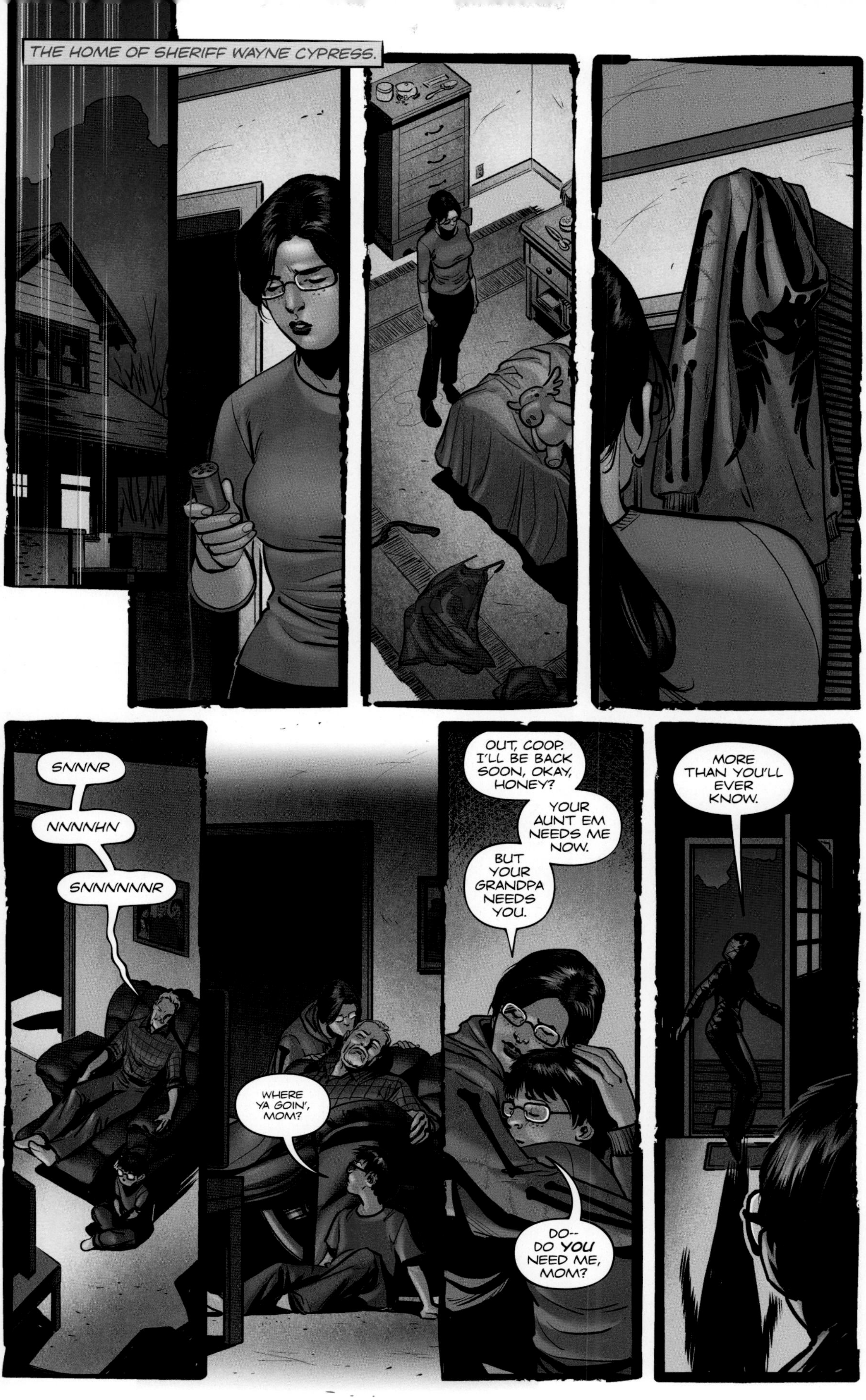
THE HOME OF SHERIFF WAYNE CYPRESS.
SNNNR
NNNNHN
SNNNNNNR
WHERE YA GOIN', MOM?
OUT, COOP. I'LL BE BACK SOON, OKAY, HONEY?
YOUR AUNT EM NEEDS ME NOW.
BUT YOUR GRANDPA NEEDS YOU.
DO-- DO YOU NEED ME, MOM?
MORE THAN YOU'LL EVER KNOW.

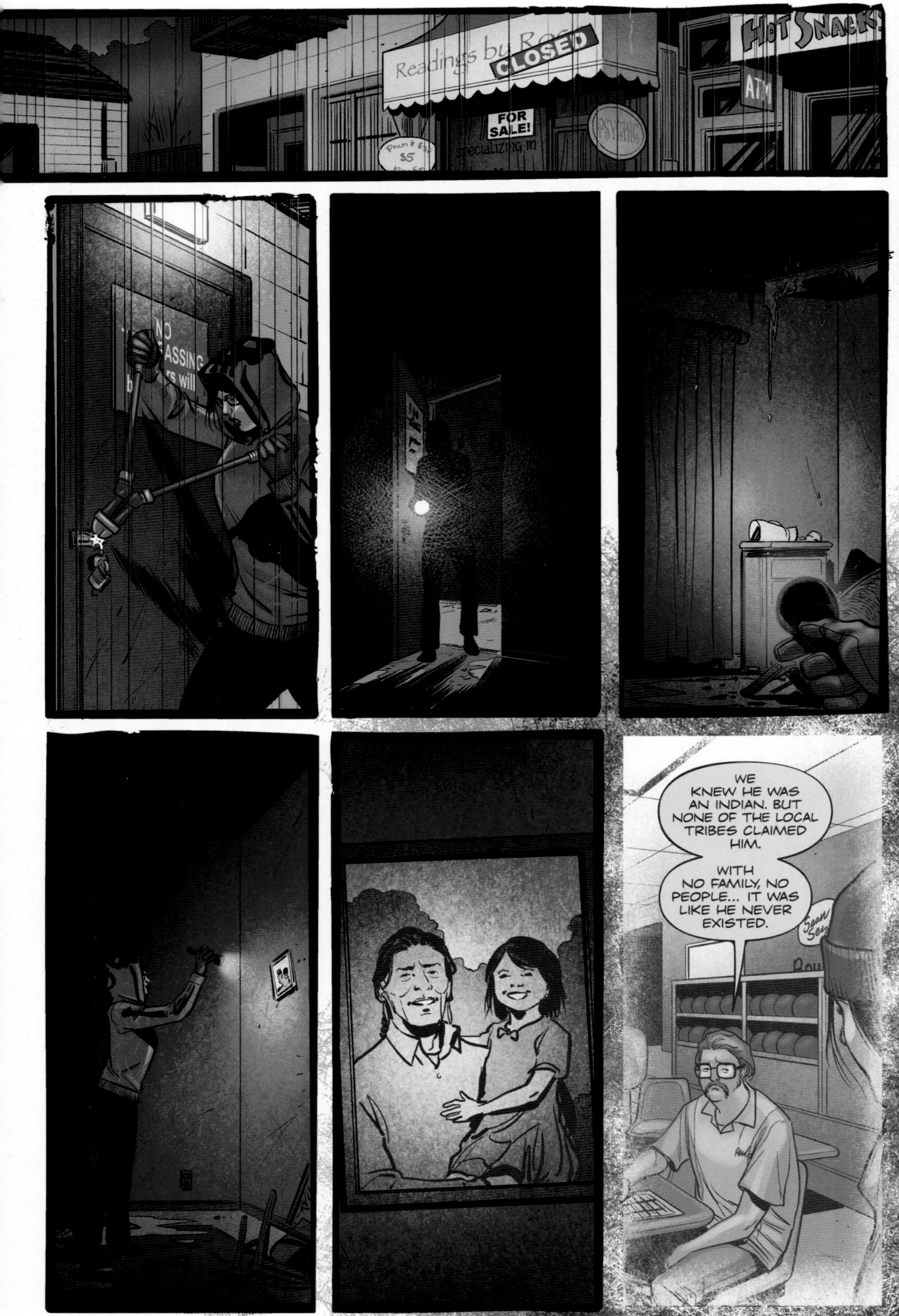
CLOSED
HOT SNACKS!
ATM
FOR SALE!
$5
SPECIALIZING IN
PSYCHIC
WE KNEW HE WAS AN INDIAN. BUT NONE OF THE LOCAL TRIBES CLAIMED HIM.
WITH NO FAMILY, NO PEOPLE... IT WAS LIKE HE NEVER EXISTED.

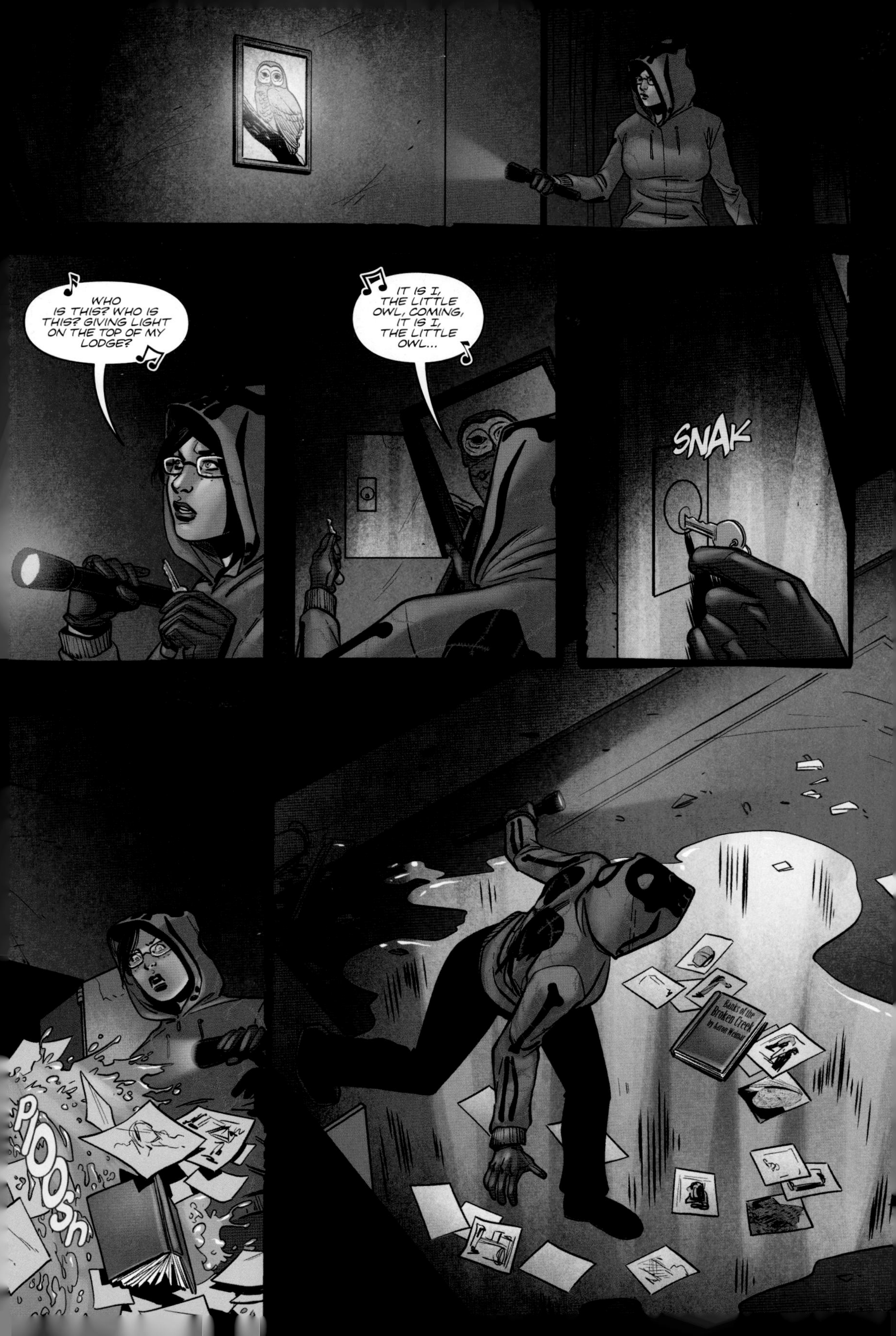
WHO IS THIS? WHO IS THIS? GIVING LIGHT ON THE TOP OF MY LODGE?
IT IS I, THE LITTLE OWL, COMING, IT IS I, THE LITTLE OWL...
SNAK
PLOOSH
Banks of the Broken Creek by Aaron Weimat

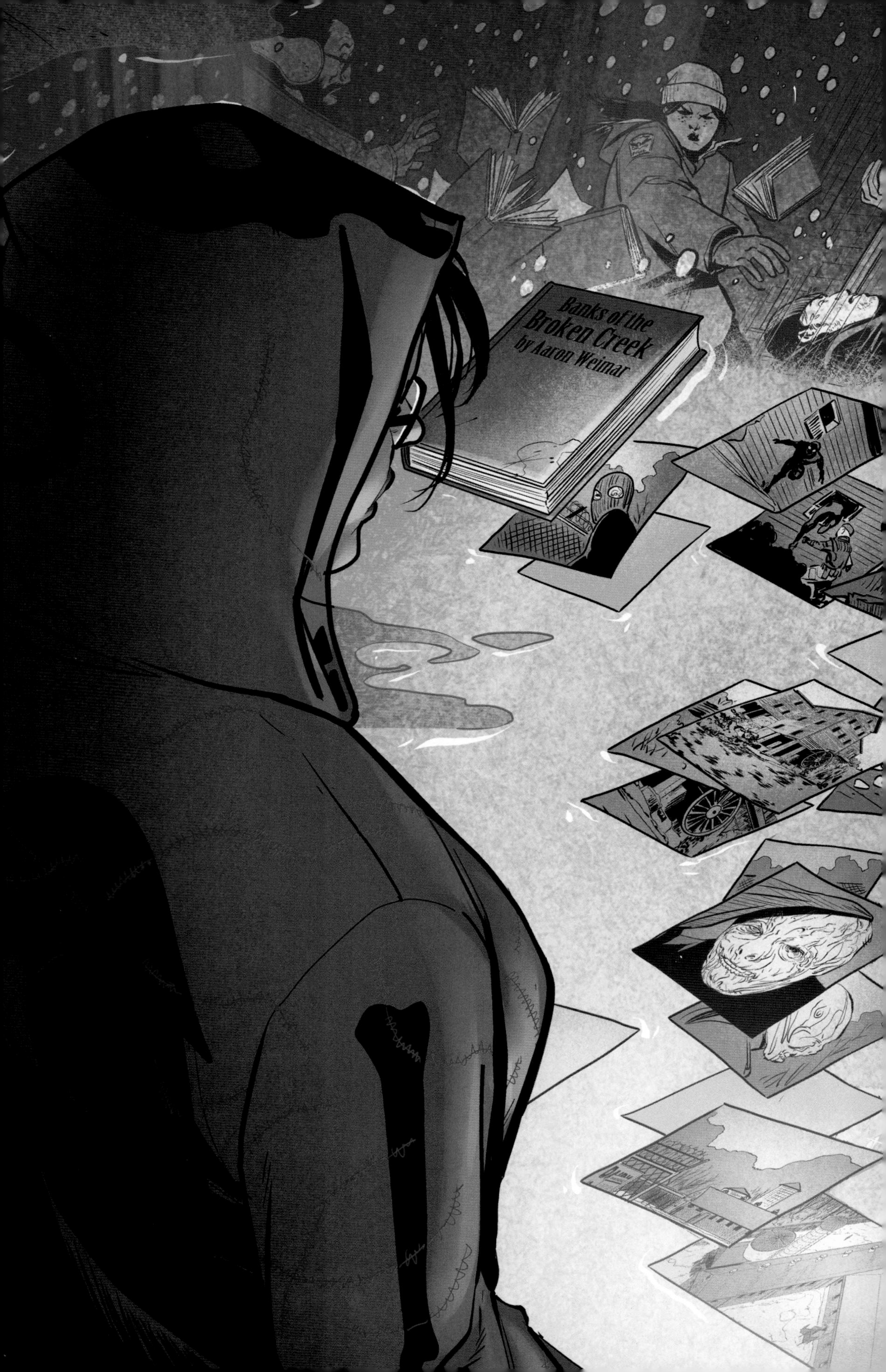
Banks of the
Broken Creek
by Aaron Weimar

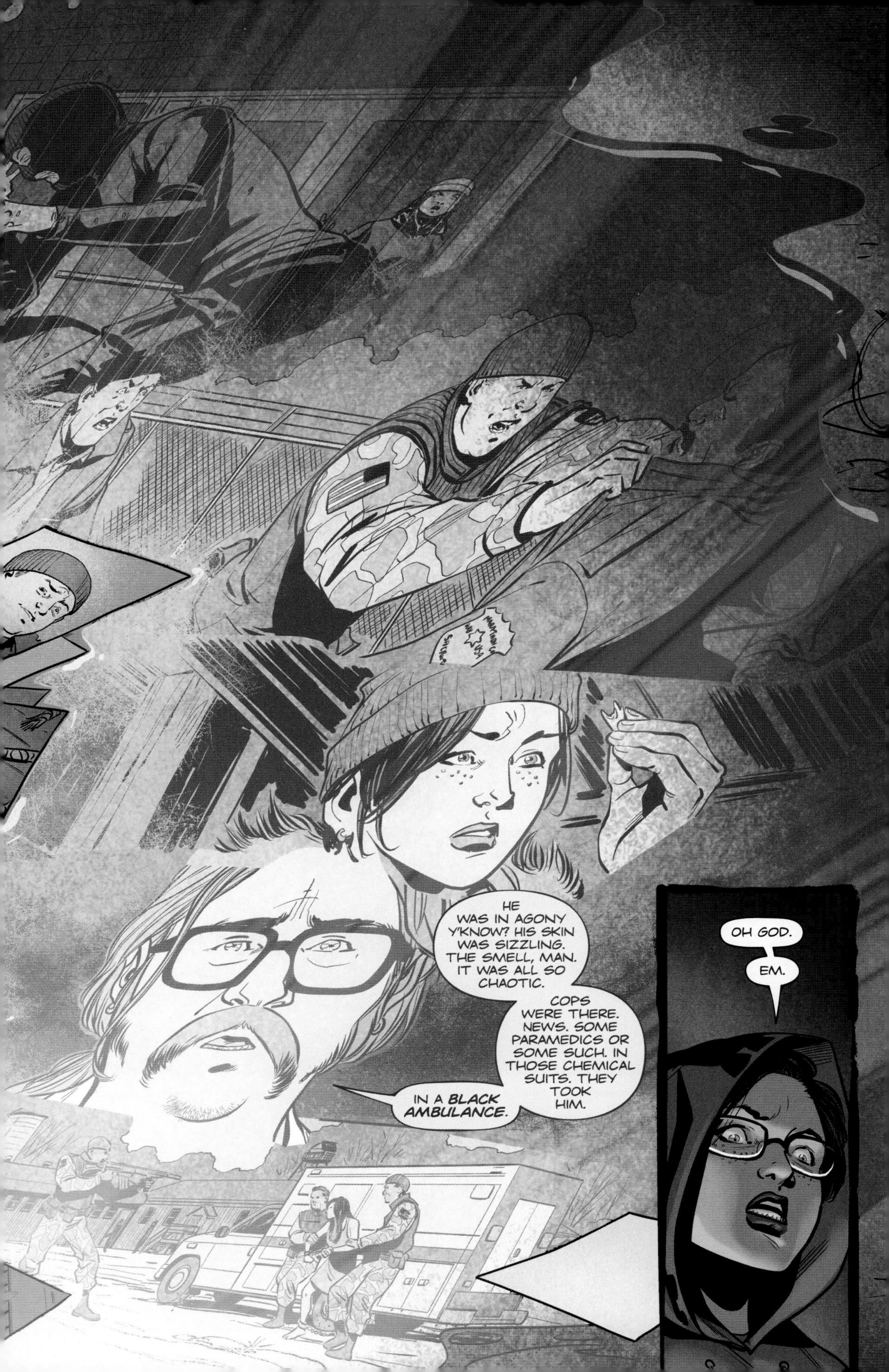
HE WAS IN AGONY Y'KNOW? HIS SKIN WAS SIZZLING. THE SMELL, MAN. IT WAS ALL SO CHAOTIC.
COPS WERE THERE. NEWS. SOME PARAMEDICS OR SOME SUCH. IN THOSE CHEMICAL SUITS. THEY TOOK HIM.
IN A **BLACK AMBULANCE**.
OH GOD.
EM.

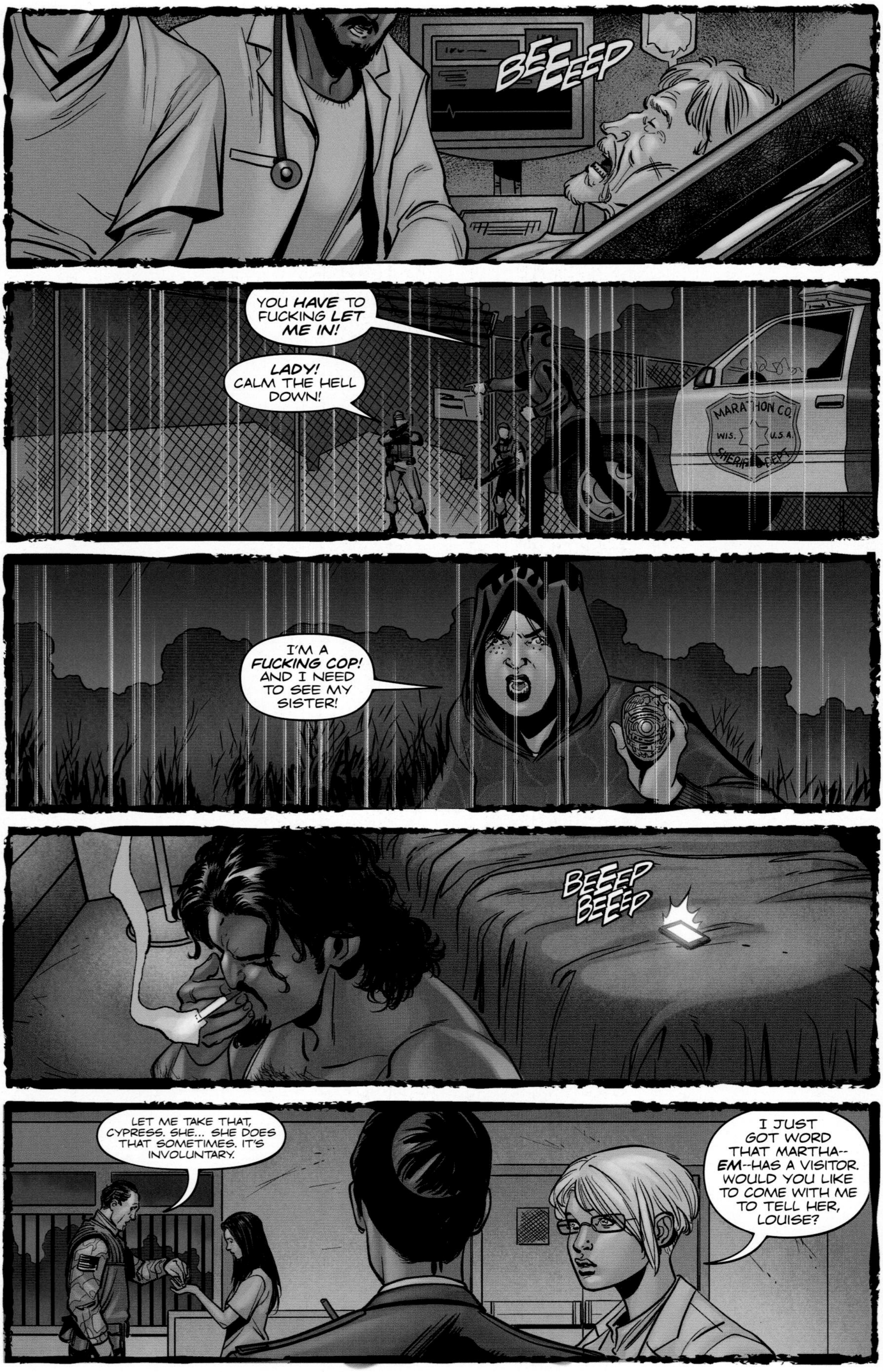
BEEEEEP
YOU HAVE TO FUCKING LET ME IN!
LADY! CALM THE HELL DOWN!
MARATHON CO.
WIS. U.S.A.
I'M A FUCKING COP! AND I NEED TO SEE MY SISTER!
BEEEP BEEEP
LET ME TAKE THAT, CYPRESS. SHE... SHE DOES THAT SOMETIMES. IT'S INVOLUNTARY.
I JUST GOT WORD THAT MARTHA-- EM--HAS A VISITOR. WOULD YOU LIKE TO COME WITH ME TO TELL HER, LOUISE?

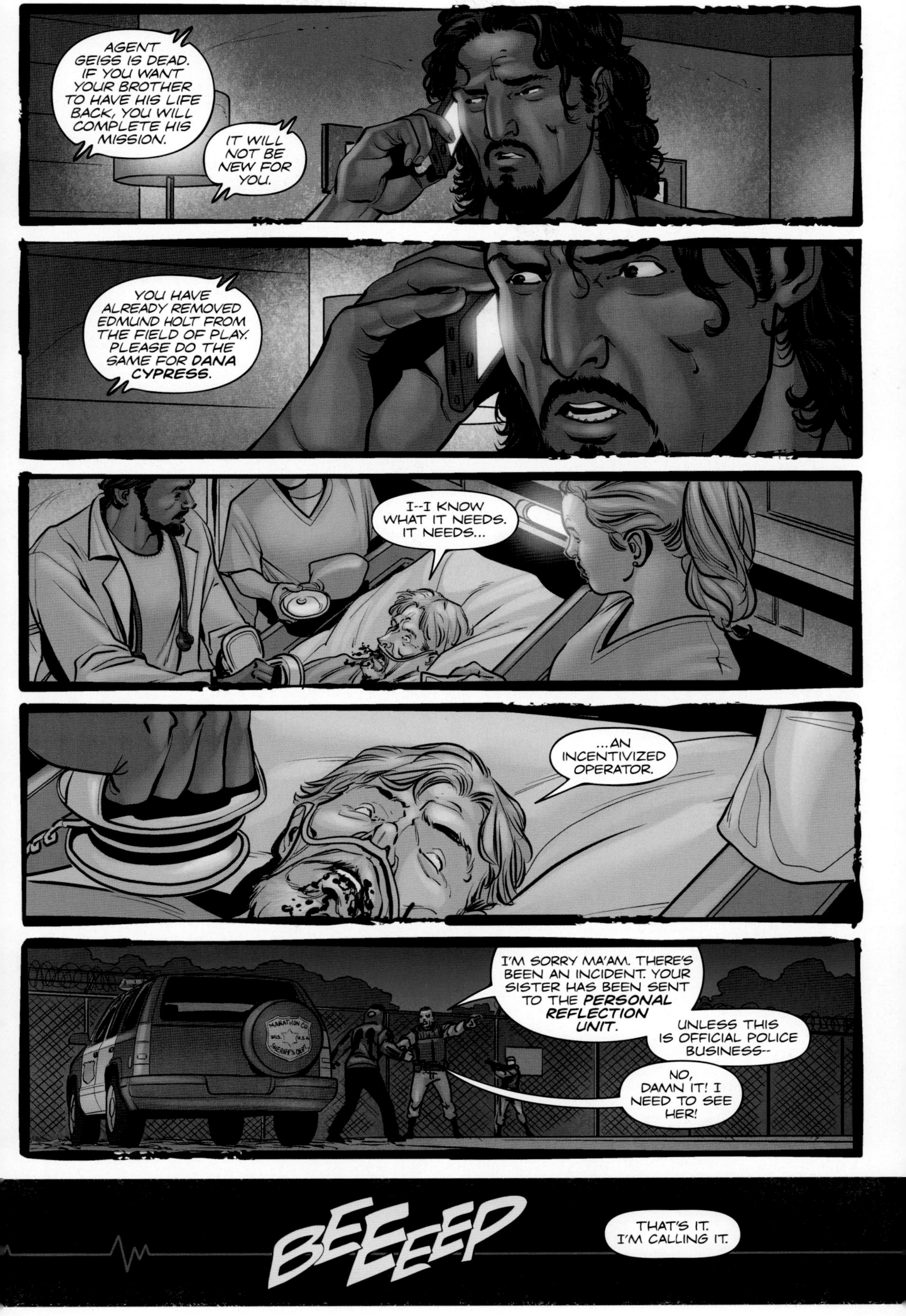
AGENT GEISS IS DEAD. IF YOU WANT YOUR BROTHER TO HAVE HIS LIFE BACK, YOU WILL COMPLETE HIS MISSION.
IT WILL NOT BE NEW FOR YOU.
YOU HAVE ALREADY REMOVED EDMUND HOLT FROM THE FIELD OF PLAY. PLEASE DO THE SAME FOR **DANA CYPRESS**.
I--I KNOW WHAT IT NEEDS. IT NEEDS...
...AN INCENTIVIZED OPERATOR.
MARATHON CO. WIS. U.S.A. SHERIFF'S DEPT.
I'M SORRY MA'AM. THERE'S BEEN AN INCIDENT. YOUR SISTER HAS BEEN SENT TO THE ***PERSONAL REFLECTION UNIT***.
UNLESS THIS IS OFFICIAL POLICE BUSINESS--
NO, DAMN IT! I NEED TO SEE HER!
BEEEEEP
THAT'S IT. I'M CALLING IT.

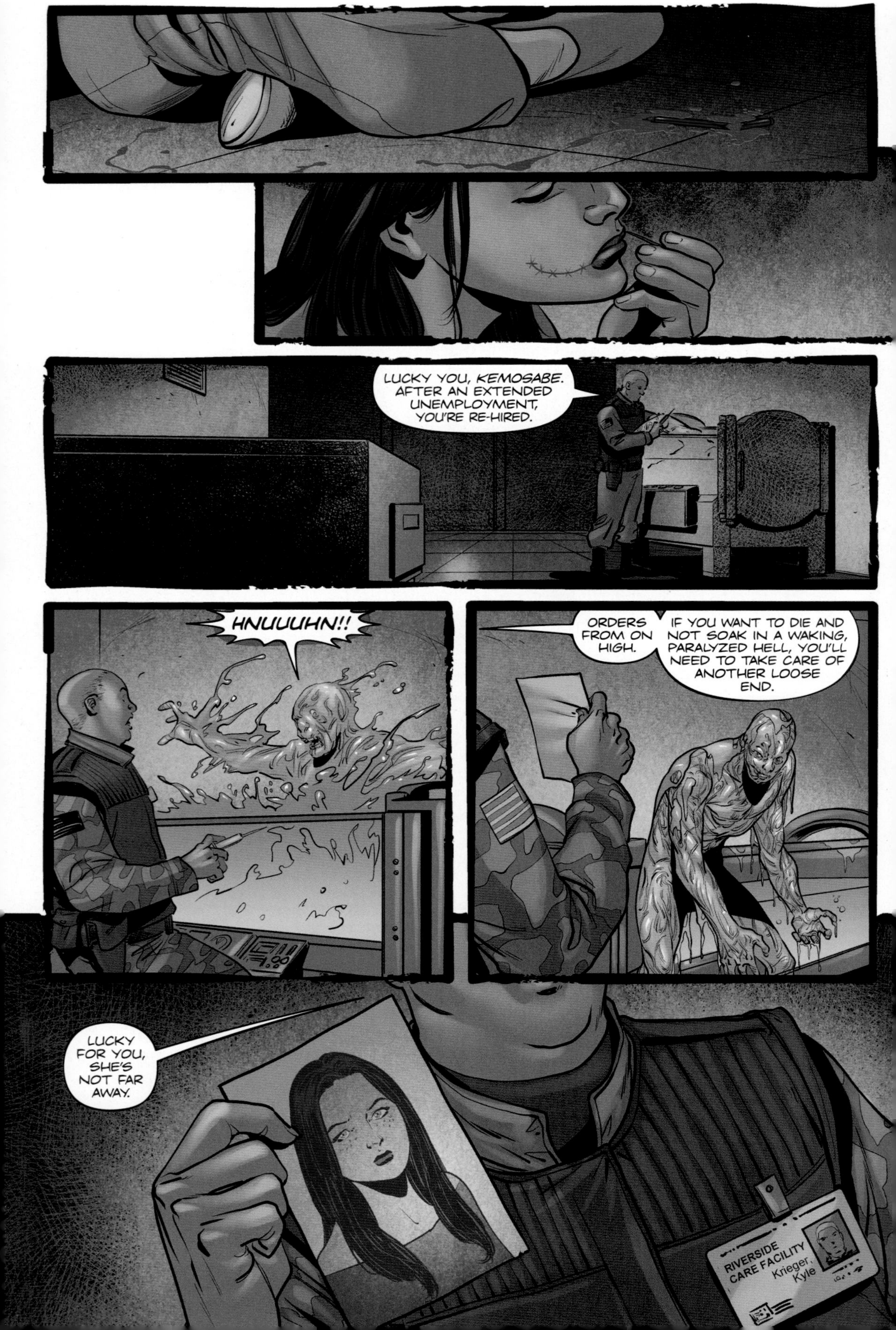

LUCKY YOU, KEMOSABE. AFTER AN EXTENDED UNEMPLOYMENT, YOU'RE RE-HIRED.
HNUUUHN!!
ORDERS FROM ON HIGH.
IF YOU WANT TO DIE AND NOT SOAK IN A WAKING, PARALYZED HELL, YOU'LL NEED TO TAKE CARE OF ANOTHER LOOSE END.
LUCKY FOR YOU, SHE'S NOT FAR AWAY.
RIVERSIDE CARE FACILITY
Krieger, Kyle

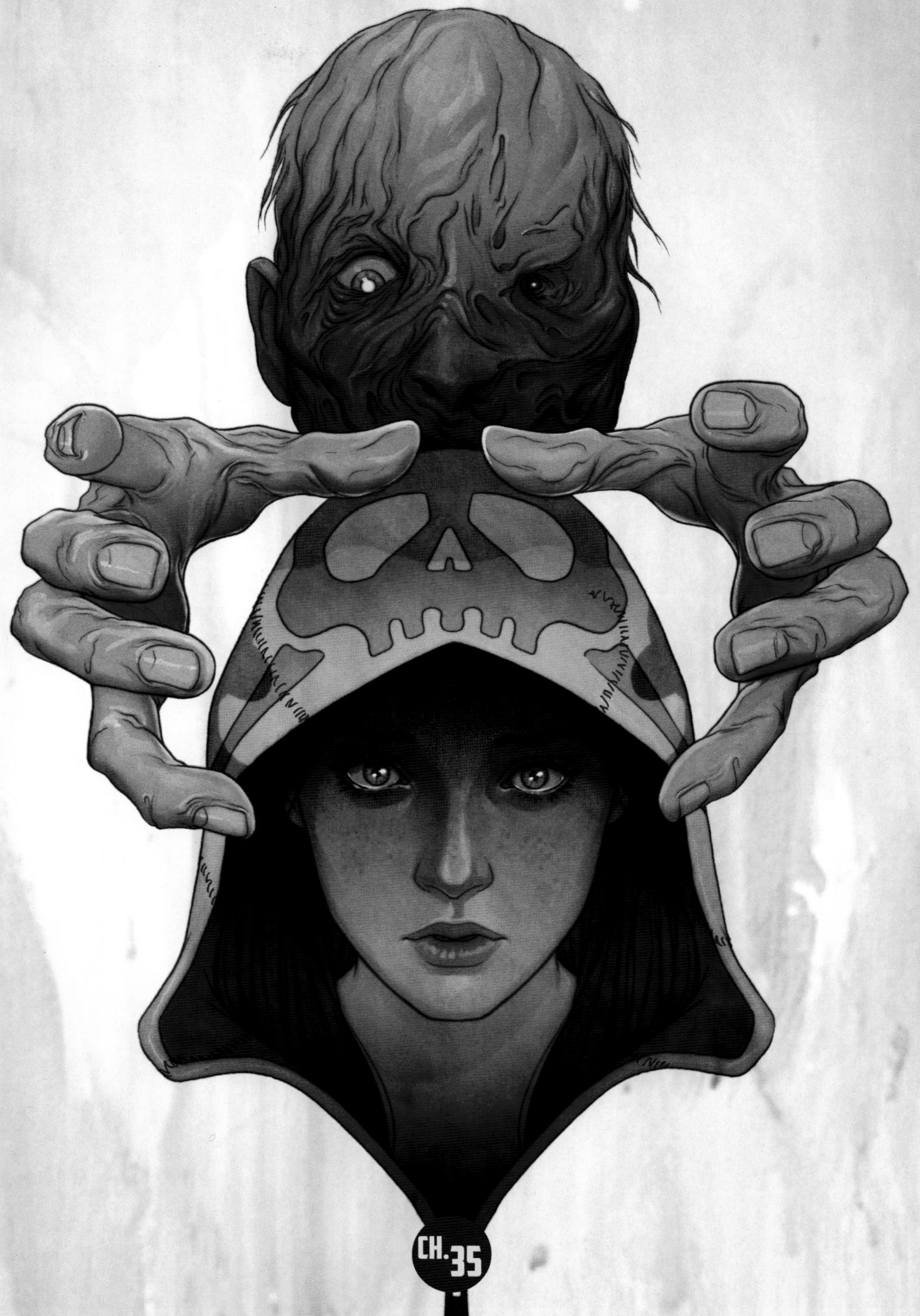
CH. 35

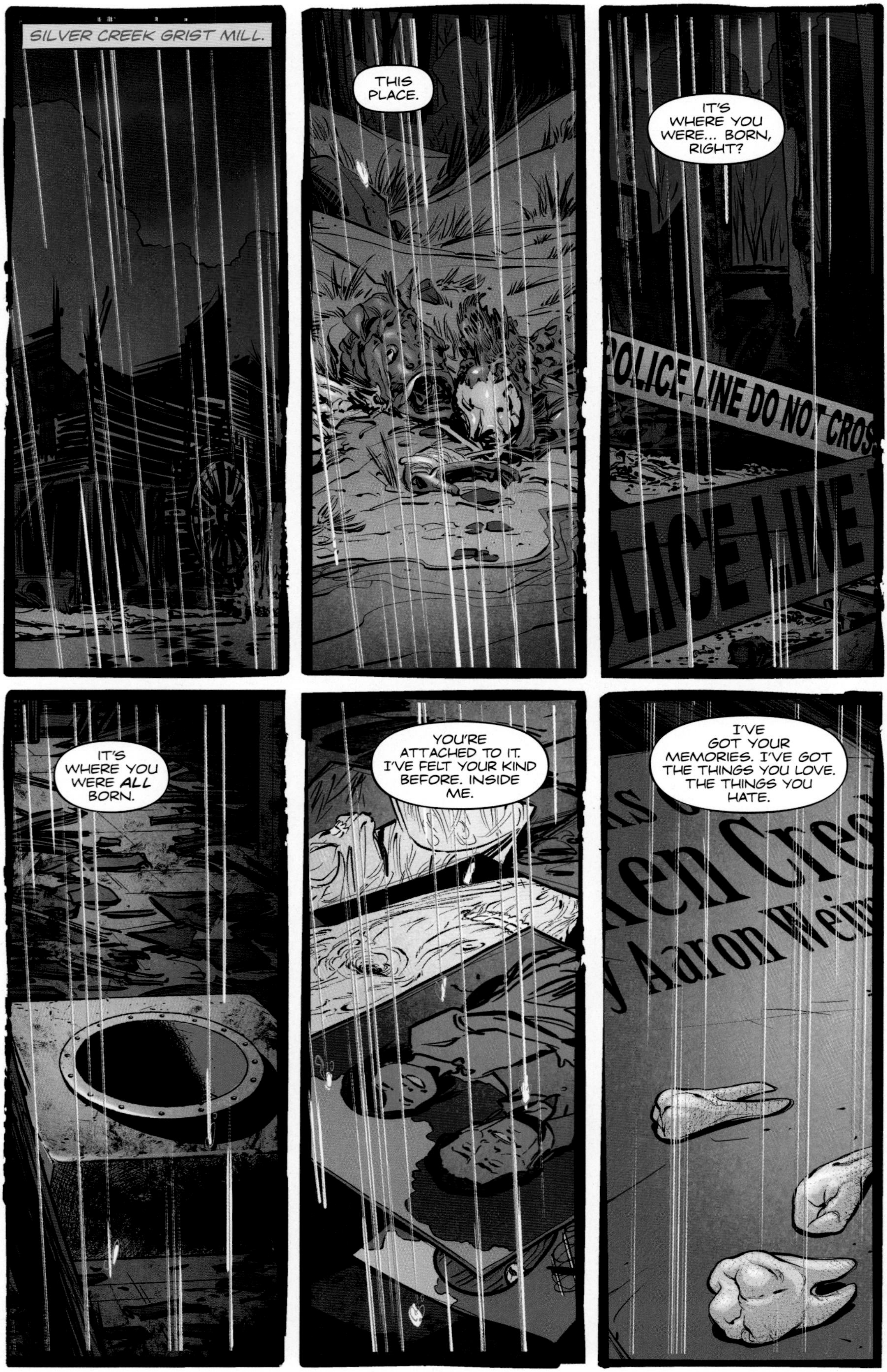
SILVER CREEK GRIST MILL.
THIS PLACE.
IT'S WHERE YOU WERE... BORN, RIGHT?
POLICE LINE DO NOT CROS
POLICE LINE
IT'S WHERE YOU WERE ALL BORN.
YOU'RE ATTACHED TO IT. I'VE FELT YOUR KIND BEFORE. INSIDE ME.
I'VE GOT YOUR MEMORIES. I'VE GOT THE THINGS YOU LOVE. THE THINGS YOU HATE.

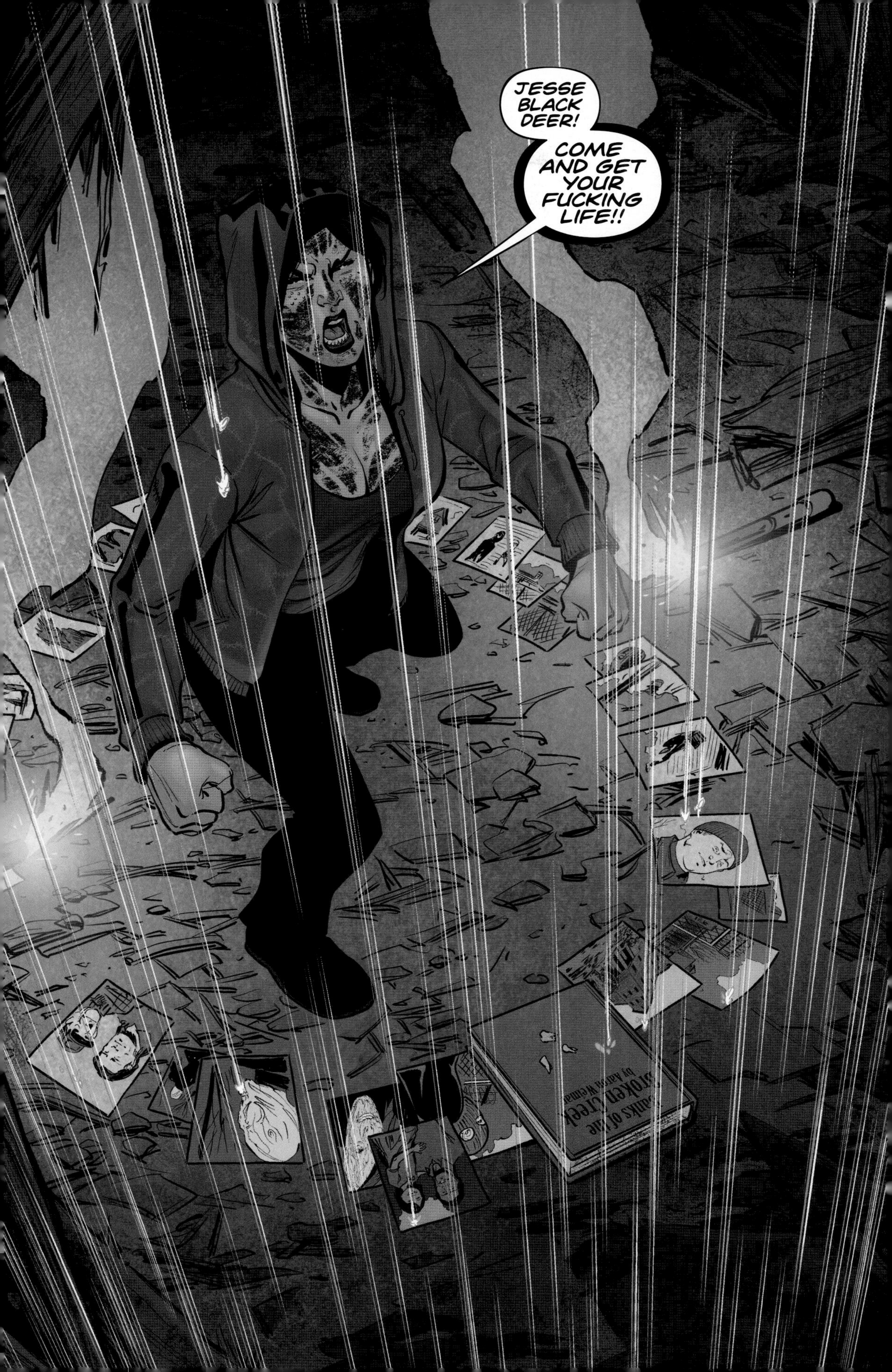
JESSE BLACK DEER!
COME AND GET YOUR FUCKING LIFE!!

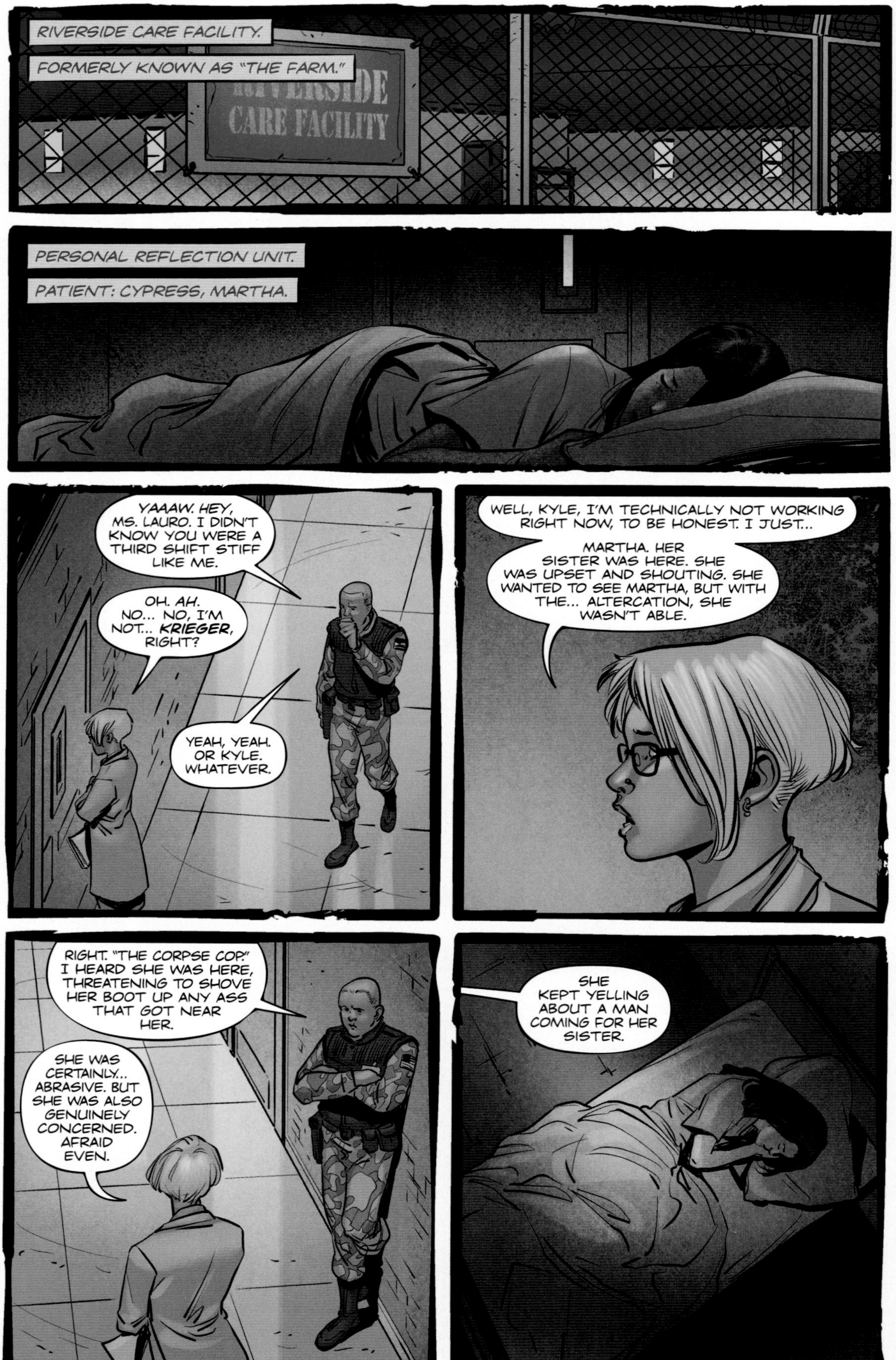
RIVERSIDE CARE FACILITY.
FORMERLY KNOWN AS "THE FARM."
RIVERSIDE CARE FACILITY
PERSONAL REFLECTION UNIT.
PATIENT: CYPRESS, MARTHA.
YAAAW. HEY, MS. LAURO. I DIDN'T KNOW YOU WERE A THIRD SHIFT STIFF LIKE ME.
OH. AH. NO... NO, I'M NOT... KRIEGER, RIGHT?
YEAH, YEAH. OR KYLE. WHATEVER.
WELL, KYLE, I'M TECHNICALLY NOT WORKING RIGHT NOW, TO BE HONEST. I JUST...
MARTHA. HER SISTER WAS HERE. SHE WAS UPSET AND SHOUTING. SHE WANTED TO SEE MARTHA, BUT WITH THE... ALTERCATION, SHE WASN'T ABLE.
RIGHT. "THE CORPSE COP." I HEARD SHE WAS HERE, THREATENING TO SHOVE HER BOOT UP ANY ASS THAT GOT NEAR HER.
SHE WAS CERTAINLY... ABRASIVE. BUT SHE WAS ALSO GENUINELY CONCERNED. AFRAID EVEN.
SHE KEPT YELLING ABOUT A MAN COMING FOR HER SISTER.

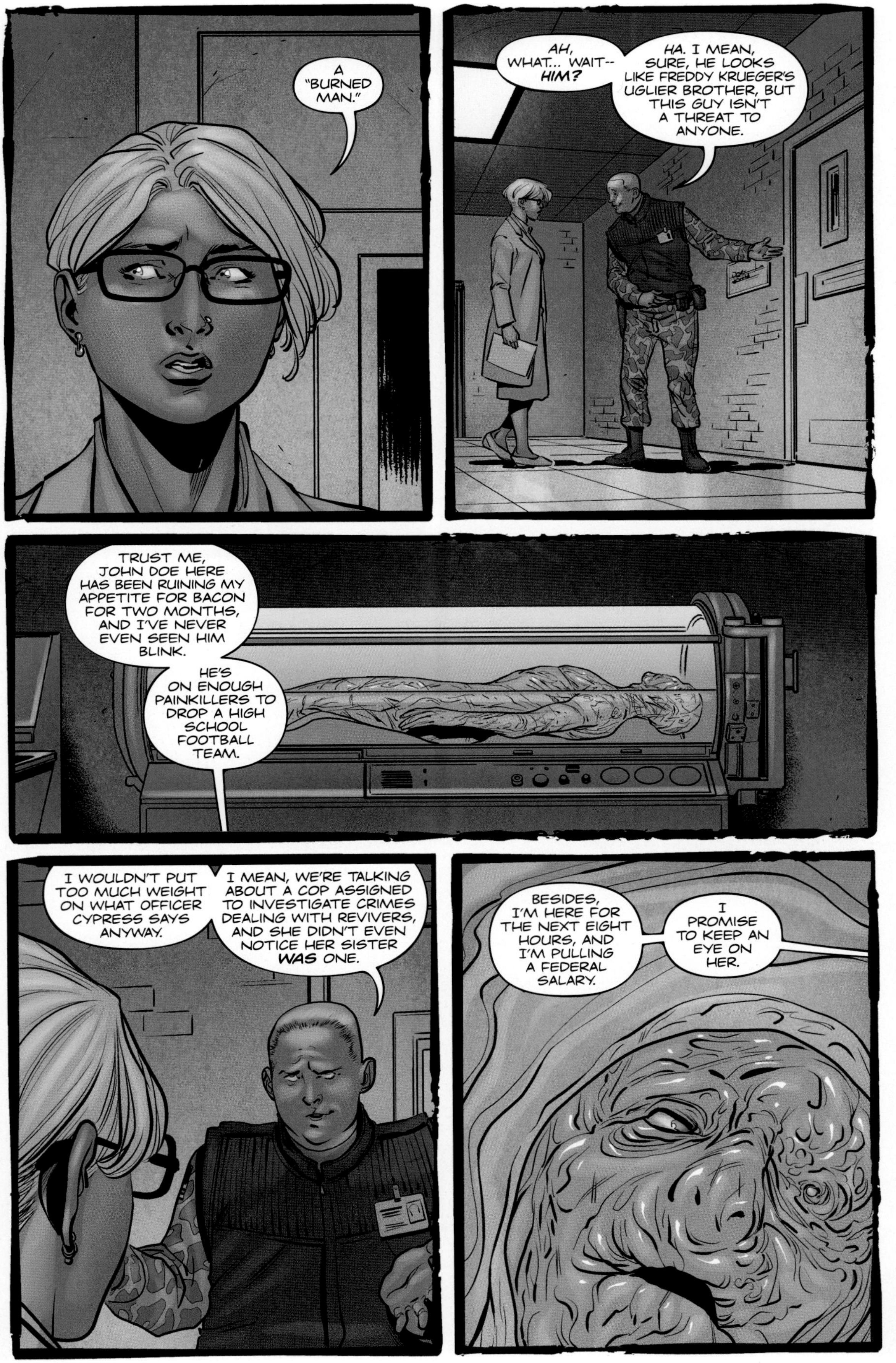
A "BURNED MAN."
AH, WHAT... WAIT-- HIM?
HA. I MEAN, SURE, HE LOOKS LIKE FREDDY KRUEGER'S UGLIER BROTHER, BUT THIS GUY ISN'T A THREAT TO ANYONE.
TRUST ME, JOHN DOE HERE HAS BEEN RUINING MY APPETITE FOR BACON FOR TWO MONTHS, AND I'VE NEVER EVEN SEEN HIM BLINK.
HE'S ON ENOUGH PAINKILLERS TO DROP A HIGH SCHOOL FOOTBALL TEAM.
I WOULDN'T PUT TOO MUCH WEIGHT ON WHAT OFFICER CYPRESS SAYS ANYWAY.
I MEAN, WE'RE TALKING ABOUT A COP ASSIGNED TO INVESTIGATE CRIMES DEALING WITH REVIVERS, AND SHE DIDN'T EVEN NOTICE HER SISTER WAS ONE.
BESIDES, I'M HERE FOR THE NEXT EIGHT HOURS, AND I'M PULLING A FEDERAL SALARY.
I PROMISE TO KEEP AN EYE ON HER.

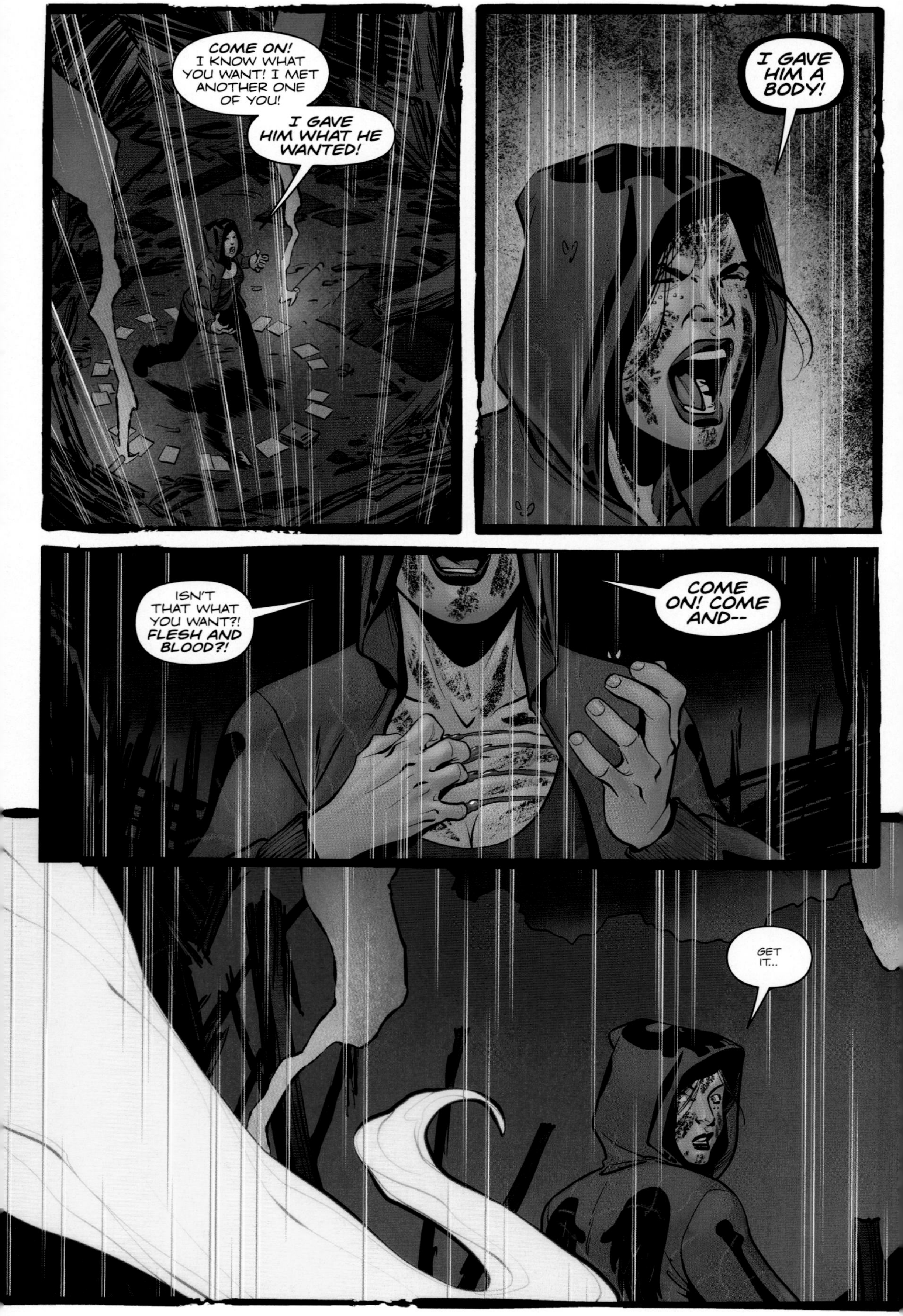
COME ON! I KNOW WHAT YOU WANT! I MET ANOTHER ONE OF YOU!
I GAVE HIM WHAT HE WANTED!
I GAVE HIM A BODY!
ISN'T THAT WHAT YOU WANT?! FLESH AND BLOOD?!
COME ON! COME AND--
GET IT...

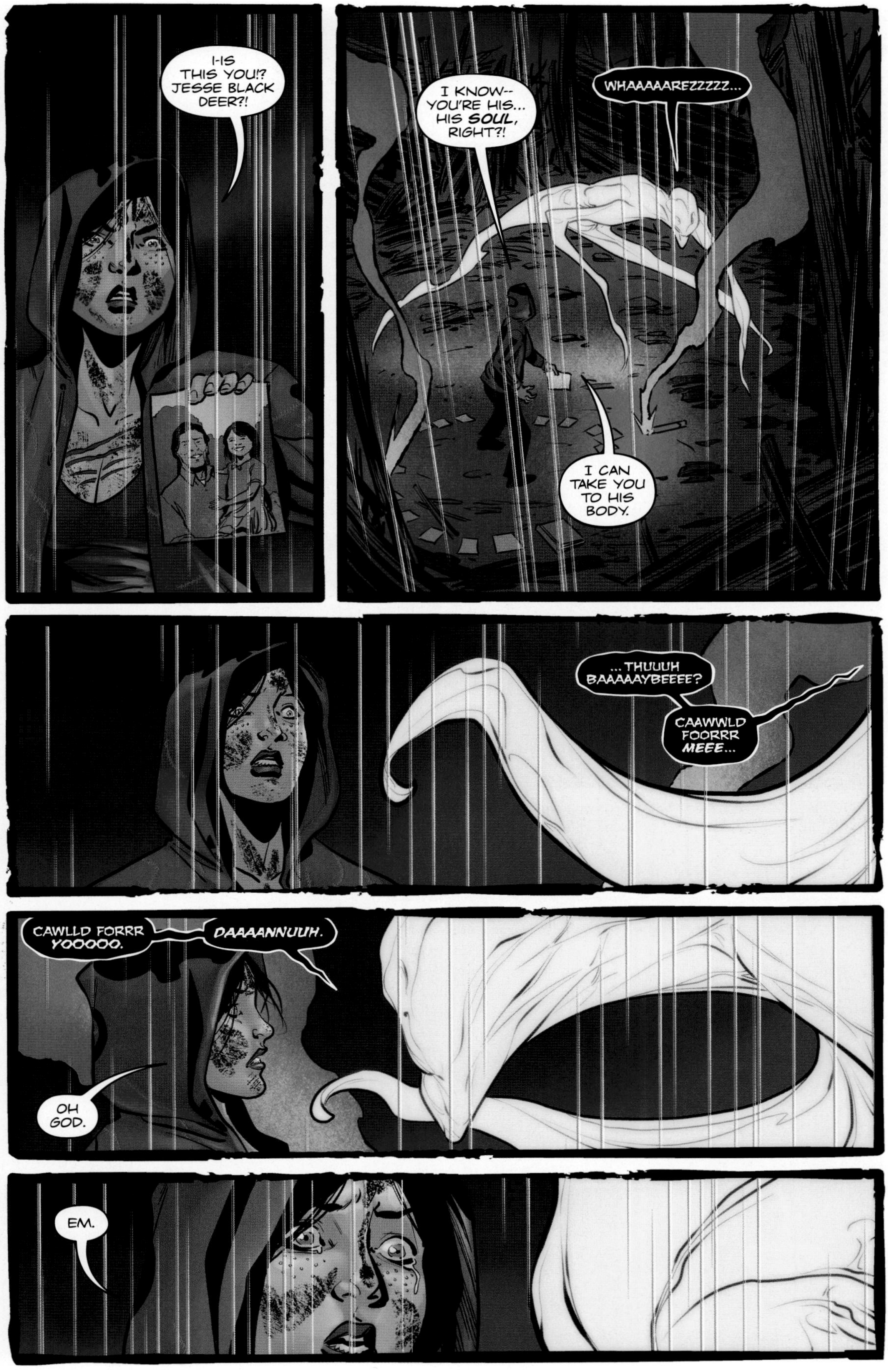
I-IS THIS YOU!? JESSE BLACK DEER?!
I KNOW-- YOU'RE HIS... HIS SOUL, RIGHT?!
WHAAAAAREZZZZZ...
I CAN TAKE YOU TO HIS BODY.
...THUUUH BAAAAAYBEEEE?
CAAWWLD FOORRR MEEE...
CAWLLD FORRR YOOOOO.
DAAAANNUUH.
OH GOD.
EM.

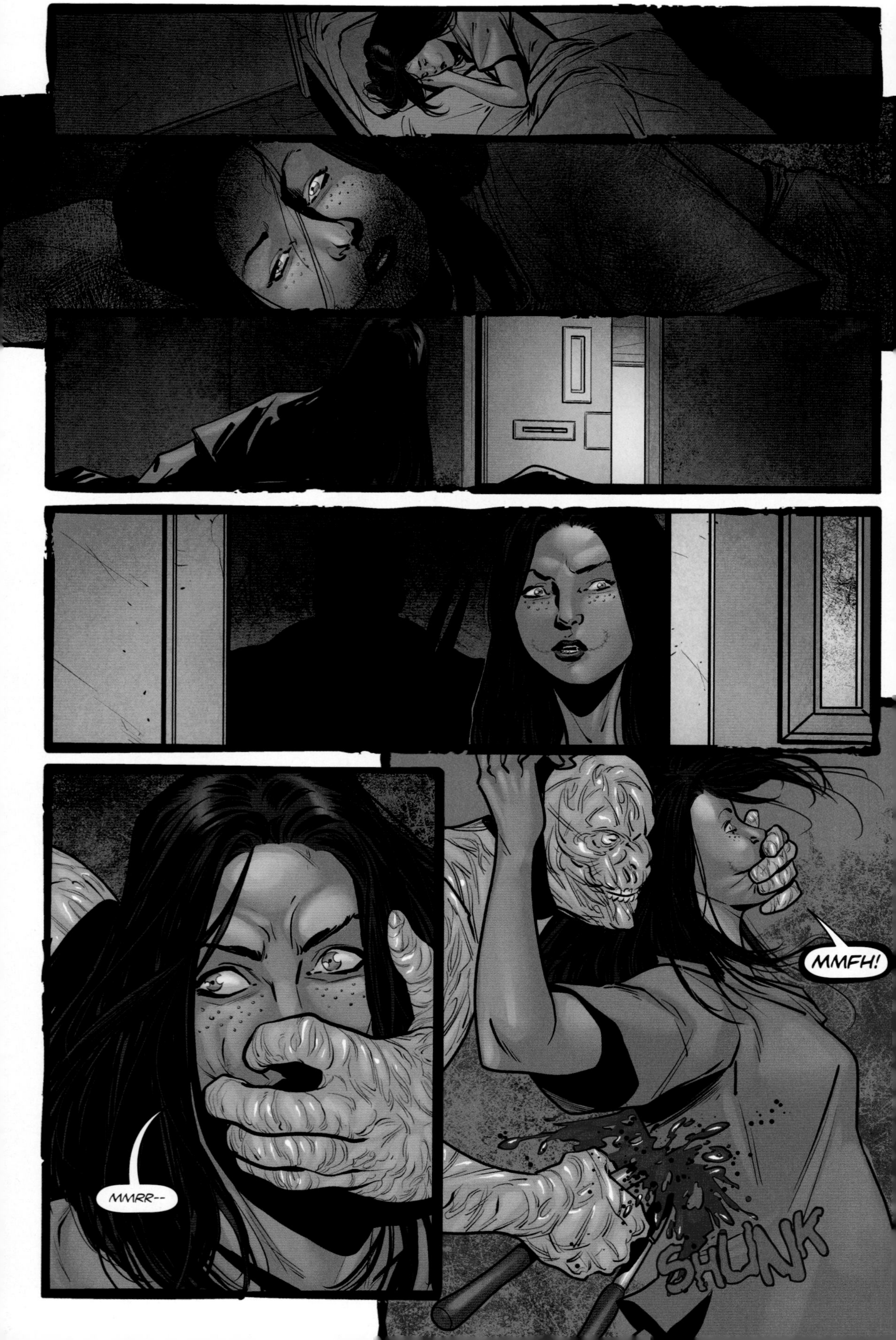
MMFH!
MMRR--
SHUNK

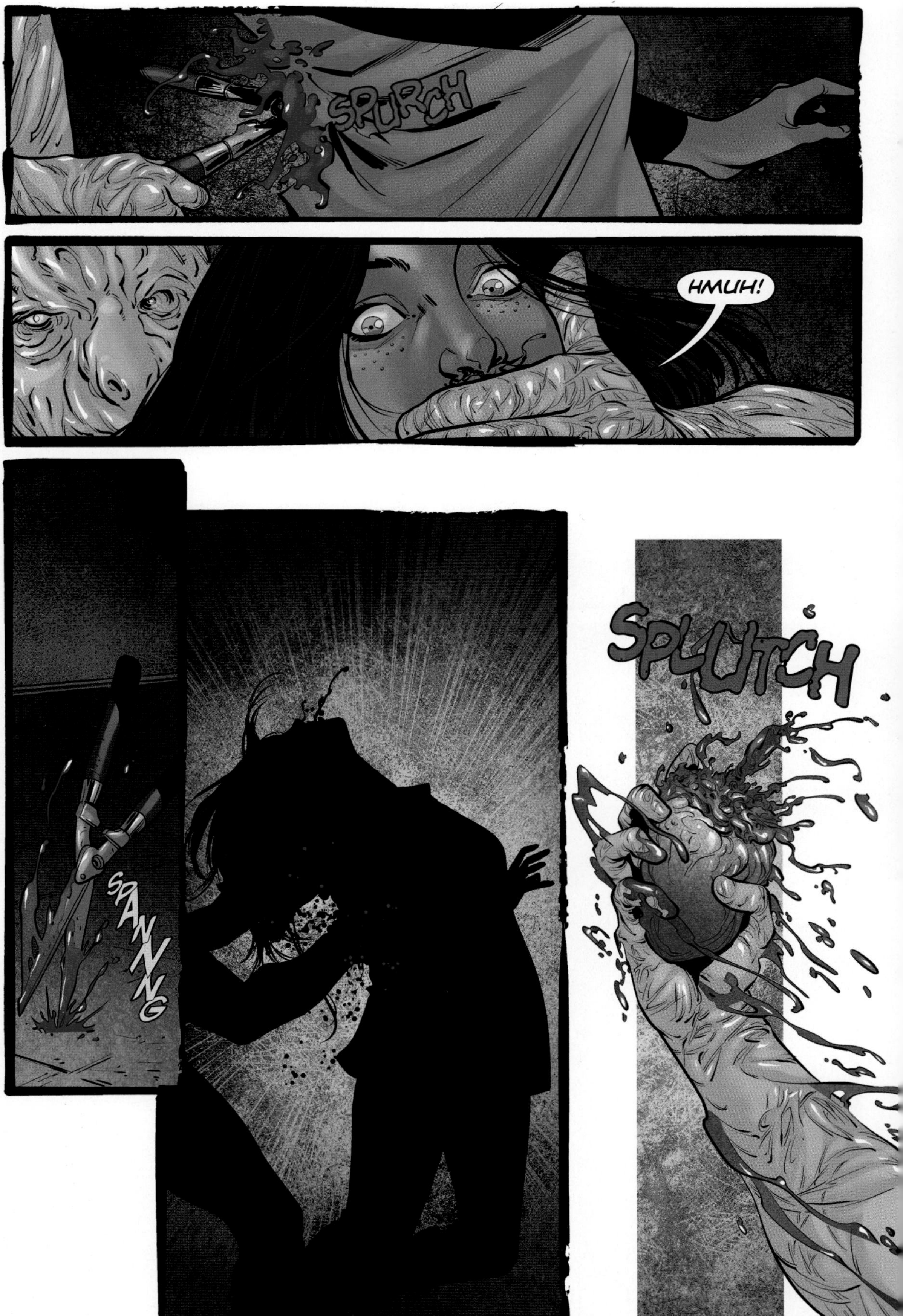
SPURCH
HMUH!
SPANNNG
SPLUTCH

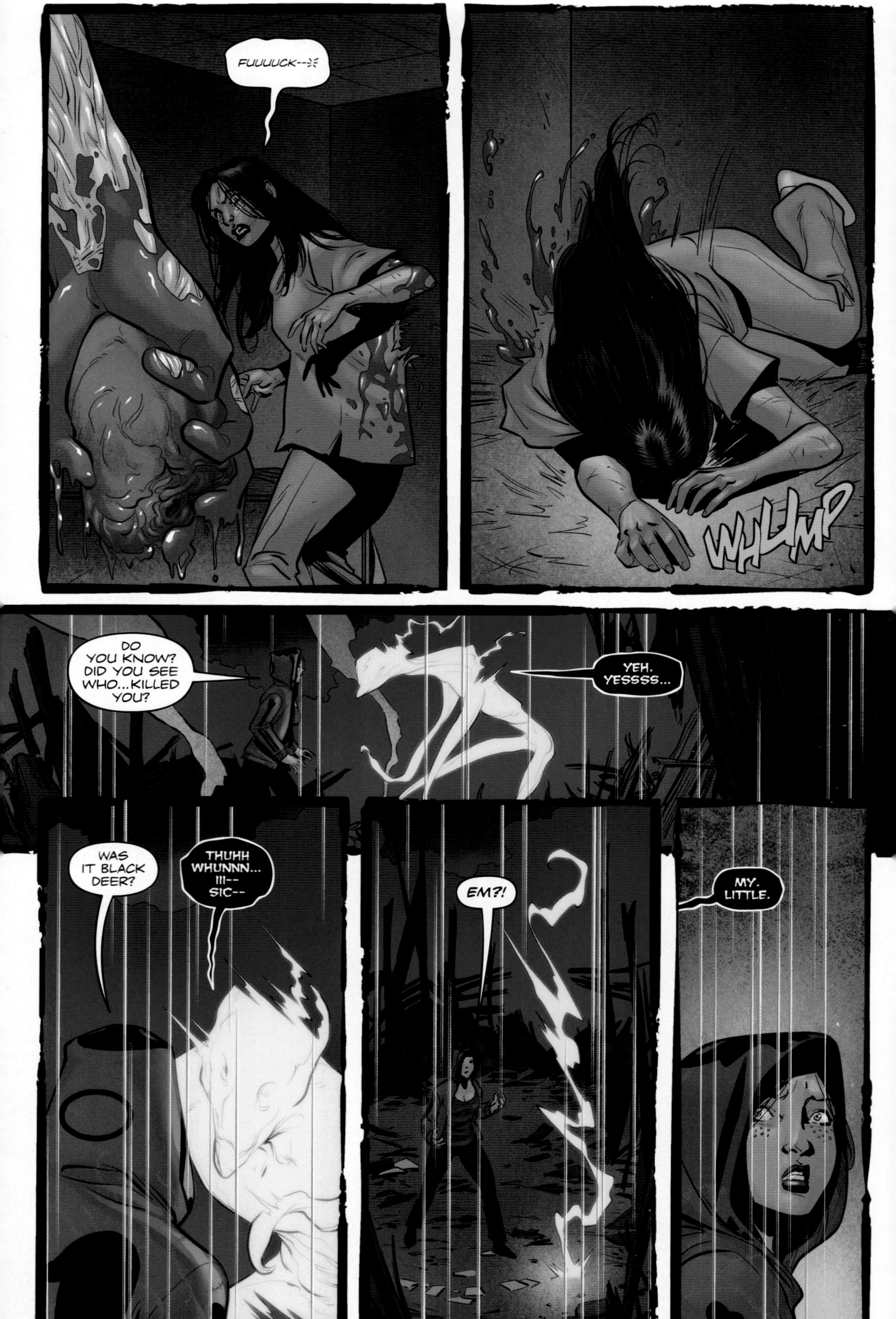
FUUUUCK--
WHUMP
DO YOU KNOW? DID YOU SEE WHO...KILLED YOU?
YEH. YESSSS...
WAS IT BLACK DEER?
THUHH WHUNNN... III-- SIC--
EM?!
MY. LITTLE.

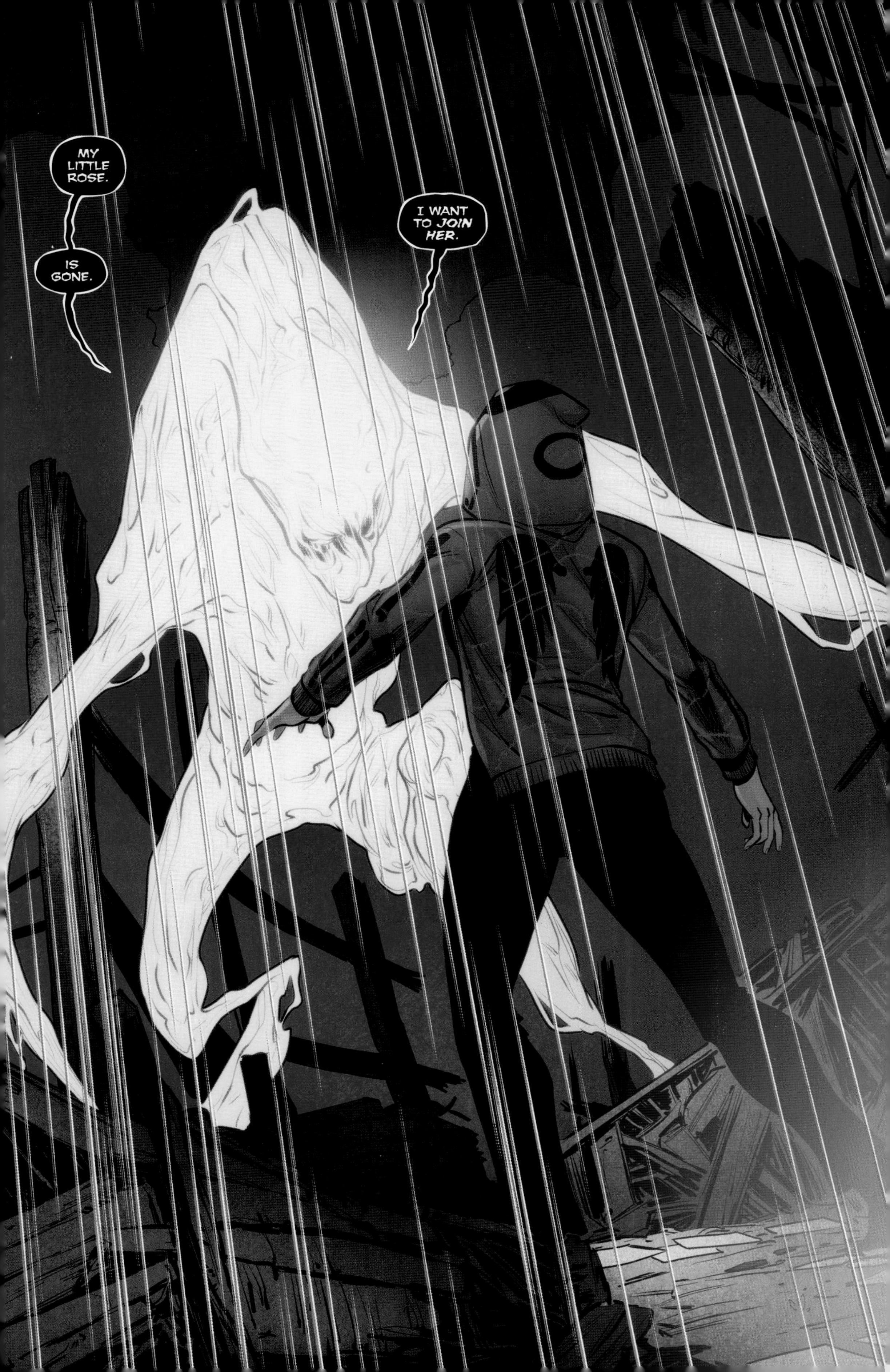
MY LITTLE ROSE.
IS GONE.
I WANT TO *JOIN* *HER*.

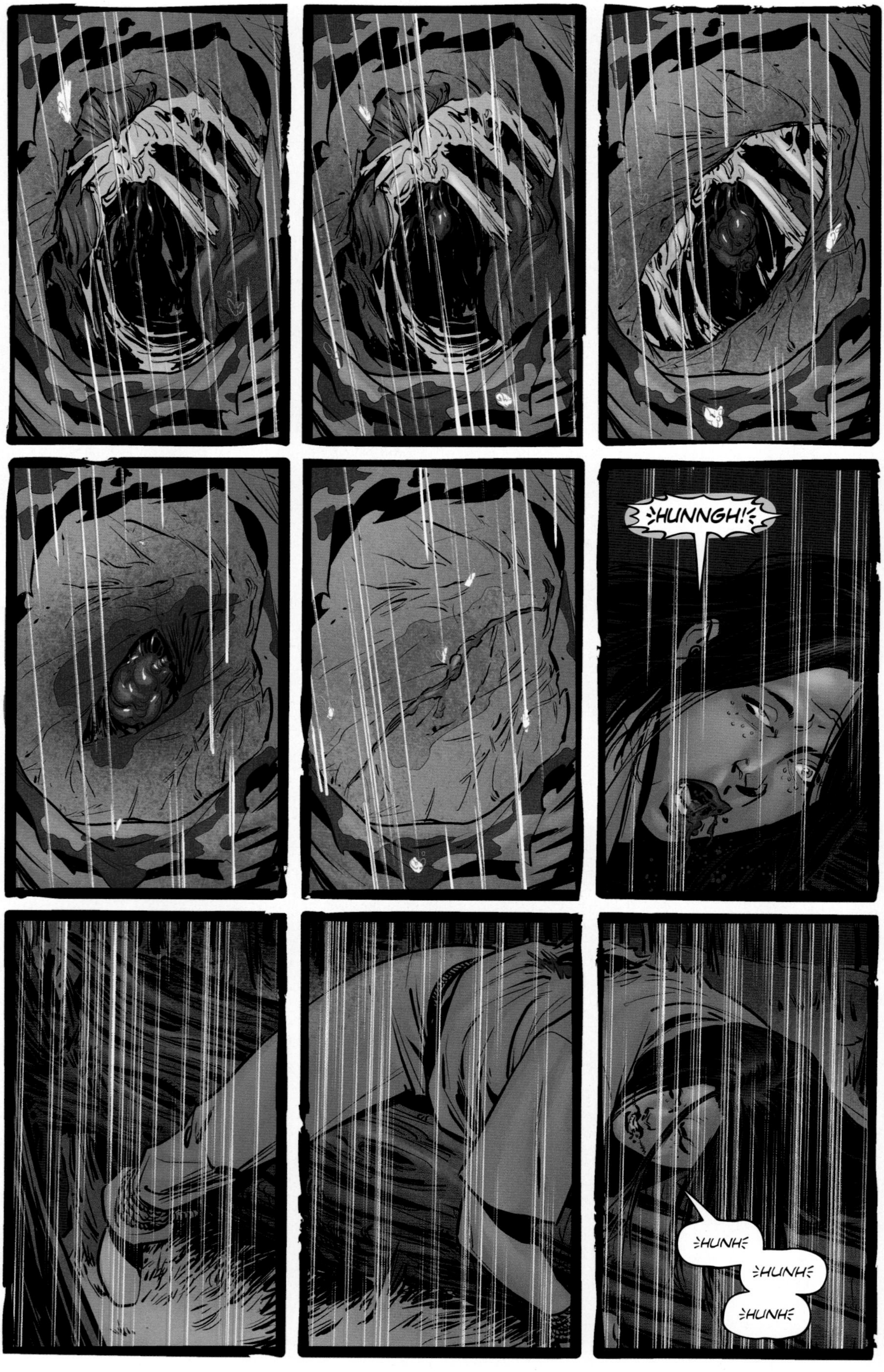
HUNNGH!
HUNH
HUNH
HUNH

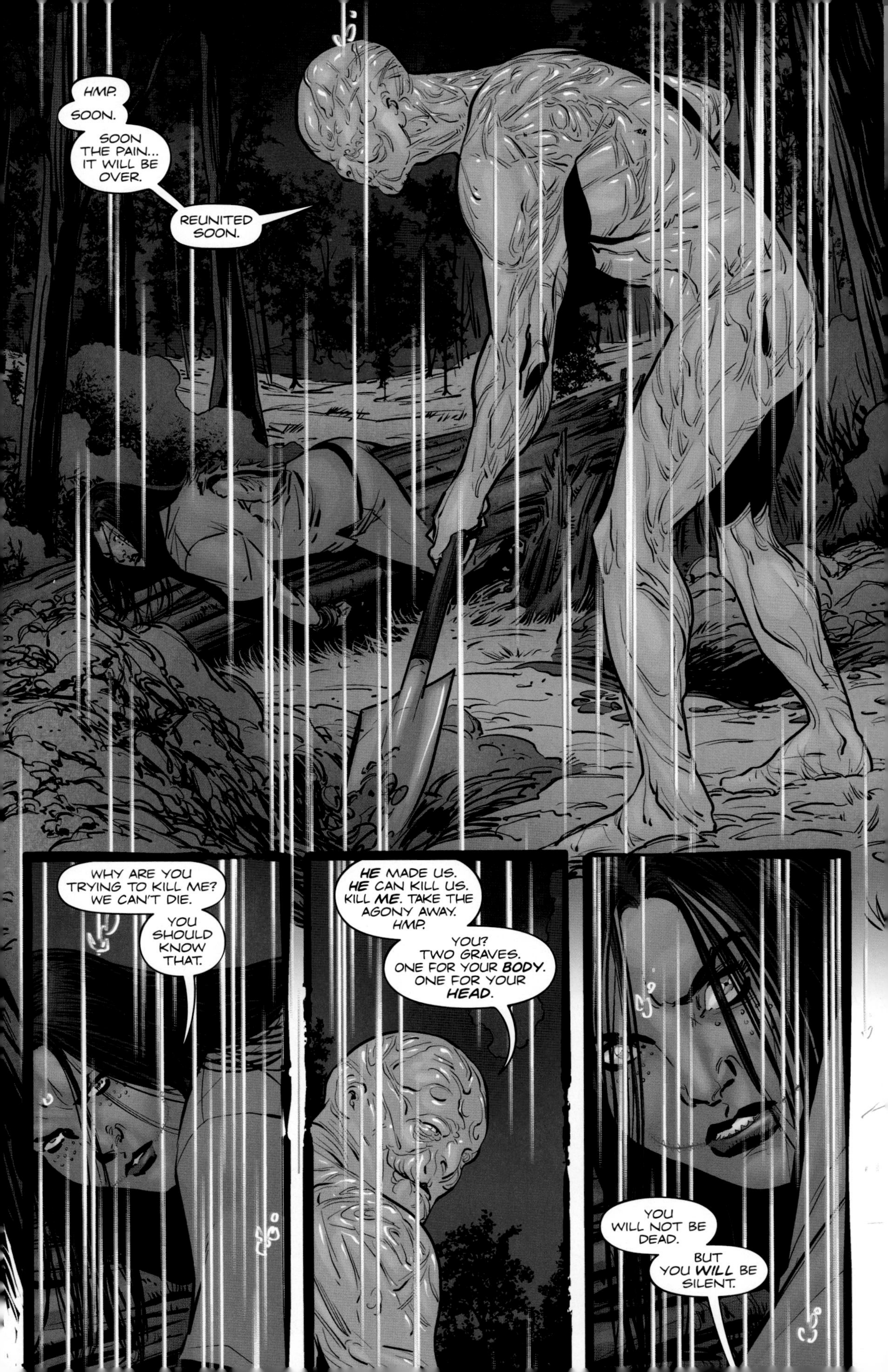
HMP.
SOON.
SOON THE PAIN... IT WILL BE OVER.
REUNITED SOON.
WHY ARE YOU TRYING TO KILL ME? WE CAN'T DIE.
YOU SHOULD KNOW THAT.
HE MADE US. HE CAN KILL US. KILL ME. TAKE THE AGONY AWAY. HMP.
YOU? TWO GRAVES. ONE FOR YOUR BODY. ONE FOR YOUR HEAD.
YOU WILL NOT BE DEAD.
BUT YOU WILL BE SILENT.

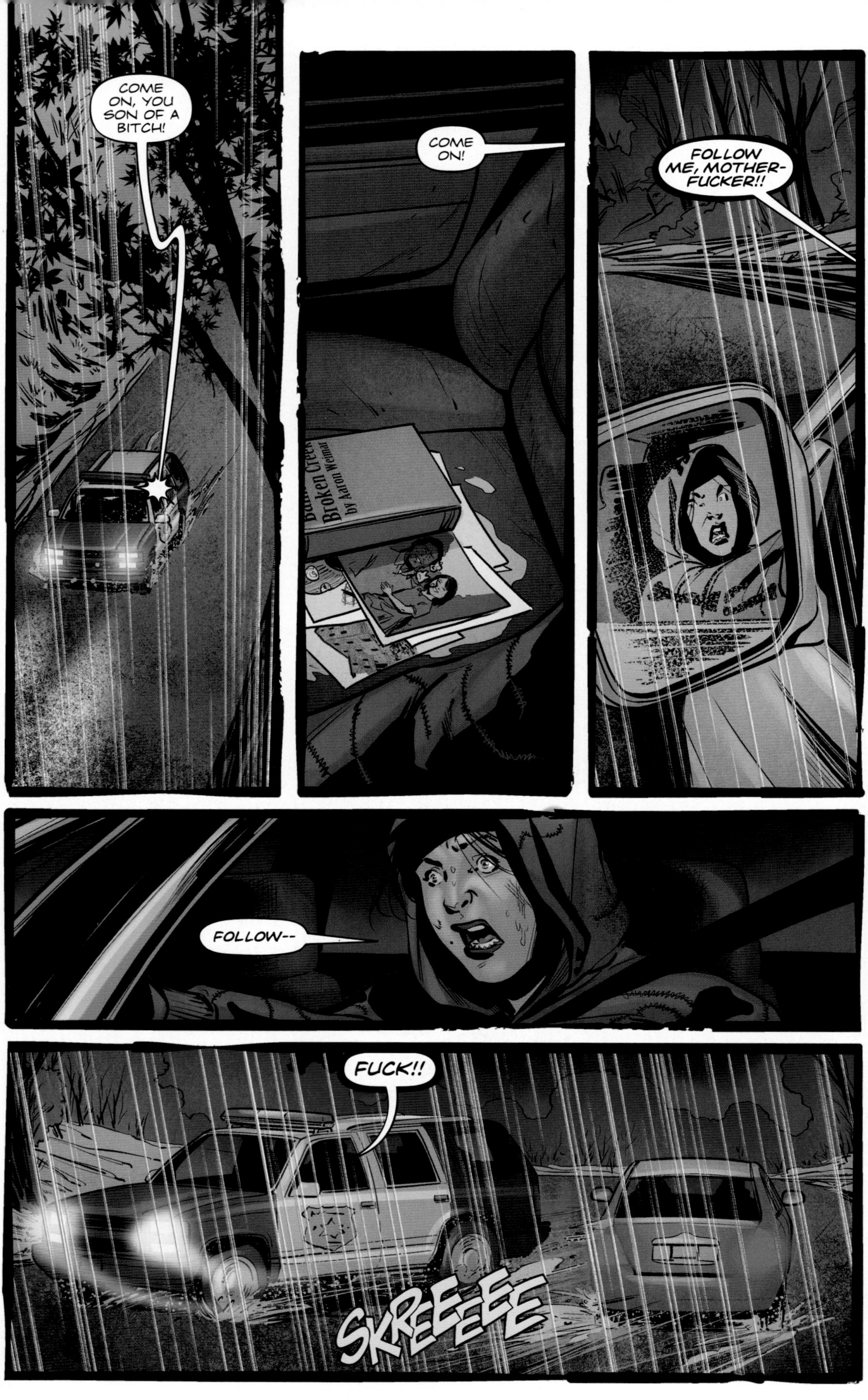
COME ON, YOU SON OF A BITCH!
COME ON!
Broken Creek
by Aaron Weimar
FOLLOW ME, MOTHER-FUCKER!!
FOLLOW--
FUCK!!
SKREEEEEE

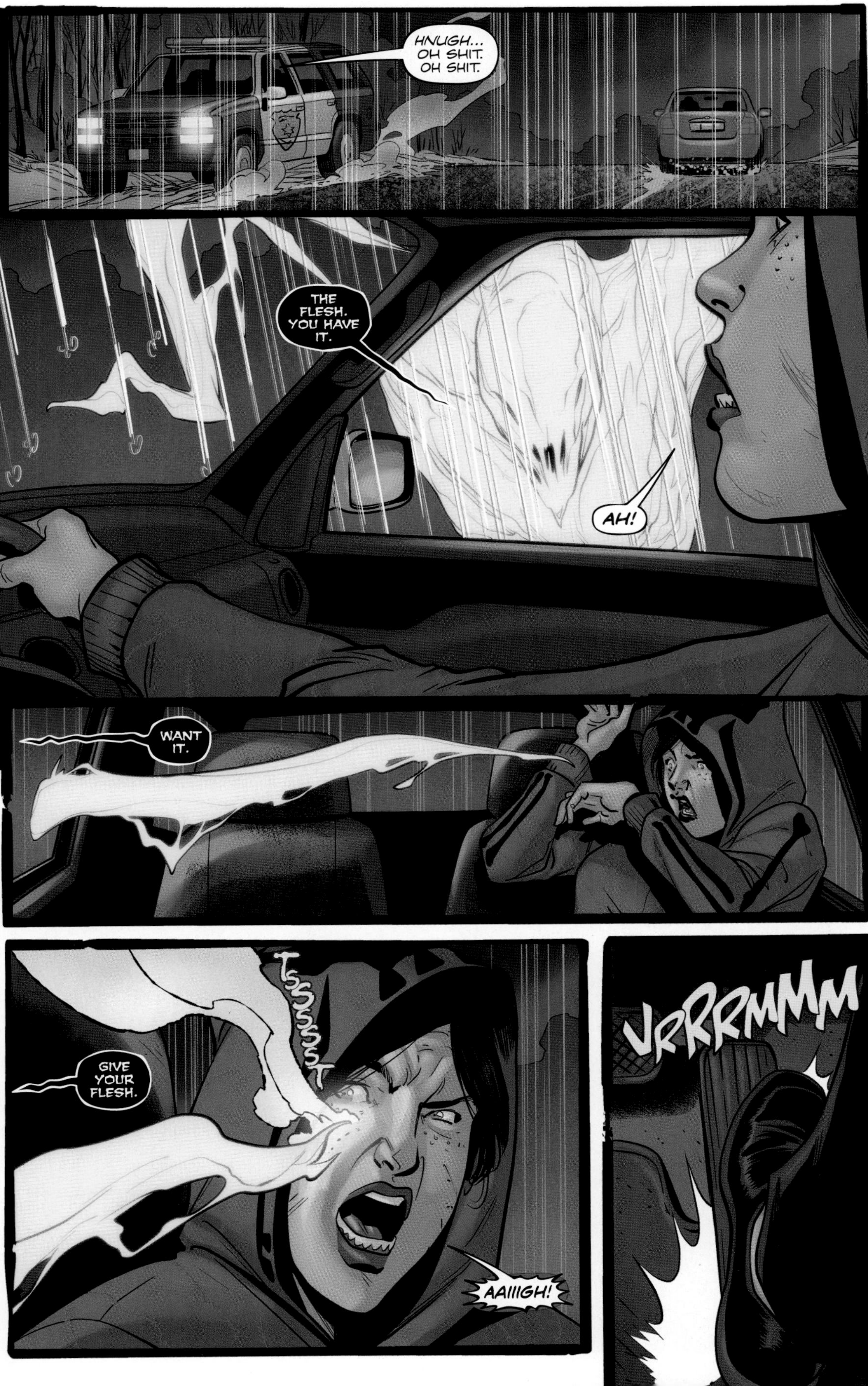
HNUGH... OH SHIT. OH SHIT.
THE FLESH. YOU HAVE IT.
AH!
WANT IT.
GIVE YOUR FLESH.
TSSSSST
AAIIIGH!
VRRRMMM

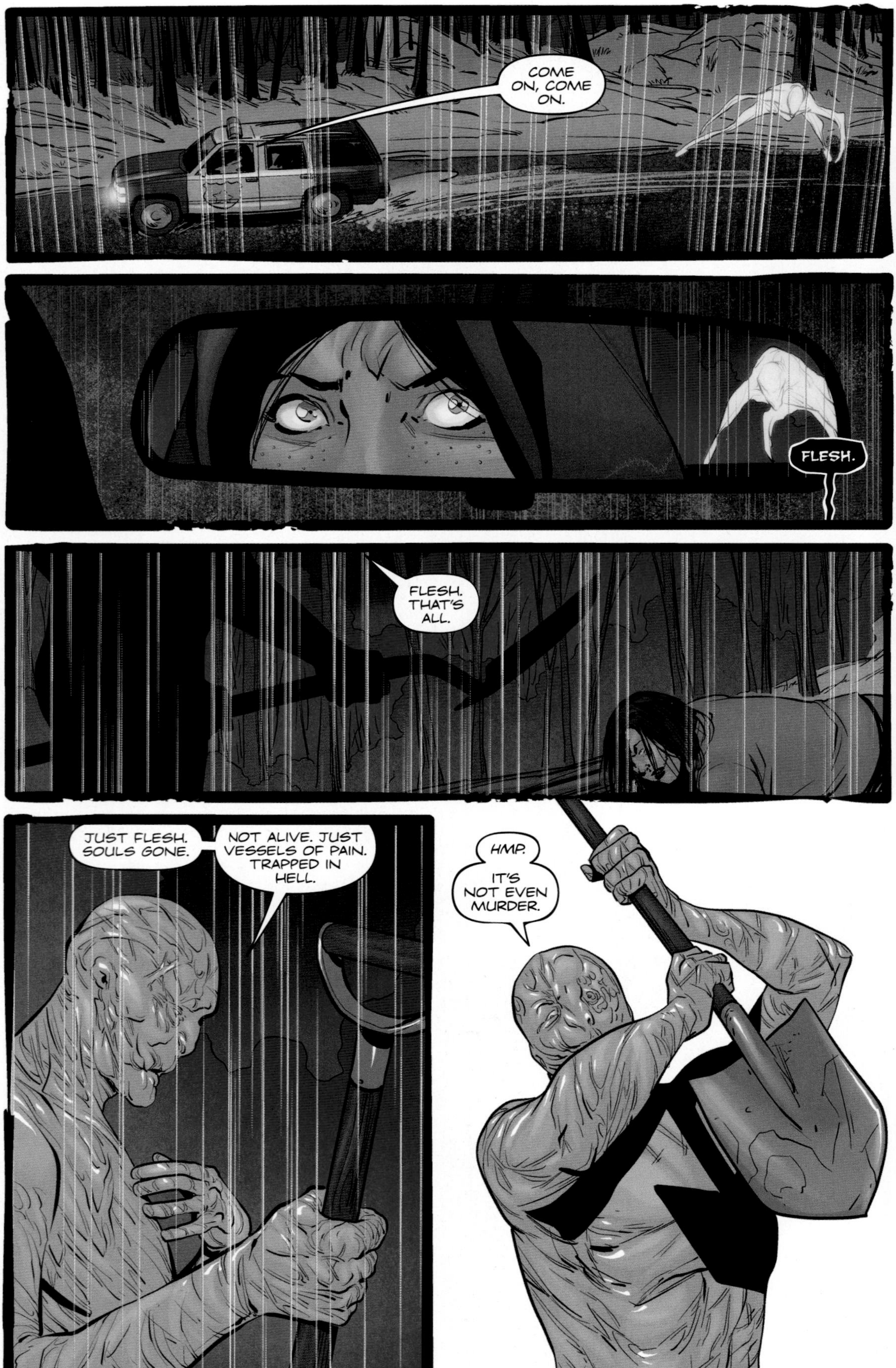
COME ON, COME ON.
FLESH.
FLESH. THAT'S ALL.
JUST FLESH. SOULS GONE.
NOT ALIVE. JUST VESSELS OF PAIN. TRAPPED IN HELL.
HMP.
IT'S NOT EVEN MURDER.

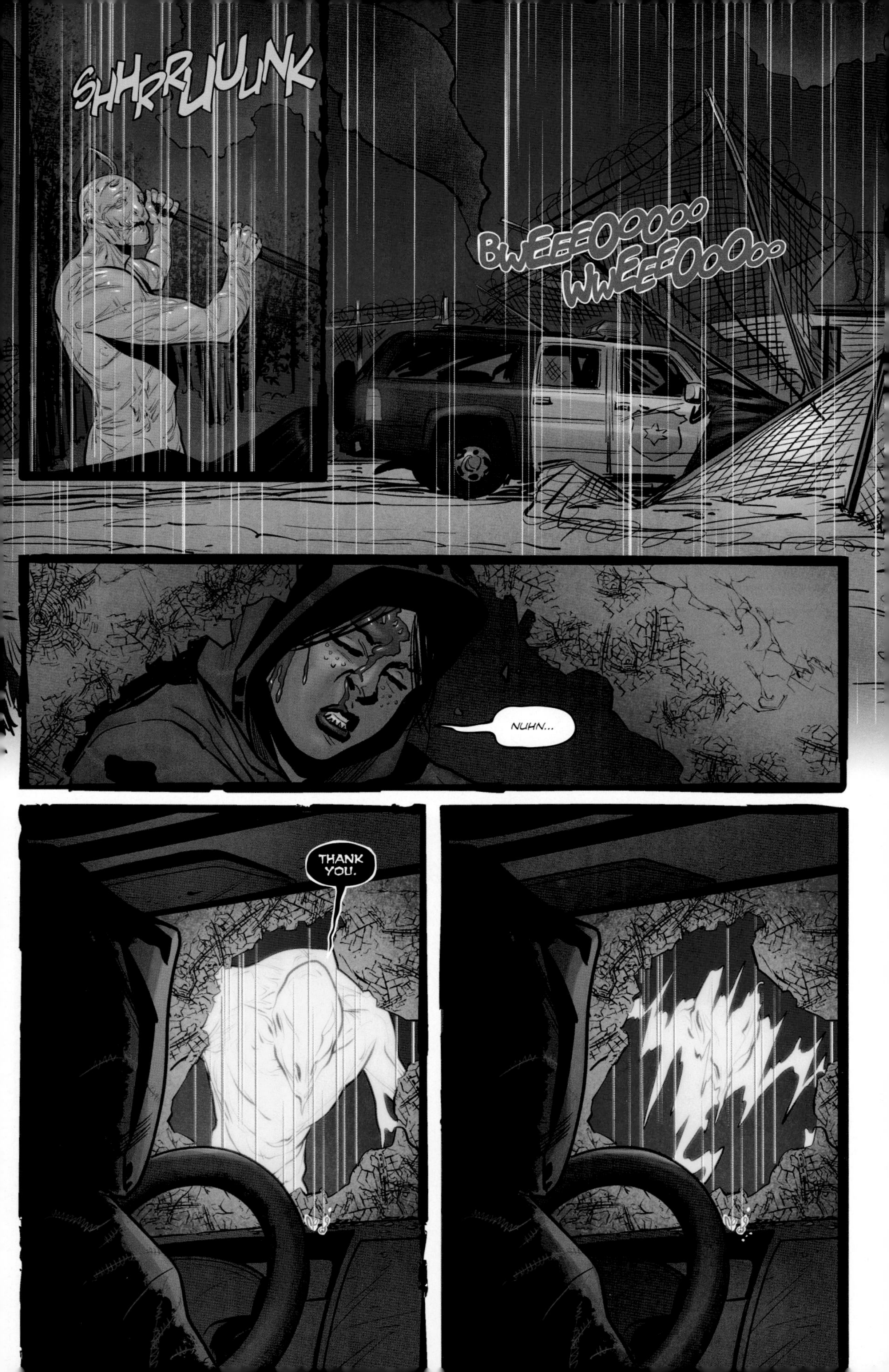
SHHRRUUUNK
BWEEEOOOOOO
WWEEEOOOoo
NUHN...
THANK YOU.

THANK YOU.

FLESH.

SOUL.

NO MORE HELL. NO MORE HELL.

EM. MARTHA.

I WAS TO KILL YOU. ONCE BEFORE.

I COULD NOT.

YOU REMINDED ME TOO MUCH OF MY ROSE.

EXCUSE ME. I... MUST SIT.

WHO... WHO KILLED ME?

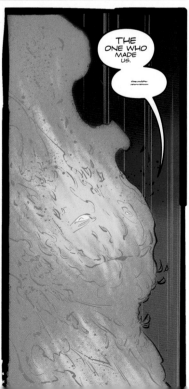

THE ONE WHO MADE US.

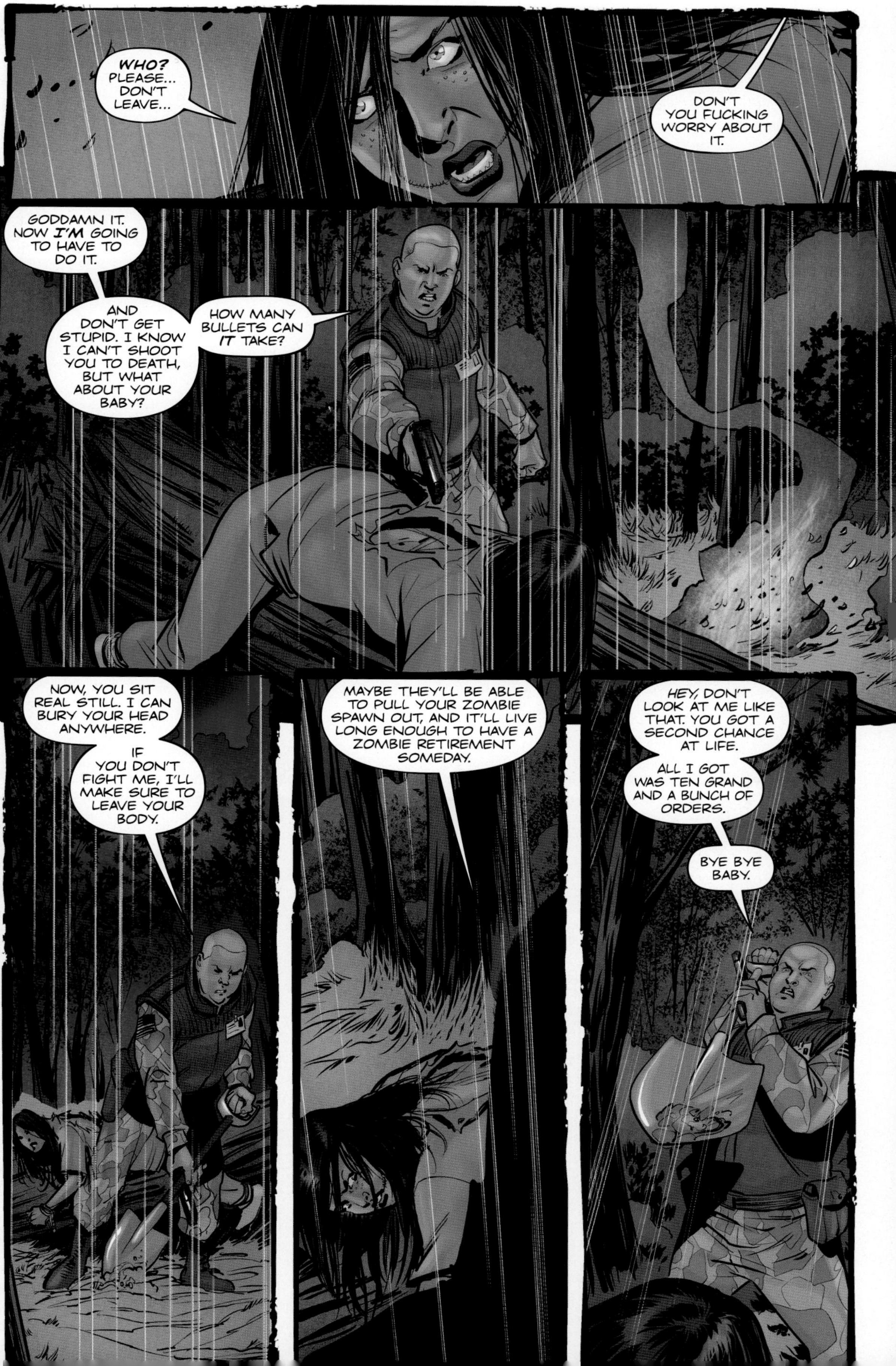
WHO? PLEASE... DON'T LEAVE...
DON'T YOU FUCKING WORRY ABOUT IT.
GODDAMN IT. NOW I'M GOING TO HAVE TO DO IT.
AND DON'T GET STUPID. I KNOW I CAN'T SHOOT YOU TO DEATH, BUT WHAT ABOUT YOUR BABY?
HOW MANY BULLETS CAN IT TAKE?
NOW, YOU SIT REAL STILL. I CAN BURY YOUR HEAD ANYWHERE.
IF YOU DON'T FIGHT ME, I'LL MAKE SURE TO LEAVE YOUR BODY.
MAYBE THEY'LL BE ABLE TO PULL YOUR ZOMBIE SPAWN OUT, AND IT'LL LIVE LONG ENOUGH TO HAVE A ZOMBIE RETIREMENT SOMEDAY.
HEY, DON'T LOOK AT ME LIKE THAT. YOU GOT A SECOND CHANCE AT LIFE.
ALL I GOT WAS TEN GRAND AND A BUNCH OF ORDERS.
BYE BYE BABY.

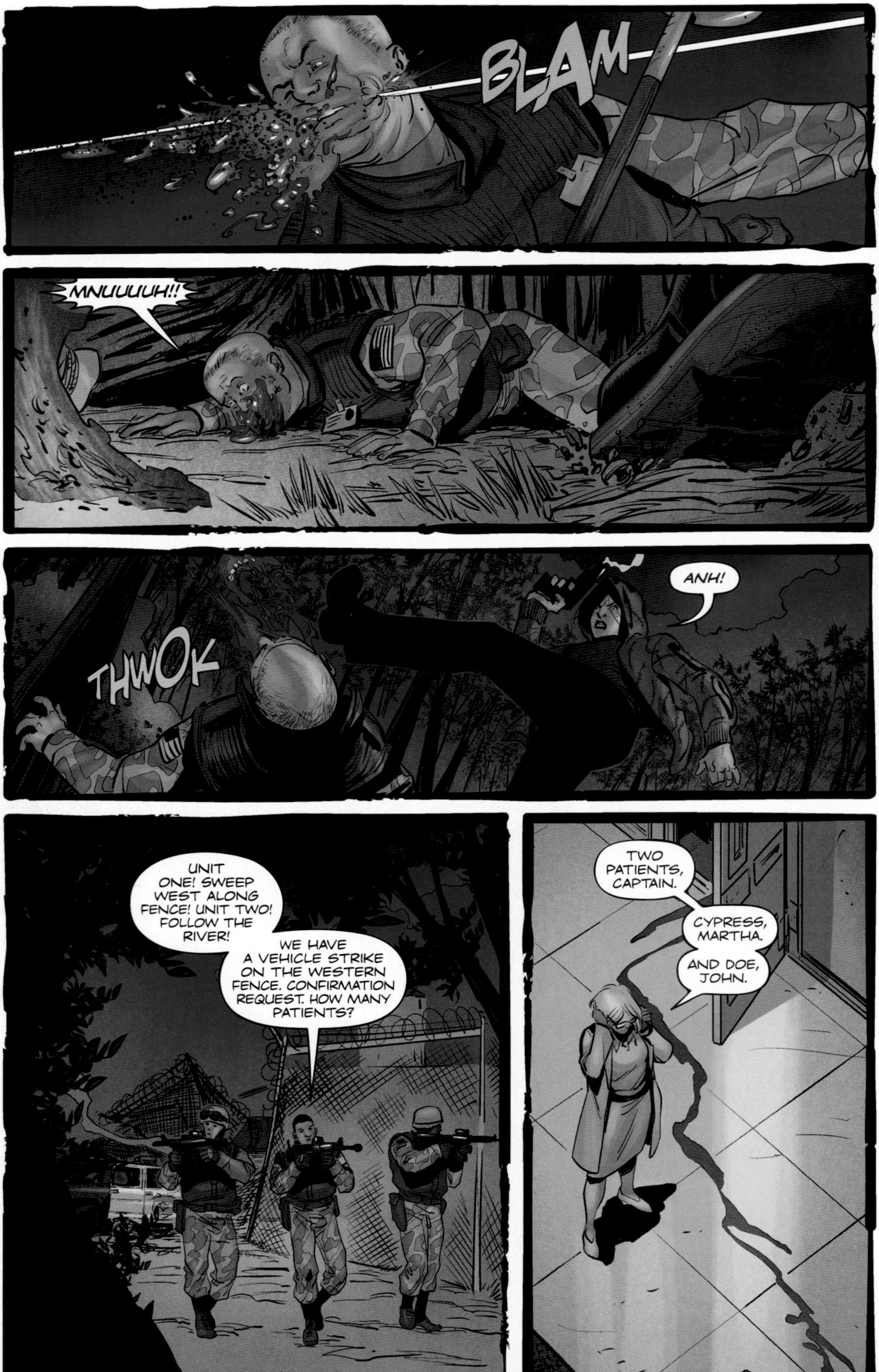
BLAM
MNUUUUH!!
THWOK
ANH!
UNIT ONE! SWEEP WEST ALONG FENCE! UNIT TWO! FOLLOW THE RIVER!
WE HAVE A VEHICLE STRIKE ON THE WESTERN FENCE. CONFIRMATION REQUEST. HOW MANY PATIENTS?
TWO PATIENTS, CAPTAIN.
CYPRESS, MARTHA.
AND DOE, JOHN.

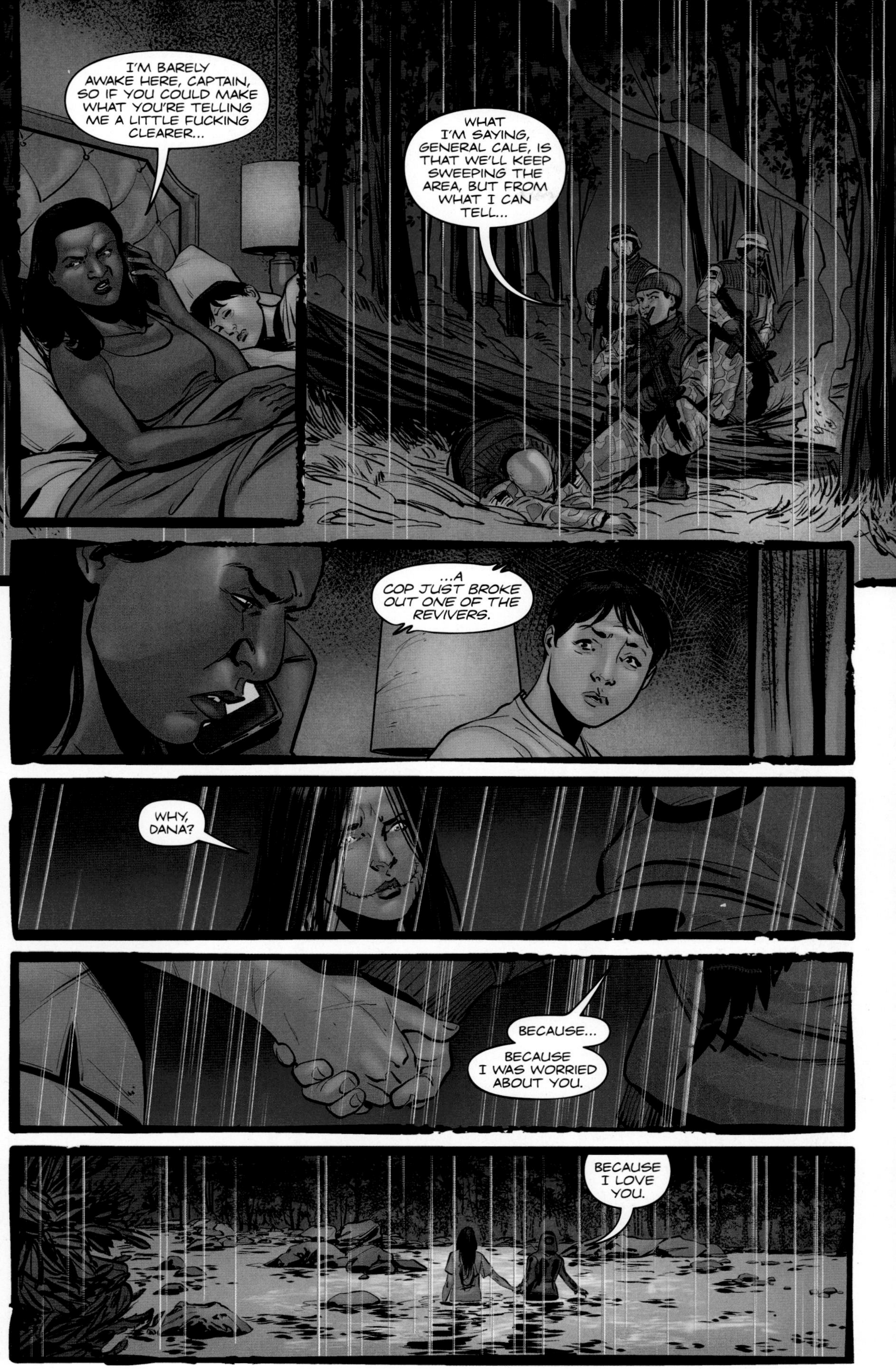
I'M BARELY AWAKE HERE, CAPTAIN, SO IF YOU COULD MAKE WHAT YOU'RE TELLING ME A LITTLE FUCKING CLEARER...
WHAT I'M SAYING, GENERAL CALE, IS THAT WE'LL KEEP SWEEPING THE AREA, BUT FROM WHAT I CAN TELL...
...A COP JUST BROKE OUT ONE OF THE REVIVERS.
WHY, DANA?
BECAUSE...
BECAUSE I WAS WORRIED ABOUT YOU.
BECAUSE I LOVE YOU.

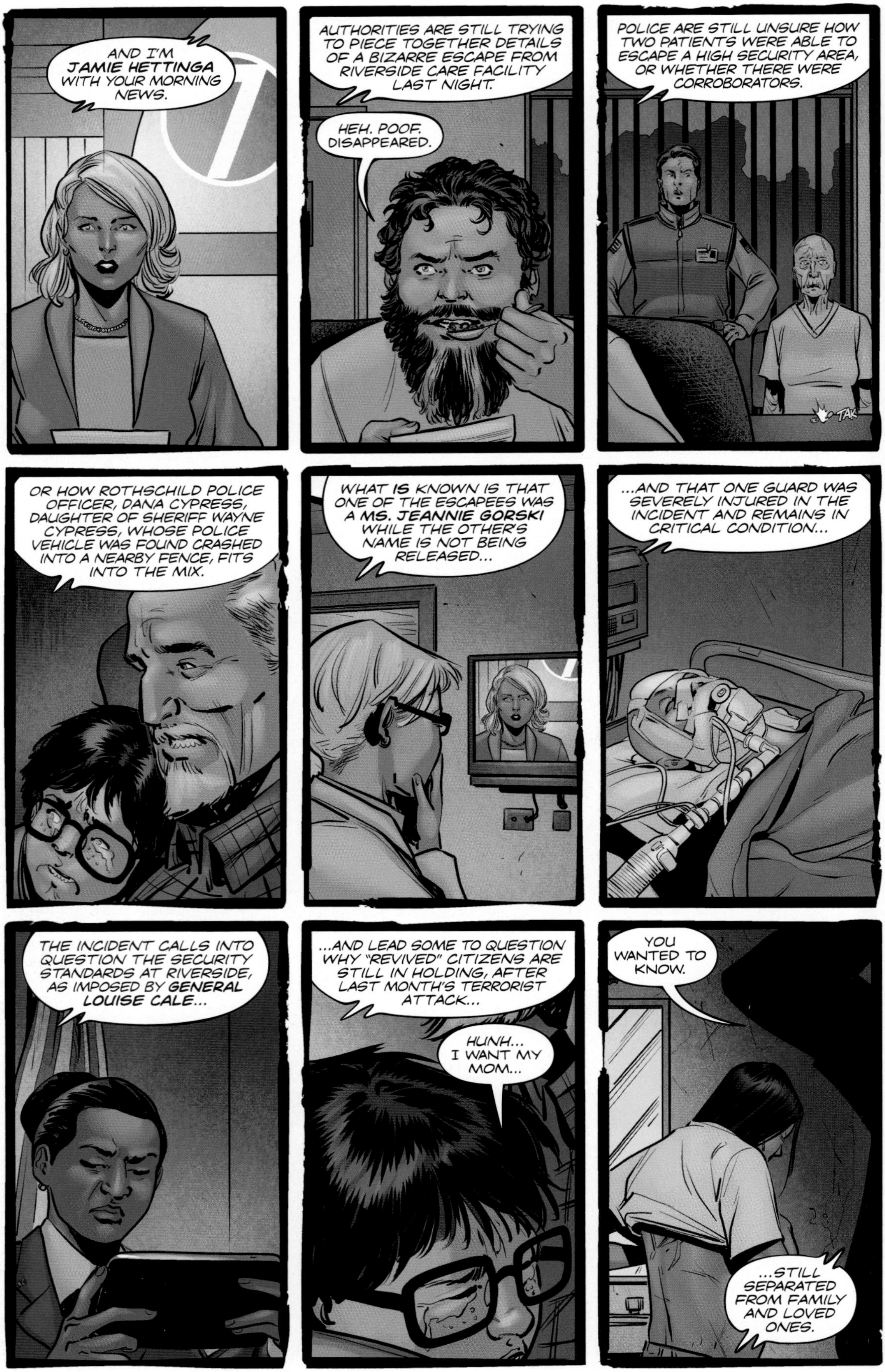
AND I'M JAMIE HETTINGA WITH YOUR MORNING NEWS.
AUTHORITIES ARE STILL TRYING TO PIECE TOGETHER DETAILS OF A BIZARRE ESCAPE FROM RIVERSIDE CARE FACILITY LAST NIGHT.
HEH. POOF. DISAPPEARED.
POLICE ARE STILL UNSURE HOW TWO PATIENTS WERE ABLE TO ESCAPE A HIGH SECURITY AREA, OR WHETHER THERE WERE CORROBORATORS.
TAK
OR HOW ROTHSCHILD POLICE OFFICER, DANA CYPRESS, DAUGHTER OF SHERIFF WAYNE CYPRESS, WHOSE POLICE VEHICLE WAS FOUND CRASHED INTO A NEARBY FENCE, FITS INTO THE MIX.
WHAT IS KNOWN IS THAT ONE OF THE ESCAPEES WAS A MS. JEANNIE GORSKI WHILE THE OTHER'S NAME IS NOT BEING RELEASED...
...AND THAT ONE GUARD WAS SEVERELY INJURED IN THE INCIDENT AND REMAINS IN CRITICAL CONDITION...
THE INCIDENT CALLS INTO QUESTION THE SECURITY STANDARDS AT RIVERSIDE, AS IMPOSED BY GENERAL LOUISE CALE...
...AND LEAD SOME TO QUESTION WHY "REVIVED" CITIZENS ARE STILL IN HOLDING, AFTER LAST MONTH'S TERRORIST ATTACK...
HUNH... I WANT MY MOM...
YOU WANTED TO KNOW.
...STILL SEPARATED FROM FAMILY AND LOVED ONES.

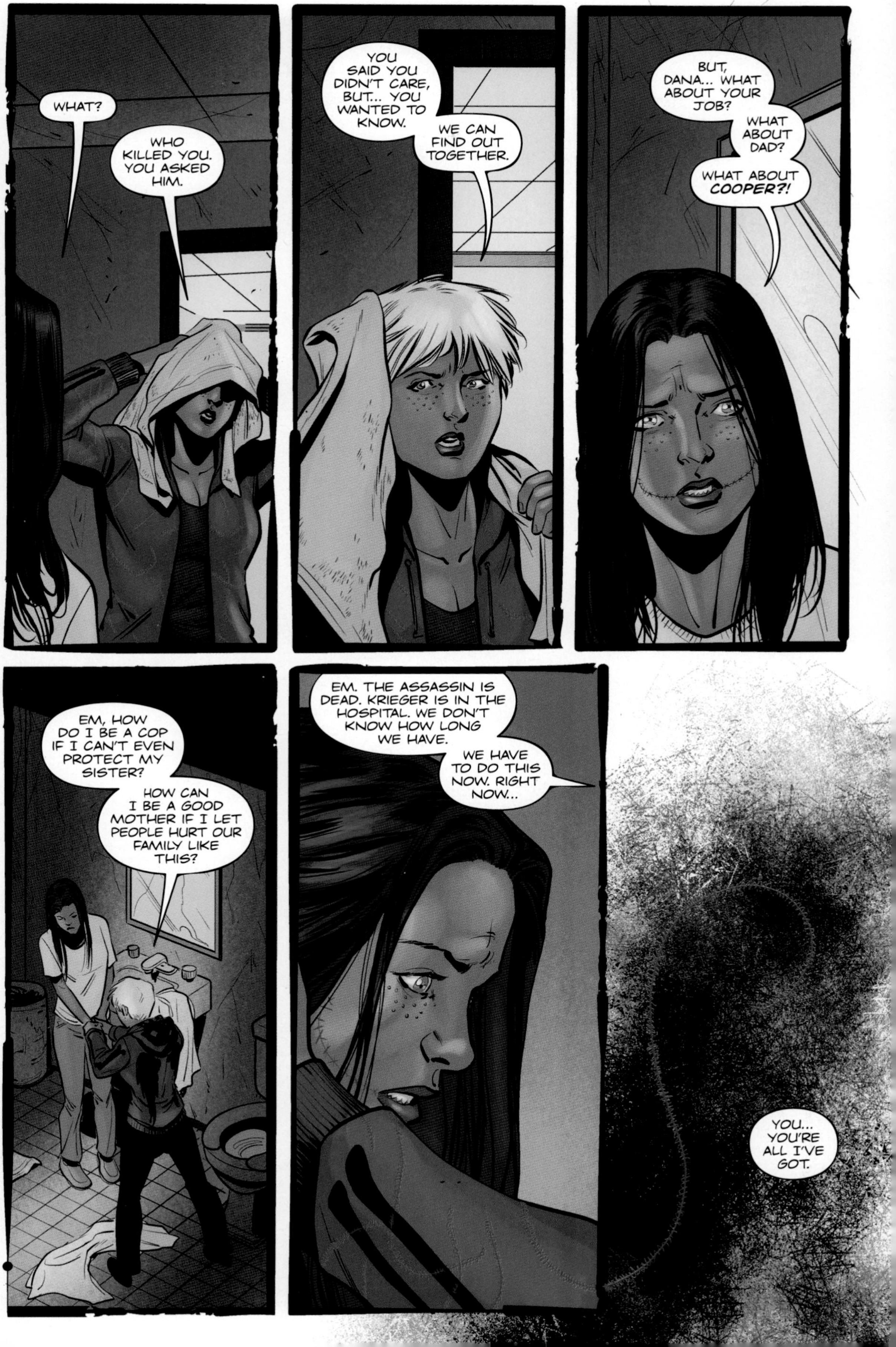
WHAT?
WHO KILLED YOU. YOU ASKED HIM.
YOU SAID YOU DIDN'T CARE, BUT... YOU WANTED TO KNOW.
WE CAN FIND OUT TOGETHER.
BUT, DANA... WHAT ABOUT YOUR JOB?
WHAT ABOUT DAD?
WHAT ABOUT COOPER?!
EM, HOW DO I BE A COP IF I CAN'T EVEN PROTECT MY SISTER?
HOW CAN I BE A GOOD MOTHER IF I LET PEOPLE HURT OUR FAMILY LIKE THIS?
EM. THE ASSASSIN IS DEAD. KRIEGER IS IN THE HOSPITAL. WE DON'T KNOW HOW LONG WE HAVE.
WE HAVE TO DO THIS NOW. RIGHT NOW...
YOU... YOU'RE ALL I'VE GOT.

COSPLAY OF THE DEAD!

We go to a lot of conventions every year, and it seems like more and more *Revival* cosplayers show up at each one! It's thrilling to see you every time, and we always try to document it. Here are a couple of the excellent fans and their amazing costumes! Looking forward to seeing more of you in the next year!

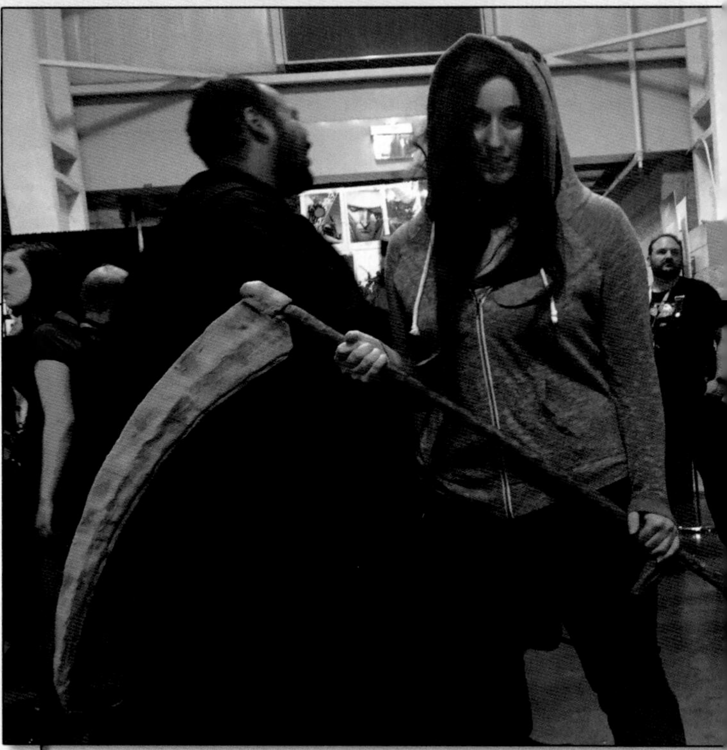

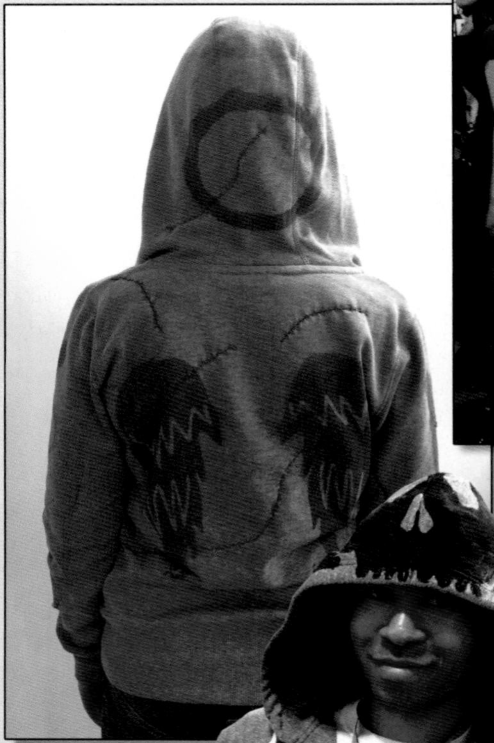

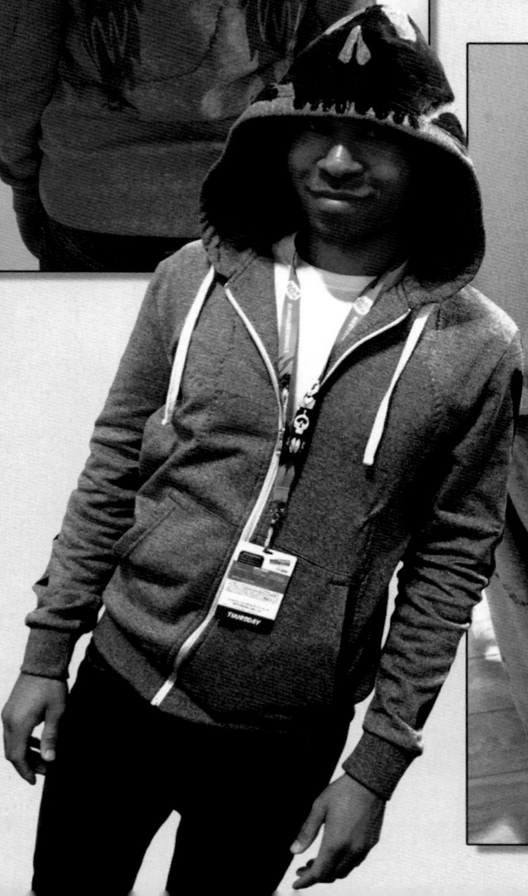

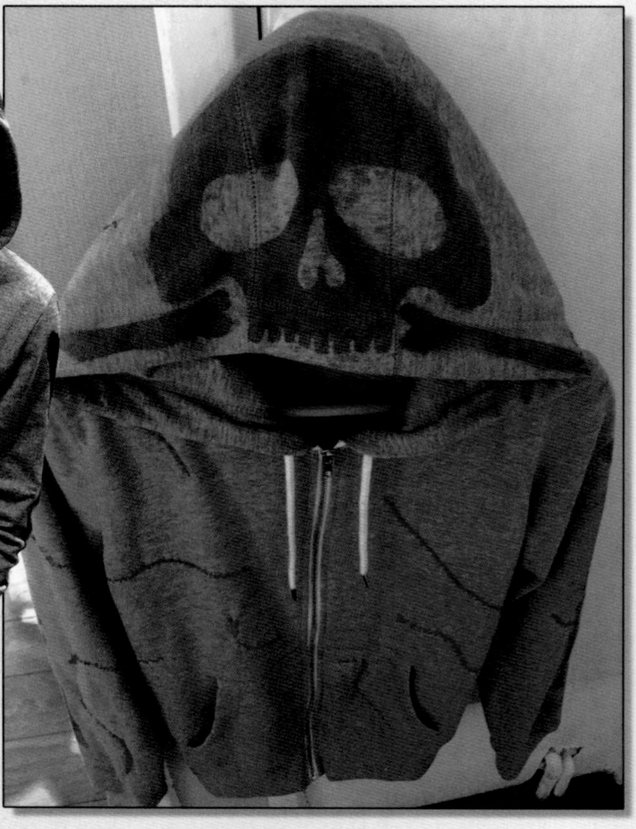

COSPLAY OF THE DEAD!

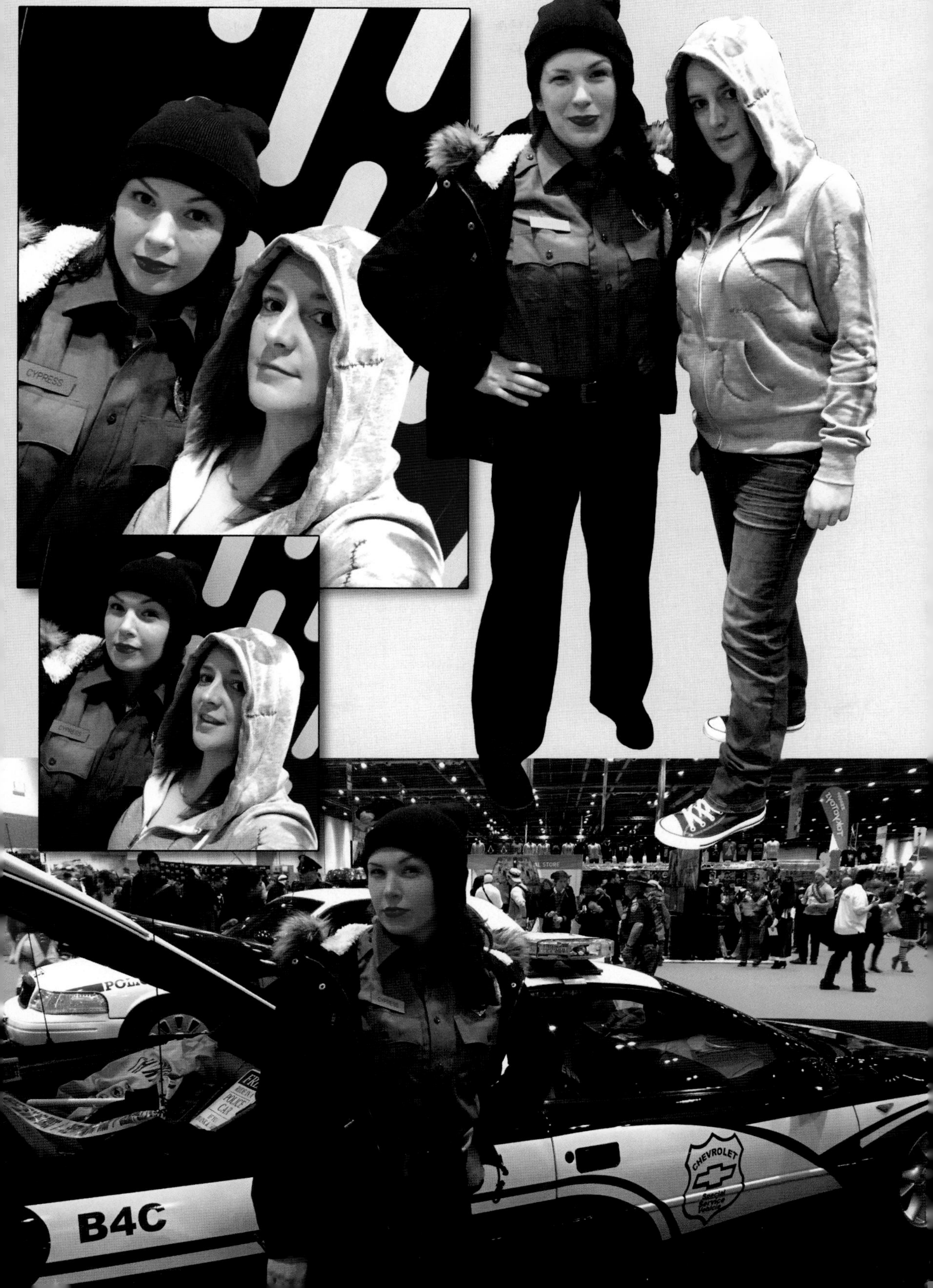
CYPRESS
CHEVROLET
B4C

TIM SEELEY is one of those "Slash" people… a writer/slash/artist. He has drawn a number of different comic book series including G.I JOE, HALLOWEEN, WILDCATS and EXSANGUINE. His writing work includes ANT-MAN/WASP, MASTERS OF THE UNIVERSE, THE OCCULTIST, WITCHBLADE and HACK/SLASH. He resides in Chicago, Illinois with his wife Gina. He works at FOUR STAR STUDIOS, never far from his 80s action figure collection.

MIKE NORTON has been working in comics for over 10 years now, gaining recognition for projects such as THE WAITING PLACE and JASON AND THE ARGOBOTS. He's made a name for himself working on books like QUEEN AND COUNTRY, GRAVITY, RUNAWAYS, ALL-NEW AT OM, GREEN ARROW/BLACK CANARY, BILLY BATSON & THE MAGIC OF SHAZAM, and YOUNG JUSTICE. He is currently drawing REVIVAL and his own weekly webcomic, BATTLEPUG, which won the Eisner Award in 2012 for Best Digital Comic. He is also very, very tall.

MARK ENGLERT has been working in comics and animation for over a decade with companies such IMAGE, MICROSOFT, HASBRO and MARVEL. Most recently, he's been making a splash in the limited edition poster scene, having produced work for BAD ROBOT, AMC, GALLERY 1988, MONDO, FOX, CBS, UNIVERSAL, PARAMOUNT, WARNER BROTHERS, IMAX and the ACADEMY OF MOTION PICTURE ARTS. To check out his poster work, head over to www.tacobelvedere.com.

CHRISTOPHER CRANK is a comics letterer currently based out of Cincinnati, OH. His recent work includes IT GIRL AND THE ATOMICS, REVIVAL, HACK/SLASH, BALLISTIC and the Eisner Award-winning webcomic BATTLEPUG! Outside of comics you can find him on Twitter @ccrank, talking about junk with Norton, Seeley, and the other Four Star fiends at crankcast.net and playing music with the Vladimirs and Sono Morti. sonomorti.bandcamp.com

JENNY FRISON is a comic cover artist and member of FOUR STAR STUDIO. She has crea ted covers for many books including ANGEL, HACK/SLASH, RED SONJA, HOUSE OF NIGHT, and I VAMPIRE. She currently lives in Chicago with her boyfriend and their super naughty cats, Demon Warrior and Ookla. She dreams of someday getting a totally awesome dog.